THE ZODIAC
FOR KIDS

CHRISTIE SANTOLI

THE ZODIAC FOR KIDS

TATE PUBLISHING
AND **ENTERPRISES**, LLC

Published by Tate Publishing & Enterprises, LLC
127 E. Trade Center Terrace | Mustang, Oklahoma 73064 USA
1.888.361.9473 | www.tatepublishing.com

Tate Publishing is committed to excellence in the publishing industry. The company reflects the philosophy established by the founders, based on Psalm 68:11,
"The Lord gave the word and great was the company of those who published it."

Book design copyright © 2011 by Tate Publishing, LLC. All rights reserved.
Cover design by Kenna Davis
Interior design by April Marciszewski

Published in the United States of America

ISBN: 978-1-61346-475-5
1. Juvenile Fiction / General
2. Body, Mind & Spirit / Astrology / General
11.09.27

Dedication

I dedicate this book to my husband, my twin flame, Dominic. You believed in my visions and turned them into a reality. I love you more than you could ever know. To my mother, Linda: you always encouraged me to use my gifts; I love you for that. To my son, Nico: you were thought of and wished for long before you arrived. You are our angel. To my guide, Lisa: thank you for pushing me to my destiny. To my brother Brian: I always looked up to you. To my brother Michael: I enjoy the signs you give me. Keep them coming. To my best friend, my brother Roger: you always know how to make me laugh. To my father, Roger: you taught me no limitations. To my stepmother, June: I could not ask for a better person to be with my daddy. To my stepfather, Kurt: this one is for you, buddy. Good things are coming.

Acknowledgements

To my sister-in-law Lisa: thank you for teaching me understanding. To my sister-in-law Pia: you've made me want to have a sister. To my niece Kayla: keep dancing. To my niece and god daughter, Mia: there is no one like you. To my niece Emma: you are the reason I wanted to have children. To my nephew Rocco: you make me look good. To my father-in-law, Eugene: you were always on my side. To my mother-in-law: Paula, you always make me feel a part of the family. To my aunt Angela: you have been a good friend. I appreciate all you have done. To Grandma Santoli: you have made my husband who he is today.

Table of Contents

Aries

March 21 to April 19

Oh, energetic Ram
Full of confidence and courage
Take care not to let your enthusiasm for adventure
Become a selfish need to be the daredevil hero
Or soon your foolhardy impulsiveness
Will make necessary your quick wits

Aries was the queen of her neighborhood, an eight-year-old tomboy beanpole with fiery red hair whose bravery and toughness had earned her the cautious respect of other girls and put boys three years her elder in awe of her. She was always the leader, no matter what game they played. For football, she was not only the sole girl, she was quarterback. For military expeditions, she was the commander, telling her troops where to go and what to do. And when they played explorer, she made the plans and decided on the goal. But whatever they were playing, even while leading, she made a point to put herself at the front of the action, a heroic, daredevil commander who made herself vulnerable alongside her charges. She even had a nickname: The Flame. Everyone had a story or two about something amazing Aries had done.

Some spoke about the time she'd jumped a twenty-foot gorge on her bike, the back wheel just barely touching down on the edge of the other side. No one thought she could do it, but her friend Randall rigged a rocket that they attached to her seat to give her an extra boost. It worked just like they thought it would—except for just barely setting her butt on fire—but that wasn't such a big deal. She just dove from the bike as soon as it touched down and scooted around in the dirt. It hurt for a week, but the adolation she received made it totally worth it.

Others talked about the legendary fake-war battle where she split up from her troops for the first time ever. In every other battle, she was always on the front lines, making sure she was there to play the hero when her side inevitably won, but not this time. For some reason, she abandoned them, or at least that's what the leader of the other side accused her of—loudly—when his troops tracked hers down and surrounded them outside the house of her friend down the street. He was gloating and laughing about how he'd always known she was weak and scared. She then jumped down on top of him from the roof of a nearby house. She captured him and won the game all by herself. The whole thing had been a ruse to draw him out so she could literally get the drop on him.

But the one that people remembered best was the football game she led the neighborhood kids in against some bully high schoolers. The older kids had been relentlessly beating up Randall and taking what they could get from him. First they took lunch money. When he stopped buying lunch, they stole his DS, then his phone, then his jacket, and finally his shoes. Aries found out and stole the tires from the leader's car one day while it was parked at school. Just to make sure they knew it was her, she soaped the car with a message: *I BEAT UP 8-YEAR-OLDS. SCHOOLED BY THE FLAME.*

They were laughingstocks at their school. Naturally, they were furious, but they couldn't just go beat up a little girl—especially now that everyone was making fun of them for being so lame that they had to beat up kids. They were trying to come up with a way to really take it out on Randall—in secret, of course—when Aries came right up to them and challenged them to a football game where everyone could hear. At first they thought she was kidding, but when they hesitated, she said she knew the only way she'd ever get them to leave Randall alone was by showing them she could embarrass them whenever she wanted and at whatever she wanted. Why? Because they were bullies and chickens and losers who were so terrible at everything in life that they had to pick on kids half their age. She had the entire school laughing at them, so finally they agreed, even setting ground rules to keep them from hurting the younger kids. No tackling, merely two-hand touch—just to show they weren't bullies. Aries agreed.

When it came time for the game, it seemed like everyone in the world showed up to watch. All the kids from the neighborhood were there, and most of the high schoolers came as well. Everyone, it seemed, was rooting for the younger kids, but no one really believed they were going to win. After all, the bullies were twice as old, twice as big, and twice as ugly as Aries's team. But somehow she made a game out of it by drawing up trick plays that made the high schoolers look like idiots. Still, the bullies were winning with less than a minute left. Aries's team had the ball, but the older kids had seemed to figure out her trickery. On the final play, she dropped back like she was going to throw the ball and then took off running straight ahead. One of the bullies got right in her way, fully expecting her to lateral it to a teammate like she'd done earlier; they had prepared for that and had one of the other bullies covering the teammate. But that was never Aries's plan. Instead of giving up the ball, she held on tight and ran right over the unprepared bully, knocking him to the ground and running in for a score. Immediately, the bully jumped up, shouting that they had won because she was down as soon as she knocked him over. Instead of arguing, Aries agreed: the bullies won when an eight-year-old girl ran one of them into the ground. Good game. All the kids started making fun of the bullies, and they ran off. They never picked on Randall again, and Aries, as always, was the hero.

Not everyone loved this side of Aries. Her parents were constantly afraid that she would hurt herself or another kid. "Be careful," they nagged her. "Don't be so impulsive." "You're going to lose a leg…an arm…an eye." "Why does everything have to be a challenge for you to win?" She knew they meant well, but they were so annoying. It wasn't like she was going to get hurt. And she always made sure everyone else was safe. They treated her like she didn't know what she was doing. But she smiled and nodded and pretended she was a good little girl, taking care not to break things or ruin clothes or do anything else that would catch their attention. And that plan seemed to work just fine until one day when she was playing baseball with her friends in the park.

It was a typical June afternoon, warm and bright, and for the first time that summer, Randall hit the ball. He not only hit it, he smashed it. The ball flew fast and far, sailing over the trees and out of sight.

"Whoa, Rand, nice one!" Aries said.

He was thrilled. "I've never hit a ball that far!"

"Lucky shot," Mark said, sarcastically. Mark was their lanky buddy who was pitching that day.

"Yeah, lucky you were pitching," Tommy, their secondbaseman said.

Everyone laughed.

"Oh, please, Tommy, you've been whiffing all day," said Aries, rolling her eyes. "Mark was pitching pretty well then, wasn't he?"

Tommy looked at the ground. "I was just kidding around."

"You bet you were kidding around," said Mark.

"Randall killed that ball fair and square. Of course," Aries said, smiling. "It wouldn't have happened if I was pitching."

Mark and Randall shook their heads and sighed.

Tommy cleaed his throat. "Well, nobody's gonna be killing any balls if we don't have one, are they?"

"Tommy has a point," said Aries. "Let's see where Randall's dinger ended up."

It was the worst possible place imaginable: Old Man McCreary's place.

Every town has a house like his. It was the most rundown, ramshackle place anyone had ever seen. Paint was peeling everywhere on the house, shutters hung loose, windows were boarded up, and holes in the roof let rain drip down, except in places where the holes were big enough for the rain to pour in. Worse yet was his messy, overgrown yard. Trees, bushes, and weeds hid most of it, casting shadows where there shouldn't be shadows and likely burying all sorts of secrets. What little of the yard could be seen from the road was blanketed in lost toys from neighborhood kids: balls, frisbees, even a boomerang Barry Mitchell had brought back with him from his family vacation in Australia the year before. Barry would have gone anywhere for that boomerang but into Old Man McCreary's place.

Mr. McCreary himself wasn't really old, but he was grumpy like an old man and always mean to the kids in the neighborhood. He lived all alone and yelled at any kids who even came near his gross yard. No one knew why; he had a tall metal fence around the place, so it wasn't like anyone was just going to wander into it. Asking to get your toys back was pointless. McCreary would either ignore you completely or laugh and say something like, "Possession is nine-tenths of the law!" Whatever that meant. He only left his house to go to his job as a gravedigger, and kids might have tried to get their stuff back while he was gone…except that Mr. McCreary being gone meant that Pitt was watching the place.

Pitt was Old Man McCreary's huge, vicious pit-bull. The dog was a monster that any number of kids reported seeing crush baseballs in his mouth and tear footballs to shreds with his claws. He had scars all over his body, and one of his ears was bitten clean off—a souvenir, it was rumored, from the days when McCreary used Pitt for dog-fighting. The old brute had killed dozens of other dogs, and one kid said he'd heard a story that Pitt only got kicked out of dog-fighting when he maimed the owner of one of the dogs he'd killed.

"Good," said Aries when she heard the story. "Anyone who makes people or animals kill each other for fun deserves what they get."

Still, there was no denying that Pitt was mean. And whether it was caused by his nature or memories of those horrible fights, like some kids said, it didn't change the fact that it was stupid and dangerous to go near him. Which is exactly what the other kids kept trying to tell Aries.

"Dude, we'll get another ball," pleaded Mark. "That ball wasn't regulation anyway. That's why Randall hit the homerun."

"I hit it because I'm good, jerkwad!"

"You haven't hit a pitch all summer!"

Tommy whistled. "Guys, focus. That is so not the point right now."

"Tommy's right," whispered Aries. "The point is that I can do this."

Her face was pressed up against the fence, and she was focused intently on the too-quiet yard in front of her. They couldn't see Pitt, but all of them knew he was in there. Waiting. Lurking.

Randall punched Aries's shoulder. Well, he tried to. He wasn't the most coordinated kid in the world, and it ended up as more of a graze than an actual punch. Still, it had its intended effect, and Aries turned around.

"This is stupid," he said simply. "Maybe you'll be fine and we'll get our ball back, but why risk it? We don't need that ball."

She smiled at him and flicked his nose playfully.

He flinched. "Hey, quit it."

"You don't need to worry about me. Have I ever gotten into any trouble before?"

They all gave her a look. She frowned.

"I mean any real trouble."

"But you could," Randall said.

"But I won't. And I'm goint to do this because I can."

Without waiting, she ran around the side of the house to a tree and started climbing. By the time the others caught up with her, Aries was already using a branch that overhung the fence like a tightrope, balancing as she crept out over it before dropping lightly to the grass. Then she stood up, turned back to them, and smiled. No dog.

The boys were breathing sighs of relief as she made her way over to Randall's baseball. Maybe she'd caught a break and Pitt was sleeping.

"Told you guys I could do this," she whispered.

Then she bent down to pick up the ball, and naturally, that's when the growling began from a tall patch of grass a few feet away. Aries immediately froze as Pitt's ugly mug emerged from the brush, teeth bared in a horrible snarl. She slowly and calmly stood up. Unfortunately, her friends weren't nearly so calm.

"It's him! It's him!"

"Ohmigosh, Aries, run!"

"Get out of there!"

She couldn't even tell who was saying what. All of her attention was focused squarely on Pitt. Thankfully, their voices divided his attention. As soon as they yelled, Pitt turned toward them, shifting his stance, and Aries bolted for the opposite side of the yard. In a flash, Pitt was after her.

There was no plan as Aries ran; she could barely form a thought. It was pure adrenaline and *faster, jump, duck, dodge, turn.* Discarded toys became both friends and enemies, slowing her down but also causing Pitt to pause and alter his course. Heavy breathing and the jangling of Pitt's chainlink collar filled her ears, and his wet, ragged breath warmed her ankles.

A thought finally sliced through the fog of her mind as she neared the fence: he'll eat me before I can climb out. As the chainlink fence loomed higher in front of her, Aries suddenly dug her foot in and changed direction, kicking up a divot of mud and grass. Pitt snapped his jaws on the air where her foot had just been but couldn't stop his own momentum, and his body slammed into the fence, giving Aries precious seconds.

She sprinted toward an old shed she hadn't even known was there from the road because giant trees hid it from sight. If she could get onto that shed and then reach the branch hanging above, there was no way Pitt could get to her. But she'd have to be fast because he was already making up the distance between them.

As she raced around the side of the shed, Aries noticed an empty metal dog bowl that had been ripped and dented from Pitt thrashing around with it and gulped. She really would be torn to shreds if he got a hold of her.

Aries pushed down her fear and made herself pay attention to her surroundings. The shed was too high for her to just jump up, but if she could a box or—there! Old Man McCreary had a pile of firewood lined up all along the back of the shed. She ran over and jumped on top of it without slowing, nearly causing the entire pile to come tumbling down. But she wasn't about to stop. Aries's feet only stayed on the firewood for a split second before she was pulling herself on top of the shed's roof. Then she picked herself up and leapt straight up, arms outstretched for the branch above her, which now looked so much farther away than it had from the ground. She missed, falling back to the roof just as Pitt reached the firewood and took in the situation with her on the roof.

Girl and dog eyed each other, knowing that this was it. This was the moment of truth. Aries stood up once again as Pitt backed up to get a running start for his jump. The dog started first, sprinting into a jump that landed him atop the firewood and then immediately bouncing upward, almost as if he was using the wood as a trampoline. He landed on top of the roof, mere feet from Aries, and almost seemed surprised. As soon as his feet touched down, Aries bent her knees and jumped with all her might, stretching like she'd never stretched before and saying *pleasepleaseplease* like a litany in her mind. Her fingers felt only air, unhelpful air—but suddenly she felt wood brush under them and laced them together before she could fall down to earth. Immediately she swung her body up and got one leg around the branch. She was saved!

Aries tried to hold in the laughter but couldn't. Her whole body shook with it, making it impossible to pull herself up farther. It took all her strength to even hold on to the branch, a thought which made her laugh even harder. If Aries had been hanging there all alone, she might have kept laughing and hanging there for another whole hour, but Pitt had other ideas, which Aries realized when she felt a sudden pain and dragging sensation in the foot she'd left dangling.

She cried out and looked down. Pitt had jumped up, grabbed onto the toe of her shoe with his teeth, and was now hanging there, an anchor dragging her back down. He hadn't broken through the shoe yet, so her foot wasn't seriously injured, but it sure didn't feel good. Aries ignored the pain, made herself ball up her foot, and shook it until the shoe came off. She tried to swing that leg onto the branch but missed; and before she could try again, Pitt sprang up and grabbed onto the leg of her jeans. She shook and shook, but he wasn't letting go this time. All she succeeded in doing was ripping her jeans. Unfortunately, they ripped in such a way that Pitt managed to lower himself to the roof while still holding on. Worse, her fingers were getting sweatier by the second.

Pitt pulled and jerked and pulled, and finally she felt her fingers slide apart before her back slammed hard into the tiles on the roof. Pitt pulled his lips back in a terrifying snarl and tensed his muscles for a pounce. He had her right where he wanted her, and suddenly Arie's mind was flooded with all the warnings her parents had given her over the years that she had dismissed. There were so many other ways she could have handled this, but she'd been stupid and impatient and arrogant, and now this dog was going to tear her limb from limb.

Pitt crouched lower, an instant away from jumping on her, when suddenly Aries heard a sharp creaking from the gate. Both girl and dog turned their heads, and the creak was followed seconds later by a bellowing voice: "Pitt!" Old Man McCreary was coming home from his shift. The dog's head lowered, and he immediately began whining. When the voice came again, he turned away and slunk off toward it without hesitation. Aries didn't dare move; she barely let herself breathe.

"Where were you?" growled McCreary. "You come when I call you, stupid dog." Aries flinched as she heard a smack, immediately followed by Pitt's pained yelp. "Maybe you won't get food tonight either, huh? What do you think about that? Maybe that will teach you to obey me, you bad dog." There was another yelp as something thumped into the dog again and then footsteps followed by a door opening and closing.

Aries didn't wait for a second chance. She stood up, shoeless on her left foot, shredded pants dragging, and again jumped for the branch. In seconds, she was over the fence and sliding down the trunk of the tree on the other side. The guys came over to her immediately from a hiding place they'd found in the bushes.

"Are you okay?"

"That was amazing!"

"We thought you were going to die for sure!"

Again the voices blended together, and Aries didn't even know who was talking. But she knew who wasn't; Randall just stood there, hands balled into fists as tears streamed down his face.

"Rand?" she asked.

"Don't," he said, quiet but firm.

"Buddy, I'm okay, Pitt didn't—"

"You got lucky. That's it. Lucky. Don't you know you didn't have to do that? Why did you have to do it? You're my best friend. Don't you know that? My best friend!"

Without even thinking about it, Aries grabbed him and hugged him, telling him over and over that she was sorry, she was so sorry, but she really was okay. Eventually, she couldn't tell which tears were hers and which were Rand's.

"It is not okay. Not at all."

"But Dad—" Aries began.

"No."

He held up a hand to silence her but, at first, didn't speak at all himself, letting the silence fill with her mother's sobs from the corner, which was so much worse. Aries hadn't wanted to come home in tears, so she stopped at the playground to pull herself together and clean up using the water fountain. By the time she got home, she was calm and in control and felt much more like her usual confident self. Which, it turned out, was a huge mistake. Her parents had taken one look at her disheveled state and calm demeanor and decided this behavior needed to stop. Clearly she didn't get how serious this was, so she needed to be taught a lesson.

"You just don't get it," her dad said for the fifteenth time; she knew, she had counted. "Forget the pants and shoes—which, by the way, your mother is going to have to pick up an extra shift at work to cover the cost on—you could have been really and truly hurt."

"I know, Dad, and I'm sorry. I just—"

"Is that what you want? Don't you know how much we both worry about you? Look what you're doing to your poor mother!"

Aries felt a surge of shame and knew that this wasn't the time for any kind of conversation. "I'm sorry," she said, lowering her head.

Her dad tore into her for a while longer, and whenever he paused, Aries repeated her apology and kept looking at the floor. Finally, he said he was fed up with her and she should go to her room and think about what she'd done. Aries didn't argue, just slunk up the stairs and went into her room.

She really did feel truly sorry, but once she sat down on her bed, she started planning a second raid to get the ball back. And this time, she knew exactly what she needed to do.

Randall shook his head and laughed, but it was a laugh full of anger and hurt. "Sometimes, Aries, you are really dumb."

"Come on, just hear me out."

They were walking to school the following morning, and Randall was scarfing down the Twinkie she'd brought along as a peace offering but, so far, not buying into a second round against Pitt.

He paused in his eating to look up at her, his mouth dotted with yellow Twinkie cake. "I thought, you know, maybe you actually might have learned something from almost getting eaten—"

"I did!"

"I thought you'd think twice next time and stop taking so many stupid chances," Randall said.

"This isn't a stupid chance this time; I've thought it through."

"I thought maybe you actually cared about how I felt and what I thought."

Aries flinched, real hurt showing in her eyes. "Of course I care what you think. Why do you think I told you about this in the first place?"

Randall shrugged. "Dunno."

"Rand, come on. Look, this is me. I like excitement and adventure and fun."

"I like fun."

"Of course you do. I'm not saying you don't. I'm just saying, you know, I don't think I'm ever not going to be me, and chances are that me is going to do some crazy stuff."

Randall kicked the dirt and crossed his arms, huffing.

"But that doesn't mean I can't be a better man. It doesn't mean I can't learn."

"Okay, I'm listening." He sighed.

"You were right before. I shouldn't have rushed in thinking I could just do whatever I wanted. It was impulsive and reckless and dumb."

"Yeah, it was," Randall said, smirking.

"Well, this time, I've got a plan."

"A plan," Randall said, confused.

"Uh-huh. It's perfect, and it's totally going to work."

"So what's this plan involve?" Randall asked.

She smiled. "The grocery store."

Randall frowned, confused.

"Oh, and twenty dollars."

He crossed his arms and glared at her.

Once again, Aries stood with her face pressed against the fence surrounding Old Man McCreary's eyesore of a house, but this time, she was carrying a grocery bag piled high with steaks.

"I'm not sure this really qualifies as a plan," Randall said.

Aries turned to him and put her hand on his shoulder. "Trust me, Rand, that poor dog is being starved by Old Man McCreary, and once it gets a whiff of these tasty steaks, he won't care about me at all."

Rand stepped in front of her. "It's still stupid to just go right in there."

She pushed him out of the way. "Duh. That's why I'm testing it first."

Aries pulled a steak from the bag, unwrapped it, and tossed it over the fence. The reaction was instananeous—Pitt's head popped out from the bush he'd been hiding in and his nose started working like crazy. He trotted over to the steak, seemingly disbelieving, and tentatively gave it a lick. Then he stopped and looked around, but when nothing bad happened, he dove right in, ripping it apart.

Randall shrugged. "Well, we know he likes steaks. Big surprise."

"That wasn't the test, genius. This is the test."

She grabbed on to the fence and began to climb slowly, watching to see what Pitt did. There was absolutely no reaction, he was so engrossed in his food. Aries looked down and smiled at Randall, and he nodded, giving permission. In seconds, she was over the fence and standing on the grass in the yard. When she touched down, Pitt looked up briefly but didn't make a move toward her and quickly went back to his feast.

Aries didn't need another invitation. She moved quickly around the yard, grabbing everything she could find and tossing it over the fence to Randall, who was carrying his own bag for the loot. There must have been twenty footballs, three or four dozen baseballs, six kites, a remote-controlled airplane, and—of course—Barry Mitchell's boomerang. All of it went flying back over the fence, free at last, until Old Man McCreary's yard looked surprisingly clean...or as clean as a dirty, unkempt jungle of a yard can look.

"Well, that's the last of it," Randall called. "Come on back."

"There's one more thing," said Aries.

Slow and cautious, she made her way over to Pitt. He growled half-heartedly, almost finished with his steak, so Aries unwrapped a second one and tossed it in front of him. He went over, sniffed it, and began tearing into it as well.

"I'm not sure that's a good idea, Aries."

"Shh." She put up her hand to silence him as she crept closer.

Pitt didn't make any sudden moves or objections as she approached, so she stood quietly next to him for a minute while he ate, then slowly reached out and put her hand on the back of his head. He paused for a milisecond, then ignored her and kept chewing, so she slowly and gently starting stroking his head. He was totally calm and relaxed as she reached into her pants pocket with her other hand and fished out a thick leash she'd brought with her, then attached it to his collar. She stood there with him while he finished his second steak, just holding the leash and crossing her fingers that this worked.

When he was done, he looked up at her, but he didn't growl or make any move to go after her. Keeping her head held high, she gave him a little tug with the leash and showed a confidence she didn't really feel. Aries felt that she was taming a lion. Inside she was shaking but trying to act like she wasn't. To her happy surprise, he followed her immediately and without trouble. She smiled but forced herself to stay calm.

After what seemed like years, they made it over to the gate, and she opened and closed it behind her. Randall rounded the corner but made sure to keep himself a safe distance from Pitt.

"Are you insane?" he asked.

"Terry Bagshaw's family in Newport is looking for a dog, aren't they?"

Terry was a kid on their baseball team who lived in the next town over. He could take the dog, and McCreary would never even see it again. Plus, Pitt would have a nice, loving home.

But Randall was shaking his head. "You can't just…he belongs to Mr. McCreary. It's steal—"

"Old Man McCreary treats Pitt awful, and you know it."

"I mean, maybe he's a little mean, leaving him outside all the time, but he still—"

"He hits him, Rand. I heard him do it yesterday while I was stuck inside. Pitt was yelping and crying, but he kept going right back to McCreary. It's not right."

"Maybe Pitt was bad?" Randall sounded conflicted.

"He didn't come immediately when Old Man McCreary called. For that he got beat. And you know what else? Know how I knew to bring food? Because that was Pitt's other punishment. No food yesterday. 'Again,' McCreary said. He's been beating and starving his own dog. No one deserves that. Right?"

Randall let out a big sigh but nodded. "Right."

"When I gave Pitt the food, he jumped on top of me and kept giving me kisses. He just wants to be loved."

They walked Pitt to the park and called Terry to explain. He and his family were completely on board. A half hour later, he came with his mom, and they drove off with Pitt, smiling and happy.

Randall shook his head and turned to Aries. "It's always going to be kind of an adventure with you, isn't it?"

"Probably, but I do promise that I won't run in without thinking things through first. Now, how about we give the kids back all their toys?"

Randall gave a small smile. "You know, I've been thinking. There's some pretty cool stuff in there. Maybe we don't have to give all of it back."

"What happened to *no stealing*?"

"Come on. Mickey Z's, what, twenty now? I don't think he wants his old frisbee back."

"You never know."

They walked off together, arguing playfully, each holding one end of the bag of long-lost toys.

Taurus

April 20 to May 20

Patient and reliable is the Bull
With warm heart full of love
But disagreement isn't recommended—
They say bull-headed for a reason
And when love is mistaken for possession
Beware the jealousy that follows
And hope lost love is fast remembered

Taurus and Jimmy had been best friends for as long as either of them could remember. They were always together—walking to and from school, sitting together at lunch; they had even managed to get all of their classes together every year at school! The two of them were together so much for so long that the other kids even stopped thinking it was weird, seeing as how Taurus was a regular kid and Jimmy was a little slow. Because of that, a lot of Taurus time was spent protecting him from other kids and trying to make them treat him like everyone else.

In kindergarten, when they had to make macaroni artwork for the class, Jimmy made the mistake of doing one of Ms. Nicklebagger, their teacher. When he took it up to her, she smiled and showed it to the class, which was the worst possible thing she could have done. Immediately, kids started laughing at Jimmy, making fun of him, and calling him teacher's pet, and poor Jimmy didn't know what to do. Thankfully, Taurus did.

"Jimmy, you forgot the best part," he said, standing. Taurus took the artwork and quickly drew something on it with his pencil. When he showed it to the class again, their teacher was picking her nose! The class howled with laughter.

Ms. Nicklebagger was furious. "Taurus Andrews, you get yourself right to the office. I can't believe you would try to blame poor Jimmy for your bad behavior!"

But Jimmy was busy with his own addition to the artwork. "Look," he said, showing it to the class again. The kids laughed and groaned at the same time.

"That's gross, Jimmy!" Alan Bigwell said, laughing.

Nicklebagger grabbed the art to find a disgusting bright green booger had been added to the finger in the drawing. Her eyes darkened, and she looked up to see Jimmy wiping his nose. Real boogers! She almost dropped the artwork.

Needless to say, they spent the afternoon in Principal Barleycorn's office waiting for their parents to come pick them up.

In second grade, when Jimmy just couldn't seem to understand the rules of soccer in gym, jerky Scott Sanderson started yelling at him. Sanderson was the best player in their grade, and he knew it. Jimmy wasn't the first—or twentieth—kid he'd yelled at, just the most defenseless. Scott and his pack of bully followers surrounded Jimmy, making fun of him and laughing like hyenas. Taurus saw what was happening and rushed over.

"I mean, I knew you were stupid, but how hard is it to kick a ball?" Scott asked.

"Hey, Scott, can I try?" asked Taurus. "He listens to me."

Scott scoffed. "Sure. Talk to your boyfriend." The hyenas laughed like this was the funniest thing in the world.

Taurus turned to Jimmy and spoke quietly. "Okay, buddy, new game."

"New game?" whined Jimmy. "I don't get this one yet."

"This one's simple, I promise. You just kick the ball at the biggest jerk."

"That's it?"

"That's it."

"I can do that." He grabbed a ball and set it on the ground.

Scott shook his head and laughed. "Nice job, nerd. He's already better than he was before."

"Kick the jerk!" roared Jimmy happily, launching a soccer ball into Scott's stomach.

He doubled over in pain, and his gang hovered around him, making sure he was okay. But it was too late.

"Kick the jerk!" said Jimmy, kicking a second ball at the group. It hit Reggie Myers in the back, knocking him into Scott.

By this point, other kids had noticed what was happening. Most simply laughed and made fun of Scott and his gang, but some kids decided to get in on the action, and soon a hailstorm of soccer balls was raining down on the jerks while they tried desperately to run away, and Mr. Cinder, the gym teacher, blew his whistle like a crazy man.

Back to the principal's office they went.

When the other kids spoke about one of them, inevitably they brought up the other. One of them, the loathesome Sally Van Pelt, had even tried to come up with a clever nickname combining their names in fourth grade.

"Look at Taurus sharing their lunch again! Are you guys in love?" The gaggle of girls surrounding her laughed.

"Are you in love with Alex D.?" Taurus replied.

Sally's face immediately turned bright red. "What? What are you talking about, nerd-face? Of course not."

Taurus shook his head. "Then why did you kiss him outside gym yesterday?"

Danielle Thomas, one of the gaggle, gasped and turned to her friend. "But Alex is my boyfriend. He gave me a valentine!"

"He's lying, Dani. Don't listen!" she snapped.

Then Jimmy started laughing and making kissy noises. "Oh, Alex, you taste like strawberries," he said, mimicking Sally's voice.

"He's always chewing strawberry gum!" Dani accused.

Sally turned and ran away, crying. Yelling after her, Dani followed, and that was the last time anyone tried to brand them with a single name.

Because they were so close, Taurus and Jimmy didn't really have any other friends, and that was fine with Taurus. He liked hanging out with Jimmy, and it also made him feel good, like he was doing something nice for someone. And Jimmy—well, he'd just never even really considered the idea of another friend. He had Taurus, and that was just the way it was. It was enough. It was great.

Until fifth grade, when a new girl moved to their school—Laurel Barrie. That year, Taurus and Jimmy finally had a few different classes from each other, so Taurus met her first, in Mr. Crumpet's math class.

She was assigned the seat next to Taurus and seemed nervous as she took her notebook out for Mr. Crumpet's lesson. He began talking while she was still digging for a pencil, and she was starting to get upset.

Taurus nudged her and offered a pencil. "Here."

"Thanks. Mine vanished. Must be magic." They smiled at each other, but neither said anything more to the other until class was over, when she tried to give his pencil back.

He waved her off. "Don't worry about it. You keep it."

"Thanks," she said, and they left in opposite directions to go to their next class.

By lunch time, Taurus was anxious to see Jimmy and go to their afternoon classes together. It was Sloppy Joe day—Puke on a Bun Day, he and Jimmy liked to joke—and he got through the lunch line pretty quickly and out to the cafeteria. Jimmy wasn't at their usual table, and at first he didn't see him at all…then he realized that Jimmy was sitting with the new girl, Laurel.

He almost tripped over his own feet, he was so surprised, but Taurus quickly regained his composure and walked over to them.

"Hello," he said stiffly.

"Taurus!" Jimmy said happily.

Laurel smiled. "Oh, you guys know each other."

Taurus sat down, forcing her to slide away from Jimmy a bit.

"Yeah," he said, "you could say we know each other. We've been best friends our whole lives."

"Cool," said Laurel. "Jimmy and I have science together, and he did the funniest thing with the rocks we were studying."

Jimmy pulled two rocks from his pockets to reveal faces he'd drawn on them, and he and Laurel immediately started laughing.

"Mrs. Beeker's face when she saw them." Laurel giggled. "I thought she was going to explode."

"She's funny." Jimmy laughed.

Taurus offered an uncomfortable laugh, unsure how to act. It was so weird to see Jimmy hanging out and having fun with someone else.

"Are you guys in any classes together?" asked Laurel.

Taurus snickered. "Um, yeah. All afternoon. This is actually the first year we haven't been in every class together. It's probably pretty weird for Jimmy."

"No, it's not," he said. "I like it."

Taurus words caught in his throat, but he coughed and went on. "I just mean, you know, because it's different than before. Because we were always together. So it's a little…strange."

After a brief, uncomfortable silence, Jimmy brought out the rocks again. For the rest of lunch, he and Laurel laughed and played with the rocks, pretending they were talking to each other, while Taurus quietly shoveled food into his mouth.

Finally, Laurel stood up. "My lunch time is just about up. Don't want to be late to classes on my first day, right?"

Taurus perked up. "Nope. You sure don't. Bye. See you in class tomorrow!"

"See you," she replied. Then she turned to Jimmy. "So you're still planning to come over to my house after school today?"

The color drained from Taury's face. He stopped breathing. *What?*

Jimmy smiled big. "Yep. I'll be there. Bye, Laurel!"

She waved and walked off, smiling.

"I like her," said Jimmy. "She's nice."

Taurus forced his hand to unclench on his fork and made himself take a breath.

"Is something wrong, Taurus?" asked Jimmy. "Taurus? Taurus?"

It was like that for the next few weeks, and Taurus walked around with what felt like a hole in his stomach, but he didn't know why. He was so mad at Jimmy. They used to hang out after school, and now he was spending time with Laurel almost every day instead.

Taurus tried to make himself be calm and rational about it. He and Jimmy never actually made real plans or anything, they just expected to be hanging out together because that's what they did. Or it was. It used to be all they did.

He'd thought it was an expectation for both of them, but apparently it was only him. Jimmy was more than happy to take their normal hanging out time and spend it elsewhere.

Without meaning to, Taurus found himself arguing more and more with Jimmy and Laurel, being mean to them for no reason at all. Jimmy mostly didn't even notice, but he could tell that Laurel was starting to think he was a jerk, which just made him even more upset. After all, she was the one stealing his friend.

Finally, Taurus couldn't take it anymore. Laurel had just left from yet another uncomfortable lunch, and he and Jimmy were alone. It was his chance.

"I don't want to hang out with Laurel anymore," said Taurus.

Jimmy frowned, seeming to have difficulty wrapping his mind around this new thought. Then, finally, he shrugged. "Okay, Laurel and I will hang out alone. But who will you eat lunch with?"

Taurus choked on his milk, spitting it back onto his tray. "No. No, no. I mean that I don't think you should hang out with her anymore. You'd really stop having lunch with me?"

"You said you didn't want to hang out with us."

"No, I said I didn't want to hang out with her."

"What's the difference? I don't understand."

Taurus was beside himself with frustration. "What's the difference? Really?"

Jimmy shrugged.

"Look, this is stupid. Just stop hanging out with her and we can be friends."

"We're not friends?" asked Jimmy. You could see the hurt in his eyes.

"I just mean…she's cutting into our time together. We used to hang out every day after school, but now you hang out with her."

"Why don't we hang out at a different time? She doesn't have to come."

Taurus shook his head. "But that was our time. Why does she get it?"

"You're making me feel weird."

"Jimmy, look, it's not that hard. You and I have known each other all our lives, right?"

"Yeah," Taurus said.

"I've always been your friend."

"That's true."

"So just tell her you can't hang out at that time," Taurus said. "That's our time." "I already told her yes."

"That's your answer?" Taurus asked.

"Come on, man, just hang out with me at some other time."

Hurt and angry, Taurus shook his head. "No. Uh-uh. I'm your best friend. If you want to hang out with me, we have to do it at that time or not at all."

"Taurus—"

"What's it going to be?"

"Taurus, don't be—"

"What's it going to be?"

Jimmy just stared at his try for a few seconds and then packed everything into his milk carton and stood. "Not at all, I guess."

Taurus watched his friend walk off, too stunned to get up and follow.

For two days, Taurus didn't even go to school. He couldn't believe that his best friend would betray him like that. After all the time they'd spent together, everything he'd done for Jimmy, to have him just turn on him like that was heartbreaking.

But Taurus tried not to let it get him down. He could still to the same things he and Jimmy used to do together, and they'd be even more fun now that he didn't have to put up with Jimmy! At least that's what he told himself. In reality, things weren't going so great.

When he went out to the woods to climb their favorite tree to their tree house, he realized he couldn't even reach the lowest branch. Jimmy was taller and had always gotten up first and pulled Taurus up after him. He tried squeezing the trunk but couldn't even get his arms around it, so finally, he gave up.

Next he went to their pond and skipped rocks across the water. At first, that wasn't so bad—he was pretty good at it and could get the rocks to hop ten times sometimes! But he quickly discovered that impressing yourself isn't nearly as fun as impressing someone else, and pretending to talk to someone who wasn't even there just made him feel silly and weird.

Even playing video games and watching TV wasn't as fun without Jimmy. There was no one to team up with or laugh with about something or even tease and joke around with when one of them beat the other. Playing against the computer was no fun at all after playing against Jimmy.

When playing by himself didn't work, he attempted to make friends with other kids at school. Everyone knew him, and he was pretty well liked, so it wasn't hard to find kids to hang out with.

He and Cam Deters read the new comic books at McGinley's one afternoon, and that was fun...until stupid Cam got into an argument with him.

"Superman?" Cam laughed, disbelieving. "Wolverine could beat up Superman in a fight any day of the week! Wolverine would be smart enough to bring Kryptonite, and then what would Superman do?"

"Wear his protective space suit because he knew Wolverine was tricky." He moved his hands in a karate motion

"Then Wolverine would just slice through it." He cut the air with his hand.

"Not if Superman used his ice breath or laser eyes—Wolverine wouldn't get close enough. Have you ever even read Superman? He and Wolverine aren't even the same class of superhero-ness. Wolverine couldn't lay a claw on him."

"Wolverine is super agile and would just avoid his breath and eye beams and jump in for the kill." He jumped around.

It was so clearly wrong that it was the dumbest thing Taurus had ever heard. Jimmy would have just agreed with him or would have made the whole thing into a joke, but Cam kept arguing until Taurus said he had to leave for dinner. He did not make plans to meet Cam again.

A few days later, Molly Marshall invited him over to play video games, but she always had to be the first player and refused to play anything that had any kind of fighting or sports or basically anything fun. Still, he tried hard to have fun playing her pony racing game, and he beat her the first game.

"No fair!" she screamed. "My controller must be broken or something. Switch me."

A little bit worried, he handed over the controller he was using and again beat her in the race. Again she screamed, so he made up an excuse. "Um, I think there's a glitch in the game. The computer let me start earlier than you. Let's try again."

"Fine," she grumbled.

They played again, and this time, he let her win by a wide margin.

"Yes!" she cheered. "I knew I should be winning."

But after he let her win a few more times, she threw her controller down in a fury and jabbed her finger into his chest.

"You're letting me win, aren't you?"

"What? No. Of course not," he lied. What was he supposed to do?

"Yes, you are!"

"You're just getting better from practicing."

"Shut up! I am not a baby, and you don't need to cheat to let me win."

"Okay."

"Play me for real!"

So he did, and again he beat her—this time by a lot. Again the controller came flying out of her hands.

"No! Fair!"

At that point, he calmly set his controller down and said that he forgot his mom was cooking his favorite meal tonight and he really should go so he was not late.

Eating dinner with his parents that night, he got an idea: they could be his best friends. It made sense, right? They had to like him; he was their kid. And he was always around them anyway, so he wouldn't have to go out of his way only to end up hanging out with people he didn't like. It was brilliant!

Except, he learned quickly, his parents were lame and boring and had no sense of humor. Watching TV that night, they not only didn't think it was funny when he repeated the lines in a high-pitched voice, they got annoyed and said he was ruining the show. Taurus didn't think that was possible with the show they were watching, but he relented and started squishing characters' heads like grapes. Which was apparently not allowed because it was distracting.

"Well, what are we supposed to do while we're watching TV?" he asked, flabbergasted.

"Have you tried actually watching it?" suggested his mom, which made Taurus howl with laughter.

"But TV's dumb."

"Then why did you ask to watch with us?" his dad asked.

"How was I supposed to know you guys didn't watch it right?" he asked. "I thought everyone knew you joked around and laughed while TV was on. Otherwise, what's the point?"

Needless to say, he gave up on hanging out with them pretty quickly.

All of this might have been bearable, but Taurus still had to sit at school and watch Jimmy have fun with Laurel. They invited him to hang out and sit with them, but he refused, not budging an inch. He didn't talk to either one of them in class, and he sat all by himself at lunch, pretending not to watch them whenever they turned his way.

That day, they had used potatoes in their science class, and both were playing with them by making them into potato creatures using sticks from ice cream bars.

"Look, mine's a two-legged dog," said Jimmy, trying to set his up to stand on its own. It kept falling until Laurel showed him to break the ice cream sticks in half and get four legs.

"Now your dog is happier." She laughed.

"The happiest."

She shoved a single stick into the "face" of her potato. "Who's mine supposed to be?"

Jimmy shrugged. "Big nose?"

"Pinocchio, silly!"

"Oh, hey, yeah. That's awesome."

As he watched them enjoying themselves day after day, Taurus began to wonder why he was doing this to himself. Maybe Jimmy had betrayed him, but so what? Refusing to back down was just making him miserable, and it certainly didn't seem to be teaching Jimmy any lesson—he was having a great time with Laurel.

When that thought occurred to him, it was like a light switch turned on. Jimmy hadn't betrayed him. Jimmy was just being his friendly self. It was Taurus who'd been jealous and demanding, Taurus who'd told Jimmy he had to hang out with him—or else.

Had Taurus been wrong this whole time? He was beginning to think he had been.

The next day, Jimmy and Laurel had lunch together, as usual, and as usual, Taurus sat off at a table by himself. Jimmy and Laurel had fun, talking and laughing and playing, and then finally she got up and left to go to class.

A few seconds after she left, someone cleared their throat behind Jimmy, and he turned to find Taurus.

"Hey," said Taurus.

"Hey," said Jimmy.

"Mind if I sit down?"

Jimmy shrugged, so Taurus sat.

Then neither one of them said anything for a long time.

Finally, Jimmy broke the silence. "Mrs. Criminy's English class yesterday made me want to fall asleep."

"You too? I had to hold my eyes open with my fingers."

Jimmy and Taurus laughed and then stopped talking again.

"Look, Jimmy, remember that soccer game we made up a few years ago?"

"Kick the jerk?"

"Yeah, kick the jerk," Jimmy said.

"That was a fun game," Jimmy said under his breath.

"Yeah. Unless you're the jerk."

"Oh, yeah. That must suck. I guess that's why you make that person a jerk."

"Yeah," Taurus said. "Well, anyway, what I'm trying to say is…I'm the jerk. If you were playing right now, you should be kicking me."

Jimmy looked horrified. "I'd never do that to you."

"I know. Because you're a good friend. But I wasn't a few weeks ago when I told you to stop being friends with Laurel. It's just...you're my best friend. My only real friend. And I got mad and stupid and stubborn, but I'm sorry."

"Is that it?"

Taurus flinched like Jimmy hit him. "Uh, yeah, I guess. Just wanted to say sorry. I was wrong. You don't have to say or do anything."

"Cool."

"Okay. Uh, I guess I'll go back to my table then."

"Okay," Jimmy said.

Taurus got up to go.

"Oh, hey," began Jimmy, "you want to come over tonight, or should I come to your house?"

Shocked, Taurus couldn't think of any words for a few seconds.

"Uh...Um...I..."

"Only if you want to," Jimmy said. "We don't have to hang out—"

"No! No, I'd love to hang out with you. Come to my house, okay?"

"Okay."

"Okay," Jimmy said.

"See you."

"Yeah."

Taurus turned to go and then turned back.

"You know, since we're going to the same class, I might as well just sit here."

Jimmy nodded. "That'smart. We should walk together too."

"Totally. Did you read the new comics this week?" Jimmy asked.

"Uh-uh. What happened in them?"

"Oh, man, it was great..."

They didn't have lunch together every day after that or hang out every night like they used to, but it turned out that most days were more than just enough, it was actually better than before. And because he'd realized he was wrong and apologized, Taurus felt like a weight had been lifted. He realized he acted this way because he was afraid of losing his best friend to Laurel. He decided to focus on the fun that he had with Jimmy instead.

He even became friends with Laurel. You know, after a long time passed.

Gemini

May 21 to June 20

Intelligence with word and wit
May win the twins great favor
And grant them fond admirers
Without an ounce of care or labor
But their superficial, nervous need
To always be on top
Could lead to evil, cunning plots
And find them unhappy with their lot

The Gemini twins, Roger and Mallory, were not only the most popular kids in fourth grade, they were the most popular kids in their entire K-8 school. Seventh and eighth graders even invited them to their parties, because it wasn't a real party unless you had the Gemini's there.

Roger and Mallory were co-student-body presidents, and they'd gotten there by working hard at it. Both of them made a point to talk to every kid from every grade at least once. Nothing special or personal, but the kid you were talking to sure felt like it was.

"Hi, there, what's your name?" one of them would ask to a random student.

The random student would give his or her name, which the twin would say was pretty or strong, depending on if it was a boy or girl, and ask a few questions that seemed somewhat personal but really weren't.

Inevitably, the other twin would be laughing at someone's joke or telling a funny story they had rehearsed nearby. "Bigger than Mr. Starterneck's belly!" the punchline would go, or something equally obvious.

They'd perfected their personas over years, molding themselves into class clowns who were always the life of the party and everyone's best friends but somehow still taken seriously. Not surprisingly, the twins came from an uppercrust, political family. Both parents were senators that they rarely saw, instead being raised mostly by their nanny, Mrs. Dewfeather. As such, they had never really formed any deep connections with anyone growing up and had difficulty understanding any relationship that was more than superficial.

Neither one had strong beliefs or convictions, because it was far easier to simply change themselves into whatever the person they were currently talking with wanted them to be. This mentality brought with it a great sadness for both of them, but neither quite understood why they were feeling the way they were, or, quite honestly, what it even was. The best description of the feeling had come from Mallory one evening, when she said she felt like she was constantly empty but never hungry.

"Weird," was Roger's one word reply.

"Yes," said Mallory.

And that was it. They behaved as empty little robot kids because it was working for them, and they craved the attention and notoriety it brought them, something sorely needed from strangers with their parents so conspicuously absent.

"Turn to chapter seven in your copies of *A Wrinkle in Time*, class," intoned Mr. Steepleberry in a monotone. He was dusty and ancient, probably older than the book they were reading. It was a perfect opportunity for the twins to practice their class clowning.

Roger raised his hand. "*A Wrinkle in Time?*"

"Yes, Roger, the book we've been reading for the past two weeks," Mr Steepleberry said.

"I think it's defective."

"Defective? However so?"

"There's a wrinkle in mine."

"A wrinkle in yours?" asked Mr Steepleberry.

"A wrinkle in mine."

Mallory raised her hand but didn't wait to be called on. "Wait, *A Wrinkle in Mine*? I don't have that."

Mr. Steepleberry turned to her. "Well, that's good, Ms. Gemini. You're not supposed to have a wrinkle."

"Not supposed to have *A Wrinkle?*" she exclaimed. "What am I supposed to be reading, then? Is it a different book?"

"Huh?" Steepleberry's brow furrowed.

A few of the kids around the class chuckled, but they were trying to keep it quiet.

"Which *Wrinkle* am I reading?" asked Mallory.

"I can't read with my wrinkle," said Roger. "Will someone switch with me? Who wants to read my wrinkle?"

A few hands, mostly female, went up, playing along.

Mallory let out a big mock sigh. "No one wants to read your wrinkle, Roger."

"Well, then, whose *Wrinkle* are we reading?" he asked.

"Mr. Steepleberry's *Wrinkle*, of course!" Mallory said.

"But which one!" he cried.

By now everyone in class was trying hard not to laugh and even harder not to think of Mr. Steepleberry's old, leathery, wrinkly skin.

"Now, children," Steepleberry said, not getting the joke at all. "While I appreciate your attempt to credit me with the work, it is Madeleine L'Engel's novel that we're reading, and that is what I would like for you to take out."

"Oh," said Roger, uttering a big sigh of relief, "so we won't be reading your wrinkles at all then?"

Steepleberry paused, and for a second, it looked like he realized they were making fun of him, but Mallory quickly jumped in with a save.

"Honestly, Roger, of course not. He just said so. It's not Mr. Steepleberry's *Wrinkle* we're reading, but Ms. L'Engel's. *A Wrinkle in Time.*"

He stood tall like a giant tree. His eyes widened as he pushed back his silvery gray hair. "Uh, yes, Ms. Gemini, that is correct. Now, if everyone would open to chapter seven of *A Wrinkle in Time*—Yes, Mr. Gemini."

"Apologies, sir, but there's a wrinkle in mine."

And the class, unable to hold it in any longer, burst out laughing.

It was an odd, superficial place of honor they held, but one that meant everything in the world to them, because their ability to charm and ingratiate themselves to people was the only thing they had going for themselves socially. They became adept at playing specific groups and cliques off of each other and learning people's fears, worries, and deep, dark secrets so that they could file them away to use if they ever needed to do so.

They engaged in a bit of playful bullying, but their allegiances shifted quickly to keep both sides happy, and more than anything, they set themselves as equal-opportunity offenders, taking on sporty cool kids and fantasy nerds in equal measure. The strategy was working quite well until something completely unexpected happened: a new boy who was their complete opposite arrived and took the school by storm.

Derrick Stone was a tall, good-looking fifth grader who was smart, funny, and way more endearing than either of the Gemini twins, because when he said something, it was clear that he meant it. The simple, gentle sincerity you could see whenever he looked you in the eyes would have probably been enough for anyone who was used to dealing with the notoriously fickle Geminis, but if there was any doubt, Derrick erased it on his first day of school.

Despite his immediate status as a popular kid, which meant he had free reign to sit wherever he wished, Derrick picked a table of clear losers to befriend. It wasn't long before one of the bullies came over to start something, and that's where the whole school saw Derrick for what he was. Johnny Barnabus, a hulking seventh grader, was making fun of Kevin Lamb and brought his hand down to smash Kevin's milk carton and splash him with milk. Derrick caught his hand and stopped him.

"I wouldn't do that," he said.

Johnny was surprised more than anything. "This doesn't concern you, man."

"Actually, it does. I like Kevin. He's my friend. So picking on him is like you're picking on me."

The entire cafeteria went silent to watch the conversation. This was not how things went down here. On any other day, Kevin would have been splashed and Johnny truimphant, but then later one of the Geminis would do something to cheer Kevin up and make Johnny feel bad or small about what he'd done. This was something new. And very, very cool.

Johnny pulled his hand away. "So what're you gonna do, man?"

Everyone in the room tensed for a fight, but Derrick quickly diffused the situation. "Do?" he asked. "Tell you what. You keep trying to smash the milk. I bet I can stop you every single time."

Johnny furrowed his brow. "Okay."

Again he swung downward to smash the milk, this time harder, but instead of stopping or blocking Johnny's hand, Derrick simply pushed Johnny's arm, making him miss the milk. Johnny tried other ways to get at it—straight on, from each side, after pretending to turn away—but each time, Derrick anticipated him and stopped him from even touching the carton. After the fourth or fifth time this happened, Johnny finally got frustrated.

"Okay, enough! What do you want, man, to fight me?"

Derrick just smiled. "How about instead I show you how to do what I was just doing? As long as you promise not to bully anyone else with it, of course."

Johnny thought about it for a second and then nodded.

"It's a deal."

"All right then."

Johnny turned to walk away and then stopped and turned back.

"You know, you're pretty cool," he said.

"Thanks," said Derrick, smiling.

Johnny nodded. "See you later."

"Later."

Mr. Septic's fifth grade science class was doing a simple chemistry assignment that day. He had provided each of them was seven different chemicals and said that it was their job to create a simple chemical reaction from the materials in front of them. Derrick raised his hand, and Mr. Septic nodded at him.

"Any of the materials in front of us?" he asked.

"Yes," said Septic. "In any amount or combination, obviously limited to what you have here in the room."

Derrick took Mr. Septic very literally, using four of the seven chemicals on his desk, as well as a piece of chalk, gum from under the desk, a hair from a male student, and some very light shavings from his desk—all things in front of him.

"*What are you doing?*" cried Mr. Septic when he came over to find Derrick's chemical green and boiling. "How did you do this?"

"I just used the things in front of me," he replied, smiling.

"But what is it?"

Derrick held up a finger. "Just wait for it. It's coming."

Suddenly, a loud, fartlike sound emitted from the beaker with Derrick's compound, followed by a wave of smelly, smelly gas that spread out to quickly envelop the room. In seconds, Mr. Septic and the other kids were gagging and choking.

"You are in big trouble, young man!" gagged Septic.

Derrick held up his hands. "Hey, I was just following instructions."

"I didn't tell you to create a stinkbomb!"

"And I didn't. This is only the first half of the reaction."

He picked up a big pink eraser and tossed it in, immediately shutting off the smell and then wiping it out around the room.

"A neutralizing agent," he said.

Within a minute, people were breathing totally normal again. Mr. Septic narrowed his eyes at Derrick, unsure what to do with him. Derrick just stood there. Finally, Septic nodded.

"Excellent job, Mr. Stone. That was some advanced chemistry you displayed there."

"All due to your excellent teaching, sir," he said, smiling.

Mr. Septic snorted a laugh. "Yes, quite."

Kids were talking and laughing about that incident the next day, even embellishing it to make Derrick sound cooler than he already was, which was kind of difficult. The whole thing was too much. Not only was Derrick a stand-up guy, he had a pretty good sense of humor.

When the twins heard this, both looked at each other at the same time. They had to do whatever they could to befriend Derrick Stone.

The twins hadn't been in the lunch room to see Derrick's performance, but they certainly heard about it. Everyone in the whole school was talking about it. They knew they needed to befriend this new kid as soon as possible. So, over the next few days, Roger and Mallory did as much research on Derrick as they could—which really meant listening in on his conversations and talking to people about him.

When they discovered he liked basketball, Roger studied up on the NBA and NCAA and made a point of mentioning some games he wanted to watch that weekend as he passed Derrick in the hall.

"Duke or UNC?" Derrick asked.

Roger stopped and turned back. A bite! "Duke, of course."

"You'd turn your back on Dean Smith and Michael Jordan?"

"For Duke, I would."

Derrick nodded "fair enough" and continued down the hall. Not exactly a homerun, but Roger thought the seed nicely planted.

Mallory found his name in playbills from his old school and feigned a love of the theatre—especially Shakespeare. She bought copies of a few of his plays—*Romeo and Juliet, Hamlet,*

Midsummer Night's Dream—and carried them with her around the school. Then she worked her connections to find out what Derrick's schedule was and made a point to bump into him so that he would see the plays. Like with the basketball, it worked like a charm. She "accidentally" ran into him coming out of class, spilling her books everywhere, and he helped her pick them up, pausing when he got to *Hamlet*.

"How old are you?" he asked, indicating the book.

"You think I'm too young to understand Shakespeare?" she asked.

"I think I'm too young to understand Shakespeare, and I'm pretty sure I'm older than you."

They continued talking as they walked to their classes, and not long after, all three of them were having lunch together and hanging out. The Geminis offered to introduce Derrick around and show him the ropes; he didn't really need that, seeing as how just about everyone had already heard of his exploits and thought he was the coolest guy ever, but he was polite or modest enough to agree.

After a few days of hanging out together, they suggested they go to Derrick's house, but he begged off with an excuse, which the twins found interesting.

"He's got to be hiding something about his parents," guessed Mallory.

"Or about where he lives," added Roger. "Either way, we give it a few more days before we bring it up again."

"Right. Don't want to seem too pushy."

So they waited.

Two days later, they had a stroke of luck—aided by a little of their own meddling—with Mr. Septic assigning Derrick to be their upperclassman advisor on their annual science fair project. The three of them had to work closely on the project, much of it in their off hours. It seemed like the perfect excuse to bring up going to Derrick's house, so they brought it up again.

"So if they're done spraying for termites at your house, we were hoping you'd be cool with us going there," Mallory said, fishing.

"Well, uh, I don't think they're quite done yet," said Derrick, nervous. "Couldn't we use your place?"

"Oh," said Roger, "our parents are out of town, and they get really angry if we have people over when they're not around."

Derrick got a sad look on his face. "Yeah, my dad hasn't been around for a while now..."

Sensing something, Mallory took a chance. "It's like they don't even care about us, just their jobs. I mean, I know they're senators, but why have kids if you're just going to abandon them?"

Roger caught on. "Oh, come on, Mal, it's not so bad. We see them...for holidays...sometimes.

But whatever, right? They chose what was important to them, and it wasn't us."

"At least your parents aren't divorced," said Derrick quietly, and individually, both twins prayed that this was not the deep, dark secret Derrick had been hiding, because if so, it was pretty lame. "Technically, I guess my parents aren't either, but all of us know that's what's happening. Dad's even got a new girlfriend. Mom can barely afford rent for us, and he's out spending money on some woman."

"That sucks, man," offered Roger.

Derrick shrugged. "Nothing we can do, right? Like you said."

"Just have to live with it," continued Mallory.

There was a long silence before Derrick spoke again. "Okay, guys, I have a confession. My house isn't off limits because of termites. It's off limits because it's not a house. Mom couldn't afford it anymore, so we moved here and started renting."

Roger shrugged. "So you're in an apartment, so what?"

"Well, you haven't seen the apartment yet," said Derrick.

That sounded promising.

It was more than promising; it was a dirty basement apartment underneath a dog grooming business called The Dog House. Yes, that's right; the new most-popular kid in school was living in a place called The Dog House. When the other kids found out about that, they'd avoid him for sure, and the Gemini's would be the top dogs again.

Mallory decided to not even attempt subtlety. She walked right into Mr. Septic's room during Derrick's class with him and cleared her throat.

"Yes, Ms. Gemini?" asked Mr. Septic. "I'm in the middle of a lesson."

"Roger and I need a new advisor."

Derrick furrowed his brow in confusion, and Mr. Septic followed suit. "But why?" Septic asked. "Has Mr. Stone not proved helpful?"

"It's less about his helpfulness and more about his living situation. Our parents don't approve."

"His living situation?"

Derrick's eyes went wide. "Mal, what are you doing?"

She ignored him. "They just think it's unhealthy for us, working in a place with all the chemicals and dog hair and who knows what else floating around in the air."

Mr. Septic puffed up and frowned at her. "Ms. Gemini, I have no idea what you're talking about, and—"

"He lives in the basement under The Dog House, that dog grooming place over on Fourth

Street. Our parents are…uncomfortable with the conditions." Mallory hid a smile. Derrick was finished, and they would have their rightful places back as the people in charge of this school. She just had to sit back and wait for the other kids to pile on.

Dan Peters, a rail-thin kid with mean eyes, opened his mouth first. "Why'd your parents decide to move into The Dog House?"

Other students leaned in, attentive.

"Well," said Derrick, "it wasn't exactly a choice, and it wasn't both my parents."

"Who was it?" asked Steph Crobel. "You?"

Carl Erickson shook his head. "No, dummy. He said it wasn't *both* his parents. That means they're getting divorced, right?"

Derrick nodded.

"That sucks," continued Carl. "Mine got divorced last year."

"Maybe they'll work it out," offered Joline Hugh. "My parents were going to separate until they saw a counselor. Now they're fine."

"Maybe," said Derrick. "But I doubt it. My dad's already got a new girlfriend."

Gasps and groans could be heard around the room. Mallory just stood there, feeling smaller by the second. This was not how the whole thing was supposed to go.

"So do you have to walk through the dog store to get to your room?" asked Frankie Missid.

"Yeah, what's it like living with all those dogs?" Beth Jones asked.

"Well," said Derrick, "the dogs don't live there, and my mom and I actually live in an apartment under The Dog House, so we've never even been inside it. I've never even seen any of the dogs."

"That doesn't sound bad at all," said Steph Crobel.

"It's not," continued Derrick. "It's pretty much like any other apartment."

Dan Peters turned on Mallory. "So then what do your parents have a stick up their butts about?"

Suddenly, she was a deer in headlights, nowhere to run, and no idea what to say. "Uh…Uh…"

"Yeah," interrupted Carl, "it sounds like they just don't like that Derrick's parents are divorced or he's poor or something."

Mallory shook her head, trying to argue. "No. No, it was our health. They were worried about—"

"Tell them to stop being so superficial and judgy," Nancy Marsh said.

"How did they even find out?" asked Derrick, and the room went silent.

"Huh?" Mallory floundered.

"You said they were out of town, right? So how did they find out?"

She was very fidgety twirling her hair. "Well, we had to tell them. About the project, you know?"

Derrick nodded. He understood. "So you told your parents about where I live?"

"Yeah."

"Then you guys are the judgy ones!" Nancy Marsh said. "You could have told them good things about the place, but you didn't because you didn't want to have to go back."

"That's not exactly true—"

"I'd never rat on a friend like that to my parents," said Carl, shaking his head.

Finally, Mallory exploded. "Look, we didn't, okay! Our parents don't know. Just Roger and I. We saw how everyone was loving Derrick and he was becoming so popular, and we thought you guys wouldn't like him as much if you knew some of the bad stuff about him."

"You mean you thought we'd turn on him if we found out he was poor?" Dan Peters glared.

Mallory's voice was small. "Maybe?"

Derrick shook his head. "Well, someone here's superficial, but it's not your parents."

A wave of angry accusations crashed against Mallory, making her take a step back. Poor Mr. Septic tried in vain to calm the kids down, but the room merely got louder and louder, and Mallory felt smaller and smaller.

The entire school had turned on them, and Mallory wasn't entirely sure she disagreed with them. She and Roger had insinuated themselves into the life of a really nice guy with the sole purpose of taking him down so that they wouldn't lose their place as king and queen of the school. More than that, they had completely misjudged their peers, mistaking their own superficial view of life for the one everyone else used. Shunning almost seemed like getting off easy.

At first, Roger blamed her. He couldn't believe she had admitted their plan and felt sure there was a way she could have turned the tide of sentiment back toward them, if only she'd been smarter. Eventually, though, he saw how bitter the other kids were toward them and knew it was from more than just the one thing. This was years of built-up resentment the kids were getting out all at once. Had he and his sister really been that bad all those years?

"We have to apologize." This from Mallory after three days of the silent treatment from everyone at school.

Roger nodded. It was a good plan. "Okay, here's what we do. We say that our parents have never been around, so we never felt love, and—"

"I've got a better idea."

"Really, what?"

"The truth."

Roger looked skeptical.

The next day, Roger and Mallory walked over to Derrick together at lunch.

"I have nothing to say to you," warned Derrick, not even turning around.

"That's fair," said Mallory. "But we have a few things we'd like to say to you."

"Starting with 'we're sorry,'" chimed in Roger. "Boy, are we sorry."

Other kids around the cafeteria started to notice what was going on and crowded over to hear.

Derrick scoffed at Roger's words. "Yeah, I'm sure you're sorry now. Sorry you lost all your friends."

"Actually, yes," said Mallory, and Derrick looked up at them for the first time.

"In a lot of ways, we know we're not very good people," said Roger. "I could probably name every single person in this room and maybe tell you one thing about them, but that's it. We're great at making friends, but not at actually being friends."

"But it's not that we don't want to be friends," continued Mallory, "we just don't know how. Being loud and smart and funny, that was always so much easier and more comfortable, so we stuck with it. And it worked out pretty well for a while, getting everyone here to know us and at least pretend to like us."

"Until it became all we had," added Roger. "Put me in front of a room full of people; I can talk for an hour, and everyone will think they know me. But if I try to talk to someone alone, they'll be bored in less than five minutes, because I have absolutely no personality."

"Me either," said Mallory. "We're both sad, empty, little human beings who probably have a good chance of being alone for our entire lives."

"Because we suck."

"At being people," Mallory said.

"And what we're really trying to say is that when you came here, and everyone started actually liking you for who you are, we panicked."

"As lame and superficial as it is, being popular and getting everybody to laugh at us—that's all we have," Roger explained. "And you were—completely unintentionally—taking it away from us."

"So we attacked."

"Because we're silly, small-minded, superficial jerks."

"But if you're at all still interested in trying to be our friend—"

"You know, after we apologize a few thousand more times—"

"—we would really, really love trying to be *your* friend."

"Which is kind of cool, if you think about it, because if it actually works out, you'd be our first true friend," Mallory said.

When they finished, they realized that the whole cafeteria was watching them, and a blush crept onto both of their faces. That, more than anything, finally sold Derrick.

"Wanna come over and hang out tonight?" he asked.

"Absolutely," Roger said, breathing a sigh of relief.

Mallory agreed. "More than anything."

Cancer

June 21 to July 22

Cancer the protector
Full of sympathy
How easy for you to give all of your love
And how difficult for you to let go
Accept that life marching on is a fact
Take care how hard you cling to the past
Lest your love grow to hate you

Cancer and Benny had bad parents.

Neither of them would have even thought of anything so horrible—they loved their parents!—but they were bad.

Now, their parents didn't mean to be bad, and if you asked them, they would have told you that they did their best. Both worked stressful jobs and made a point of trying to spend time with their two children.

Trying, unfortunately, is the key word in that sentence. Both parents were young and full of life, and it was not uncommon for them to call and cancel plans with their children or simply forget them altogether when their friends called to hang out with them. Over the years, Cancer had gotten used to it.

"Cancer, dear," her mother would say, "I know I was supposed to go to the movies with you and your brother, but Madeline really needs a girls' night out. She's been feeling dreadful lately. Can I get a rain check?"

"Of course, Mom. Tell her to feel better. I'll make sure Benny gets his medicine and goes to bed on time."

"Oh, you are a dear!"

When Benny was really little, he'd been incredibly sick. Every day, it seemed, they'd had doctors coming to their house or they were rushing him in to the hospital. No one could ever quite tell them what the problem was, just that it was bad, and it wasn't getting better.

"You don't even have a guess about what it is, Dr. Glassfarden?" their father had asked again and again.

"No," said the doctor. "But it's bad, and it's not getting better. His muscles aren't growing the way they should be, leading to general weakness, which is unfortunately being compounded by ear aches, migraines, fevers, and a really runny nose."

"What can we do?" asked their mom.

"Protect him," Dr. Glassfarden had said, turning away from Cancer's parents to look at her directly. "Whatever you do, protect him, always and forever. It is your solemn duty." Technically, that last part hadn't actually happened, but that was the way that Cancer felt. As his older sister—by four whole years—she knew that it was up to her to keep him safe.

She took her job seriously, setting up her own baby monitor that went from her room to Benny's so that she could be the first one on the scene. That was how she stopped him from crawling down the stairs when he was one and somehow escaped his crib. He was right at the edge of the top step when she caught him and scooped him up, right in the nick of time. Benny wouldn't have even made it that far except that she had gone to great lengths to make his room safe—pillows covering everything, even the floor, and that was why he hadn't gotten injured falling from the bed.

When his fevers were really bad, she slept with him in his room, getting up several times each night to check on him and make sure he had medicine when he needed it. For meals, she carefully prepared his food so that there was no chance of him choking on anything too small or hurting his tender gums on anything too hard. It was she who ran his baths, she who dressed and changed him, and she who made his appointments at the doctor and reminded her parents so that they would be there to take them.

Cancer became so good at protecting and taking care of her little brother that her parents came to take it for granted that she would handle everything.

"We'd help out more," her father said, "but you're just so good at it."

"I understand," Cancer had replied.

"Your mother and I would probably just mess things up."

"No probablies," her mother added. "We would definitely mess things up."

"Definitely."

"Okay," said Cancer.

"But you can let us know if you ever need anything," her mother said.

"Of course. And if you do—you don't, do you?—we'll try really hard to help you out."

"If we can," finished her mother.

"Thanks," said Cancer.

Truth be told, she liked being responsible for Benny and knowing that he needed her so completely. She loved him desperately and wanted nothing from life but to keep him safe, and in Cancer's mind, he was much safer with her than with her parents. He was her job, her responsibility—her life. If she did nothing but keep Benny safe for the rest of his days, she was just fine with that.

Then, the unthinkable happened: Benny got better.

"It's completely and utterly unexplainable," explained Dr. Glassfarden, "but Benny is getting better."

"That's unfathomable!" said their father.

"Unthinkable!" added their mother.

"I don't believe it," muttered Cancer. "How do you know he's really better? How do you know he isn't faking?"

Dr. Glassfarden pulled out files full of indecipherable documents and sheets and sheets of x-rays. He pointed here, there, and everywhere as he spoke. "Benny faking is a scientific impossibility. As you can see here and here, the problem has dispersed, and the diffusion opened up his ability to feel completely better."

Cancer had no idea what he was talking about. "So he's just better now, always and forever? There's no chance of him being sick again?"

"Well, I suppose a relapse is possible, but I'd say it's highly unlikely."

"Relapse means he could be sick again?"

"Yes. Possible, but highly unlikely."

"So a relapse could happen at any time."

"Well—"

"So I need to keep Benny safe."

And that's exactly what Cancer did, continuing to care for her little brother as she had always done, making sure that nothing ever happened to him. She was good at her job, and nothing ever did.

Years went by, and the very unlikely relapse still hadn't happened. Benny was about to turn nine years old, and he was the very picture of health. Despite this, Cancer still continued to protect him as she always had, much to his dismay.

"This is stupid," he would tell her. "I don't need to tie pillows to myself when I sleep."

"But what if you fall?" Cancer would ask.

"I won't."

"But what if you do?"

"Then I fall."

Whenever he said something like this, Cancer's eyes would widen in horror. Then she'd scrunch her face up in anger.

"Benny Masterson, you stop that. I haven't kept you safe your whole life only to have you be stupid now!"

And Benny would feel bad and back down, knowing how much his sister had given of herself to keep anything from ever happening to him.

Still, it was frustrating. He liked his sister, appreciated her help protecting him from bullies, and enjoyed playing the games she invented, but sometimes he wanted more. Why couldn't he ever play with other kids? Were all of them really trying to hurt him, like she said? He was starting to suspect that maybe—just maybe—his sister might be wrong. Some of those kids she said were trying to beat him up had seemed like maybe they just wanted to play a game. His suspicions got even stronger when Richie Gilmore stopped by one night.

"Hello," said Richie after his sister had reluctantly opened the front door. "Would Benny like to come over and play some video games?"

"Yeah!" Benny had answered, excited, but his sister had just laughed.

"Come over? I'll have you know that Benny is very sick, so *coming over* is out of the question."

"I'm not—" began Benny, but Cancer shushed him.

"Okay," Richie responded. "What if I bring my games over here?"

"That sounds reasonable—" Benny had tried again, but again his sister stopped him.

"I don't think you heard me right. He's sick. You coming here is just as bad."

"Why?" asked Richie.

"Because of your dirty, gross, stinky germs," she said, aghast. "Why do you think?"

"But I don't have germs," Richie argued.

"Yeah," said Benny, "Richie doesn't have germs."

Cancer just shook her head sadly. "The fact that you believe that is more than enough to show me that you two shouldn't be playing together. I'm sorry, Richie, but Benny can't play."

And with that, she shut the door in his face and on whatever social life Benny might have hoped to have as an even halfway normal nine-year-old, and suddenly he found himself angry.

"Why'd you have to do that?" he yelled.

Cancer was maddeningly calm. "Because, Benjamin, you're sick and need to stay safe."

"But I'm not sick. I haven't been sick in years!"

"Ah, but you forget that you could relapse at any time."

"You say that, but every time I see Dr. Glassfarden, he tells me I'm doing great."

"Well, he told me that you could relapse."

"When?"

"I don't know. A while ago."

"Years ago, I'll bet."

"Maybe. But that doesn't mean it couldn't happen."

"Well, you know what? Good. At least something would be happening, then."

"What are you saying?"

"I'm saying that I'm nine years old, and you don't ever let me do anything."

"Because I'm responsible for you. I have to make sure nothing ever happens to you."

"Well, you're doing a good job so far. Because there's definitely nothing happening to me."

And with that, he stormed off, leaving Cancer shaken and utterly surprised.

Over the next few days, things got worse. Benny, who up till now had always followed their plan of waiting for her to help him around and make sure nothing happened, started going off on his own.

She came to his class one day to find him already gone and immediately panicked. Cancer's breath caught in her throat, and she felt her pulse racing, but she forced herself to calm down for Benny's sake and get to him before something horrible happened. First, she grabbed another kid by the collar as he passed by.

"Hey!" he yelled.

"I need you to check the bathrooms."

"I have to get to class."

"It's a matter of life and death! Benny could be in grave danger!"

"Okay, okay, which bathroom?"

"Bathrooms!"

"Which ones?"

"All of them, of course!"

"You're crazy."

"Just do it," she said, shaking him.

He nodded and ran off, glad to get away from her.

"Meet me in the nurse's station afterward!" she shouted after him.

But he wasn't in the nurse's station, and she hadn't seen him all day. Cancer was in the middle of yelling at the nurse to convince her to put together a search party when the boy she commissioned for the bathroom search returned.

"Did you find him?" Cancer asked, desperate.

"Yes."

"Where? Which bathroom? Is he okay? You called 911, and they're already with him, right?"

"Which question do you want me to answer first?" asked the very overwhelmed boy.

"Which bathroom?"

"None of them."

"Then where is he?"

"Mr. Lowinsky's math class?"

"He collapsed in math class?"

"What? No!" said the boy, but Cancer was already off and running.

She burst into Mr. Lowinsky's class right in the middle of a lesson, interrupting integers.

"Where's Benny? Is he okay?"

Mr. Lowinsky looked upset. "What is this? You can't just run into my classroom like this."

"My brother's in trouble!"

"Uh, no, I'm not," said a voice from the back of the class, and Benny stood up. "I'm fine. You're the one who's running around like crazy."

Cancer stood there, sputtering, while Benny's class laughed at her. Finally, Mr. Lowinsky escorted her out and shut the door behind her. He'd gone to class without her? What was Benny thinking?

"I was thinking that I didn't need you to hold my hand everywhere we go anymore," Benny said later that night at home.

"But you didn't wait for me! You didn't tell me."

"Because I didn't need to. And I didn't tell you because you would have argued."

"That's ridiculous," Cancer said.

"No, it's not. You never listen to me."

"Of course I listen to you."

"Okay. From now on, I'm walking to classes myself."

Cancer bit her lip and fidgeted, clearly wanting to argue but trying not to. Arguing won out. "But something could happen to you."

"Good! I want something to happen to me. Anything! My whole life, you've been 'keeping me safe' by not letting me live."

"What are you talking about? You live."

"Your life. By your rules."

"Fine. Tell me what you want to do, and I promise I'll let you do it.

"For real?" he asked, excited but disbelieving.

"Promise," she said.

"Okay," he said. "Here goes. Today in gym, for the first time ever, I actually played with the other kids."

"What?" exploded Cancer. "But something could have…" She trailed off as she saw the look her brother was giving her. "That's nice. How did it go?"

"Coach McGill said I'm a natural soccer player."

She bit her lip. "That's fantastic," she made herself say. "Good for you."

"It is good for me. I felt good. Really good."

"I'm glad," she said, surprised to discover that she really was. Maybe she had been too restrictive on Benny, keeping him away from being a kid. Maybe it was good that he did stuff that made him feel normal once in a while.

"Good," said Benny. "I'm glad you're glad, because I'm joining the soccer team."

Cancer felt her jaw drop to the floor, along with her stomach. If Benny had said he was going to join the army, she didn't think it would be any worse.

"Joining the soccer team?" she said.

"Yes," he replied. "It starts tomorrow after school, so you can walk home without me."

And with that, Benny turned and walked up to his room, leaving Cancer speechless and terrified and more helpless than she'd ever felt in her life.

The next day after school, Cancer snuck out to the soccer field, pulling her hoodie up over her head to hide her face. Benny had told her to walk home without him, so she didn't think he wanted her there, but she couldn't bring herself to just go home. It was still her job to make sure nothing happened to him, and if she had to hide to do it, so be it.

Bleachers stood next to the field, and a few kids and parents were hanging out there, Cancer noticed, thankful that she wouldn't be completely conspicuous. She climbed up them quickly and took a seat in the back, trying to make herself small so that she wouldn't be noticed.

On the field, her brother was listening intently while Coach McGill gathered the entire team around him for instructions. He looked so small out there, she thought, noting that several of the other boys were a lot bigger than him. Didn't they have weight classes or something? Her thoughts were interrupted by the conversation of the two mothers in front of her.

"Last year, Billy darn near broke his arm," one was lamenting, shaking her head. "We had to take him to the emergency room."

"That's nothing," said the other mother. "My Darryl got two concussions, and once they had to call the ambulance to cart him off the field."

The two women laughed. "Boys will be boys."

Cancer gulped, a knot of fear tightening in her stomach as Coach McGill blew the whistle and the team took their positions to start practicing. This game was going to give her a heart attack. A real one. She was going to have a heart attack right there in the bleachers and die, and then who would take care of Benny? She forced herself to breathe slowly and calmly as the coach blew the whistle again, and the boys began.

Then, as she watched, a most surprising thing happened: Cancer discovered that Benny was good. Really good. He ran circles around the other boys and worked the ball with grace and elegance, like he'd been doing it his whole life. She didn't know where the skill came from, but he really was a natural. While the other kids had difficulty not using their hands, Benny was a master at using his body. She stared in awe as he bounced the ball off his knees, chest, and head, effortlessly passing to other players and sometimes even to himself. And when he kicked the ball—oh, it was a thing of beauty. It was as if he had found a way to control the ball's flight in midair, so accurate and powerful were his kicks.

He was so good that she forgot all of her fears, simply enjoying watching him be one with the ball. Maybe she'd been wrong. Maybe he was ready to take some chances and be a real kid. She was just starting to accept that idea as a reality in her mind when it happened: one of the other boys went for the ball at the same time as Benny, and there was a midair collision, both boys knocking heads and crashing to the ground.

In a flash, Cancer was up and racing to her brother's side, screaming his name. By the time she reached him, he was sitting up and smiling while he held his head.

"Cancer, what are you doing here?"

She grabbed his hand and started dragging him off the field. "I knew this was a bad idea. You can't handle something like this. It's just not for you. It's too dangerous."

He shook her hand off and stopped. "Quit it. I'm fine. And I'm staying."

"No, Benny, you don't know how weak and frail you really are. I saw you when you were a baby and you almost died. You're just not meant for stuff like this."

"I'm not leaving, Cancer. Look at me. I'm fine. I'm not a baby anymore."

"Stop being so stubborn! I've sacrificed so much for you," Cancer snapped.

"Oh, stop it!" Benny said. "Don't blame me for you not having a life. You keep saying I'm too weak to do things, but really, it's you. Taking care of your poor, frail little brother is such a great excuse for not ever having to do anything. But I want to do things, and you can't stop me. Now leave me alone!" He walked away angered.

He ran back to his teammates on the field, and she slowly backed away, hurt and shocked, and then broke into a run and got away as fast as she could.

That night, after Cancer cried herself out on her bed with the music blasting, there was a knock at her door. When she didn't respond, Benny let himself in.

"Can?" he asked.

She pulled her blankets up over her head and burrowed as deeply as she could go. "Leave me alone," she said.

After a pause, her door closed, but when Cancer popped out from under the covers, Benny wasn't gone. He was over by her iPod deck, turning off her music.

"I thought I told you to go," she muttered.

"Sorry," he said.

She shrugged.

"No," he said. "That's what I came to tell you. I'm sorry."

"For what?" she grumbled.

"You know for what," he said. "I was really mean and jerky to you earlier. You didn't deserve that, and I'm sorry."

"You mean that?" she asked.

He nodded. "Yeah. You've always done everything to take care of me, and I shouldn't have said that."

"Thanks," she said, "but you're wrong."

Benny blinked and shook his head. "What?"

"You're wrong."

"So...I shouldn't be apologizing?"

"Oh, no, you were really awful to me today."

"Hey, I said I was sorry!"

"But it was deserved."

"Still—"

"No. You were right. I look at you and still see my baby brother who could die if the wind blows too hard."

"Was I really that bad?"

"Worse," she said, smiling.

He smiled back. "Jerk."

"But you've come a long way since then, and I'm sorry I had trouble seeing that. Let me rephrase that: I'm sorry that I'm still having trouble seeing that, but I really am going to try hard to be less protective of you. You're growing up, and I need to let you grow up."

"Thanks," he said, smiling.

"You're welcome," she replied and then pointed at him. "Don't think I'm still not going to protect you. You don't get off that easily. I'll just be more selective with my protecting."

"Fair enough," he said, laughing. "But if you get out of line, I'm going to tell you."

She nodded. "That's fair, too." Then she held her arms out for him. "Now get over here and hug me."

He ran over and wrapped his arms around her, both of them squeezing each other tight. Finally, Benny pulled away, or, rather, tried to pull away. "Uh, sis, you know you eventually have to let me go."

"I know," she said, "just give me a little longer."

He did.

Leo

July 23 to August 22

Warmhearted Leo lives to help
With enthusiastic generosity of wallet and ideas
But take care when accepting his assistance
Because patronizing Leo always knows best
And you may find that help comes with strings

Leo LeMeur knew that he was a very lucky boy.

His wing alone on his parents' estate had a swimming pool, a video game room, a movie the-atre, a basketball court, and a sound-proof music room full of instruments he'd grown bored of playing after a few attempts. And his bedroom, of course. He had every toy you could imagine in there—from video games to high tech flying airplanes.

But more than that, Leo just seemed to have the perfect life. He was smart and athletic, popular at school, and his mom and dad were two of the nicest people in the world. They doted on him, yes, but they also made sure he grew up appreciating the things he had and often took him to their many charity events and fundraisers to show him the necessity of giving back and helping one's fellow man. To them, it was an ideal at the very core of responsible wealth. If you had money and opportunities, it was your duty to share with the rest of the world. This was something that Leo took very much to heart.

Now, just because they were good, warm-hearted people didn't mean that Leo's parents were in touch with the way the world worked. They had so much money that they had forgotten its value, providing Leo with an enormous allowance each week that he couldn't possibly use himself without starting up several multinational corporations.

But because he was generous and warm-hearted himself, the thought of lording his money over the other kids in his class never even occurred to Leo. Instead, he showed how greatly he had internalized the message of giving his parents had instilled in him by sharing.

As with most things, it started with something small.

On his very first day of kindergarten, Leo overheard Mrs. Merriweather, his teacher, speaking to Mr. Longbottom, the principal.

"The payment was supposed to be in yesterday," Mr. Longbottom said, sounding annoyed.

Mrs. Merriweather patted his hand to calm him. "Ansel's mother is well aware, and she's trying to scrape together the money as soon as possible, but we can't very well just not feed the boy."

"I know that. But I also know that the budget is tight as it is, and giving away free lunches in the hopes that they'll eventually be paid for gives me an ulcer."

Leo tugged on his teacher's pants leg to get her attention. "I can pay for Ansel."

She smiled kindly at him but shook her head. "That's very sweet, Leo, but I'm not sure your parents would approve."

Mrs. Merriweather turned back to continue talking to Mr. Longbottom, but Leo tugged on her pants leg again. "I am," he said simply and then dug twenty dollars out of his pocket and presented it to her. "Is this enough?"

Before his teacher could say anything, Mr. Longbottom snatched the money from Leo's hand. "Enough? My dear boy, this will feed Ansel for the week!"

"Two weeks," said Mrs. Merriweather, shooting the principal a glare.

"Ah, yes," he said uncomfortably. "Quite right. Two weeks."

Leo's teacher smiled down at him again. "That was a very kind thing you just did, Leo. You're sure your parents won't mind?"

"My parents always say that giving back isn't a master of choice; it's a responsibility."

Mr. Longbottom frowned, confused. "Master of choice? Oh, matter of choice. Quite right, young fellow, quite right." He reached down and ruffled Leo's hair. "I only wish we had more people like your parents. We might even be able to pay off the money we owe for the lunch program."

"You mean more kids don't have money and might not eat?" Leo asked.

"I'm afraid so, my boy," answered Mr. Longbottom. "We do our best, but it is the way the world works, you know."

Leo looked thoughtful for a second and then pulled a giant wad of twenties out of his pocket. "Is this enough to make sure everyone gets to eat all year?"

Their eyes went wide, and their mouths dropped, and five minutes later, Leo was sitting in the principal's office while his parents were being called. After ensuring Mr. Longbottom that their son had not stolen the money, that it was part of his weekly allowance, Leo's parents said that he was free to do with it as he wished. When the principal told them Leo's plans for the money, they were overjoyed and offered to pay for the lunch program themselves right then if the principal would just send over a contract. Without hesitation, he agreed.

From that day forward, everyone—kids and adults—knew Leo was the person to ask if they needed anything. But what was even better was that they didn't need to ask; if Leo ever overheard anyone talking about being in need, they had what they required moments later. Because of this great generosity, people actually found themselves trying not to talk too openly about their desires, lest Leo have it waiting for them when they got home.

Jen Grady, a girl in Leo's class, found this out the hard way after wishing for a kitty cat. Leo got her the best one he could find, but it didn't take Jen long to discover that she was utterly allergic.

"I'm sorry," she said the following day, bringing the cat back to him. "I love Skittles, but when

I'm around her, I can't breathe. I have to give her back."

Leo thought and then offered a solution. "Maybe you can get allergy medicine from your doctor."

Excited, Jen said she'd ask her parents, but Leo offered to pay for her to go to his doctor right then. Jen didn't see why not, so they had the test, and she was given a prescription.

"Thanks," she told Leo through her stuffy nose. "I'll try the medicine as soon as I get home."

"Great," said Leo. "See you tomorrow. I'm sure you'll be right as rain."

But the next day, Jen was worse. It was even harder to breath, and her eyes were puffy and sore. Again she offered to give the kitty back, but again Leo refused, saying the doctor could do more tests.

"There has to be something he can do," offered Leo.

Reluctantly, Jen agreed.

This time, the doctor had to use a big needle. "We want to make sure we know exactly what the problem is, don't we?" he asked.

"Uh-huh," Jen said, scared.

The needle was painful, and she almost cried, but it seemed worth it when he gave her a different medicine that he promised would work. "Guaranteed or your money back," he joked.

"It's not my money," she replied.

It also wasn't the right medicine, she discovered, coming to school the following morning feeling somehow even worse than the day before. Again she tried to give back the kitty.

"But he loves you," said Leo. "I'm sure one more trip to the doctor—"

"No! No more trips to the doctor. What I really want is for Skittles to go to a kid who won't get sick and will love her."

Leo thought for a second and then nodded. "That's a great idea." He took the cat and found her another home with a girl who had no allergies at all and told Jen he was sorry the cat made her sick.

Stories like that became abundant over the years.

It could be as small as Leo buying the new Spider-Man comic book for someone who lamented not being able to get it, to as big as him offering to pay for a friend's family's medical bills when he knew they were having difficulty.

Leo really was a genuinely good guy, and often, with the bigger "gifts," he involved himself way past money. Flowers and hospital visits were not uncommon if someone was sick. Once he had a house built for someon over to check to make sure thing smoothly. Startup money for businesses was provided, along with advice.

By the time he was ten, Leo had not only given his school district the newest, most-advanced school buildings, loaded with technology and staffed by the brightest—and most well-paid—teachers, he'd also become the youngest person on the school board, involving himself in every decision he cared to. It was pretty hard to say no to someone who was doing so much good for them, so the board let him have his say and bore his whims.

As for his friends at school, they learned to be careful what they said around him, lest they inadvertantly found themselves under his well-meaning thumb. They developed a code and warning signals and did very well with it overall.

Until, that is, Remy Duveril got so excited about his newest idea for an invention that he just blurted it out, right in front of Leo.

"Edible books!" shouted Remy. "Why hasn't someone thought about it before?"

It was lunch period for the entire fifth grade, and they were all sitting in the fancy new cafeteria Leo had bought for them, eating healthy but tasty gourmet lunches prepared by the world's best chefs.

All the boys at the table knew Remy's mistake the second he made it, but there was nothing to be done now. Still, Denny Miller tried to quickly change the subject.

"I really like popsicles," he said, too quickly and too loudly. He was not a master at changing the subject.

"Books you eat?" Leo asked.

"Exactly."

"Why would anyone want to eat books?"

Apparently Remy was too excited to stop himself, because he just kept right on going.

"Why wouldn't they? Think about it. What's more useless than a book you've already read? It just sits there. It's not like you're going to read it again."

"Of course not. Who would want to do that?" Leo asked.

"No one! So it just sits there, taking up space."

"Right," Leo said.

"But what if it didn't just sit there? What if you could eat it? Then it would solve two problems— getting rid of the book and getting rid of your hunger."

"This is one of the best ideas I've ever heard, Remy." Leo smiled.

"Thanks," Remy said.

"So let's do it."

Remy turned to him, confused. "Huh?"

"I'll hire some scientists and get them started working on the problem."

"Oh, I don't know—"

"Don't be silly. This is a great idea, and you'll be in charge. Each step of the way, you'll have total control."

"Yeah?" asked Remy, a little confused

"Yeah."

"Well, uh, okay; let's do it," Remy said.

"Yes! This is going to be so much fun."

"I'm going to be a real inventor!" Remy said excitedly.

"More than that, your idea might stop world hunger when people can eat books as entire meals."

"Well, uh, I was thinking more that the books would just be candy or something."

Leo clapped Remy on the shoulder. "I wouldn't worry about it too much. I'm sure the scientists will figure it out."

"Yeah," said Remy, a note of discomfort creeping into his voice.

The rest of the boys at the table shared a look. It was beginning. Remy's name might end up on it, but this was going to be Leo's invention.

Over the next few weeks, Leo thought the project was moving along swimmingly. He had had a bunch of notes and ideas for the scientists, and they were busy carefully crafting and implementing his thoughts. Remy had called several times, and Leo kept meaning to call him back, but it was just so busy that he hadn't been able to do it.

As he finished another song on Rock Band in his video games room, he made a mental note to try to return Remy's call that day.

Just as he had that thought, the doorball rang.

He lifted the guitar over his head—a real Fender he'd had customized so that he could use it to play video games—and carefully set it down in the cradle next to the couch before heading out to the door.

On the way, he passed by the music room, basketball court, and movie theatre—where *Fred: The Movie* was playing on a loop—and it occurred to him that the front door was really far away. This thought cemented itself when the doorbell rang again before he was halfway there, and Leo resolved to fix the situation. Perhaps another door? But then how would people know where to go? Maybe a moving sidewalk built in to the floor? Or a golf cart to drive around the hallways?

The doorbell rang for a third time just as he rounded the corner to the foyer, and he pushed those thoughts out of his mind for the time being.

"Who is it?" he asked.

"Remy," said a voice.

Immediately he brightened and opened the door to find his friend.

"Remy! I was just reminding myself that I had to call you back today. How are you?"

Remy, who had come to the door resolved in his anger at being kept out of the loop on his own invention, was momentarily taken aback by Leo's friendliness.

"Uh, good, mostly. I guess."

"Well, then I guess that's good," Leo said, smiling. "Come in."

Remy entered the house and was immediately intimidated. Everything was so large, so ornate, so... grand. He'd set his mind to come over and yell at Leo, but maybe that was the wrong way to take this. Maybe he was overreacting.

Leo waved him into the nearest room, a huge, open space full of books and couches. "Sit down. Want a drink? Want to play a game?"

Remy sat. Still taking in his surroundings, his reply was short. "Uh, no."

"Well, then, what's up, man? So sorry I haven't called you back. I'm so bad at stuff like that sometimes."

"Actually, that's what I wanted to talk to you about."

"Me being bad at things?"

"Sort of. I haven't been able to get in to talk to the scientists about my invention."

"That's ridiculous!"

"They said you set up security access that required your verbal permission to get in."

Leo smacked himself in the forehead. "Oh, right. Clearly I didn't mean you. Those guys are such idiots. I'll clear it up."

"Oh. Okay," Remy said. "Thanks."

"Was that it?"

"Well, could you do it now?" Remy asked. "The project's due in a week, and I'd really like to get started on it."

"Get started, are you kidding?"

"Uh, no. Why would I be kidding?"

"Well, you don't have to worry about that," Leo said.

"Why wouldn't I have to worry about that?"

"Well, because my scientists have been working on it since that first day I called them," Leo explained.

Remy jumped out of his seat. "*What?*"

"Yeah, you don't need to worry. I went in and gave them some thoughts on the best way to do it right away."

"You...you?"

"It's going fantastic, they tell me."

"But this is my project!"

Leo laughed. "Duh. Of course it's yours. I wouldn't steal it or anything. We're buddies. And besides, that's just not me."

Remy started pulling his own hair in frustration. "Don't you understand? That's exactly what you're doing!"

Leo looked at him like he was crazy. "No, I'm not. I'm just helping."

"Helping?"

"Yeah. Isn't that what you wanted me to do? Isn't that why you took my money?"

Remy held up a finger in Leo's face. "No. No, you don't get to do that. That's not fair."

"What am I doing?"

"Do you really not see?" asked a shocked Remy

"I guess not."

"You've completely taken over my idea," Remy yelled.

"Oh, I wouldn't say—"

"Really? Are the books paperback or hard-cover?" Remy asked.

"Uh, hardcover."

"Paperback is smaller and easier for kids to take with them for snacks," Remy said.

"Ah, but it's not a snack; it's a meal."

"Exactly. This whole meal thing. You wanted that," Remy said. "And I even told you I didn't, but you went ahead and did it anyway."

"I didn't know you felt that way."

"Everyone feels that way. This is what you do, Leo. You come in like the nice guy just wanting to help out, but then you start taking things over."

"No I don't."

"Mike Wilson's tree house."

"Exactly. I helped Mike out, and he loves it," Leo said.

"Where did Mike want it?"

Leo narrowed his eyes. Was this a trick question? "Uh, where it is."

"No. He told you he wanted it in the tree right next to his bedroom so he could go in and out at night, but you liked the tree in the corner of the yard, so that's where it is."

"If that's true, why didn't Mike argue with me?"

"Because you are a nice guy, Leo, and because we all feel guilty when you give us money to do stuff, even though none of us has ever asked you for any of it."

"So people are afraid to tell me what they really think?" Leo's voice became quiet, thoughtful.

"You want to be this good guy who just lets people do the things they want to do and give people everything they need, and that's great, but you can't say you're just letting people do what they want and then butt your nose in whenever you feel like it."

Leo crossed his arms, pouting, unable or unwilling to believe people thought about him this way; he so clearly wasn't that person Remy was describing. The more he thought about it, the more upset Leo became, and he couldn't believe that Remy was being so ungrateful about all the help Remy had given him. He allowed anger to flare up in his heart and said something he'd never thought he would say.

"Well, maybe I should just take my money back, then."

Remy just stood there for a second, his expression unreadable, and then one single word came out: "Fine."

Then he turned on his heel and stormed from the room, and Leo was still sitting there wondering what just happened when he heard his front door close.

All that night, Leo raged about how stupid and mean and unfair Remy was being to him. He didn't take things over. That was just silly. He helped people. Didn't he have a whole slew of people he'd assisted to prove it? Weren't there a dozen programs with his name on them and wings in schools that had been dedicated to him because he'd paid for them himself, all to make the school better?

He thought and he thought.

Leo remembered the good feeling he'd had when Louise Colgate's mom was finally diagnosed as being completely free and clear of cancer after he paid for her treatment. He recalled the smile on Ray Charlotte's face when Leo bought them a new house after a tornado took theirs.

But then he thought again.

The slightly uncomfortable smile Louise and her father gave him when he started showing up every day to ask for updates on their mom. The surprise and confusion on Ray's face when Leo unveiled that he hadn't recreated their former home like they'd spoken about, but made improvements on it. Were there tears that his friend had held back? And were they tears of sadness, rather than joy? What right had he to decide that his vision of their new home was better than their own? If he was truly gifting people out of selflessness, shouldn't he simply hand over the money and not look back?

He started shaking so badly that his fingers started missing the notes on Rock Band, and he ended up with the worst score he'd ever gotten. It made his stomach churn to even think it, but maybe Remy was right.

The next morning, when Remy left his modest house for the daily walk to school, Leo was outside waiting for him in his limo.

Remy took a deep breath and walked over to him. "I'm not so sure I really want to talk to you right now," he said.

Leo nodded. "That's understandable. I just wanted to give you this." He reached into the car and pulled out a document.

"What's that?"

"Take it," said Leo.

"What is this, a contract or something?"

"Yup. You can read it, but basically it says that I offered you the money free and clear, and henceforth—that just means from now on—I won't have any involvement in making the invention. Oh, and it also says you have to sign off on every single part of the invention, and you can change whatever you want."

Remy looked up at his friend. "Why are you doing this?"

"Because it's right, man."

"I don't want you to—"

"And because I realized that you were right. I always take things over, and they're not mine to take over. I didn't realize it, but I was being really selfish, pushing my way into things where people didn't really want me."

Remy smiled at Leo. "Thanks. You saying that really means a lot."

Leo nodded and started to turn away.

"Hey, wait, I have an idea."

Leo turned back and watched as Remy pulled a pen from his back and wrote something on the contract. Remy handed it over to Leo, and he read it aloud.

"Remy and Leo share this invention fifty-fifty, and they both have to sign off on every single part of the project."

Leo looked up at his friend, shocked. "Why?"

"Because I don't want to do this without my friend. I never did; I just wanted to work together. Will you work together with me?"

"Of course I will!" said Leo, excited.

"Sweet," said Remy. "I was hoping you'd say that."

"You wanna ride with me to school so we can talk some ideas through?"

"That's a great idea."

And with their friendship restored, the boys tumbled into the back of the limo and rode off, arguing happily all the way.

Virgo

August 23 to September 22

Oh, brilliant Virgo
So meticulous and diligent in your tasks
So reliable and practical in your execution
If only your own quest for perfection
Didn't leave you overcritical and harsh
Toward the rest of the world

Virgo was a nerd.

She knew that was how everyone else in the ninth grade saw her, and she had to admit—in this one thing, at least—they were probably right.

After all, while her classmates spent their time talking about parties and drinking and who was hotter than who, Virgo diligently worked and read ahead on her class assignments, getting her homework done early. The previous semester, she had actually completed the work for three of her six classes halfway through the quarter.

Naturally, she always got straight As and was currently number one in her class, though that brown-noser Rachel Salinger was breathing down her neck because of all her weighted grades.

Some people thought that Virgo herself was a brown-noser, and she could certainly see why, but it wasn't true. She couldn't be blamed if teachers saw her as the responsible one and always chose her for tasks that involved trust, could she? Virgo never asked to be the attendance taker, and she had no burning desire to be the one passing out and collecting tests. What was she supposed to do, tell them no? Talk about an awkward conversation. So she did it without fail, taking the glares from some of the other students as par for the course.

Besides her unsolicited teacher's assistant duties, she was one of the few in classes who was not only paying attention but raising her hand. So far, she'd calculated 73.5 percent of Mr. Donald's history questions had been answered by her, and a whopping 82 percent of Miss Jenkins's biology questions. By the end of the year, she estimated, she would have answered more questions than everyone else in any of her classes combined.

Virgo didn't take her smarts for granted though. She knew that she could slip at any time, which was why she was such a hard worker. Practice made perfect, and perfection would always be her goal, so any time she got the opportunity to do extra work, she took it.

Unfortunately, her classmates had easily picked up on the fact that she would never turn down work and used it to their advantage. There was one time she was the most popular person in the room:

"Group project time!" announced Mr. McShane.

Immediately, a sea of faces surrounded Virgo, clamoring for her attention.

"Pick me, and I'll do your hair," begged Darlene Mark, a gum-popping, big-haired fool of a girl that Virgo wouldn't let touch her hair with a ten-foot pole.

"I'll do your nails," offered William Bigsby, a cute and not-very-well-closeted gay boy she remembered had once been nice to her when some jocks were picking on her.

She raised her hand and pointed at him, eliciting a shriek of excitement from William and groans of frustration from the others.

"You can go to the homecoming dance with me," Dillon Murphy said, a suggestion that immediately discounted him.

Jenna Farren pushed through the crowd to lean in to her at the desk. "Pick me, and I'll pretend to be you in gym class for a month," she whispered.

It showed how little Jenna knew about Virgo that she would think that suggestion a motivator for her. She might not be the best, but Virgo's need for perfection didn't stop at her studies; sometimes she even stayed after school just to practice jumpshots for basketball or sliding into bases for baseball. Still, Jenna's offer showed ingenuity and a certain care for Virgo's well-being, so she pointed to her as well.

This time, the groans of disappointment were even louder. There was only one more person allowed in her group. People clamored for her attention so that she couldn't even make out what was being said, let alone who was saying it. Through the tumult, she noticed that Art Binkle was just sitting and reading a fantasy novel at his desk, oblivious to the scene. For some reason, that made her like him.

"Art," she said, pointing.

As everyone moaned and groaned their disappointment, Art gave her a thumbs up to show that he had heard.

Mr. McShane shook his head at the downtrodden, dispersing mob. "You're shameless, people. The rest of you, find a group quickly and sit together."

While the rest of the class did just that, Art and the others grabbed a chair nearby. Virgo laid down the ground rules.

"We all know why you chose me. I actually care about my work, and I don't mind doing this entire project one hundred percent by myself if I have to. That being said, I'm sure Mr. McShane wants all work to be written out by hand, so don't ever make a photocopy of work I've done and turn it in as your own. You will recopy it in your own hand. If you have trouble doing that, I am willing to help you read or understand anything confusing, because it will just mean more practice for me. Any questions?"

"Are you, like, a robot or something?" asked William.

Virgo sighed and shook her head. "Don't I wish."

Her classmates weren't the only ones who'd caught on to Virgo's incredible willingness to pile work on herself.

Virgo's mom and dad both worked full-time jobs, and in an industry where full time sometimes meant fifty, sixty, or even seventy hours a week. Because of this, they relied a lot on her to make sure that the housework got done and her little brother, Sammy, was well taken care of.

Every day after school, Virgo came home to a routine. With four people in the house, there was always laundry of some kind, so the first thing she always did was toss a load in. While that was going strong, she prepped whatever meal they were having that night. Usually, by the time she had finished that, the wash was finished; she could turn it over to the dryer and then begin doing whatever was on her chore list for that day. She'd broken down and organized the main list so that she could rotate through the chores and keep everything at a minimum level of cleanliness. One day she might clean the bathrooms; another, she was mopping the floors. After that, it was back to actually cooking the meal for that night, with varying levels of intensity required, depending on the meal. Some of them she could just throw in the oven and put a timer on, but others forced her to stand there, stirring or flipping or something equally boring.

At some point in all of this, Sammy would come home, and she'd have to make him a small, healthy snack and get him set up to work on homework. In the beginning, she'd trusted him to do it if she set it out for him, but after several times discovering him playing video games or watching TV, Virgo decided to put him at the kitchen table, where she could watch him more closely. Still, usually little of his work got done until after they had eaten dinner—usually just the two of them—and washed the dishes together.

Some people might have thought that all of this responsibility was a bit much for someone her age, but Virgo welcomed it. Though she never would have told her parents this—or, for that matter, her group members who so desired her help to do all of their work for them—it was when she wasn't in charge that Virgo started to worry about things. When she was doing them herself, at least she knew they would be done right. But if others were working on things, who knew what could happen? She wasn't about to risk herself in that way when she could just as easily do the work herself.

Plus, as with her after-school basketball sessions alone or her willingness to read and work ahead, Virgo welcomed any and all opportunities to practice, because she believed it brought her that much closer to the perfection she sought in all areas of her life.

One area where she needed quite a bit of practice, it turned out, was human interaction, and for that discovery, she owed a debt to her little brother and to her parents for making her the de facto babysitter.

Babysitting Sammy was not an unusual thing for Virgo, and she took her job very seriously. There were rules, he was expected to follow them, and when he didn't, she would both punish him and give him a stern talking to.

"You're being a passive receptor," she'd say when she caught him watching television instead of working. "All that thing teaches you is how to buy things."

"I know," he'd say. "I know."

"When are you ever going to need to throw fireballs?" she'd ask if he snuck to play a video game instead. "Hand-eye coordination there shows little correlation to real life coordination."

"Yes, sister," he'd intone. "You've told me."

Punishment might be sitting quietly in the corner, or it might be extra chores; it really just depended on how much needed to be done in the house on that particular night.

For the most part, Sammy didn't mind Virgo getting after him for those kinds of things, and even doing chores could sometimes be fun. Sometimes. The truly bad part came when Virgo didn't have any work of her own to do and helped him with his homework.

She was smart and all, obviously, and could break down everything very clearly once he made her understand that he needed to know every single step—no skipping—but sometimes it was difficult for him to deal with her, and he was really hoping against hope that it wasn't going to be one of those nights. He'd been thoroughly confused by his teacher in class but hoped that it would become clearer when he had a chance to slow down and sit and look at it by himself. So far, no such luck with the assignment *or* his sister.

Try as he might, Sammy could not make the fractions on the page in front of him make any sense at all. Three-halves divided by two-thirds gave you a big hunk of nothing so far as he was concerned. But he had to have some kind of answer, so he kept struggling through it.

To make matters worse, Virgo was hovering over his shoulder, watching intently and making him feel extremely uncomfortable.

He looked at the equation again and suddenly thought he understood something. Sammy leaned forward to write the answer, but his sister stopped him.

"Not that."

"But that's the only way that it makes sense to me," Sammy said.

"There's an easier way."

"So, wait. Is it wrong, or are you just telling me that there's an easier way to do it?"asked Sammy.

"If there's an easier way to do it, then you are doing it wrong."

"I'm doing it my way," Sammy said. "At least, it's a way that I understand."

"That's a mistake."

Sammy ignored her and solved the equation, taking twice as long as he'd hoped. Behind him, he heard Virgo sigh, so he flipped to the back of the book to check the answer key. He was right!

"Ha! Look at that. My method works."

"It's still wrong."

"But it makes sense to me. Plus, I got it right."

"It's wrong because it's way too slow. You're going to fail because you won't finish the test."

"I'll get faster."

She scoffed. "Not with that method."

He set his pencil down and took a deep breath. "Okay, show me your method."

In a flash, she had picked up the pencil and was writing so furiously that he couldn't understand a single step. In seconds, she was finished.

"There, you get that?"

Sammy looked at her like she was crazy. "What, are you kidding? No. Show it to me step by step."

She let out a big sigh but sat down and wrote down the first step for him. He didn't get it.

"I don't get it."

She scrunched up her face at him like she couldn't believe what he'd just said.

"What's not to get?"

"I don't get it, okay?"

"What about it?"

"Well, why does the X move from here to here and replace the four?"

She tapped a number on the question with her pencil. "That's this number."

"Why?"

"What do you mean, 'why'?"

"Why is it that number?"

"Sammy, did you even read the question?" She leaned back and shook her head. "You're never going to pass this test if you're not reading the questions."

"Don't be a jerk, Virgo. I read the question."

"Then how in the world can you not see why it's that number?"

"I just don't, okay?"

He stood up and stormed away from the table and up the stairs, where Virgo could hear his door slam shut.

"That's not going to help you learn any faster either, Sammy!" she shouted up after him.

After taking a moment to pause and shake her head, Virgo stood and cleaned up the drinking glasses they'd been using, busying herself with work.

When more than a half hour passed and Virgo still didn't see Sammy come back down, she decided to go investigate.

If he kept up this kind of behavior, he was never going to learn. He had to be able to push through it, be stronger. She was working up a whole speech to tell him about how she worked so hard because she didn't understand some things either, and sometimes you just needed to put in the work to be the best, but when she approached his door, she was surprised by what she heard. Sammy was praying.

She pushed in on the door ever so slightly and saw him kneeling there on the side of his bed, pajamas already on, hands clasped in front of him, head halfway bowed.

"…don't talk to you much, I know," he was saying, "but I really need to start understanding this fraction stuff soon. I've really, really, really been trying, but it just doesn't make any sense to me, and I have to figure it out. I have to."

He stopped and took a deep breath, and Virgo realized that Sammy was crying.

"I have to because I'm sick of Virgo treating me like she thinks I'm dumb. I'm not dumb, but that doesn't mean I understand everything, and sometimes she's just so mean. She says that she had to work really hard too, but I don't really believe it, because if that were true, she'd be a lot more understanding instead of such a jerk."

Virgo's eyes went wide. Was she really being so horrible to him? No, he had to be overreacting. She was just being rational and honest with Sammy. Surely he'd see that when he calmed down and looked at things better.

"I need you to help me, God, if you're up there, because I'm so angry with her, and I don't want to be angry. I know she's just trying to help and that she doesn't know any better, but sometimes she hurts me so much. And I'm not stupid, and she makes me feel stupid. Can't you do something to make her see that I'm not stupid, God, but still be able to help me? I guess... I guess what I'm really asking is for you to help her. Make her a better, more understanding person."

Virgo closed the door carefully behind her and crept down the hall, finally slumping down on the top stair before she started crying.

Her brother hated her, and it was her fault because she didn't realize she was being so mean and dismissive to him. Well, for Sammy to feel this way was not acceptable, so she had to figure out some way to fix it.

But what?

Virgo came home the following evening energized. She knew exactly what she was going to do, and she was convinced it would work. Probably. Hopefully.

She and Sammy went through their usual routines, doing chores, getting dinner ready, and in general just working to get to the point where they could work on homework. Sammy thought Virgo must have a lot of it that night; she was working so fast at everything else to get to it, but when everything was done and he sat down to do his own work, she didn't open her bag at all. Instead, she grabbed flashcards out of the hall closet and wrote on them, working intently.

"What are you doing?" he asked at one point.

"Just a project."

"What kind?"

"You'll see."

"For what?"

"You'll see. Do your work."

So while Virgo wrote and organized her flashcards, Sammy oranized his thoughts on his math assignment and tried to wrap his brain arond the still-fuzzy equations. Finally, Virgo was finished, but Sammy still had about half his homework to go.

"Wanna take a break?" she asked.

This was unheard of. Virgo didn't take breaks. Her method was more to power through everything; being done was her method of destressing. Sammy would be a fool to pass this opportunity by.

"Sure," he said, "what did you have in mind?"

She held up the cards, and for the first time, he could see that she had made fraction flashcards for him … but also, it appeared, for herself. At least, he hoped so.

"Those are for you, right?" he asked.

The cards he had dubbed "hers" were way more advanced than anything he'd ever been taught. She nodded.

"I made a set for you and a set for me."

"Okay. Why?"

"I thought we could have a little race—handicapped with harder questions for me because it's only fair—where I use the method I was trying to show you yesterday, and you can solve them however you're most comfortable."

He shrugged. "Sure, why not?"

She separated the cards out for each of them and then grabbed the timer from off the stove and set it.

"Ready?" she asked.

He nodded.

"Set...Go!"

She hit the timer, and each of them were off, racing as fast as they could through the cards...or at least, Sammy was. Maybe it wasn't the most honest she'd ever been, but Virgo had decided that what Sammy really needed was a burst of confidence, especially after what she'd done to him the night before.

"Done!" yelled Sammy, knocking her out of her reverie.

"What do you mean, done?" she asked. "With all of them?"

He laughed. "No, just the first one."

"Oh, so we're doing that, then?"

Sammy shrugged. "I thought it might be fun."

"Well, in that case," she said, taking just a few more seconds to write, "done."

It went on like that for a while, Sammy always just barely out in front, but as they neared the end, Virgo made a point of catching up with him and pulling into the lead.

"Ha!" she said. "Good luck catching me."

"I don't need luck," he answered. "I've been beating you all night! Done!"

Now, essentially, he was caught up, so Virgo took her sweet time on the equation in front of her, timing it beautifully.

"Done!" they both said at the same time.

Sammy seemed to be totally into it. The game had been a fantastic idea, and she kicked herself for not thinking of it sooner.

Her last equation was actually a truly tough one, so there was very little faking involved in the length of time it took her to solve.

"Done!" Sammy yelled, triumphant.

He had finished mere seconds after she was done herself. He really had gotten faster with his method.

"I knew I shouldn't have given myself this question." She laughed, turning it over for him to see.

His eyes widened. "Wow. Glad I've got a few years before I get to that."

"You'll learn more things along the way that will make it a little less daunting."

They looked at each other, last night's animosity all but forgotten—not by Virgo, though.

"So, Sammy, listen. It's not easy for me to say this, but I think I was probably kind of a jerk to you last night, and I'm really sorry."

He lowered his eyes to the table and shrugged his shoulders. "S'okay."

"No," she said. "It's not. It's really not, and I'm sorry."

He didn't do anything for a few seconds except squirm in his seat, so she continued.

"So what I'd really like to do—or try to do—is if you're up for it, I want to try to teach you the equation from last night. Only this time, I promise to go slow and not be such a meanie about it."

He looked at her and smiled. "I'd like that," he said.

"You know, Sammy, forget all this math stuff."

"What do you mean? You don't want to do it?" asked Sammy.

"Oh, no, I really want to try to teach you the equation."

"What then?" asked Sammy.

"I just mean … whenever you start feeling like math is tough, remember that you're my brother."

"Sometimes, sis, you are really, really confusing," said Sammy.

"Actually, that's exactly what I'm talking about. You think math is hard? Ha! Someone should give you a medal for being smart and patient enough to put up with me."

Sammy cracked a smile, and she grinned back.

"Come on," he said. "You're just stalling because you don't think you'll be good enough to teach me."

"Wow," she said, "you are learning. You really know how to push my buttons."

"Well," he replied, "I did learn from the master."

Then she moved over to sit beside him, and they got down to business.

Libra

September 23 to October 22

Easygoing and sociable
Idealistic Libra loves people
Gullibly believing in their general goodness
And that no problem is too strong to resist
Her urbane diplomacy
And flirtatiously charming nature
But her tendency for self-indulgence
Leaves her easily influenced

Libra Friedman actually kind of liked it when her friends fought.

Not because she liked fighting—she thought it was stupid and pointless—but because it gave her an opportunity to play peacemaker. It was a role she thoroughly enjoyed. Getting in between two people and calming them down, listening to opposing points of view, and then coming up with a solution that satisfied both of them—Libra had a hard time imagining anything more fun or exciting.

That was why her eyes nearly popped out of their sockets when Mrs. Feldtopper announced the creation of a new Beakersman Middle student group—Peer Mediators.

"They are looking for older students, so you seventh graders might have a harder time getting in, but I thought some of you might be interested in trying out."

Davey Johnsman, an arrogant, preppy kid, piped up from the back of the room. "Why would I want to spend my time talking about other people's problems? What's in it for me?"

Davey clearly meant it as a kind of joke, but Mrs. Feldtopper elected to take him seriously. "Being able to communicate with other people is an invaluable skill that will look great on college transcripts, might resonate with employers, and is just useful to have in life."

"But I already know how to communicate," Marty Fess said, snickering.

"Debatable, Mr. Fess," said Mrs. Feldtopper wryly, "but no one has to try out if they don't want to."

Libra's hand shot up. "When are the tryouts, Mrs. Feldtopper?"

As they walked down the hall after class, Libra's excitement overwhelmed Melanie Torv, Libra's best friend.

"Can you imagine a better person, Mel?"

"Nope," said Mel, sure she had answered this question at least twice before.

"I mean, I do this kind of stuff anyway, but to do it professionally..."

"I don't think you can call it professional."

"Yeah, yeah, I know. But you know what I mean."

"Yes."

"This is going to be amazing."

"Probably."

Suddenly, Libra stopped dead in her tracks, falling behind Mel. Her face drained of color.

"What if... What if I don't make it?"

Mel rolled her eyes and took a deep breath before turning around to face her friend. "This morning, I turned on the TV to find out that my stupid little brother deleted my *Next Top Model* season pass so he could record some stupid Nickelodeon show."

Libra's demeanor immediately changed. "Did you confront him about it?"

"If you mean 'did I yell at him,' then yes."

"Did he say why he did it?"

"Yeah, some garbage about the DVR only recording two shows, so he had to delete mine to record his. Dad had another show recording at the same time."

"And what did you say?"

"That if he did it again, I'd punch his nose so hard it would go inside his face."

"Mel, you should know that's not helpful."

She shrugged. "Made me feel better."

"What if one of you watched your show when it's actually on?"

Mel shook her head. "Both out. I have my tae kwon do class, and he's got piano."

Libra thought for a second. "Did you check to see if either of your shows was on at different times?"

"No. Huh," said Mel, her brow furrowing in thought. "That's a good idea."

"Might work," said Libra. "If not, there's always Hulu and stuff like that. A solution is always hiding there somewhere if you're just willing to look hard enough for it."

Mel smiled. "Exactly. And that's why you don't have to worry."

Libra narrowed her eyes. "What are you talking about?"

"Libra, I just threw a random problem at you and you found a solution in less than a minute. Trust me, you're going to be fine at this try-out thing. If they don't want you, they're just dumb. Now come on."

Libra nodded, unsure, but followed after her friend. "But, uh, what if you're wrong?"

Mel gave an exasperated groan and kept walking.

There were only two other students at the try out, both eighth graders.

The three of them stood waiting in a line while Mr. Resnick, the eighth-grade English teacher, sat at a table reading statements each of them had had to write for the try out, wondering what in the world he would ask.

While they waited, Libra did her best to size up her competition, trying to figure out the best way to convince Mr. Resnick to take her over them.

One of them was an overweight kid with glasses named Reg who kept scratching the outside of his nose and tugging at his shirt. He seemed nice enough but none too bright, and she couldn't understand what had made him want to try out for this.

The other half of her competition was Joanna Starks, a real brain who was at the top of the eighth-grade class and participated in every club.

She was serious, meticulous, and seemed to look at everything analytically.

Mr. Resnick was another story. He was an English teacher, so Libra thought that meant he probably cared about people and emotions and…themes maybe? Psychology? What did English teachers care about? She thought her best bet was probably appealing to his sense of drama and showing that she knew how to talk to people. That and maybe highlighting her difference as a seventh grader. Younger kids would see her more as a peer. Or maybe bringing up being younger was stupid.

She was just starting to formulate an actual strategy when Mr. Resnick looked up from the table and smiled. "Congratulations, you're all in."

"Woo-hoo!" yelled Reg, raising his arms in victory.

Joanna merely gave a cordial nod and walked off.

But as Mr. Resnick gathered his things to go, Libra just stood there, dumbfounded.

"Really?" she asked. "That's it?"

Mr. Resnick smiled at her. "That's it."

"But I was preparing a whole thing. Don't you want to know why I'm perfect for this?"

He finished putting his papers in his bag and closed it up. "Not really. See you tomorrow."

"But Mr. Resnick—"

"Libra. Out of the entire school, you three are the only ones who cared enough to even show up for a group that's all about helping your peers. That alone tells me that you're the best ones for the job."

Libra thought about it for a second and then nodded. "That actually makes a lot of sense. Thanks for staying to explain it to me."

"You're welcome. See you tomorrow."

"Ugh," said Joanna a week later in the mediation office, putting a file away into a cabinet. She had just finished handling a particularly tricky argument between two eighth-grade football players. "Doing this just makes me think the human race is doomed. We fight over so many stupid, petty things. People are just mean and vindictive and spoiled."

Libra thought that she could not disagree more as she waved to Reg and tossed her backpack onto the couch. Over the past few days, she'd helped people work out four different arguments and even stopped a fist fight in the cafeteria. Sure, the arguments could seem silly, but no one was fighting out of malice; they just thought they were right and the other person was wrong. And usually, that came about because they had stopped listening to each other.

In the fist fight, Brad Metzger had gotten angry because Aaron Simpson refused to let him copy his homework anymore. By the time she got there, fists and screams were flying.

"I won't do it anymore!" Aaron said, ducking a punch.

"This isn't fair! I need it!" yelled back Brad, putting up his arms as Aaron rushed him.

"Whoa!" said Libra, rushing between them to pull them apart.

"Beat it," sneered Aaron. "Who do you think you are?"

"The person who's going to keep you from getting suspended," said Libra, nodding to the school security guard approaching.

Immediately both boys stood up straight and fixed their clothes.

"You boys grab your stuff and come with me," said the guard.

"But he started it," whined Brad.

"That's a lie!"

"I don't care who started it. Get your stuff."

Libra tapped the guard's arm and whispered something in his ear, flashing her student mediator card. As first the guard just shrugged, but as the two boys watched, his demeanor softened. Finally, he nodded at Libra.

"As long as you guys go with her, I'm letting you go. For now. But if I hear about anything else happening, I won't let it go."

"Yes, sir," both boys said simultaneously.

Out in the hall with her, the boys were wide-eyed with excitement and confusion.

"How did you do that?" asked Aaron.

"Yeah, that was amazing."

Libra put on her business face and gave each of them a look. "It's not going to be so amazing unless you two fix whatever's wrong. He won't look the other way next time. So just tell me what the problem is."

Brad pointed at Aaron. "He's the problem."

"What, because I have a conscience?" Aaron asked.

"Right, conscience. Where was that the last three months while I was paying you?"

Libra whistled to get them to shut up. "Okay. Aaron, why was Brad paying you?"

Aaron looked away. "I'd rather not say."

"Okay, Brad. Why were you paying Aaron?"

"Because he's smart, and I wanted his homework."

Aaron shook his head. "Dude, are you dumb? We can get in trouble."

"No," said Libra, "that's not what I do. I help people work through problems, not cause more. Are you mad because he stopped paying you, Aaron?"

"I didn't stop paying him!"

"No, and that wasn't the problem," said Aaron. "Like I told him, I just felt wrong about it. I even gave him his money back from this last time."

"I don't need money, man. I need to pass. Just give me your work," Brad said.

"I can't do that anymore," Aaron said. "Judy says it's—"

"This is about your little girlfriend? Come on, man."

"You come on."

Libra waved her hands in front of them to get their attention.

"Okay, so let me see if I understand. Brad, you really need to get a good grade in this class, whatever it is."

"History."

"Doesn't matter. Aaron's work is helping you get a good grade. Right?"

"Right."

"And Aaron. You had a deal with Brad that was working out fine until you grew a conscience."

"Exactly!" Brad said.

"I wouldn't put it that way," muttered Aaron.

"But the moral part of it is the only thing that's bothering you, right? If you feel better about it, you'd probably love to still get money from Brad?"

"Sure, I guess. But I can't cheat."

"Yeah, now."

"That's in the past, Brad. Things have changed. If you want to pass history, you need to move on. Do you want to pass?"

Brad's reply was meek. "Yes."

"Answer's simple, then. Brad, you're going to pay Aaron to tutor you. Think about it. Solves all your problems."

Both boys looked slightly uncomfortable with the idea.

"That would take a lot more time," said Brad.

Aaron was nodding. "Yeah. I don't know."

Libra shrugged. "We could always tell the guard you'd prefer to be suspended."

The guys looked at each other and nodded.

"Okay," said Aaron, "we'll do it your way."

Yesterday she'd run into Brad in the hall, and he'd excitedly showed her the B he got on his most recent history test.

"It's so cool," he'd said. "I never knew learning would cost the same as cheating."

Scenes like that made her feel more adult, like she wasn't just one of the regular students anymore but something more important. She was doing something meaningful. She was helping people.

Even better, she could tell that they appreciated her and all her hard work. Yeah, Joanna was just wrong. Maybe she'd had some bad experiences, or maybe she just wasn't as good at her job as Libra was, but she was wrong. People were generally good, and almost everyone wanted to be good, even if they were doing something wrong. She opened her mouth to have a constructive conversation with Joanna about it, but the older girl grabbed her backpack and quickly left, waving as she went. *Oh well*, thought Libra. *Next time I'll get her to see how wrong she is.*

As she turned back, Reg handed her a file.

"Four girls are here in the office."

"You're not handling it?"

He shrugged. "They asked for you."

Libra suppressed a smile as she took the file and walked toward the mediation room. She was good. People already knew. And she suspected that most of it was due to the fact that she respected people and knew they were good and wanted to do the right thing. When she got older, maybe she'd write a book about it.

By the time she reached the mediation room, she couldn't suppress her smile any longer.

Libra immediately recognized two of the girls in the mediation as the participants in her very first mediation, Erica Malloy and Tina Bellstadt. She had successfully convinced them to stop fighting over the same table at lunch, which each claimed had a special meaning to them. Basically, they'd both met—and broken up with—their first boy-friends there. Once they discovered that commonality, Libra's demand that they just share the table went down a lot easier. It wasn't fair, she'd argued, for one to get the table over the other. Now, from the looks of it, they were best friends.

"I trust this isn't another problem with the lunch table," she said jokingly as she walked in and sat down.

"Actually," said the third girl, whose leg was up on the coffee table in a cast, "that's exactly what it is."

Libra turned to her, puzzled. "I'm sorry, I don't think I know you."

"Tammy Keaton. I just moved here."

"Yeah, and already she's trying to steal our lunch table," accused Erica.

"We offered to sit there with her and share it like you said with us," said Tina, "but she won't do it."

Libra turned to Tammy. "Is that true?"

Tammy nodded. "Because there's not enough room. The table's meant for two people, and right now I'm two people because the doctor says I need to keep my leg up when I'm sitting."

Libra sat. "Okay, but these girls were sitting at that table first. Why do you need this particular one?"

Tammy tapped the cast. "It's the closest table to the door, and if I don't sit there, I can't get to class on time."

"Huh, that's tough," said Libra, frowning.

"It doesn't matter," broke in Tina, "because it's not fair for one person to have the table over another. Right, Libra?"

"Yeah," said Erica. "That's what you told us."

Libra let out a big sigh. "Well, that's true, girls, but this is a bit of a different situation."

"What's that supposed to mean?" asked Tina, already getting annoyed. "She doesn't have to compromise because she broke her leg? That's not our fault."

Tammy snickered. "Jeez, sorry my broken leg is such an inconvenience to you."

Libra put her hands up. "Okay, okay. Look, it doesn't mean we can't compromise; it just means that the compromise is going to have to be different. Erica, Tina, her leg is broken. That's a physical fact we can't change. And it just makes sense that she get the table closest to the exit because of her condition, at least until the leg heals."

"I don't want it any longer than that anyway," said Tammy.

"The compromise I'd suggest for now is to sit at the table before Tammy gets there or after she leaves."

Erica and Tina's jaws dropped, but they didn't say anything.

The following day, Erica and Tina were back in the mediation room again, this time fighting with each other.

"You two just can't get enough of me, can you?" Libra joked. Neither one laughed, so she continued. "Okay, what's the problem this time?"

Both girls started yelling at the same time, so Libra held up her hand to stop them.

"Come on, guys. One at a time."

"We're working on a science project together," said Erica.

"Which would be great, except that her idea for it is stupid, and she won't listen to mine."

"My idea is perfectly fine," Tina said.

"Yeah, if you want something lame."

"Okay," Libra said. "Erica, what's your idea?"

"I want to show a cool chemical reaction that's exciting."

"Sounds good. And you, Tina?"

"Everyone's been worried about earthquakes lately, so I want to show the aftermath of an earthquake with lots of facts and figures."

Libra laughed. "Guys, the solution's simple. Make a mini city block and then use a chemical reaction to create a tiny earthquake and destroy the city. You both get to do what you want."

Both girls looked at each other skeptically and then frowned at her. "Uh, that's impossible," said Tina. "No one can do that."

"Sure you can." Libra nodded.

"Uh-uh," Erica disagreed. "You're wrong. Mr. C. told us."

"No way. That doesn't make sense. The formula to do that is simple."

"If you can't help us with our argument, just say so," Tina said.

"Yeah," Erica said, "I think I'll take Mr. C.'s opinion over yours on what you can and can't do."

"Right. I'll believe that earthquake thing when I see it," Tina said.

"We should just stop working together and tell Mr. C. we're doing separate projects," Tina said.

"Guys, I'm right on this. Look, I'll do it tonight and show you tomorrow. Be in the mediation room first thing tomorrow morning."

The girls both stood up. "Okay, Libra," said Erica, "you do what you want, but I think I'm going to go ahead and start my own project."

"Me too," said Tina.

And with that, the two girls left.

Libra shook her head and narrowed her eyes, a fire lit in her belly.

Sleep deprived but successful, Libra arrived the next morning carrying a large diorama of a city block over her head to keep it from getting broken. In her backpack, glass bottles clinked together.

Erica and Tina were both waiting with arms crossed when she reached the mediation room, and she gave them a triumphant smile.

"Prepare to be wowed," she said.

They gave each other a look, as if to say "we'll see," which made Libra even more determined. She sat the diorama down on the coffee table and pulled the glass bottles out of her bag.

"This one," she said, holding up the bottle in her left hand, "goes in first, right here under the soil layer."

They came around, and she showed them where a hole had been left to put the chemicals. She poured in a bit of the first substance. Nothing happened.

"Uh, nothing happened," said Erica.

Libra frowned at her. "That's because it's not supposed to happen. The chemicals have to mix. That's what causes the earthquake."

"Whatever," said Tina.

Biting her lip, Libra picked up the other chemical and poured it in. Nothing. Then, suddenly, the ground of the diarama started to bubble up in different places, making the buildings shake.

"Ha!" she said. "Told you!"

The girls both looked sufficiently impressed.

"Cool," said Erica. "Consider me wowed."

"Double wowed," added Tina.

"There's always a compromise if you're willing to look for it," Libra said boastfully.

"You are totally right," agreed Erica, picking up the chemicals to check them out.

"Yeah," said Tina, lifting the diorama to do the same. "We're sorry we didn't listen to you."

Libra smiled and shrugged. "Don't worry about it," she said, smug. "As long as you see now, it's okay."

"We absolutely do." Erica nodded. "Thanks for showing us."

"Anytime."

Then they took the project and left Libra feeling quite satisfied with herself.

It was only when she heard the two girls talking in the bathroom later that Libra realized how stupid she had been.

"I can't believe how stupid Libra is," said a voice Libra recognized as Tina's. Libra had just closed the stall door, and now she pulled her feet up onto the toilet seat so that she wouldn't be discovered.

"I know, right?" added Erica. "Talk about gullible. She did our whole project for us for free."

"Serves her right for giving away our lunch table. Jerk."

"Totally. Especially after she fed us that line about it not being fair for one person to have it."

"Right. It was like she had one set of rules for us and another for Tammy. But whatever. We showed her."

"And got a good grade, I bet."

"No kidding. She really went all out, didn't she? Maybe we should tell her we can't agree on our next project too."

Both girls laughed loudly as they left the bathroom, the door closing behind them.

A month later, Erica and Tina returned to the mediation room, saying they were fighting about another project.

"*Oh, no,*" thought Libra, knowing exactly where this was going.

She followed the script from the last time, allowing them to maneuver the conversation to the place where she told them she'd prove them wrong by bringing in the project and showing them.

As before, they expressed disbelief that what she was saying was even possible, and she pretended to get fired up over their disbelief.

"Meet me here first thing tomorrow morning," she demanded.

And that's where the script changed.

When Libra arrived the following morning, she came empty-handed and was happy to watch the smiles fade from the faces of Erica and Tina as she entered the mediation room.

"Hey," said Erica nervously, "did you leave the project in your mom's car or something?"

"Yeah, maybe you should call her," added Tina. "Now."

Libra held her hands out apologetically. "Sorry, you guys were right. I couldn't do it."

"Wait, for real? But this is our grade we're talking about."

"Well, good thing you guys didn't believe me and did your own things last night, right?"

Erica and Tina just stood there speechless, unsure what to do, and then finally walked out.

For the most part, Libra still believed in the goodness of people and that just about everyone wanted to work things out in the best way for everyone. She believed that, but she also wasn't going to be a gullible little sap anymore, letting people take advantage of her. As she sat down on the couch in the mediation room, she allowed herself a smile.

Scorpio

October 23 to November 21

Exciting and magnetic
Passionate Scorpio draws people in
Attracted to his power and determination
But beware if jealousy should come
For she brings with her his worser nature
Giving rise to secrets and obsessions
That drive others away

Every school has its thing that gives rise to popularity and notoriety. For some schools it's a particular sport—football or basketball, sometimes even cheerleading. Others—there are a few—are known for their arts programs, and being one of those few chosen to act or sing or play the flute isn't social suicide; it's a fast pass to friends. At Ridgemont Junior High, video games were the thing, and Miles "Scorpio" Revis was the king of the gamers.

A block away from the school was Mr. Nicky's Universal Games Lounge and Emporium, a long-winded name that the kids all just shortened to Nicky's. Nicky's store was a place to buy and rent video games, but to the kids at Ridgemont, it was so much more.

First off, while most places only carried the newest, hottest games, Nicky's had everything. No, really—everything. On any given day, you could walk into Nicky's and buy or rent any video game for any system from any era. Playstation 3 games mingled with classics for Atari 2600. He even had games from all over the world that hadn't been released in their town and cheap converters to play them. Plus, Nicky was cool. No games left the store without him getting paid, but he didn't care at all if you played the games in the store. And that last part is the beginning of why the kids really loved Nicky's so much.

Not only was Nicky cool with kids playing games to try them out, he'd created an entire gaming lounge in the back that was bigger than some people's houses. On the side walls, it was outfitted with several medium-sized flat-screen TVs, each one connected to two or three game systems with controllers, and video game chairs where you could sit and play against friends, using headphones that jacked into the chairs so gamers wouldn't get confused when there were twenty games going on at once. There was even a snack and drink bar set up where gamers could, as they said, "power up," and Nicky's prices usually weren't much more than double what you'd normally pay. Not bad to avoid having to leave gaming paradise.

But the real showpiece was the rear half of the room. The back wall was dominated by a giant movie screen that was hooked up to play video games with a projector, and it was lined on all sides by smaller flat-screen TVs that had been rigged up to show player stats. On either side of those smaller TVs and above the giant screen were huge surround-sound speakers, both on the floor and mounted on the wall. A half-circle of super comfy couches faced the screens, each with hidden compartments in the arms that held controllers and built-in spaces to hold drinks. No headphones were used for this set up because people were supposed to both see and hear every life lost, weapon fired, and power-up obtained. It was meant to be a spectacle, and it was, drawing dozens of Ridgemont kids for hours each day after school and often for entire weekends.

Over the last few years, Scorpio had become the biggest part of that spectacle, developing into the best gamer anyone in Ridgemont had ever seen. He could beat anyone and anything, blasting through the latest Mario game in just over an hour as crowds of kids cheered him on, but Scorpio's favorite games were real-time strategy games. There was just something so satisfying about crafting a strategy and anticipating your opponents' moves so that you could outsmart them, and Scorpio did this ruthlessly, preying on the weaknesses of other players to take out their armies as quickly and efficiently as he could while being very mindful to protect himself.

A few months after his string of victories began, the other players began to realize that he was the strongest and decided to team up against him, but Scorpio found ways to use their plotting against them and set up traps to kill off several armies at once, shocking everyone. Now it was commonplace to team up against him, and his opponents rarely fell for the same thing twice, but still, Scorpio found ways to defeat them using his brilliant strategic mind, refusing to lose despite the odds heavily favoring the others.

Because of his constant winning, you might think that the other kids at Ridgemont would hate Scorpio, but it was actually the total opposite. He was beloved by his peers and praised around school, something of a hero. In large part, this was probably due to his magnetic and engaging personality and the passion he clearly felt for gaming. He didn't lord his wins over the others, and he genuinely wanted everyone to be better, even the kids who were less than gracious about him beating them.

"Good game, Todd," said Scorpio, seconds after wiping the floor with another opponent.

Todd Veryman, his competition, tossed down his controller. "You're cheating!" he said. Todd was nine, three years younger than Scorpio, and an only child that his parents couldn't help spoiling a bit. As a result, he'd gotten used to having things his way.

"I promise you, I'm not cheating," Scorpio said.

"You have to be. There's no way you could be building armies that fast."

"Sure there is."

"Uh, no there's not. I timed it, and a base can only give you ten units a minute."

"Yes, but that means three bases can give you thirty units a minute."

Todd's eyes opened wide. "You had three bases? But how? We were only playing for ten minutes."

So Scorpio explained his strategy to Todd. How he split his forces and attention early, only building things he absolutely needed and quickly spreading out to other areas. He was very specific, more or less giving Todd the tools he needed to beat him.

They played again, and naturally, Todd followed Scorpio's instructions to the letter. This time, it only took five minutes for Scorpio to beat Todd.

Todd was livid. "No fair! You tricked me! You knew I was spreading out and attacked me too fast."

"Todd, you did great. If I didn't completely change my strategy, you would have overwhelmed me. I had to kill you fast or I knew I was a goner."

"Yeah, but you knew what I was doing."

"Technically you're right, but that's why you shouldn't have used the strategy I just gave to you."

"So you admit you cheated!"

"It's not cheating to anticipate what your opponent's going to do, man."

"But—"

"Look. I did guess that you would follow the strategy, but I don't do anything based on guessing."

"Okay...so how did you know, then?"

"I scouted you right at the beginning of the game, and once I knew you were following the strategy I'd given you, I knew how I had to play. Here, I'll show you."

And Scoprio patiently began showing Todd a second strategy, once again making him a better and more versatile player. This time, Todd declined a rematch, but he left much happier.

"Thanks for showing me all those things. I'm totally going to beat all my friends now."

"Just don't kill them too bad, or they won't want to play with you."

Todd smiled and left, and it was easy to see why the other kids loved Scorpio so much. He was just a genuinely nice guy, and you always learned something from a game with him.

It got to the point that so many kids were asking Scorpio for pointers that he worked out a deal with Nicky to teach a sort of class at the store on the weekend, letting people pick his brain without him having to beat them first. Nicky even offered to pay him because Scorpio's class quickly became the most popular event at the store, but Scorpio declined. He loved being able to talk to the other kids about games and answer their questions. It was almost more fun than actually playing the games and winning.

Then, one day, everything changed.

Cho Lee moved to Ridgemont from Korea, and his English wasn't very good at all, so the school felt they had to put him in remedial classes or he would never catch up. Because of his English difficulties, he ran away when kids tried to talk to him, and they started thinking he was slow and stupid and started making fun of him, especially his thick accent. It didn't help that he was uncoordinated in gym and didn't seem to care much about how well he did in his classes. Everyone decided Cho was a total loser.

Everyone, that is, except for Scorpio.

Sad to see the way the other kids were treating him, Scorpio brought Cho to Nicky's in the hopes of showing him a little bit of fun. He also wanted Cho to see that not everyone in his town was a mean jerk.

As soon as they entered the store, Cho became a different person. He ran excitedly over to the racks of games and began babbling something that was half-English and half-Korean, neither of which Scorpio understood.

"This *yoshinokimishantangvu* exciting very *mookappa* space gun berries!" he said excitedly.

"Uh, okay. Cool." Scorpio nodded. "Well, if you like that, you're gonna love this. Come on, I'll show you."

He motioned for Cho to follow him and walked through the curtain into the back room. Cho ducked in after him, and immediately, his eyes went wide and his jaw dropped. When he had recovered, he turned to Scorpio and shook him by the shoulders, laughing.

"Best!" he said. "Best!"

"Yeah, I think so too," Scorpio said. "I can't imagine anything better."

Then Cho's eyes got even wider, and he pointed at the game on the big screen. "Spacecraft!"

Scorpio looked. It was true; three of his buddies were playing his favorite RTS, Spacecraft. "You play?" he asked Cho.

"Best!" he said, pointing to himself.

Scorpio smiled and laughed. "Really? That's great. Want to play when they're done?"

Cho nodded vigorously.

When they sat down to play the game, the usual crowd started to gather to watch Scorpio play, and he started to feel nervous for Cho.

"We don't have to do this with everyone watching," he said.

Cho laughed. "You…scared?"

A couple of kids in the audience laughed.

"Yeah, you scared, Scorp?" joked Ernie Biggs.

Scorpio turned to Cho and handed him a few dollars. "Can you get us some Cokes?" He pointed at the snack counter behind them. "Cokes?"

Cho nodded and bounded over.

Scorpio turned to the crowd and spoke quietly while he was gone. "Just be nice, okay? Try to imagine living in a place where you can barely tell what people are saying most of the time and you don't know anybody."

Several in the crowd nodded, and he thought they might actually be taking him seriously. Oh well. There was nothing more he could really do.

Cho returned, and they both picked up their controllers and got their game faces on. Right before the game began, Cho turned to him. "Be…scared," he said, and Scorpio had to laugh.

Then the game was on, and he was in an entirely different world. He quickly built the early required structures for minimal defense and then thought he would try to expand and upgrade his forces, giving Cho time to establish himself a little bit before he took him out. He sent a scout just to make sure all was well and saw that Cho had only just begun building his base. Yeah, exploring and expanding was a good idea. He wanted to give the guy a chance.

He had just started to build a second base when a siren alerted him to the fact that his first base was being attacked. Scorpio went there immediately, and what he saw shocked him—he was being overrun! With his lack of soldiers, there was no way he'd be able to turn back Cho's forces there.

Immediately, he gave it up for dead and decided he would concentrate his efforts there and refocus himself. He'd thought Cho an easy win, and that had made him sloppy. Unfortunately, he returned to the second base to discover that it was under attack too.

Scorpio looked around frantically for a way to build more soldiers, but it was over. Cho had taken away his ability to do anything but watch as his army burned. It only took another thirty seconds for Cho to completely destroy everything he had built, but to Scorpio, it felt like a fiery eternity.

"CHO WINS!" came up on the screen, and Scorpio finally pulled himself out of the game world to realize that the entire room was sitting in shocked silence.

Cho turned to him and smiled. "Again?"

Scorpio blinked twice and shook his head to clear it. "Yeah. Yeah, again. Definitely again."

Someone's hand clapped his shoulder, and voices he couldn't place offered him encouragement. "Shut up!" he said. "We're trying to play here."

Again, he blotted out the real world and went into that of the game, determined to take Cho out. This time, he would build defenses and a quick-attack bum-rush army, leaving nothing to chance. He had just sent his armies out to attack, confident that his base was well-protected, when an earthquake ravaged the base defenses. In a flash, he'd ordered his armies back to guard the base, but a loud explosion and screams told him he wouldn't be seeing them. Cho had set a mine-field booby trap, and he'd run his troops right into it. Immediately, he began building new troops, but he knew it was already too late. Cho had positioned his troops close by, and again, everything

was destroyed before he could do anything.
"CHO WINS!" flashed.

"Again!" he yelled, starting a new game without even waiting for Cho's okay.

"Dude," said Todd from behind him, "calm down. It's just a game."

Scorpio didn't answer. He was going all out this time.

His fingers flew over the buttons as he pulled out all the stops, using every shortcut he knew to get to the strongest army units as fast as possible and loading up on them while expanding and defending everything. He'd discovered Cho's location early on and tailored his armies so that they could annihilate that exact threat. Careful to protect against long-range attacks, he set his own booby traps to kill off anyone before they could get near him. To avoid any booby traps Cho might have set for him, Scorpio created a flying army and sent it off to destroy Cho's base. Within seconds of that attack, Cho sent his armies to destroy Scorpio's base. He had expected this and made defenses against it. Unfortunately, Cho had too many soldiers, and each of them destroyed the bases of the other. Scorpio smiled. This was his failsafe plan. All that was left was for the remaining soldiers to fight, and his flying army would easily wipe out Cho's ground-based forces. Cho seemed to realize that and had his soldiers run away, with Scorpio's flyers in pursuit.

Scorpio laughed. "Can't run forever—" he said and then choked on his words.

Cho had created another hidden base that Scorpio hadn't discovered, and it was solely designed to rip a flying army apart. Very quickly, "CHO WINS!!!" flashed again.

Scorpio stood up, tossed his controller across the room, and stormed out, leaving everyone behind him shocked.

When the usual group of kids returned to Nicky's the following day, this time laughing and talking with Cho—whose English seemed improved—they found Scorpio already there, playing Spacecraft alone.

Immediately, they quieted down and then huddled up and started whispering.

"Do you guys mind?" asked Scorpio without turning around. "I'm trying to play a game here."

Frankie Hammond was pushed forward by the others. "Oh, uh, sorry, Scorpio. Didn't mean to bother your playing."

"Don't apologize, just be quiet."

"Right. Sure. Sorry."

Frankie turned back to the others and shrugged, not knowing what to do, but they waved him on to try again. Reluctantly, he cleared his throat.

"Uh, see, the thing is, me and the other guys were hoping to learn a few tricks about the game."

Scorpio paused and turned around to face them. "Dude, I just told you, I'm a little busy playing the game. I can't stop whenever anyone wants just to teach them something."

"Oh, we didn't want you to teach us."

"What?

"Cho said he could show us a few things."

From behind Frankie, Cho smiled and nodded his head vigorously.

Scorpio was silent for a long beat.

"So...I guess you just want me to let you use the big screen, then, huh?" Scorpio's voice was small and tight, not at all what they were used to hearing.

Frankie's mouth just kept opening and closing like a fish, so Tim Morrow stepped forward. "Not now, of course. I mean, you can finish your game. I mean, we don't even need to use the big screen, really. Since you're using it."

Scorpio looked at the screen, back at them, and then back at the screen again. Then he shut off the game, stood up, and walked over to one of the smaller screens, pulling the privacy curtain closed so they couldn't see anything.

Altogether, the boys let out a huge sigh.

Only Cho was unfazed. "Come, I show tricky trick," he said, walking over and plopping down on the couch.

The other boys followed, glancing back at the closed curtain as they went.

It was like that for the next several days with Scorpio.

Kids would leave immediately from school to go to Nicky's, but somehow, Scorpio was always there first, and he was still there when they left.

When one unlucky kid decided he would try to ask Scorpio a question about the game, he quickly wished he hadn't.

"You want to know my strategy for a full-on three-prong attack on waterways?"

"My brother always beats me," said the boy, "and I just want to show him finally."

"Why would I tell you something that you can use against me?" asked Scorpio, incredulous. "You'll probably tell everyone else how I do it."

"No, I wouldn't. I promise."

"Don't you understand that this is a game? There are winners and losers, and I am not a loser!"

And then he closed the privacy curtain in the boy's face, leaving the kid standing there confused and upset.

It was getting way out of hand. They left the back room and found Nicky out front, as always.

"Night, boys."

"Night, Nicky," they all intoned as they went out the door.

Frankie lingered there, holding the door, and then turned and went over to Nicky.

"Mr. Nicky?"

He was opening a shipment of new games for the following week behind the counter and jumped a little when Frankie called him before turning.

"Frankie, my boy. What's going on?"

"I just wanted you to know that Scorpio's still back there."

Nicky turned to toward the back room. "Huh. He's not going home with you guys?"

Frankie shook his head.

"That's odd. Okay, thanks for telling me." He went back to his work.

"And, Mr. Nicky?"

"Yes, Frankie?"

"He's acting weird. Normally, Scorpio's really nice, but ever since Cho beat him, he's just been quiet and mean."

"Cho beat Scorpio?"

Frankie nodded.

"Okay," said Nicky, "don't worry about Scorpio. Thanks for telling me."

"G'night, Mr. Nicky!" Frankie ran out the front door and off down the street.

Nicky finished unpacking the box in front of him and then cracked his neck and headed into the back room.

"Yo, Scorpio, you in there?"

No answer.

"I'm close to closing up, buddy. Unless you want to take inventory or something."

As he got closer to the curtain, he smelled bad body odor and noticed the stepped-on remains of chips and sticky footprints that were probably from spilled soda. He shook his head.

"Scorpio, you can't spend all your time in there."

He whipped open the curtain, expecting to find his best customer greasy and dirty, absorbed in a game with headphones on, but Scorpio was facing him and writing in a notebook. As the curtain opened, he looked up and smiled.

"Hey, Nicky, sorry I didn't answer you. I was just finishing something up."

"What do you got there, buddy?" Nicky reached for the notebook, but Scorpio snatched it away and held it to his chest.

"Whoa, whoa, whoa. No one can see that."

A little taken aback, Nicky crossed his arms. "Oh, really? And why is that? What is it that's so important?"

Scorpio's eyes gleamed, and he laughed maliciously. "The ultimate Spacecraft strategy. It's going to help me destroy Cho once and for all."

Nicky frowned and narrowed his eyes at his young friend.

"Cho Lee, I challenge you to a duel," said Scorpio the next day at lunch, slapping Cho with a glove.

Cho stood, angry. "What you deal?"

Scorpio laughed and put his hands up. "Hey, easy, I was just kidding around. I wanted to play you in another game of Spacecraft tonight."

"Spacecraft?"

"You up for it?"

Cho nodded. "You on."

"Fantastic. And this time, you be scared."

Scorpio flashed a big grin and then turned and left the lunch room.

Everyone came out for the game that night, even high schoolers.

Scorpio watched as Cho chattered and joked around with people before the game, shaking his head at his opponent's lack of focus. Frankie and Todd both tried to talk to Scorpio before the game, but he just held up his hand to stop them. He would not be distracted and risk losing again.

As they sat down on the couch, Cho held out his hand for Scorpio to shake.

"Luck may you win the best man," he said.

Scorpio scoffed. "Luck won't have anything to do with me destroying you."

Then they sat down, the game began, and both of them were lost to its rhythms. Scorpio employed a strategy no one had ever seen before and few of them even remotely understood. What they did understand, however, was that very quickly, he had Cho on the run. He lost his main base to Scorpio early on; then most of his soldiers died in a raid on Scorpio's secondary base. All he was doing was hanging on, so Scorpio did the kind thing and put him out of his misery, ending the game in all of twenty minutes.

Cho stood up and put his hand out for Scorpio to shake. "Good game," he said, smiling. "Look forward play again."

Scorpio put his hand out but pulled it away before Cho could shake it and laughed at him. "Just kidding, man. Just kidding. But I don't see the point in another game unless you want to lose again. I've got you totally figured out."

Cho just looked at him, confused.

"Don't worry about it, man." He turned to the room. "Anyone else want to play? Or want me to help them with strategy stuff? No? Okay, I'm getting a drink."

As he walked over to the snack bar, still riding high on his win, he heard something that truly disturbed him.

"Excuse me, Mr. Cho," said Frankie. "Todd and I had a question and were hoping you'd help us."

Cho nodded. "Certainly."

Scorpio bit his lip. They always came to him. Why weren't they asking him these questions? He stole a look over his shoulder and saw that there was a line already stretched around the room to ask Cho questions, but no one even came near him.

"But I won," he said, almost to himself.

Nicky put his hand on Scorpio's shoulder. "You won the game, but you didn't win them."

"What do you mean?"

"Think about how you've been treating them lately. Think about how you just treated Cho. I know, deep down, you're one of the nice guys, but I gotta tell you, if I'd met you a week ago, I would just think you were a big jerk."

Nicky walked off, allowing Scorpio to process his words. After a few seconds, Scorpio took a deep breath and walked over to Cho.

"Hey, man," he began. The other kids got out of his way to let the two of them talk. "Look, I know I've been a jerk the last week, and I just wanted to tell you I'm sorry. Until you beat me, I hadn't lost in a long time, and it was really hard for me to take it. But I don't mean that as an excuse, and I just...I guess what I'm trying to say is that I hope we can still be friends. I'd like to be your friend."

Cho smiled. "Let you in on secret. I'm used to losing. Older brother. Beat me every night."

Scorpio barked a laugh. "No kidding?"

"No kidding. You should play him?"

Scorpio held up his hands. "I think I'll hold off on that for a while."

They regarded each other for a second, and then Cho stuck out his hand. "Friends," he said.

Scorpio shook his hand. "Friends."

"Now," said Cho, "who have questions for me or my friend?"

They smiled at each other as hands went up all over the room.

Sagittarius

November 22 to December 21

A jovial and good-humored optimist
Sagittarius believed in truth above all
Trusting in the welcomeness of honesty
But everything has a time and place
And tactless, superficial truth
Can be more dangerous
Than careless lies

When Sagittarius was a little boy and his parents were getting a divorce, his mother sat him down and told him the secret of life: always tell the truth.

"If you always tell the truth," she said, "people will respect you for your honesty and know without a doubt that you are a person they can trust."

"What if the truth gets someone hurt?" he asked.

"Not telling the truth will eventually make the truth worse," she replied, casting a withering look over her shoulder at his father, who was packing his things to move out of the house.

"What if the truth seems mean?" he continued, trying not to think about his dad leaving.

His mother smiled at him. "Well, you're a sweet boy, and the truth always goes down nicer with a little bit of sugar, just like medicine."

Sagittarius smiled back, completely understanding his mother.

Over the years, Sagittarius always remembered her words and tried to live by them, making him someone teachers loved.

"Who threw that?" a teacher would ask about an especially noticeable spitball.

Without prompting, Sagittarius would raise his hand. "Jason Meadows, ma'am. But he wasn't aiming at you. Casey Andrews surprised him by ducking."

The teacher turned a stern eye to the two boys. "Jason, Casey, go to the principal's office now."

Shoulders slumped, the two boys shuffled out of the room and down the hall.

Because of his unfailing honesty in this regard, you might think that the other students would hate Sagittarius, but in reality, it was quite the opposite.

Part of this was because Sagittarius's honesty had cut both ways for most of them, sometimes getting them into a jam and sometimes helping them out of one, like the time in second grade with Miss Everly, the young playground monitor who was trying hard to get a teaching job at their school. One day, she blew her whistle to call them all together.

"I found cigarettes over by the woods," she announced, holding up a plastic baggy of butts. "Either whoever did this comes forward, or the entire grade has recess inside for two weeks—in the library."

There was a chorus of groans and moans.

Marcus Rellias, in typical fashion, whined the most. "But that's not fair, Miss Everly. How can you punish all of us for something we didn't do?"

She shrugged. "Then maybe you should come forward and tell me who did it."

"But I don't know who did it. None of us do."

Naturally, she turned to Sagittarius. "Sagittarius, can you honestly tell me you didn't see anything?"

"No," he said simply.

"Well, then, how about you tell me about it?"

He shrugged. "Okay, but I don't think you'll like it."

"Out with it, Sagittarius. It's not like you to hold things back."

"I saw you and Mr. Sandlebroth kissing under the bridge while you were patrolling."

Miss Everly's mouth dropped and just hung there for what felt like a full minute. When she finally picked it up, the bell had rung, and all of the students had already gone inside.

The kids never heard another word about the cigarettes, and no more were ever found.

Another reason was because they knew that they could trust Sagittarius.

Not with secrets, of course—that would have been the height of stupidity with someone who always told the truth. In fact, most of the kids had learned the hard way to create rules around Sagittarius. One, they never invited him in on any pranks or jokes or adventures that were against the rules. Two, they made sure that he wasn't anywhere near them when they were engaging in these illicit activities. Three, they never talked to him about these activities or anything else that they wanted to keep private, just in case someone were to ask him, making him feel obligated to reveal it.

But they did trust him with information that they wanted to know.

"I think Roger Lawrence likes me," Sarah Adams whispered to Lisa Gilfried, her best friend, one day in fifth grade. "He looked over at me and winked in gym yesterday." The two girls giggled excitedly and then decided to put it to the test.

"Let's ask Sagittarius," Lisa said.

Sagittarius, who had in fact been walking right in front of them, stopped suddenly and spun around, almost causing them to run into him. He shook his head. "Actually, he was winking at Kevin McDonald to tell him that he was successful getting Mrs. Crabtree's answer key for the science test tomorrow."

"How do you know?" asked Lisa.

"Because I heard Kevin talking about it in the locker room."

Lisa squeezed her friend's arm. "That doesn't mean he doesn't like you. Kevin could be wrong."

"That's true," said Sagittarius, "but I wouldn't waste your time. I saw Roger kissing Audrey Reynolds last week, and I heard he was kissing Rachel Biars the week before that."

Sarah's face fell, and she started to cry.

Sagittarius shook his head. "You should not be sad about him. You are so much better."

"That doesn't make me feel better."

"Well then, maybe this will: I know who really does like you."

He smiled at them, and Sarah wiped away her tears, curious.

Then there was Gary Williams, Sagittarius's best friend.

Through thick and thin, whenever Sagittarius said a bit more than he should or accidentally ruffled the feathers of the wrong person at the wrong time, Gary was there to protect his buddy.

They'd grown up together, literally from birth. Gary's mother gave birth to him at 6:01 p.m., and Sagittarius barely missed out on having the same birthday by taking his time and arriving at 12:01 a.m. the following morning. Their parents joked that the two of them were best friends even in the hospital baby ward, turning toward each other in their beds so they could coo and cry at each other, ignoring the other kids.

Along the way, they'd done just about everything together: school, sports, Cub Scouts—their parents even had embarrassing baby pictures of the two boys bathing together, which had proven to be very effective blackmail.

Because Gary knew Sagittarius so well, he never took any of the hurtful things he said in the wrong way. He knew that they came from a good place. Even more than that, he knew that Sagittarius just didn't know how to behave in any other way. Also, perhaps because he was the older brother of a sort, Gary felt an obligation to protect and stand up for his friend.

Luckily for Gary, he'd been gifted with the perfect attributes to make friends in grade school: he was outgoing, fun, athletically gifted, and good looking. Now, it might seem weird to think that kids care about good looks, but in a world where every odd thing about you can be picked on, looking good, at the very least, saves you from being picked on for being fat ... or pimply ... or just simply weird looking in some way. In short, Gary was popular, and that popularity gave him a certain leverage and pull with the other kids, something he was more than happy to use to Sagittarius's advantage.

So when he heard kids talking about how weird and annoying Sagittarius was, Gary made a point of disagreeing and talking about something cool Sagittarius had done the other day, which was even true once in a while. In class and at lunch, he always made a point to sit next to his friend. During recess and in gym, Sagittarius was always the first person he picked when playing games. It didn't always work with everyone, but at the very least, it kept Sagittarius from becoming a social outcast during some of his more blunderingly truthful moments.

But the biggest reason most kids liked Sagittarius was because of how positive and optimistic he usually was about life.

It was hard not to like someone who was so open and good natured about everything. Even when he was telling you something you didn't want to hear, he coached it in something good. And what was even better was that you knew it was true because Sagittarius telling a lie would be like Mr. Hampton, the civics teacher, ever missing a day of class—it just didn't happen.

So while you might hear from Sagittarius that you weren't going to pass earth science unless you studied a lot more, in the same breath, he would give you a compliment on how smart you were in history or how talented you were on the baseball field.

Above all, there was just this aura of "right-ness" around him, someone who felt entirely sure about his view of the world and was one hundred percent comfortable being who he was. That was something the other kids all respected and admired, even if they didn't know exactly what it was or why they felt the way they did.

However, over time, that "rightness" veered left and became tinged with overconfidence. And like all people who are a bit full of themselves, Sagittarius got more intense with the truths that he would tell.

"I think that blouse is very pretty" was small comfort when it followed "you're too overweight to make the cheerleading squad," or even worse, "That girl is way too pretty for you, but your article in the school paper was very good."

Somehow, in Sagittarius's mind, the truth had become more about his subjective point of view than actual facts and figures, but he felt obligated to share his thoughts with everyone, lest he risk lying to them.

It had come close to getting him into trouble at the most recent school football game. The team was losing 45–0, and as he left the field with his players, Coach Harrison tried to pump them up.

"There's still a half to go, fellas. We can fix what's wrong at halftime; come back out and whip these jerks!"

Sagittarius was passing by them when he heard this and scoffed. "No, you can't," he said.

Coach Harrison stopped and turned to him. "Excuse me? What did you say?"

"I was referring to you saying you can fix what's wrong at halftime. You can't."

"Where do you get off telling us what we can and can't fix?"

"It's just logic, Coach. That team is a lot more talented."

A few of the players heard and turned around. Those who knew Sagittarius were offended and hurt, which was bad enough, but the players who didn't know him were just mad, and they looked ready to take on whoever was talking crap about them.

"Maybe you'll have a different opinion of our talent after I suspend you for a week, huh? What do you think about that?" asked the coach.

Sagittarius thought about it for a second and then shook his head. "No, I don't see how a suspension would raise the talent level for the team. That just doesn't make sense. Although, I suppose it's possible, if the level of coaching improved significantly over that week."

The coach's face got bright red, and a vein on his forehead began to throb. "I have had just about enough of you, you little—"

"Oh, Coach Harrison, thank you!" said a voice from off to the side. Everyone turned to see Gary approaching.

Harrison shook his head. "Thank me? For what?"

Gary grabbed Sagittarius by the arm. "He just wandered off from us and we couldn't find him."

Harrison's eyes narrowed. "This little trouble-maker is your friend?"

"Cousin, actually."

"No, I'm not," said Sagittarius.

Gary continued as if nothing had been said. "Has he been trouble? So sorry. He can be a hand-ful, especially when he's off his meds." This last part was said in a whisper, almost conspiratorially.

Harrison took his ball cap off and scratched his head thoughtfully. "Meds, huh?"

The players who knew Sagittarius crossed their arms over their chests, annoyed. Vic McAfee tried to speak out. "Coach, that's not—"

But Harrison held up a hand. "McAfee, was anyone speaking to you?" He turned to his play-ers. "No, no one was speaking to any of you, so there's no reason for you to be standing here. Get into the locker room. Now!"

Frustrated but knowing not to argue with Coach when he gave an order, the players jogged away. Harrison turned back to them.

"Look, just get your little friend out of here and try to be more careful with him next time, okay? Running his mouth like that, he's going to get himself in trouble with someone eventually."

"But not telling you would be lying, Coach," said Sagittarius, genuinely confused.

Gary started dragging his friend off before Harrison could respond. "I promise, Coach. I'll have a shorter leash next time."

"See that you do!" Harrison shouted as they hurried away from him.

There were a few more close calls, but things pretty much went on that way without trouble for several more months and might have continued forever, if not for The Incident.

Though Gary was almost constantly at Sagittarius's side, one day after school, Sagittarius couldn't find him. Not one to worry much, he simply made his own way out of the school and rounded the building to the back, heading for the shortcut they always took on their walk home. He was passing the overgrown hedges by the tennis courts when he heard Gary's voice coming from inside the hedges. It sounded like Gary was reciting something. He crept closer and saw that Shannon Murphy was in the hedge, too, and Gary was intensely reading to her from a creased piece of paper.

"...eyes are like the morning dew, glistening under the sunlight of your really bright blond hair—"

Sagittarius couldn't help barking a laugh. "Gary, that's awful. It sounds like something you pulled out of a poetry cliché book."

Shannon stifled a chuckle, and Gary's face turned bright red. "Dude, that's not cool," he said.

"What's not cool are those terrible similes. You're great at lots of stuff but not this. There's no way it's going to get you a girl."

Gary advanced on his best friend and shoved him. "Sagittarius, what's your problem? She's standing right there."

"Actually," said Shannon uncomfortably, "I think I should probably go."

"No, please," begged Gary, but she backed off.

"Sorry," she said. "Thanks for the...thing." Then she turned and hurried off around the corner.

Gary was furious. "How dare you?" he growled. "After all I've done for you, you go and ruin that for me."

"Your poem was already doing that."

Suddenly, Sagittarius found himself on the ground and his face throbbing. What happened? He looked up to see Gary glaring at him with clenched fists.

"You hit me," he said, rubbing his jaw.

Gary put his fists down. "Yeah, well, you sucker-punched me first."

And with that, Gary turned his back on his friend and walked away.

Things for Sagittarius were harder after that.

Without Gary around, he had lost both his protector and, he soon realized, his only real friend. Having spitballs constantly launched at him and his locker repeatedly defaced was bad enough, but not having anyone to hang out with was so much worse. Gary's defection meant an almost instant loss of every supposed friend Sagittarius had thought he had, from Jay Dowd to Marylin Shaw to Darnell Reeves. They all abandoned him at once very publicly as he tried to join them at their lunch table; they simply stood and left.

He didn't get it. He wasn't doing anything wrong, just telling the truth. It was what his mother had told him to do. Wouldn't these people rather just know than have someone lie to them? He knew he would.

On the way to study hall that afternoon, he watched as two jocks tripped uber-nerd Lawrence Baumgarten in the hallway, causing him to fall on his face and sending his books flying everywhere. As the jocks laughed and high fived, already walking down the hall, Sagittarius sighed and bent down to help Lawrence with his books.

"Thanks," he said.

Sagittarius picked up a thick fantasy novel and made a noise of disgust. "They'd make fun of you less if you didn't read stuff like this."

Lawrence shrugged. "I like it. Besides, those guys are just jerks for making fun of me."

Sagittarius sighed and looked Lawrence up and down. "They are jerks, but they do have a point. Your clothes are all old and ratty, and you kind of smell."

Lawrence shook his head. "You know what? You're a jerk."

"Because I'm honest?"

"Being honest is not the same thing as pointing out everything wrong with every person, place, or thing. You might not think it, but you are mean."

"I... I don't mean to be."

"I know. Which is almost sadder. You don't even know how big of a jerk you are."

Lawrence snagged his fantasy novel out of Sagittarius's hand and continued down the hall to study hall.

Sagittarius just stood there, thinking hard.

The last thing Gary expected when he shut his locker was to see Sagittarius standing there.

"What do you want?" he asked, already annoyed. "I have to get to my art history class."

"I'll walk with you," Sagittarius said.

"Whatever," said Gary. He began walking toward his class without waiting.

Sagittarius turned and hurried after him to catch up.

"You come to tell me how my hair's wrong or I'm not going to make the wrestling squad or something else jerky?" asked Gary.

"Actually," said Sagittarius. "I came to say I was sorry."

Gary stopped. This was new.

Sagittarius continued. "I was trying so hard not to lie that I said a lot of things that didn't need to be said."

"A lot," Gary said.

"A whole lot," Sagittarius said.

"And you were mean."

"Needlessly mean," added Sagittarius.

"Yeah, why is that?"

Sagittarius shrugged. "I guess…I guess I felt justified. I felt like it was my duty to tell people the truth, so if I did my duty and they got angry, well, that wasn't really my fault, was it? How could I be responsible for doing my, you know, job?"

"Your mom really did a number on you."

"Maybe, but I'm responsible. And I'm sorry. I'm so, so sorry. I can't promise I won't do it again from time to time; it's kind of ingrained in me at this point, but I do promise that I'll try not to do it."

"Don't do that. Don't try to stop entirely. You just need to, you know, think first. About what the point is. About what good is going to come out of saying it."

"Okay. I'll do that."

"Okay. So I'm guessing you want to be friends again?"

Sagittarius smiled. "Not yet."

He pointed behind Gary to where Shannon was standing shyly. They both waved at each other awkwardly.

"Okay," said Sagittarius, "so this might go against everything I just said, but I feel responsible for the other say. Shannon, you know about my craziness with the truth, right?"

"Yeah."

"Then you know this is real. Gary here really, really likes you. He's liked you since fifth grade." Gary blushed and turned away. "And though he may not be the best poet in the world, he is a great guy. He's smart, kind, funny—he's my best friend. And believe me when I say it takes someone pretty amazing to put up with me."

Shannon and Gary both laughed.

"If you give him a chance, I know that you'll see how amazing he is too."

"Okay," Shannon said, looking into Gary's eyes.

Gary stared right back at her. "Guess there are some advantages to having a friend who always tells the truth, even if it is embarrassing."

Shannon took his hand. "Trust me, you have nothing to be embarrassed about."

Sagittarius smiled at both of them and slowly backed away.

Capricorn

December 22 to January 19

Disciplined ambition can take her far
With patience, prudence, and care
That will see her through to her goals
But when a fatalistic mind
Brings an allegiance to those goals
A grudging, miserly attitude can follow
Leaving Capricorn all alone

Charley Caramel's Candy Cornucopia had the best sweets in the world.

Or so thought the children of East Lake Elementary School in the town of Charming. Each day after school—and oftentimes on the

193

way to school as well—the store would be packed with children of all shapes and sizes, clamoring for a treat or three.

Allowances in Charming were not measured in dollars but in candy canes and chocolate fudge mallow pop bars. Children would not beg their parents for an extra dollar but another bag of circus peanuts, and it was not uncommon to hear them complaining about a friend's larger allowance.

"But Mom," one might whine, "R. J. Snelfield's parents give him four Fizzy Rizzle sodas, five dark chocolate caramel peanut malt bars, twelve feet of Chewy Chews Jawsnapper gum, and a bag of mints! How am I supposed to face the other kids with just a dozen chocolate peanut butter banana bites?"

"Sorry, dear," the mother would inevitably reply. "You'll just have to learn to cope with what you have."

"But I don't want to cope with what I have!"

In fact, the candy insanity was so pervasive that it had claimed every child in the town but one: Capricorn Daniels. Unlike the other children, Capricorn rarely bought candy, not even from Charley Caramel's Candy Cornucopia. In fact, Capricorn rarely bought anything with her allowance.

"What do you do then?" asked Betsy Randall one day after Capricorn told her this astonishing news. Betsy did not seem impressed, as Capricorn had hoped, but horrified.

"I save it," said Capricorn.

Betsy, who didn't know how to respond, just frowned at Capricorn, shook her head, and walked away.

Capricorn had always been a frugal girl, setting aside a portion of any money she received for what she called a rainy day.

If she had told other children this little saying, they would have immediately called her out as a liar; they had been with Capricorn on rainy days, and she didn't spend her entire allowance then, either. She never spent the whole thing.

"You still have four strawberry chocolate peanut butter dips there, sweetheart," Mr. Caramel would tell her.

"One creamy crunch dip surprise is enough for me," she'd reply, making Charley frown and leaving the other children scratching their heads. How could one of anything ever be enough?

Needless to say, other kids thought she was a little weird, and Charley himself thought of her as his least favorite customer.

Recently, however, she had become even more frugal, refusing to spend even a little bit of her money.

It started because of Mr. Floom's environmental science class, where they learned that the earth—or at least the human race—was going to be destroyed.

"Mark my words, children," he said, pausing to ensure that they were indeed marking his words, "the earth is doomed. It's going to be destroyed."

Audible gasps could be heard around the room, but Capricorn merely nodded, sad and serious; she had expected as much. This only confirmed it.

Timothy Farcry, disbelieving, raised his hand.

"Yes, Timothy?"

"How is the earth going to be destroyed?"

"Why, by us, of course. We'll use up all the resources and dirty the air and sea so much that all living creatures will first mutate into terrifying monsters and then eventually die out, along with the planet itself. Not going to be pretty. No, sir."

Then Mr. Floom, seeing the principal pause in the hallway, listening to the lecture, altered his statement ever so slightly. "Or if not the earth itself, at least the human race will be destroyed." He nodded to the principal.

The principal nodded back and continued on his way. This statement was apparently more acceptable.

Capricorn raised her hand.

"Yes, Capricorn?"

"If the human race is destroyed, does that mean that every single one of us dies?"

Mr. Floom chuckled and shook his head. "Oh, no, no, my dear girl. There will definitely be small pockets of poor, destitute survivors eking out a miserable existence. Nothing to worry about."

"What if you prepare ahead of time?"

"Oh, right, I'd forgotten about that," he said. "Yes, there most certainly will be a privileged class that has hoarded food and supplies. They'll live far more comfortably than everyone else and quite possibly rule over the rest of us ruthlessly."

Well, thought Capricorn, *that is definitely preferable.* Then the wheels began turning in her brain, coming up with the perfect plan to thrive when the apocalypse inevitably arrived.

"Nothing at all today, Capricorn?" asked Mr. Caramel, slightly peeved.

"No, sir," she said. "I'm saving my money for something important."

He smiled a smile that did not reach his eyes and then slid down the counter to the next child, content to put the conversation behind him.

After she refused to buy anything for the next four days, he was not quite so content.

"Capricorn, you haven't purchased any candy in a week!" he said, flabbergasted.

"Wow, you're right," she said. "It has been a week."

"Well?" he said.

"Well what?" she asked.

"Do you plan to ever buy any candy from me again?"

"Of course I do."

"Just not today."

"No, not today."

"Tomorrow, then?"

She thought about it, looking around the store, as if she was sizing it up. "I doubt it," she finally said.

Mr. Caramel let out a big sigh. "Well, then. Any idea when you might finally start buying again?"

She shrugged. "I'm guessing it's going to be a long time."

His shoulders slumped. "That's what I thought." He slid down to the next child and then slid back to her before speaking to him. "But you'll still come in here every day and take up a seat that a paying customer could be using, I take it?"

She smiled at him. "Of course I will, Mr. Caramel." She laughed. "It's not like you're going to lose me as a customer."

"Right," he said and again slid down to the next child.

Capricorn's plan for the apocalypse—a plan that she had shared with no one in the world—was to save up enough money to purchase all the candy in the world.

Because he was her friend, she promised herself that she would start with Mr. Caramel's entire supply of candy. As she put that week's allowance into the hidden compartment in her music box with the rest of the money she'd been saving, she looked at the medium-sized pile and wondered how long it would take to get enough money. At the current rate she was saving, she thought it would take years and years.

"That's way too long," she said to herself.

Oh well. Maybe she could convince people it was her birthday again. That would quadruple what she already had. She'd still be years away, but at least it was something. Capricorn would just have to keep thinking of ways to get money faster. After all, with the apocalypse looming, it was definitely the most important thing.

After a month or so of saving and at least three un-birthdays she'd made up to get cards from various relatives, Capricorn wasn't happy.

Her stack of money was now so large that she'd taken it out of the secret compartment of the music box and moved it into an empty coffee can that she'd hidden in the back of her closet under all the dirty socks her mom had been telling her to clean up for as long as she could remember. She was happy with how well she was doing saving it, but she knew that it was still far too little for her to buy even an entire shelf of Mr. Caramel's candy, let alone the whole store. This just wasn't working.

But because she didn't know what else to do, Capricorn vowed to try to find other ways to make money. That and keep saving. She couldn't give up now.

Unfortunately, Alexander Copeland, one of her best friends, didn't know anything about her plan, and she certainly wasn't going to tell him. Every once in a while over the course of her saving, he had asked her to loan him some small amount to get a candy bar or something like that from Charley's store, but he'd always backed off when she refused without giving her any grief.

Then, one day while they were sitting on stools at Charley's, grief came calling.

"Buy me a mallow fudge bar?" he asked.

"Sorry," she said. "You know I can't."

"Right," he said. "Because you're *saving it*." He said the last two words with such disdain that she was momentarily taken aback, but she pulled herself together to continue.

"That's right," she finally said.

"Why?" asked Alexander simply.

"I told you," she said. "I'm saving it."

"Yeah, but for what?"

"Something important."

"What though?"

Capricorn got quiet for a second and then sighed. "If I tell you, do you promise not to laugh?"

He held up his right hand and put his left over his heart. "Promise. Totally."

"Remember Mr. Floom telling us about the end of the world?"

"Sort of. Yeah. Yeah, I remember."

She looked at him as if to say, "Okay, then."

He shook his head. "I don't know what that means."

"He said that the people who would live the best would be stocking up on stuff."

"Okay, and...? What, you're stocking up on money?"

Her brow furrowed, and she laughed disdainfully. "No, of course not. That would just be ridiculous." Then she thought about it for a second. "Okay. Well, I mean, I guess technically, I'm doing that right now, but that's only to pay for something."

"Jeez, enough with the suspense. Just tell me what it is already."

She spread her arms wide in an all-encompassing gesture. Alexander still didn't get it.

"The candy, dummy. I'm going to buy up all the candy in the world, starting with Mr. Caramel's store."

Alexander just sat in utter silence for a few moments. Finally, he spoke.

"So, then," he said, "you're not really using it."

"Well," she finally said, "thanks for not laughing, I guess. What do you mean I'm not using it?"

"If you didn't want to tell me the truth, you could have just said so."

"You don't believe me?"

He frowned. "Come on, really?"

"It's the truth," Capricorn said.

"I've never turned you down when you've asked me for money."

"I've never asked you for money," Capricorn said.

"The point is that I wouldn't turn you down."

"I'm sorry, but I really feel strongly about what I'm doing," Capricorn said.

"What's that?" asked Alexander. "Being stingy?"

"Alexander!"

"I thought you were a good friend, but you're not," Capricorn snapped.

"Based on me not buying you candy?"

"Based on you hoarding your money for something that might not even happen.

You've always been careful, but this is…Wow. I mean, you have to actually live life. Right now, you're just finding excuses to put it off."

"No, I—" said Capricorn.

"Deep down, I bet you don't even believe in this whole thing."

"I do."

"No, you want to."

"Why would I want to believe in something like this?" asked Capricorn.

"Because you like worrying. Like withholding."

"I am thinking about the future, Alexander."

"Yeah. Well, maybe you should start thinking about the present."

And with that, he stood and walked out, leaving her sitting there.

That night, she sat in her room, thinking.

Was Alexander right? Was she just using Mr. Floom's apocalypse as an excuse to do something she already enjoyed—saving money?

No. He couldn't be right. She was trying to be responsible. She was trying to look out for herself. And for him, if he survived the apocalypse.

"I'm just being smart and careful," she said aloud.

She went over to her closet and opened the door. It was a mess. Clothes were piled on the floor and strewn over shelves and other clothes that were still on hangers. She couldn't even tell what was clean or dirty anymore. *Mom might have a point*, she thought and then pushed that thought away for another time as she bent down and rifled through the clothes.

Capricorn uncovered the coffee can, pulled it out, and then went back over to her bed and dumped out the contents. Her first thought was amazement; she'd saved more than she even realized. The bills covered her bed, a green blanket that was a patchwork quilt of different numbers and faces.

See? Alexander was wrong. She'd already saved so much. She couldn't just stop now that she was so close. And he'd be thankful when she was able to go through with her plan.

She decided to sit and count it all to make herself feel better, so she pushed the money over to one side of the bed and plopped down. The feel of the wrinkly bills between her fingers was fantastic at first, and she felt excited at the thought of all the money just sitting there.

But as she started to get close to the end of her count, apprehension set in: she had nowhere near as much money as she'd thought. How was that possible with all the weeks and weeks of saving she'd done? With all of the candy she'd sacrificed?

She finished her count, disappointed but not defeated. Within seconds, she was counting a second time. Maybe she'd messed up?

But it was the same.

So she made a chart to check against her count, starting to think someone had stolen from her. But no, the number of weeks she'd been saving matched the amount of money there. The count was right; it just felt low.

It felt wrong.

She sat there, just staring at it for a few seconds, disappointed. Then she stood up, wadded the money together, grabbed her jacket, and walked out the door.

Charley was just closing up when she arrived.

"Excuse me, Mr. Caramel," she said. "May I buy some candy before you close?"

He turned, already exhausted from a long day of work, and if possible, his shoulders slumped farther when he saw who it was.

"Capricorn?" he asked. "What are you doing out so late?"

She shrugged. "Just had a craving for some snacks."

"Well, listen, darling. I just closed everything down for the night."

"Please, Mr. Caramel?"

"It's not really worth it for me to open the store just to sell you one piece of candy, child. I'm sorry, but if you come back first thing tomorrow, I promise I'll set aside whatever it is you want."

"What if I wanted more than one piece of candy?"

He shrugged. "Even if it's four or five pieces, and I know darn well you never order that much at once, opening up the store just isn't worth it."

"Well, how many pieces would make it worth it?"

Caramel sighed. "How many do you want, child?"

She shrugged. "Not sure. How much will this buy?"

Capricorn fished bills out of her jacket pocket and pressed them into his hand. His eyes got wide.

"Capricorn, you want to spend all of this?"

"Actually," she said, "hold on. There's more."

Without another word, Mr. Caramel turned back, unlocked the door, and held it open for her.

"My dear girl, please come in."

"Thank you," she said.

Alexander and Capricorn always walked to school together, but when he stepped out of his house the next morning, Alexander didn't see her at all.

He waited around for a while, worrying that he had been too mean and made her mad when they fought. Immediately after he'd left, he'd been sorry, but he felt too embarrassed to go back in and tell her. Maybe this was her way of telling him it wasn't okay.

Finally, Alexander went back inside and had his mom call her house. Capricorn's mom answered, saying she'd just dropped her daughter off at school. Guess that answered Alexander's question: if she was asking her mom to take her to school rather than walk with him, she was definitely angry.

"Do you want me to take you?" his mom asked.

"No," he replied. "I'll just be fast."

And with that, he left, running most of the way there just to make sure he wasn't late.

Much to his surprise, a huge bag awaited him at his locker when he arrived.

As he stood there wondering what it was, Capricorn came up behind him.

"Sorry I didn't call," she said.

"What do you mean?" he asked.

"About not walking to school with you."

"Yeah, what happened? I just thought you were mad. You're not?"

"No, of course not."

"Then what did happen?"

"I realized when I got up that Mom had to take me because the bag was way too heavy to carry all the way here."

Alexander turned back to the bag.

"Oh, so this is you?"

"Yup."

"What is it?"

"Open it and see."

He smiled, excited, and turned back to the bag. As he lifted it off the hook she'd hung it with on the outside of his locker, he realized she was right.

"Wow, it is heavy," he said.

He lowered the bag to the ground and peaked inside—candy. All candy!

"This is more candy than I've ever seen!"

She smiled and nodded back toward her locker. "Wait till you see mine. I split it evenly between us."

"How did you get all of it?"

"Convinced Mr. Caramel to stay open a little late for me."

"So you paid for all of it? But how—your savings! You used your savings?"

"I realized you were right. I like waiting and planning and holding back, so I was letting myself believe what I wanted to as an excuse to save everything instead of actually living life. I was wrong."

"Well, me too. I'm sorry I was such a jerk to you, and I shouldn't expect you to give me money whenever I want it. I'd just gotten so used to you offering that I guess I started to forget that it was yours to offer in the first place."

"Don't worry about it."

Alexander nodded toward the bag on the ground. "We should probably get this put away so we can save it for later," he said.

Capricorn smiled mischievously at him. "Jeez, Alexander, all this talk of saving." She reached into the bag, tossed him a candy bar, and then grabbed one for herself. "How about we live for now?"

He smiled back, and they both dug into their candy bars.

Aquarius

January 20 to February 18

Aquarius, the creator
The loving humanitarian
Bestowing her amazing inventions
Upon a grateful populace
Because she always knows what's best
Based on logic and reason
Regardless of their wishes

In a remote part of Montana—which is kind of redundant—there existed an amazing town by the name of Gilead.

Now, in most ways, it was like any other small town in America. There was a Main Street, where most of the local businesses operated and the townsfolk gathered for celebrations and meetings and such. The local elementary school down on Three Fork Lane fed into the local middle school, which gave the local high school its students. It was an even easier "feed" from middle to high school, since they were attached to each other over on Simpson Avenue. People went to the local grocery, Millet & Sons, when they needed food, or to the farmers' market that was set up on the football field each weekend. For entertainment, they watched the high school teams play, went to the lone movie theatre on Main, which played as many old movies as new ones, and in the summers, they boated on the lake.

But if you looked a little closer, Gilead was a most different town. The bulbs lighting all the streets gave off a slightly different light. No actual buses ever arrived at the bus stops, but people always seemed to manage traveling from one stop to the next. Players for Gilead teams always seemed to run a little faster and jump a little higher than anyone rightly should be able to do—but only in practice. Once games against other teams began, they were painfully average. And the weather was always exactly what they needed it to be; rain came for the crops, but otherwise, it was always pleasant and comfortable, and games never had to be canceled.

All of this came about because of one very bright young girl, Aquarius. This girl, you see, was a brilliant inventor, more brilliant than the top minds of the top scientists of the top schools in the world. At age thirteen, she had already done more good for Gilead than other scientists had done for the world in the last half-century.

The reason those bulbs gave off a slightly different light was because they were all running on one hundred percent renewable, environmentally safe power. In fact, everything in Gilead ran off of this power. It was clean, safe, and so far seemed to have no limits to what it could power.

Athletes were able to run faster and jump higher because of a revolutionary new shoe-and-sock combo Aquarius had created that worked with the muscles to enhance natural abilities. And actually, that had been a side effect—the real purpose of the device was as a physical-therapy tool to help people heal faster who were recovering from leg and foot problems. It worked so well that the teams had adopted it to make players' legs stronger and more durable. But Aquarius wouldn't let them have them until they promised never to use them in games—only for practice. The first time a Gilead player jumped over the backboard during a basketball game, she swore she would destroy the shoes herself.

Weather was perfect because of what she called her *umbrella*. Really, it was closer to an upside-down umbrella, since ultimately what it did was collect the weather they didn't want and keep it away from the town until they needed it. If that sounds like an imperfect explanation, it's because it is. When Aquarius had tried to explain it to the adults in the town, they'd all just sat there, scratching their heads. But this was Aquarius doing the talking, so they let her implement her idea, and lo and behold, it worked, just like everything else she came up with. Hopefully, as she grew older, she would actually be able to explain *how* her inventions worked.

This was especially desired for what might have been her most amazing invention of all— the personal transporter. Those bus stops without buses were not bus stops at all but travel points across town. People could enter one, sit down on the bench, use the built-in keypad to type in their desired location, and they would be immediately transported there. There was no need for buses! In fact, there was no need in Gilead for people to have cars of any kind unless they needed to haul something or go outside of town altogether. And that last "limitation" was a personal choice by Aquarius. She was constantly perfecting her inventions and didn't think the world was quite ready to be given the power of instantly traveling to anywhere they wanted to go, not unless she could find a way to take away all the guns and bombs first.

That last part was really Aquarius's guiding principle of inventing: her efforts were humanitarian, improving the good of everyone while trying to minimize the bad. Because of this, she'd had to turn down a lot of frivolous and potentially dangerous inventions from townsfolk.

"Robots to work my fields," Angus McReedy had requested, sure she'd have no problem with that. Naturally, he was wrong.

"But real people would lose their jobs."

"The work would be done more efficiently."

"The robots could have an uprising."

"Not with your careful programming."

"They could if someone else got a hold of one and learned how to reprogram it."

"Come on. It'll save me money, which will make food cheaper and easier for people to afford."

She considered this for a second. "Nothing will be affordable if they're out of jobs because robots took them. Sorry, Mr. McReedy."

Susanne Tulliver had thought she'd had an unstoppable idea too.

"Flying cars," she said with a flourish. "Can't you just see it?"

"I can," Aquarius said. "The skies would be a mess."

"But it would help with traffic problems and let people get places faster."

"People would have to get flying licenses just to be able to use the cars. There aren't enough places for that if everyone gets a flying car."

"All the more reason. New jobs for people."

"That's true. But the infrastructure would take years to build, and there would need to be a lot of training for people to give flying tests. Plus, car accidents on the ground are one thing. Can you imagine how many mid-air collisions there would be with millions of people flying around? And if they crash and fall out of the sky, what's to protect the people on the ground?"

Susanne was beside herself. She was so sure she'd had a winner. "But something big needs to change in the way we get around."

"You're right," said Aquarius, nodding, the wheels already turning in her brain. That was how she came up with the personal transporter and why she'd thanked Mrs. Tulliver when she unveiled it.

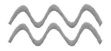

Worse yet were those projects that even the proposer couldn't pretend had any real value to society other than the person wanting it for him or herself. Aquarius set aside time each day for people to make suggestions, and there was always a ridiculously long queue. Sometimes people would wait for days on end if they couldn't talk to her within the allotted time. Aquarius was always surprised by how silly some of the suggestions were.

"A five-dollar home tanning bed," Mrs. Chiklins suggested.

"No."

"Blankets that turn into pillows and vice versa," said Ted Billings.

"What? No."

Randy Marquette wanted a two-way gun.

"What does that even mean?" she asked.

"You know. You put it on your shoulder, and it shoots in front of you and behind you."

She just stared at him. "No."

"Adding a projector device into smart phones so you can project videos onto a wall and watch them get bigger," said Renee Montaine.

"Cool, but I don't see how it really helps people."

"It helps people have a bigger screen … ?"

"No."

Harold Simons didn't seem to realize that people knew he was a thief. "You know how they have DVD-copying devices so you can back up your DVDs?"

"Yeah."

"What about one with an X-ray feature so you could copy the DVD right through the case? And instantaneously, too, because it can take a long time sometimes."

"One, I don't see how that helps people. Two, what's to stop someone from going into a store and just copying a bunch of DVDs they don't even own?"

Harold scoffed. "What? That's crazy. Who would try that?"

"No."

Most people knew that Aquarius was just trying to do the right thing and respected her decisions, but a few thought she was a witholding bully, using her power to keep them from getting what they wanted. And even more people at least thought that she was a little bit annoying and pompous about making her decisions on what to create. Some of the things she'd turned down were fantastic ideas but didn't meet her standards for one reason or another. She was a bit of a busy-body, giving them what they thought they needed and ignoring their wants, saying it was all for the greater good. The only reason more people hadn't turned against her yet was that they had to admit that, usually, she was right and they were wrong.

A great example was when the Phillipses asked for a self-sustaining swimming pool in their back yard. They even tried to play by her rules, saying that it would be good for the community because they would invite everyone over to use it, but still Aquarius had refused.

At first, the Phillipses had been angry, blaming her for the loss of a pool they not only never had but that she was going to have to make for them if she agreed. But that anger evaporated when she unveiled the lake. Yes, the town lake that people went boating on in the summer was one of Aquarius's creations, one hundred percent renewable, chosen in a spot that all the science said would not harm the environment, and full of self-cleansing microorganisms that she'd made sure were completely safe for people and animals. If those microorganisms ever came into contact with dangerous chemicals or toxic materials, though, they would secrete a substance that turned that area of the lake red and then go about the task of breaking down and destroying the hazardous material so that the lake would be clean and pure again. Once that happened, the color would return to normal.

It was an amazing piece of engineering that the whole town could use, not just the Phillipses and their neighbors. Aquarius also made a point to credit the Phillipses with giving her the idea, never mentioning that their original request had been a swimming pool for themselves rather than the end result.

In short, most of the townsfolk respected Aquarius because she had proven time and time again that her way of doing things—giving people what she thought they needed rather than what they knew they wanted—was usually right, and they ended up with something better than what they'd first asked for.

Not that Aquarius would have changed, even if everyone in town got mad at her. She not only believed what she was doing was right, she had little inkling that anyone had ever been annoyed with her, thinking she was wrong. Aquarius, you see, was not especially attuned to emotions and social behavior, being more of the cool, intellectual sort.

What was amusing was that she considered herself an expert on human behavior. Perhaps that was true on a larger scale; she was certainly able to see the big picture on what the town as a whole would use and enjoy and what would be helpful to them, but picking up on when individual people were happy, sad, or mad was not her strong point. Because of this, it was not at all uncommon for her to offend someone without knowing it, leaving a trail of slightly peeved neighbors in her wake. Luckily, they all knew her and understood her vast abilities and surprising limitations, so nothing had ever come to a head.

One person who had always been there for Aquarius, reminding people of all the good she'd done and defending her latest pompously thoughtless remark, was her best friend, Jessa.

Because of her clearly vast intelligence—not to mention their desire to keep her working on new and amazing inventions—the town council had decreed that Aquarius didn't need to attend school like the other children, provided she could pass a few tests. Not shockingly, she aced them all, testing herself all the way out of high school classes at the age of five.

As such, she didn't have school as an opportunity to socialize and make friends like other kids. Her parents, not wanting her to grow up friendless, had tried throwing parties for her when she was younger, inviting the neighborhood kids over. Mostly, these were a disaster.

Even at a young age, everyone already knew that Aquarius was a genius inventor, so the parties mostly consisted of kids begging her to invent cool toys for them, or worse, things that their parents had clearly told them to ask for. Aquarius, being so young and impressionable at first, had actually made a few of these in the beginning, leading to some of the town's darker days. Let's just say that there are downsides to giant, fast-growing plants and jetpacks.

But at least one good thing came out of it because Aquarius met Jessa, a little girl her age who took to Aquarius immediately, treating her like any other kid instead of someone to use to get what she wanted. Jessa was very patient with Aquarius when they first met.

"Rick Mester is a stupid jerk," Jessa said, escaping into Aquarius's room and announcing angrily to no one in particular.

"Boys his age tend to enjoy immature jokes and silly physical play," agreed a voice from under the twin bed in the room. Jessa jumped and then bent down to look under the bed. Aquarius waved at her.

"Is that supposed to mean Rick isn't a jerk?"

"It just means that he's engaging in typical behavior for a boy his age. Or at least, I'm assuming. I don't know exactly what he did."

"He pulled my hair and chased me. Which is jerky."

"My observations lead me to believe that might mean he likes you."

"Eww, gross."

Aquarius nodded. "Quite gross."

"And I still think Rick is a jerk."

"Okay."

There was a pause while the girls just regarded each other.

"I thought the room was empty," Jessa admitted.

Aquarius shrugged. "You were wrong." She slid out from under the bed and shook Jessa's hand. "Hi, I'm Aquarius."

"Isn't this your party?" asked Jessa.

"Technically. But really, my parents are the ones who wanted it. Apparently I need to make friends and socialize."

"Me too! My parents keep trying to make me join teams and clubs and stuff so I'll make friends. They're so annoying."

"They're merely trying to do what they think is best for us."

"Yeah, but they're wrong."

"Clearly."

"You're kind of weird."

"Do you want to be friends?"

"Yes."

From that day forward, Aquarius and Jessa hung out constantly, Aquarius making her friend see things in a more rational, intellectual light, and Jessa working to make Aquarius see that people didn't like being seen as a collection of electrical impulses whose behavior could be predicted by study and science. Neither was incredibly successful, but each made the other a better, more interesting and complicated person.

For Aquarius's thirteenth birthday, Jessa had taken her to the local science museum, just the two of them, and they'd spent the afternoon looking at things Jessa didn't care about and reading things she didn't understand. But it seemed to make Aquarius happy, and that was all she cared about.

In two weeks, it was going to be Jessa's birthday, and Aquarius had caught her hinting more than once that she would love an at-home workstation to design clothes.

"It would just be so great to be able to make my own things, you know?" she would tell Aquarius.

"I do know," she would reply.

"Exactly. You do. Because you make things. My parents just don't get it though."

Jessa had become more and more interested in fashion over the last year, and Aquarius knew that she was dreaming of becoming a designer, though for some reason, she'd yet to admit it to Aquarius.

If Jessa had her way, her birthday gift would enable her to creatively express herself with a myriad of fabrics, colors, and designs that included intricate sewing, beads, buttons, studs, and anything else that added, as she would say, "flavor."

Aquarius thought that was a great place to start, but she had an even better idea. Rather than Jessa spending her time figuring out which silly beads to put on which way-too-flowery blouse, Aquarius would design her a workstation to create the perfect clothes. They would be everlasting, stain-proof, and one size fits all—from infant to large adult!

"It's brilliant!" she said.

Immediately, she set about making it, so happy that she could make her best friend a part of something that was greater than she was. She had just wanted to make clothing, but Aquarius was going to give her a much better gift—the gift of changing the world!

The night of the party, Aquarius found herself surprised at how many other people came to celebrate Jessa's birthday. Apparently, Jessa had become much better at making friends over the years. There was dancing and laughing and playing around, and all of it made Aquarius uncomfortable and left out at first.

But Jessa, great friend that she was, noticed her friend's discomfort and made a point to bring her into the celebrating, introducing her to everyone and telling her friends about all the cool stuff Aquarius had done. Much to Aquarius's surprise, some of them were quite intelligent, and she ended up having a few halfway-decent conversations about quantum mechanics and the silliness of the space elevator, among other things.

When it was time to open the gifts, Aquarius sat at the back while the other guests had Jessa open fairly typical things: new clothes, jewelry, and music and movie theatre gift cards. Aquarius scoffed at the lack of imagination and frivolity behind the gifts, but Jessa seemed very appreciative of all of them. *If she likes these,* Aquarius thought, *I can't wait until she sees mine.*

Hers was saved for the very end because it was huge and already set up in Jessa's room. The entire room full of partygoers migrated to Jessa's bedroom and gasped in appreciation as Jessa flung the door open to reveal her new design station taking up most of the back wall.

Jessa squealed in excitement and hugged her friend before running over to it.

"How does it work?" she asked. "Where's all the fancy fabric? How do I add sequins? How do I attach beads? Studs? Lace frills?"

"Let me show you how it works," Aquarius said.

She went over, flipped a switch, and a low humming could be heard coming from the machine. The entire room leaned forward in expectation, so curious to see how this amazing device would work. Humming changed to whirring and the *pock-pock-pock* of sewing, and within a minute, a tiny blue jumpsuit slid out of one end of the machine.

Jessa forced a big, patient smile. "Ooh! Cool. Now, how do I add the actual designs I was talking about and change the fabric and everything?"

Aquarius completely missed her friend's somewhat tight voice and waved off Jessa's worries. "This device creates the ultimate piece of clothing. The fabric is practically indestructible, stain-proof, unisex, and it can stretch to fit anyone, but will never stretch out so that someone smaller can't fit into it." She demonstrated by taking the tiny, infant-sized jumpsuit and climbing into it herself. It fit her perfectly. You know, for a jumpsuit. "This device means that we'll only ever need one piece of clothing our entire lives!"

The other guests weren't sure how to react, but Jessa couldn't hold it in any longer. "Aquarius, I wanted something so that I could design my own clothes. Something with style, with creativity, with flair and flavor."

"I know," said Aquarius.

"You know? But…Then why would you give me this? I can't design anything with this. It's already done for me. Besides that, it's ugly!"

"Who cares what it looks like?"

"I do! I want to make pretty clothes, clothes people want to wear."

"But this is so much better. Don't you see? This jumpsuit could change the world."

"I didn't want to change the world!"

"I know. But I thought you should."

"Don't you care what I want? I didn't want this."

By now, the room had nearly emptied of the other guests, who had been slowly trickling out as the argument continued.

"But Jessa," she said, confused, "this is better than what you wanted."

"That's not the point, Aquarius. It's my birthday. The one day of the year you're supposed to care just about me. Like when I took you to the science museum."

"Yeah, so that I could see things that would give me ideas about how I could better change the world."

"What? No!"

"But why, then?"

"Because you like it! And I know you, so I did something for you that I knew you would like. That's it!"

Aquarius just stood there for a minute on the brink of comprehension. Everyone else had left. Even Jessa's parents had decided to give them privacy by going to their room. Aquarius shook her head. "Here, give me a second."

She bent down behind the design center, opened a panel, and tinkered around inside for a minute. Then she closed the panel and stood.

"Ta-da!"

Jessa looked at her incredulously. "What do you mean 'ta-da'? You just flip a few switches, and now the machine will do what I wanted it to do?"

Aquarius nodded. "I'll have to train you a little bit on the design process for the machine, but once you have that down, it's pretty simple."

"Thanks," said Jessa.

Aquarius shrugged. "I'm sorry. I guess I was trying to give you what I thought you needed instead of what you wanted."

Jessa put her hand on her friend's shoulder. "Aquarius, what I needed was to know that you actually cared about what I thought."

Aquarius's eyes opened wide. "I…I've never thought about that."

"I know." Jessa laughed. "And I don't hold it against you. I know you're always trying to look at the big picture and think about how everything you do will affect people overall, but sometimes…sometimes it's important for a person to know that you care about them individually."

Aquarius nodded. "Thanks for that. Sometimes I'm such a know it all that I forget I still have things to learn. Want to try to get people back and finish the party?"

"How about we just hang out and have fun by ourselves?"

"I like that idea."

Pisces

February 19 to March 20

*Sensitive, compassionate, and kind
Pisces idealistically trusts in others,
Easily following where they go
Even if they lead her astray.
But what happens when she's selfless
To the point of self-destruction?*

All parents worry about their children. That is a fact as sure as night following day or spring sliding in after winter.

Some parents worry that their children are too lazy, always sitting about and happy to just breeze by and let others do as much of the work as possible. Other parents worry that their children are too meek, letting opportunities pass them by, or too bullying, reveling in pushing people around to get what they want.

Pisces's parents worried about her being too nice.

Now, this may seem a strange thing to worry about. After all, one of the first things every child learns is to be kind to others and share. Parents want their children to learn these lessons so that they'll be able to get along in the world, make friends, and in general just be good people and citizens. Being nice is a good thing to learn.

However, Pisces wasn't just nice, she was an angel. When another kid from the neighborhood wanted the last jumbo vanilla graham crisp from the ice cream truck, Pisces offered to give him her place in line. When Janie Lammers complained that she wanted to do a book report on the same book Pisces was reading, *The Wind in the Willows,* Pisces offered to let her do it and read a completely different book, even though she had already finished her report. If a classmate forgot lunch money, Pisces was the one they went to because they knew she'd give them hers, even when it meant not eating herself. But it wasn't out of meekness or an unwillingness to fight or argue; Pisces genuinely loved helping people.

Outside of school, it was even more striking. It wasn't uncommon for Pisces's parents to come home to any number of stray animals their daughter had befriended and adopted. First, it was the odd dog or cat, usually in some state of distress that they would need to help out with. Fleas, injuries, starvation, illness—you name it, they'd seen it. They would feed the animal or patch it up and then return it to its owners, if they could find them, or to the nearest no-kill shelter. But after a while, it seemed like dogs and cats had become too easy; they started returning home to discover wilder denizens—birds at first, then squirrels and raccoons, then snakes, and eventually they walked into their den one evening to find their daughter tending to an injured mountain lion.

"Hi, Mom. Hi, Dad," she said, waving from the couch. The monstrous mountain lion was lying next to her, his right front paw resting on her lap.

"Pisces! Get away from there!" her dad exclaimed, terrified.

"I can't," she said, shaking her head. "I have to help him." She lifted the paw to make her point, showing them the giant thorn that had lodged itself deeply into it.

"But, honey, that creature is dangerous. A professional needs to deal with that."

"Don't worry, Dad. I know what I'm doing. I'm using this damp cloth filled with ice"—she held it up—"to numb the paw so that I can remove the thorn."

Luckily, Pisces's mom knew her daughter, and while her husband freaked out and attempted to talk sense into Pisces, she crept into the kitchen and called animal control from the phone in the kitchen. Before Pisces could do anything rash, they arrived and sedated the mountain lion, saving everyone and safely removing the thorn.

Needless to say, animals were off-limits after that.

Unfortunately for Pisces's parents, that just meant that she moved on to people in the wild. One day, she decided to take a different route home from school and was amazed when she came upon an entire community of people living under the Meadowbrook Bridge.

The following day, she told her friend Melanie about it.

"Weird," Melanie said.

"I know, right?"

"Why would they live there?"

"I don't know. But I want to."

"Let's ask Mr. Jobs. He'll know."

So they did. He was the school guidance counselor and always seemed to know things like that.

"Well, Pisces, they certainly don't want to be living there," he said.

"Then why do they do it?"

Mr. Jobs scratched his head. "It's probably a little bit different for every person, but it boils down to the fact that they don't have money to pay for a house or an apartment."

"Why don't they get jobs?"

"Many people older and wiser than you have asked that very same question, kiddo, and there's no simple answer. Some of them are looking for jobs but just haven't found one yet. Some of them are too sick—in a variety of ways—to get a job."

"Why doesn't somebody help them?"

"People do what they can. Why, do you want to help them?"

"Of course! I'll do anything."

"I take some of the older kids to a soup kitchen once a week. If you get your parents to sign a permission slip, you can come with us."

"Oh, thank you! I'll do that."

Pisces's parents were so excited to have their daughter going out to her new pet cause rather than bringing it home with her that they happily signed the form, and Pisces went on the very next soup kitchen trip.

The place was amazing. So many big-hearted people came out to help the kitchen feed the needy that it made Pisces swell with pride. That first night, she personally fed 212 people! She also got to go around and talk to everyone, learning their stories and earning thanks and praise.

It was such an incredible experience that the weeklong wait for the next trip was agonizing for Pisces. Her second night at the kitchen was just as fantastic, and the following day at school, she moped around all morning, knowing how painful it would be to wait yet another week before going back. She was complaining about that very thing when Melanie had a brilliant idea.

"Why don't you just go without the group to volunteer?"

It was so simple that Pisces couldn't believe she hadn't thought of it herself. She and Melanie both told their parents they had to stay late for choir practice and then hopped on the number seven bus downtown and arrived at the soup kitchen just in time to help out. Both of them loved the experience and decided to return the following night. In fact, they ended up going every night that week and every night the following week. They were running out of excuses to tell their parents.

Still, though, it wasn't enough for Pisces. She just knew she could be doing more.

"You're already doing more than anyone I know," Melanie said.

But Pisces just told her that wasn't the point.

When they went back to the soup kitchen the following night, Pisces noticed a boy her age that she
had never seen before waiting in line to get food.

"What are you doing down here?" she asked
him when he reached her station.

"What do you mean?" he asked.

"Are you homeless?"

"For now. We had to leave our house. Dad lost
his job."

"What's your name?"

"David. You?"

"Pisces."

"Weird name."

"I know, right?"

"But at least it's not boring. I know seven
Davids."

"I guess. So ... you don't have anywhere to stay?"

David shook his head, and Pisces smiled.

"Would you like to have one?"

That evening, Pisces's parents returned home
from a hard day at work to find her cooking a
meal for four homeless people: David, his sister,
and their parents—the Braverman family. Being
good people themselves, Pisces's parents couldn't
rescind their daughter's offer to the Bravermans
of a nice meal and a place to stay the night. They
even helped her finish cooking dinner, and all of
them had a nice meal together, talking about the
state of the world and staying positive and fighting on even when you didn't want to.

The Bravermans were friendly, and Pisces's parents were quite taken with them.

"We're glad to have met you and happy you could share a meal with us," said Pisces's mom.

"Believe me," said David, "we're the ones who are glad."

"Yes," said Mrs. Braverman, "thank you so much for your kindness."

"Thank our daughter," said Pisces's father. "I know that she's offered our guest room for you to stay in, and I wanted to second that. You are welcome to stay."

"Thank you so much!" said Mr. Braverman.

"For tonight," Pisces's father said. "That's all we can offer."

"I understand." Mr. Braverman nodded. "We appreciate your kindness."

But Pisces did not understand. Not at all.

"They have nothing," she argued, "and we have so much."

Pisces's father opened his mouth, but it was her mother who spoke.

"You're right, Pisces; we have more than others: a house, a car, and good jobs to keep those things."

"Exactly! So why can't we share some of the good things we've been given to people who need them?"

"We do, Pisces, and you know that. Every year, we donate to several charities, which is more than a lot of people do. But we can't bring four more mouths to feed into this house, or all of that 'more' that we have will disappear very quickly."

"Plus," her father added, "that family in there was just like us. A year ago, they had what we had. Then the father lost his job, and it all went away. What's to stop that from happening to us?"

Pisces pouted. "So you won't help them because you're afraid? That's just dumb."

"That's the way it is," her mother said, tucking her into bed.

Not one to give up easily, Pisces decided that if her parents wouldn't let the Bravermans stay, she would find a way to get them enough money to get a place herself.

"How are you going to do that?" asked Melanie the next day at lunch.

"I've got an idea," Pisces said.

"Does it involve selling your lunch?" Melanie joked, pointing at the food Pisces hadn't even pretended to start eating.

"No, that's silly. From now on, I'm just not eating lunch, so I can give the extra food to the Bravermans."

"Pisces, don't be dumb. What are you gonna eat?"

She shrugged. "I'm fine. I'll just have bigger breakfasts and dinners."

"But you'll be hungry all day."

"So? There are worse things. Besides, the Bravermans are hungry all the time, and they don't have any money to get food at all."

"Whatever, but I think you're being dumb."

The next day, after Pisces told her how she'd gotten money, Melanie thought dumb might have been an understatement.

"So you don't have *anything* anymore?"

Pisces frowned and shook her head at Melanie dismissively, like she was being really stupid. "Of course I have some things, Mel. Don't be so dramatic. I didn't sell off all my clothes or anything."

"So what did you sell?"

"Toys, books, my old baby clothes—not like I was going to be using those again—my TV, my computer, my iPods, the toy chest, since I didn't have any toys left, and my computer desk and chair because—duh—why would I need it without a computer?"

"Does your room have anything in it anymore?"

"Of course it does. I didn't sell my bed or my dresser."

"That's nothing!"

"Well, Dad's been telling me to clean up my room for a while now. This is my way of doing that."

"I think you're going too far, Pisces. I like helping people, but this is getting crazy."

"Why is it crazy? Because I got rid of some stuff I don't really need to help out people who really do need help?"

"Yeah, but still. It's weird. How much did you get for all of it, anyway?"

"Enough so the Bravermans could move into a hotel."

"Well, that's at least good."

"Yeah, for an entire week."

"A week! You sold everything you own to give them one week in a hotel?"

Pisces stood. "Ugh! You just don't get it."

That evening at the soup kitchen, David thanked her for the money to stay at the hotel when he reached her station in line.

"Don't worry about it," she told him. "What did your parents say?"

"Some of it I told them I found, and I said I got the rest doing odd jobs for people."

"And they believed you?"

He shrugged. "I don't think they wanted to question it much. It's been awhile since we've had even a little bit of money."

"Well, whatever I can do to help, I will."

He smiled. "I'm glad to hear that, because what would really help is Dad having some nice clothes to look for jobs."

Pisces bit her lip. "I'd love to help, but I'm not sure where I'd get the money. I kind of used everything to get you the hotel."

"Oh," he said. "Well, no big deal. I just thought with all the stuff you guys have, there had to be something lying around you could use that you don't need."

Pisces thought about it. "Let me see what I can find."

When she got home that night, Pisces went on a scouting mission around her house, taking inventory of things she knew they weren't using and her parents wouldn't miss. She filled an entire box just with stuff from the garage: more old toys, tools, and clothes. She was shocked how much unused clutter they had just lying around.

She sold it, getting just over a hundred dollars, and brought that to David the next night at the soup kitchen.

"You're a lifesaver," he said. "This is fantastic."

"I found some extra stuff we had lying around the house."

"Great. Now if only he had money for buses so he could go to any interviews he gets."

David looked at Pisces pointedly, and she knew she would be scrounging around the house again.

Over the next week, as David asked for money to print resumes, for walking shoes (because his dad couldn't walk from business to business in his nice new shoes or they would get scuffed), and for cough medicine for his sister, Pisces worked harder and harder to scrounge up valuable items around the house. She uncovered some old paintings in the attic her parents had never hung up, but then the well of unused goods ran dry. Pisces found herself taking more expensive vases and just hoping her parents wouldn't notice. She grabbed collectibles from shelves and rearranged things to make it look like nothing had changed.

Whatever she did, it was never enough. David always had a new request, and Pisces wanted so badly to help that she always agreed. She took jobs around her neighborhood mowing lawns and cleaning houses. She emptied her personal bank accounts.

But when he asked for a computer (silly her for selling hers to get them into the hotel) and a second week's worth of hotel expenses, Pisces knew she would have to take more drastic measures.

When her parents were gone one afternoon, she snuck into their room and found a checkbook. Pisces flipped to the last check, thinking it was less likely her parents would look there, and wrote a check for David.

He was thrilled and said she was amazing for giving them so much help and that he'd never ask for anything again. But of course he did, because there's always something new to ask for.

Checks disappeared at an alarming rate until Pisces had used up almost an entire book.

Throughout all of this, Melanie watched as Pisces grew more and more exhausted and became sicker and sicker, running herself ragged with all of the work. Increasingly, she was late with homework, her grades dipped on tests and quizzes, and she even missed days of school—but never a trip to the soup kitchen.

"Pisces, this is killing you," Melanie finally said after she couldn't take it anymore. "You have to stop it and take care of yourself."

"Maybe you need to take care of yourself," Pisces sniped back.

That night, her parents confronted Pisces about the missing checks. Turned out that, once they hit the bank account, it didn't matter where in the checkbook she'd taken the checks from, and now they were overdrawn. Very, very overdrawn.

"What were you thinking?" her mother said.

"I was thinking that helping people who need it was more important than letting money pile up in a bank account," Pisces shot back.

"Don't you get it?" her father asked. "This is serious. We can't pay the mortgage on our house. We're going to have to use credit cards to pay our bills and hope we can pay them off."

"Will you listen to yourselves? David's family is wondering where they're next meal will come from."

"I doubt that," said her mother, "because all he has to do is ask you."

"Pisces, if we don't find a way to pay these bills off, we'll be homeless too."

Pisces eyes widened in shock. "Okay. Okay, I promise I'll stop."

But the next day, David asked her for something that seemed completely reasonable.

"Dad got a job, and things are really turning around," he said.

"That's great," she replied, feeling happy and justified in her decisions.

"They're even offering him a promotion, but he needs a car, and his next check isn't going to come in time."

"You need money."

"One last time."

Pisces pulled the checkbook from her back pocket, sure it was empty, and that would be that. But there was a single check left, and before she thought about it too hard, she signed the check over to him.

After that, things happened quickly.

David or his father must have cashed the check because her parents found out about it. They told her it was the final straw, pushing her parents' debt past what they could afford.

"What does that mean?" Pisces asked.

"It means," her father said, "that soon, we're going to be homeless."

There was no yelling this time. No accusing. Her parents seemed beaten down and defeated, and Pisces didn't know what to do.

So she left.

Her thought process, if it could even be said that Pisces had one at that point in time, was that maybe—just maybe—her parents would be able to make it through if they had one less mouth to feed. It wasn't hard. She just packed up the few things she had left and headed out. She already knew exactly where to go—the bridge. The people there knew her and welcomed her, giving her one of the warmest, cleanest spots at the center of their little camp, and for a while, it seemed okay.

At least from Pisces's point of view. Her parents were worried sick and made everyone around them worried sick by canvassing the neighborhood and telling every single person they came into contact with to keep an eye out for her. People were horrified and more than happy to help. Everyone knew what a giving girl Pisces was, and most of them had benefitted from her kindness, either directly or indirectly. A few even discovered the financial situation that the family had gotten itself into and started helping Pisces's parents pay down their bills, not even waiting to ask for their permission. Pisces had helped them when they needed it, so there was no way they were going to let this opportunity to help her out pass them by. Pisces's parents were touched that so many people loved their daughter with such ferocity.

When Melanie finally saw Pisces a few days later at the soup kitchen, she started bawling. Her friend looked awful.

"Pisces, you need to let someone help you. Please. Go back home."

"I can't do that. My parents can't afford me because I ruined things."

"No, they're fine now. Everything has changed."

"You're crazy."

Pisces took her food and tried to leave, but luckily, the adult workers there had heard the conversation and called over their security officers. Despite her protests, they held Pisces there until her parents could show up to take her home.

She argued with them the whole drive back, pleading for her parents to drop her by the bridge because she knew they couldn't afford her anymore, but they simply ignored her.

As soon as they opened the door to the house and turned on the lights in the living room, people leapt out from their hiding places. *"Surprise!"*

It was everyone Pisces had ever helped. One by one, they came to her and told her thank you, that she had done something amazing for them and meant a lot to their lives.

"Don't be afraid to ask for help," Mr. Francis from down the street said.

"We're always here for you," chipped in Maureen Dowd.

Finally, David and the rest of the Bravermans came over and handed over a check. "Obviously, that is only a small part of what we owe you," Mr. Braverman said, "but I wanted you to know that it goes both ways. And we would never have taken money if we thought it was hurting you. The world needs more people like you, which means you need to take care of yourself first so that you're able to keep helping others."

Pisces turned to her parents. "I'm sorry," she said. "I thought it was selfish to keep anything for myself when I knew somebody out there needed it more, but now I see that me giving away everything of ours was just putting us in the same position of needing help, which doesn't help anybody."

"We're sorry we didn't realize how important this was to you," her mother said.

"Yeah," her father said. "We want to figure out how we can help people more but without emptying our bank accounts."

"It's a deal, Dad!"

They all hugged.

Praise for *Serve to Lead*

"Leadership as service is so obvious once one has pondered the idea and its application—and, alas, so rare in current practice. This is a superb book."

—TOM PETERS
Author of *The Little BIG Things* and *In Search of Excellence*

"*Serve to Lead* distills timeless leadership principles into readily accessible, actionable practices that you can put to work today."

—WARREN BENNIS
Distinguished Professor of Business, University of Southern California
and author of *On Becoming a Leader*

"*Serve to Lead* is the essential guidebook to 21st century leadership. On a personal level, this book has changed my life. I urge men and women who aspire to make a difference in the world to let it change theirs as well."

—MARTI BARLETTA
Author of *Marketing to Women* and *Prime Time Women*

"*Serve to Lead* is a book of far-ranging insight, as much about life as it is about business. It is concise, thoughtful and—perhaps most importantly—useful."

—FRANK BLAKE
Former CEO, The Home Depot

"*Serve to Lead* is a really great book."

"*Serve to Lead* will be one of the greatest leadership books of this decade."

"'Who are you serving?' is the question at the heart of *Serve to Lead*, and it is the question that will change your entire vision of how you lead. If you are committed to being a truly effective leader in the twenty-first century, read this book—today."

"*Serve to Lead* has inspired me to actually change my leadership behavior: it's powerful stuff and gets results! It should be required reading for all aspiring CEOs."

"*Serve to Lead* is one of the few business books I've read that offers a truly democratic vision of leadership—a vision that can help leaders of every kind better serve their colleagues, their clients, and their community. Pick up a copy now and use Strock's insights to turn the raw material of your life into a masterpiece of service."

"Leadership is about service. *Serve to Lead* shows us how. Organizations today need leaders at all levels throughout the enterprise, not just at the top. This book is a must-read for everyone who aspires to lead through service."

—BILL NOVELLI
Former President & CEO of AARP

"This inspirational book offers a heartfelt, revolutionary approach for twenty-first-century leadership. With its vision for our transition from a transaction-based to a relationship-based world, *Serve to Lead* is a blueprint for leadership success."

—ROBIN GERBER
Author of *Leadership the Eleanor Roosevelt Way: Timeless Strategies from the First Lady of Courage*

"*Serve to Lead* is much more than a stake through the heart—if it exists—of fossilized hierarchies everywhere. Putting service before self, Strock has written an invaluable guidebook to the purposeful life. Boy, do we need it now!"

—RICHARD NORTON SMITH
Presidential Historian and author of
On His Own Terms: A Life of Nelson Rockefeller

"*Serve to Lead* is filled with principles that inspire us to the highest level of leadership. I highly recommend this book to those who want to make a lasting difference."

—SKIP PRICHARD
Author of *The Book of Mistakes: 9 Secrets to Creating a Successful Future,*
CEO, OCLC, Inc.

"Brilliant and absorbing! I couldn't put it down. Illuminates what is needed to lead in today's world. Strock's insights come to life through hundreds of real-life examples. An important book that belongs on the desk of anyone who aspires to lead (or influence) others."

—JESSE LYNN STONER
Coauthor of *Full Steam Ahead!*
Unleash the Power of Vision, and *Leading at a Higher Level*

"Great leaders stand apart by how they put others before themselves. *Serve to Lead* provides a road map for how everyday leaders can accomplish the same, allowing us to help those we lead, along with ourselves, to achieve our own form of greatness."

—TANVEER NASEER, MSC.
Award-winning leadership writer,
Inc. 100 leadership speaker, author "Leadership Vertigo"

"The call to develop transformational leaders has never been greater. *Serve to Lead* is a catalyst for great leadership in all times."

—IRENE BECKER
Founder, CEO, Just Coach It

"*Serve to Lead* is one of the finest books I have read on leadership in my lifetime. It will change the way you think about leadership, life, success and service."

—PROFESSOR M.S. RAO, PHD.
Father of "Soft Leadership" and International Leadership Guru

Serve to Lead

SERVE TO LEAD

LEAD 2.0

JAMES STROCK

With Admiration and Appreciation

**To the United States Armed Forces
Past, Present, Future**

THE FOUR QUESTIONS

Who Am I Serving?

How Can I Best Serve?

Am I Making My Unique Contribution?

What Am I Learning?

Contents

Preface to the
Second Edition

The early twenty-first century is a disruptive moment. It's debatable whether we're living through changes as significant as a century ago.

There can be no doubt that familiar, longstanding institutions and expectations are being re-created.

Five hundred years ago, the world was rocked by what we now call the Reformation. The information revolution wrought by the spread of the printing press found expression in the dissent of Martin Luther against the Catholic church doctrine and hierarchy. His heresy went viral, finding fertile ground across Europe. Luther's transformational leadership would not have been possible in earlier times, when the capacity to communicate was limited to a privileged clique.

We cannot know what the verdict of history will be for our present moment. Yet we can turn to history for context as we seek to navigate unfamiliar waters. Like our ancestors and predecessors, we must make fateful decisions based on incomplete knowledge.

Our Digital Age is distinct from twentieth-century norms and experiences. The last century was a time of centralization. Tremendous value was created by unifying human endeavor through large organizations: corporations, unions, government, mass political movements, the military.

The initial decades of our new century are marked by decentralization and disruption. Individuals and task-centered teams are challenging and changing the range of bureaucratic institutions. Mary McCarthy's twentieth-century "rule of nobody" is being supplanted by the twenty-first-century age of accountability. The "organization man" is receding in memory. The demands of our entrepreneurial moment are real, yet there is little nostalgia for the cloying conformity and suppressed individuality of the era of centralization.

Serve to Lead offers a system to approach the new challenges of leadership in the twenty-first century. Many aspects of our current circumstances appear uncertain and unfamiliar from the mid- and late-twentieth century.

Yet there is a magnificent compensation. The individual empowerment and accountability of our moment has resonance with earlier times, including the nineteenth century. Thinkers who were neglected in the past century, such as Ralph Waldo Emerson, are being rediscovered as we update familiar, longstanding customs and institutions.

This new edition includes information and insights gained in recent years. I am grateful to many generous readers who've sharpened the ideas.

The fundamental messages are ever more relevant:

— Servant leadership is the essence of effective leadership in our Digital Age;
— Everybody can lead, because everybody can serve;
— Transactional thinking and approaches are being superseded by creating and sustaining relationships;
— Networks are replacing hierarchies;
— Advancing the values of customers unlocks untold value;
— A primary task of leaders is to create more leaders;
— Twenty-first-century leadership integrates life and work.

Many readers have noted the consistency of the *Serve to Lead* approach with Christian values. I see servant leadership, properly understood, within Dietrich Bonhoeffer's prescient formulation of "religion-less Christianity." It represents an approach to life and work congenial with numerous traditions and philosophies.

What is emerging, in real-time, is the tightening nexus between ethical, other-directed conduct and value creation. In our ever more interconnected moment, sustainable value creation does not come from "winning" transactions so much as nurturing mutually beneficial relationships. My greatest hope is that this book adds value in a practical way, constituting a compass that readers can customize to navigate the vistas of challenge and change before us.

Thank you for reading and reflecting on the notions of *Serve to Lead*. Your continuing encouragement and insights are inspiring and deeply appreciated.

JMS
June 2018

Note to Readers:
How to Use this Book

////////////////////////////

"Books are for use."

— SHIYALI RAMAMRITA RANGANATHAN

"Men more frequently require to be
reminded than informed."

— SAMUEL JOHNSON

"First, say to yourself what you would be,
then do what you have to do."

— EPICTETUS

////////////////////////////

There are many types of books. There are as many ways to read them as there are readers.

Some regard books as delicate, cultivated creations. They are to be treated as other-worldly, fragile, precious. Thus Henry Wadsworth Longfellow's nineteenth-century, timeless evocation of

The love of learning, the sequestered nooks,
And all the sweet serenity of books.

Serve to Lead is not intended to sit on a shelf in graceful repose. It would be against the very notion of this book for it to lay idle—*who would it be serving?*

This book is intended to become your sturdy companion as you embrace the *Serve to Lead* approach to living.

To that extent, *Serve to Lead* is inspired by Theodore Roosevelt's "Pigskin Library." Roosevelt was one of the most consequential and vital leaders in the unruly pageant of American history. He was a learning machine. Nothing escaped his rampant curiosity. He read voraciously, often several books in a single day.

Even in the White House, as president of the United States, he would wring out moments for reading amid the most crowded hours imaginable. With pardonable hyperbole, TR's youngest son exclaimed to other children that his father, the president, read every book in the Library of Congress.

In the words of his world, Roosevelt was the epitome of the man of action, as well as the man of thought.

As he left the presidency in 1909, TR planned an expedition to Africa. It was then that he conceived the "Pigskin Library." Roosevelt methodically catalogued a collection of books he wanted at his side as he undertook a new chapter of his life's "Great Adventure."

Looking back after his return, Roosevelt reflected on the role his books played in unifying his thoughts and actions in the wilds of Africa:

> I almost always had some volume with me, either in my saddle-pocket or in the cartridge-bag which one of my gun-bearers carried to hold odds and ends. Often my reading would be done while resting under a tree at noon, perhaps beside the carcass of a beast I had killed or else while waiting for camp to be pitched; and in either case it might be impossible to get water for washing. In consequence the books were stained with blood, sweat, gun-oil, dust and ashes; ordinary bindings either vanished or became loathsome, whereas pigskin merely grew to look as a well-used saddle looks.

This book is intended to serve you in the same way. Let it become well-worn, reflecting your life. Carry it with you. Scuff it up. Mark it up. Underline ideas you agree with. Add your thoughts, add your examples. Follow quotations to their sources.

Make this book truly your own. Make yourself the coauthor. Create a journal of your daily, monthly, quarterly and annual goals and milestones. Use the *Serve to Lead* System to turn the raw material of your life into a masterpiece of service.

> *Life's most persistent and urgent question is,*
> *"What are you doing for others?"*
> —MARTIN LUTHER KING, JR.

Serve to Lead opens with an exploration of twenty-first-century leadership. Succeeding chapters focus on specific competencies ranging from casting a vision, to management, customer service, general communications, to sales, marketing and other persuasive communications. The book concludes with an eight-week program, presenting specific strategies to incorporate the *Serve to Lead* approach into all aspects of your life.

> *A man is what he thinks about all day long.*
> —RALPH WALDO EMERSON

> *Learning how to think really means learning how to exercise*
> *some control over how and what you think. It means being*
> *conscious and aware enough to choose what you pay attention*
> *to and to choose how you construct meaning from experience.*
> —DAVID FOSTER WALLACE

Many of your existing thought patterns were set by yourself or others in your early years. Your ways of thinking may be as out of date as the clothing and hair styles of those days. Yet they may still occupy prime space in your mental closet. You may have become so accustomed to long-standing, familiar notions that you've come to assume they are just the way things are.

The fact is, your thoughts are, ultimately, the result of *your choices, your decisions.*

Every minute of every hour of every day of your life represents a decision.

Going forward as a twenty-first-century leader, your fundamental question in illuminating those decisions, great and small, should be: *Who Am I Serving?* This query can be redirected to hold others to account.

> *If I had an hour to solve a problem and my life depended on the solution, I would spend the first fifty-five minutes determining the proper question to ask…for once I know the proper question, I could solve the problem in less than five minutes.*
>
> —ALBERT EINSTEIN

> *I beg you, to have patience with everything unresolved in your heart and to try to love the questions themselves as if they were locked rooms or books written in a very foreign language. Don't search for the answers, which could not be given to you now, because you would not be able to live them…. Live the questions now. Perhaps then, someday far in the future, you will gradually, without even noticing it, live your way into the answer.*
>
> —RAINER MARIA RILKE

LEADERSHIP IS THE KILLER APP

Leadership is the killer app that can transform all aspects of life and work.

The *principles* are universal. The *applications* vary, depending on whom one is serving, and how one can create the greatest value in the circumstances at hand.

Whether one is young or old, male or female, rich or poor, of any race or ethnicity or nationality or religion, the principles are the same. So, too, whether one is serving the world, a nation, a community, a corporation, a non-governmental organization, the military, or one's family and friends.

The application of the principles may vary greatly. Effectively serving is based on the relationship of the leader and those to be served. It is that relationship, rather than the preferences of the leader, that will determine the how value can best be created.

In a world of tumult and unprecedented competition and connection, leadership profoundly based on service enables anyone to create value in any circumstance. Anything less is not sustainable.

EVERY DAY'S A DECISION.

The next step is yours.

Are you prepared to commit? To fully engage your unique combination of talents, experiences and inspirations to serve more effectively—and live more fully—than ever before?

The risks and losses of change may be very real. The hoped-for results are necessarily uncertain. Will you summon the courage to commit to transformation?

Faith is taking the first step
even when you don't see the whole staircase.
—MARTIN LUTHER KING, JR.

God will not have his work made manifest by cowards.
—RALPH WALDO EMERSON

Many people undertake commitments lightly. Even the most solemn, public undertakings—such as marriage vows—are, all too often, taken casually.

When you engage the *Serve to Lead* system you are deciding to alter your approach to leadership and life. It requires stretching and growing and openness to change—sustained by relentless dedication.

In the words of the Stoic philosopher Epictetus, you must "distinguish yourself from the mere dabbler, the person who plays at things as long as they feel comfortable or interesting. Otherwise, you will be like a child who sometimes pretends he or she is a wrestler, sometimes a soldier, sometimes a musician, sometimes an actor in a tragedy."

If one determines to overcome the obstacles, the results can be remarkable. To be sure, they may be entirely different from what one anticipates at the start. It's not about you. You may reach unforeseen destinations. Your experience and imagination and limitations may all be transcended.

There are no guarantees of "success" in conventional terms. What one can seek, is the fulfillment immortally evoked by Roosevelt in 1910:

> It is not the critic who counts; not the man who points out how the strong man stumbles, or where the doer of deeds could have done them better. The credit belongs to the man who is actually in the arena, whose face is marred by dust and sweat and blood; who strives valiantly; who errs, who comes short again and again, because there is no effort without error and shortcoming; but who does actually strive to do the deeds; who knows great enthusiasms, the great devotions; who spends himself in a worthy cause; who at the best knows in the end the triumph of high achievement, and who at the worst, if he fails, at least fails while daring greatly, so that his place shall never be with those cold and timid souls who neither know victory nor defeat.

I don't know what your destiny will be, but one thing I do know: the only ones among you who will be really happy are those who have sought and found how to serve.

—ALBERT SCHWEITZER

PART 1

////////////////////////////

Everybody Can Lead
Because
Everybody Can Serve

1

Everybody Can Lead
Because Everybody Can Serve

"Everybody can be great, because everybody can serve.
You don't have to have a college degree to serve.
You don't have to make your subject and your verb agree to serve....
You only need a heart full of grace, a soul generated by love."

— **MARTIN LUTHER KING, JR.**

"[W]hoever wants to become great among you must be your
servant, and whoever wants to be first must be slave of all.."

— **MARK 10:43**

We are living in a golden age of leadership.

There are more opportunities for more people to serve—and lead—than ever before. Individuals are empowered to express their visions and views through the internet. Value can be created in unforeseen ways by unheralded innovators in unexpected places. Political and cultural change can be focused, intensified, and spread through social media. Longstanding controversies such as same-sex marriage and marijuana legalization are resolved, with public sentiment transformed amid deep public engagement. Traditional political alignments are swept away as citizens demand that their government reflect their values, rather than the interests of politicians and pressure groups.

Only in our time could the entire world be inspired by the courage of a theretofore unknown Pakistani schoolgirl who overcame a brutal assassination attempt. Her offense: refusing to be deterred from seeking a full education solely of her gender. Malala Yousafzai became the first high school student summoned from class to receive news of being awarded a

Nobel Prize. The impact of her leadership will surely be greater than that of many holding high positions in government or corporations.

The early twenty-first century also feels like the worst of times for leadership. Poll after poll confirms widespread dissatisfaction, discontent and cynicism. Political turbulence is endemic. Great organizations, spanning the private and public sectors, face existential challenges from empowered individuals and networks. Authority in all forms can be discredited and displaced with ruthless speed. CEO's and celebrities, previously seen as untouchable, can face a rude awakening or a grievous reckoning. From government to corporations to the not-for-profit sector, the missteps of self-serving individuals and organizations abound. High position can be perilous. One tweet, one selfie, one moment of anger in an unguarded moment can result in ruin.

THE EMERGENCE OF TWENTY-FIRST-CENTURY LEADERSHIP

In Search of Excellence co-author Tom Peters declares: "Leadership in the twenty-first century A.D. is exactly what it was in the twenty-first century B.C.... *Nothing* has changed!"

Peters gets so many things right that one hesitates to disagree with him. Just this once, he doesn't have it quite right.

Twenty-first-century leadership is markedly different from what came before it in the Industrial Age. The empowerment of individuals through the Information Revolution is a change of transcending importance. It marks a decisive historical moment as significant as the introduction of the modern moveable type printing press by Johannes Gutenberg in 1440.

In the recent past, to one degree or another, centralized information and expertise constituted the foundation on which leadership systems were based. The closely held authority of Industrial Age organizations was based on the methodical aggregation of resources, directed by a small number of individuals.

In the words of Clay Shirky, author of *Here Comes Everybody*, "Media is now global, social, ubiquitous and cheap." There are innumerable ways in which people can connect. Leadership and management are being redefined even in (or perhaps, *especially* in) established, tradition-bound organizations.

Authoritarian police states are not exempt from disruption occasioned by social networks in their midst, with incongruously frivolous names such as Twitter.

> *Group action gives human society its particular character,*
> *and anything that changes the ways groups get things done*
> *will affect society as a whole.... The ways in which any given*
> *institution will find its situation transformed will vary, but the*
> *various local changes are manifestations of a single deep source:*
> *newly capable groups are assembling, and they are working*
> *without managerial imperative and outside the previous*
> *structures that bounded their effectiveness. These changes will*
> *transform the world everywhere groups of people come together*
> *to accomplish something, which is to say everywhere.*
>
> —CLAY SHIRKY

Until recently, attaining high position entailed achieving a status with a degree of permanence, built on a foundation of prior performance. Increasingly, persons in high positions recognize their circumstances to be precarious—at least if they don't adapt to the new realities. The lack of security and control they encounter arises from the heightened accountability imposed by the empowerment of others, inside and outside their enterprises. To the extent those they're ostensibly serving conclude they're being well served, those in positions of authority can feel secure. To the extent stakeholders conclude they're *not* well served, "leaders" in high positions will, rightly, be insecure.

Gandhi and other historic leaders who challenged great institutions could achieve significant power based on their moral authority. If such authority was conferred by those "below," it would have power because it was consistent with the values of those "above." Today, armed with Information Age tools, more and more individuals can realistically aspire to attain both moral and formal authority—even within institutions resistant to change and accountability.

If it's a challenging moment for those holding formal positions of power, it's altogether exhilarating for those who effectively serve others. To an unprecedented extent, it's possible for *anyone* to become a leader. Those who serve most effectively can serve more people, in more ways, than ever before.

What leaders *do*—hour by hour, day by day—is in the midst of tremendous change. Persons entrusted with high positions of authority in the twenty-first century who aspire to be effective *leaders* are quite different from the *bosses* we all know and disdain.

The creator of *Dilbert*, Scott Adams, provides a good definition of a boss:

> He's every employee's worst nightmare. He wasn't born mean and unscrupulous, he worked hard at it. And succeeded. As for stupidity, well, some things are inborn. His top priorities are the bottom line and looking good in front of his subordinates and superiors (not necessarily in that order). Of absolutely no concern to him is the professional or personal well-being of his employees. The Boss is technologically challenged but he stays current on all the latest business trends, even though he rarely understands them.

Adams' "Boss" has a long and unlamented past, a shaky present, and a bleak future. The empowerment of customers, and the imperative to empower employees as the primary means to serve customers effectively, is transforming organizations and individuals. As we will explore throughout this book, what leaders do is indeed changing radically, along with who can be leaders.

At the same time, there are timeless aspects to effective leadership. Tom Peters is absolutely right in this respect. Paradoxically, in the twenty-first century, those timeless aspects are, if anything, more important than ever before.

What changes have you experienced or observed in twenty-first-century leadership? Are you seeing leadership from unexpected people, in unexpected places?

What effective leaders *do* is changing dramatically; what they *are* in terms of character is the same as in distant times.

---◆---

What effective leaders do in the twenty-first century is quite different from recent times. What they are remains much the same as in distant times.

---◆---

Throughout history, "character" has been recognized as decisive in evaluating leaders' potential and effectiveness. Its definition is elusive. It's akin to Justice Potter Stewart's characterization of pornography: you know it when you see it.

Theodore Roosevelt robustly emphasized three elements of character: honesty, courage and common sense. In ways large and small, traits of character indicate that one is serving others before oneself—often at great personal cost.

Bill Novelli, the recent, highly regarded CEO of the roughly forty-million-member AARP, notes that a leader's personal character may be *more* important today than in the twentieth century. The wide availability of information and the empowerment of various stakeholders have altered the leadership landscape irrevocably.

In this sense, as in others, there is a growing convergence of leadership roles. In the twenty-first century, corporate CEOs and others in high positions find their personal lives being held to public scrutiny and judgment in ways long familiar to elective and appointive politicians.

When one steps back, this isn't surprising. The tools which enable leaders to serve ever more people in ever more aspects of their lives also open them to the judgment of more people, and in more extensive ways.

Individual and organizational ethics are moving from the periphery of business strategy to its center. Ethical practices are necessary for sustainable success, even in the most rough-and-tumble business sectors. What it means to *lead* is merging with what it means to *serve*.

From the vantage point of those being served, this makes perfect sense; from the vantage point of those striving to lead, it points toward significant change. We're in a new era, with new rules, new ways to serve—and much greater accountability.

Reflecting the new realities, the *Serve to Lead* System is based on the following definition of leadership, that applies to individuals and organizations: *Twenty-first-century leaders inspire others to alter their thoughts and actions, in alignment with an empowering vision.*

This understanding of twenty-first-century leadership has numerous aspects and implications.

TEN PRINCIPLES OF TWENTY-FIRST-CENTURY LEADERSHIP

1. EVERYBODY CAN LEAD, BECAUSE EVERYBODY CAN SERVE.

Service—evaluated from the vantage point of those served—is the essence of leadership. When service is the basis of leadership, *anyone* can be a leader.

> *Organizations exist to serve. Period.*
> *Leaders live to serve. Period.*
> —TOM PETERS

Leadership within our definition is entirely separate from your position. A CEO may be a leader—or not. A person holding a subordinate position on an organization chart might well be a tremendously effective leader.

Whether you're a leader is not determined by your age or gender or race or ethnicity or your past or others' expectations. The decision of whom and how to serve is entirely yours.

In a world where everybody can lead, because everybody can serve, *a critical mission for organizations is to continually develop the leadership capacities of their employees (and others with whom they are associated in networks, supply chains, projects, etc.).*

Leadership is lifting a person's vision to high heights,
the raising of a person's performance to a higher standard,
the building of a personality beyond its normal limitations.

—PETER DRUCKER

◆

Everybody can lead because everybody can serve.
Your decision. No excuses. No exceptions.

◆

This is not a matter of choice. It's a matter of survival in today's ruthlessly competitive, global markets.

No matter how strong their past or present performance, any individual or enterprise *not* committed to developing leadership will *not* retain a preeminent place.

2. THE MOST VALUABLE RESOURCE OF ANY ENTERPRISE IS ITS PEOPLE.

We've all suffered through the mind-numbing mantras of corporate training, to the effect that "our people are our greatest resource." We've then watched as many of the same organizations routinely disregard the welfare of their employees. Their slogans are no more reality-based than the bloodthirsty tyrant Mao Zedong's grotesquely ironic slogan: "Serve the People."

To be sure, most enterprises have not regarded their people as their most valuable resource. Their management systems are built around their actual, rather than their proclaimed, values.

In the Industrial Revolution, going back to the late 1700s, natural resources—such as wood, coal and metals—were generally held to be the fundamental source of wealth. A privileged elite directed others with the goal of extracting maximal value.

Human labor was necessary to create value, but it was widely available. Individual workers often were treated as interchangeable. Those who directed them tended to regard laborers much as they regarded machinery. Indeed, many viewed human capital as less reliable than machinery. The goal was the same for each: to increase production and value through efficiency. Those in charge didn't so much want new pairs of hands; they saw others as extending their own reach.

One of my favorite examples of this kind of thinking is from Australia. It comes in the form of a striking monument in downtown Sydney. It honors an early governor of the state of New South Wales, the Lieutenant General Sir Richard Bourke. The memorial "records his able, honest, and benevolent administration from 1831 to 1837":

Selected for the government at a period of singular difficulty, his judgment, urbanity, and firmness justified the choice, comprehending at once the vast resources peculiar to this colony.

He applied them, for the first time, systematically to its benefit. He voluntarily divested himself of the prodigious influence arising from the assignment of penal labour, and enacted just and salutary laws for the amelioration of penal discipline. He was the first governor, who published satisfactory accounts of the public receipts and expenditure.

Without oppression, or detriment to any interest, he raised the revenue to a vast amount, and, from its surplus, realized extensive plans of immigration.

He established religious equality on a just and firm basis, and sought to provide for all, without distinction of sect, a sound and adequate system of national education. He constructed various public works of permanent utility, he founded the flourishing settlement of Port Philip, and threw open the unlimited wilds of Australia to pastoral enterprise. He established savings banks, and was the patron of the first Mechanics' Institute. He created an equitable tribunal for determining upon claims to grants of lands. He was the warm friend of the liberty of the press. He extended trial by jury after its almost total suspension.

For many years, by these and numerous other measures for the moral, religious, and general improvement of all classes, he raised the colony to unexampled prosperity; and retired amid the reverent and affectionate regret of the people; having won their confidence by his integrity, their gratitude by his services, their admiration by his public talents, and their esteem by his private worth.

This adulatory recounting of one person's "leadership" might as easily move today's reader to laughter or anger. Its claims of individual accomplishment are ludicrous from our vantage point. That it is carved in stone reflects the overweening entitlement of the "leaders" of an earlier generation, presuming the permanence and inevitability of their values and institutions.

Echoes of this kind of thinking reverberate in our midst. Mainstream twentieth-century American management was premised on the view that value is primarily created by the few directing the actions of the many. The greater the extent to which people could be directed, the greater the value created.

The ultimate expression of this approach is identified with an influential early-twentieth-century American management theorist, Frederick Winslow Taylor. Taylor conceived systems by which industrial managers would control and direct their employees. Their time and movements were monitored, clocked to the minute, sometimes to the second. Complex tasks were deconstructed into multitudes of simple, repetitive tasks, readily translatable into metrics for increasing output.

There was literally no time for thought or reflection by employees in many industrial settings. No matter. Little or no value was placed on their observations or capacity for improving their own output, much less that of the larger enterprise. Workers were manipulated to conform to the machinery to which they were appended. Assembly lines were designed by theorists and accountants, directed by clerks.

[I]n almost all of the mechanic arts the science which underlies each act of a workman is so great and amounts to so much that the workman…is incapable of fully understanding... without the guidance and help of those who are working with him or over him, either through lack of education or through

insufficient mental capacity....Those in the management...
should...guide and help the workman in working under it, and
should assume a much larger share of the responsibility for results
than under usual conditions is assumed by the management.
—FREDERICK WINSLOW TAYLOR,
THE PRINCIPLES OF SCIENTIFIC MANAGEMENT (1911)

Fritz Lang's classic silent film, *Metropolis* (1927), presents an unforgettable, futuristic vision of Industrial Age dystopia. A gray, monochromatic, densely populated urban area warehouses untold masses of indistinguishable drones. Their waking hours are trance-like. They are zombies—physically alive, spiritually dead. They shuffle listlessly, in affectless anonymity, to and from their dreary, interchangeable jobs. From the multitude of mechanical tasks performed with unnatural regularity—such as moving a clock arm on cue—emerges a system devoid of humanity. At the top, amassing the lion's share of the profits, sits a chief executive. He is well-coiffed, nattily dressed. He exhibits the sleek lines and heedless vitality of a vain, unconscious carrier of evil.

Metropolis remains compelling. Its memorably beautiful sets, manifestly from another age, underscore its timeless resonance.

This business leadership model had its analogs in politics, culture, and religious practice. What they shared was the assumption that the most effective way to create value was to have an elite direct the exertions of the many.

As alien as it now appears, this approach no doubt seemed reasonable to many in an era when education and information were scarce commodities. By the dawn of the twentieth century, the United States led the world in education. In that pre-GI Bill time, perhaps 5 percent of college-age Americans were enrolled in post-secondary education.

For most of the twentieth century it was widely accepted that communications from those holding authority as "leaders" would be largely one-way. People in power would announce; they would declare; they would broadcast. This was bolstered by the emerging technologies of radio and television. Until the turn of the twenty-first century, there were no corresponding tools for listening and receiving actionable information from employees, customers and other stakeholders.

In retrospect, that model of leadership—familiar, hierarchical, patriarchal—was in decline by the mid-twentieth century.

Prompted by management theorists, most notably the legendary Peter Drucker, those at the top of some farsighted enterprises recognized their workforces to be a vast, largely untapped resource. They began to see that CEOs and others in positions of authority could serve their organizations most effectively by empowering and exchanging information and ideas with their employees, rather than primarily directing or controlling them.

In the aftermath of the Second World War, vanquished Japan and Germany had no alternative but to rebuild from the ground up. Dire necessity afforded the opportunity to comprehensively revamp their management practices. With nothing to lose, they were open to change. It is a quirk of fate that these two nations, marked by longstanding traditions of hierarchy and obedience to authority, found competitive advantage from empowering employees.

In contrast, American companies enjoyed market hegemony in the immediate aftermath of the Second World War. Flush with unprecedented success and unchallenged by international competition, many were initially slow to recognize the new opportunities to create value in their midst.

Nonetheless, greater forces of change were in train. One of the transformative trends of the second half of the twentieth century was the increasing value created by previously underutilized segments of our population. This had causes and consequences throughout American life—economically, financially, culturally and politically. As the century closed, the Information Revolution occasioned and accelerated fundamental change.

Today, nearly everyone recognizes—at least in theory—that the human capital of an enterprise is its most valuable resource. This is obvious in certain sectors, such as professional services (law, medicine, engineering), high technology, as well as marketing and sales. It's no less true in modern manufacturing and retailing, where the most advanced and financially successful companies, such as Toyota and Costco, are notable for extraordinary efforts to nurture their teams.

Knowing something and acting on it are different things. In a recession, when financial capital is scarce, human capital is liable to be treated in a short-sighted manner. This is exacerbated by the absence of agreed metrics relating to human capital. The costs of counterproductive practices occasioning employee turnover or disengagement are routinely underestimated. Traditional accounting practices reflect the values of another era; a consistently effective twenty-first-century leader must master the demands of the balance sheet while not becoming captive to its limitations.

We need to break away from the Industrial-Age psychology
that labels people as expenses and cell phones as assets.
Jobs should cater to our interests.
Instead of telling people what they're hired to do,
we should ask them what they love to do.
Then create a marriage between that passion and your needs.
—STEPHEN COVEY

Managing winds up being the allocation of resources
against tasks. Leadership focuses on people. My definition
of a leader is someone who helps people succeed.
—CAROL BARTZ

◆

In the twenty-first century, effective management
is based on recognition of the preponderant value
of human capital. Management is not only in
service of leadership; it's increasingly merged.

◆

A Leader's Top Priority is to Serve the People Who Constitute and Create the Preponderant Value of the Enterprise.

The traditional understanding of leadership as based on "leaders" and "followers" is no longer apt.

In the twenty-first century, when the essence of leadership is service, a leader serves by enabling others to create value. The relationship dynamics are from the *bottom-up* rather than the top-down; from the *outside-in*, rather than the inside-out.

> *Twenty-first-century leadership relationship dynamics are from the bottom-up rather than the top-down; from the outside-in, rather than the inside-out.*

Our view of leadership has changed correspondingly. A leap of imagination is required for us to comprehend the reality of the serried, robotic ranks of hundreds of thousands of interchangeable troops at Hitler's hypnotic Nuremberg rallies. We would not acknowledge, much less countenance, such a "leader."

In the past, leaders were often compared to film directors. To execute their visions, directors would supervise every detail of every scene. The stereotype was barked commands, followed by unquestioning obedience.

We now look to exemplars whose task is to elicit extraordinary performance from others. Thus we often turn to the lessons of coaches. A great sports coach, such as the legendary John Wooden, obtained outstanding team performance by assembling and training individuals with the raw materials of serviceable talent. He relentlessly instilled habits of thought until they approached the inevitability of instinct. Wooden explicitly inculcated character—the combination of virtues by which individuals achieve excellence through serving others.

It is often said that networks are orchestrated. Benjamin Zander and Rosamund Stone Zander unite the perspectives of symphony conductor and executive coach. The conductor, who elicits outstanding individual and team performance in a coordinated setting toward a shared vision and product, is another archetype of twenty-first-century leadership. So, too, the talents and team leadership skills of a music producer, such as Sir George Martin (known as "the fifth Beatle"), resonate far beyond the recording studio.

Even the most stereotypically hierarchical of organizations, the military, is altering its leadership approach. War correspondent Robert Kaplan chronicles the dramatic changes underway. Some are wrought by the applications of new information and weapons technologies. Others emerge from the retrospective consideration of failures from command-and-control operations in the Vietnam conflict. Officers recognize that an increasing part of their role is to teach leadership to those who report to them. As a result, today's troops on the ground are entrusted with an ever-rising number of life-and-death judgment calls. Those closest to the action also can transmit more valuable information to their commanders, enabling them to make better strategic and tactical decisions.

This is a historic change. In the American Revolution, General George Washington contended with rambunctious troops who resisted discipline and order. One officer grumbled, "The privates are all generals." What earlier generations saw as a disadvantage is being transformed into a strategic asset. A recent Marine Corps commandant summarized his mission as creating "strategic corporals."

Whether one is dealing with citizens or colleagues or employees or customers, twenty-first-century leadership is more and more about influence and persuasion. It's less and less about formal authority and orders.

There are fewer and fewer "followers" in the old sense. More often there are "followers" as with Twitter; they choose when to "follow," and can disengage or simply ignore those they are "following" at any moment. In many situations today the "leaders" are better understood as "followers"; the "followers" are now the "leaders."

In the past, "servant leadership" was viewed as a variant on "leadership." Robert K. Greenleaf, the founder of the modern servant leadership movement in the mid-twentieth century, explained: "The leader-first and the servant-first are two extreme types."

Today, the *only* effective leadership is focused on serving others. It is no longer an option or a modifier; it's the very definition of leadership.

> *Today, the only effective leadership is serving others. It's no longer optional. It's the essence of twenty-first-century leadership.*

Collaboration is the Primary Means of Joint Enterprise.

The word "collaboration" was damaged in the twentieth century. Memorably, it was used to characterize the activities of many in France who declined to resist the Nazi occupation during the Second World War.

It's often seen as antithetical to, or at least separate from, leadership. This is expressed in a 2009 *Wikipedia* entry: "Collaboration does not require leadership and can sometimes bring better results through decentralization and egalitarianism."

That may have been a reasonable twentieth-century view, but it's wide of the mark today.

Collaboration—from the Latin, literally, *working together*—is a pillar of twenty-first-century leadership. When the information and insight creating value is reposed in the larger group rather than a select few, collaboration becomes essential to leadership.

The days of maintaining power through hoarding information are waning. Collaboration is inconsistent with the older, hierarchical model; you don't collaborate with a Dilbert-style "boss."

This has many consequences. To lead any enterprise effectively, you must enable the most productive collaboration of the greatest number of people. This begins with employees. It can also encompass customers and a range of other stakeholders. To create value, those you're serving should be, to the maximal extent, your collaborators.

We hear many effective leaders constantly refer to their "teams." Teams imply equality; they also require leadership. It can include leadership from a coach or a fellow participant with a specific title or task. It can arise spontaneously from any team member. It can flow from one team or member, toward another—or emerge simultaneously among several.

Such fluidity and energy, well-channeled, can generate tremendous power. One can imagine almost any role being played consistently in such teams, at the highest level of performance—other than "boss."

In terms of improving performance, gathering information, or even spurring insight, two heads can be better than one. Or as John Lennon wrote, a million heads can be better yet. Networks whose participants continuously improve their performance can create extraordinary value. John Hagel, co-chairman of the Deloitte Center for Edge Innovation, writes of a steep, rising "collaboration curve."

Command-and-control approaches are less and less effective. What is needed is not direction, but management in service of leadership. The most productive collaborations are more than unions of equals; they are unions of leaders, serving in dynamic relationships. Participants resemble skilled dancers. Methodical choreography and direction enable them to move in concert—maintaining space for individual contribution and creative collaboration, including spontaneous improvisation.

◆

Collaboration—working together as equals—is not antithetical to leadership. It's the primary working relationship fostered by twenty-first-century leaders. The most effective collaborations are more than unions of equals; they are unions of leaders, serving in dynamic relationships.

◆

3. WE ARE IN TRANSITION FROM A TRANSACTION-BASED WORLD TO A RELATIONSHIP-BASED WORLD.

We are in transition from transaction-based world to a relationship-based world. This represents a fundamental change in leadership and service.

In the past, people might reasonably conclude their self-interest would be advanced by seeking unilateral advantage in any given transaction. To be sure, they might choose to take an ethical approach, either from conviction or with an eye toward the longer term. Nonetheless, their perceived self-interest and the interests of those on the other side of a transaction were routinely viewed as at odds.

This state of affairs has been in transition for some time. In 1916, during another period of rapid advancement in communications, Orison Swett Marden observed, "There was a time when the man who was the shrewdest and sharpest, the most cunning in taking advantage of others, got the biggest salary. But today the man at the other end of the bargain is looming up as he never did before."

> *We are moving from a transaction-based world to a relationship-based world. Transactions often have been occasions to seek unilateral advantage over others. Relationships, to be successful and sustainable, incline invariably toward cooperation, collaboration and service.*
>
> *In a relationship-based world, your self-interest moves ever more tightly into alignment with serving others.*

The internet is taking Marden's vision to the next level. In a relationship-based world, one's self-interest moves ever more tightly into alignment with serving others.

In the past, isolated interactions might well remain isolated interactions. If a company chose, for example, to treat a customer shabbily, that might be the end of the matter. Most consumers were not empowered to respond effectively. If a fuss were raised, the company might well have a surpassing advantage in terms of credibility and influence. The "relationship," such as it was, strongly tilted one way.

On the other hand, if a company treated customers notably well, the benefits of isolated interactions or individual relationships might be difficult to scale into additional value creation.

Today, there are limitless possibilities to deepen and broaden relationships arising from all manner of interactions.

Amazon continually breaks ground in creating new relationships with and among its customers. Its reader reviews have become an invaluable resource. Likewise, a key to the phenomenal success of eBay is its insight that relationships among strangers could be created by enabling buyers and sellers to rate one another online.

Social networking sites and apps connect millions of people in new, evolving ways. School alumni can retain or restore relationships which in the past ended at graduation. Devotees of hobbies or causes can find one another. Human resource functions within large organizations can be electrified through web-based social networks.

The new relationships—and new kinds of relationships—arising amid social networking are in an early phase of evolution. Their impact is already significant.

Any Interaction Can Be Transformed into a Relationship.
As law professor, radio talk show host and blogging pioneer Hugh Hewitt summarizes, "There are no insignificant actions in the Internet Age." He might well add, any interaction can be transformed into a relationship by the decision of one party (even someone who merely observed the interaction).

> *There are no insignificant actions in the Internet Age.*
> —HUGH HEWITT

The internet can be used by those outside of positions of formal authority or power to establish new relationships, or redefine existing relationships. A leader can emerge by attracting and focusing widespread attention to an idea or product. The political insurgencies of Barack Obama in 2008, and Bernie Sanders and Donald Trump in 2016 elaborated such approaches.

Another striking example comes from the world of advertising: Dove Soap's "Campaign for Real Beauty." Dove's advertising firm, Ogilvy & Mather, estimates the campaign has reached 400 million people. It utilizes the range of information technologies to expand notions of female beauty. Suddenly, many women are engaged in a relationship arising from a basket of products ordinarily viewed as commodities.

The technological capacity to create relationships from otherwise disparate interactions represents a breathtaking opportunity for enhanced service.

On the other hand, self-regarding actions can occasion more peril than ever before. These include actions which in the recent past might have been regarded as private or trifling.

New York Times columnist Thomas Friedman provides a light but telling example. As he was picking up periodicals at a newsstand while on the road, he inadvertently moved ahead of another customer waiting in line for the cashier. She admonished Friedman: "I know who you are." Friedman immediately comprehended that this stranger had the power, with today's communications technologies, to let the world know if he comported himself as less than a gentleman. A breach of shared values in such a universally comprehensible situation might undercut Friedman's credibility on much more complex, entirely unrelated matters.

In his useful book, *Sticks & Stones*, Larry Weber recounts the customer service story of Michael Arrington, a web luminary whose blog is followed by approximately twelve thousand fans. Arrington's internet service provider, Comcast, was providing notably ineffective customer assistance—and he was offline for nearly two days, with no end in sight. Arrington blogged about the problem and fired off a Twitter entry "tearing into Comcast." The result: within twenty minutes of his tweet he was called by a Comcast executive in Philadelphia, eager to assist. Comcast rapidly dispatched a repair team, fixed Arrington's connection, and "apologized profusely."

Arrington transformed a transaction into a relationship that continues to have aftershocks for Comcast long after the event.

Former U.S. Senator George Allen of Virginia learned this lesson the hard way in his 2006 reelection campaign. He was understandably annoyed by the presence of an uninvited guest who trailed him relentlessly, recording his every move with a handheld video camera. The persistent visitor was acting on behalf of an opposing candidate. On one occasion, during a speech, Allen berated and mocked the young camera-man. The senator dismissed him with the epithet "Macacca." The word, unknown to most Americans, was soon identified—surely by Google and *Wikipedia* searches—as an ethnic slur. The video recording of Allen's words flashed across the world via the internet.

The young man was of Indian descent. Allen carried the burden of a preexisting reputation for bullying. Fairly or not, the incident was devastating to his previously strong reelection campaign. The capacity to create a relationship from an interaction enabled a college student with a camera to play a critical role in the upset defeat of a sitting United States senator and former governor who was preparing to run for the presidency. The outcome of the Virginia election had broad ramifications, altering the partisan balance of the closely divided U.S. Senate.

A decade later, we are inured to the reality that a single, momentary lapse in demeanor, or an errant tweet, or a tasteless selfie could have devastating consequences in our wired world.

Implications of a Relationship-Based World.

Aspects of the transaction-based world are so familiar that one can be forgiven for assuming them immutable. Organizations and individuals seek to "win" in a given transaction. In many cases, they keep score based on simple, short-term metrics such as dollars expended. In transactions the participants tend to seek an advantage vis-à-vis others. Information relating to outcomes is held tightly, not shared. "Spinning" of facts or even dishonesty is endemic or assumed. "Hard skills" such as analytical reasoning and other traditionally "male" attributes are prized. To the extent longer-term relationships with the other parties are considered, it is largely to calculate value within the transaction at hand.

In a relationship-based world each of these aspects is upended. Transactions are increasingly comprehended in the context of relationships. The relationships may reach beyond the participants themselves, including various other stakeholders. The value of seeking to "win," to obtain advantage, to prevail over another party is diminished. The mentality is one of abundance rather than scarcity. Information is more valuable if it is shared, rather than held close. There is more value to be gained from cooperation, collaboration pointing toward new, perhaps unforeseen directions. "Soft" skills—interpersonal skills—are prized. These have traditionally been seen as "female."

These changes have many consequences, which will be seen throughout this book.

Actually I think this is one of the most profound changes
that more openness and transparency brings: It puts
more weight and importance on building better social
relationships and being more trustworthy.
—MARK ZUCKERBERG, FOUNDER, FACEBOOK

4. LEADERSHIP IS A RELATIONSHIP BETWEEN EMPOWERED, CONSENTING ADULTS.

As is evident in considering collaboration, twenty-first-century leadership is a relationship between empowered, consenting adults.

As such, it has all the characteristics associated with consensual relationships generally. It's based on mutuality and reciprocity. It involves risk. It involves vulnerability. It involves negotiation. It involves constant change.

In the past, consent was often more theoretical than real. In the Information Age, the relations between those who hold power and those who consent to it are being fundamentally altered.

The potent combination of empowerment and accountability enables people to have meaningful consent in their leadership relationships. To an unprecedented extent, people can enter, withdraw from, or alter relationships. These are not the capacities ordinarily ascribed to "followers."

There are three important aspects of consent in a twenty-first-century leadership relationship:

Consent Must be Earned on an Ongoing Basis.

Many CEO's are finding that the benefits they receive from information technology—such as greatly increased mass investing—come with significant strings attached. The expectations of an expanded array of stakeholders—from institutional shareholders to the general public and activist groups—have risen dramatically.

This does not mean that every aspect of life has become a direct democracy. It does mean that stakeholders, including customers and citizens, are empowered as never before.

In the past, the benefit of the doubt often went to authority. This was true even in the most anti-authoritarian nations, such as America and Australia. Consent was often presumed. If people were dissatisfied in various relationships, believing they were not well-served, they had limited means of redress.

Unionized employees might go on strike. Aggrieved consumers might boycott or join in a class action lawsuit. Shareholders or citizens might petition or complain. Such options tend to be too unwieldy or expensive to be relied upon routinely.

Today, organizations and their top officers receive continuous signals about perceptions of their service.

Shareholders monitor their management teams to an unprecedented extent. Some publicly challenge boards of directors who act in their name.

Even non-unionized employees have many means to affect the management of their organizations. They can communicate with one another, or the outside world, through internet sites and chat rooms. They can readily obtain information on compensation and benefits inside and outside their companies. Those on the lower end of an organization chart can have access to information formerly held close by the highest officials. They are thereby empowered, in today's digital world, to materially affect the value of a company's brand.

Similar stirring is occurring in the marketplace. Consumers have something more than a buyer's market; it's becoming a buyer's world. They can find alternatives to almost any offering, whether in a brick-and-mortar store or an online storefront. If they are aggrieved, they need not suffer in silence. Citizens can interact and join forces of their own volition. They need not wait for governments or mass political parties or established interest groups to speak in their name. If they are concerned that their views are not being reflected in public policy, they can mobilize thousands if not millions of their fellow citizens.

The common theme: individuals are ever more empowered to grant or withhold their consent. This does *not* necessarily mean power relationships are equalized. It *does* mean relationships premised on service must earn the ongoing consent of those they would serve. The evaluation of the relationship is increasingly based on the views of those served, not defined primarily by people occupying positions of authority.

Consent Excludes Power Based on Force or Other Coercive Means.

Consent means consent. One is not serving another when exacting consent by force, duress or lies. No matter what the rationalization, such a relationship is not one of service; those holding power thereby are not acting as "leaders."

Under this definition, Hitler's "Third Reich," despite his self-proclaimed "leadership principle," was not an exercise in leadership. Initially, Hitler participated in the electoral process and achieved power within its rules (more or less). The German people were soon prevented from directly influencing policy; shortly thereafter they were barred from questioning or otherwise challenging the regime acting in their name.

There are numerous ways to characterize such a relationship, but "leadership" would be inapt.

Any relationship where one party has no alternative—in the economic or political marketplace, or otherwise—is not based on meaningful consent. This applies to monopolies (private sector as well as some government services) and cartels. It applies to publicly held companies where the voice of the shareholders is distorted by self-serving boards of directors. It includes thumb-on-the-scale political arrangements, such as electoral maps drawn to serve office holders, interest groups, or political parties rather than citizens.

The Determinant Metric is Service—from the Point of View of Those Served.

Unless something is measured, it's often said, it's unlikely to be done, at least to a high level of effectiveness.

This is surely true of simple management measures. Measuring outputs (e.g., sales) or in some cases inputs (such as how many cold calls are placed), can be significant.

Yet Albert Einstein was correct: many of the most important things cannot be reliably measured. The contribution of one holding a leadership position is often hard to quantify usefully. The higher the level of responsibility, the more difficult precise measurement becomes. Did a company's profits soar because of the CEO's leadership—or because of competitors' errors, changes in the broader economy, government policies, currency fluctuations, demographic changes or altogether unpredictable natural events?

In contrast, leadership failures often appear unambiguous, though some of the same questions may arise.

A defining fact today is that the evaluation of the contribution of leaders, including those in high positions, is increasingly based on the judgment of those they serve. There can be debate and disagreement about the contributions of individuals. Those being served are in the best position to render judgment. They may not be infallible, but, more and more often, their verdict is final.

A defining fact today is that the decisive evaluation of the contribution of leaders, including those in high positions, is increasingly based on the judgment of those they serve.

There are as many ways to incentivize and evaluate leaders as there are people and causes to serve. In recent years, many companies utilized stock options to reward key executives. The assumptions include: the executive's value is reflected by the enterprise's overall financial performance; the stock price will reflect performance; the interests of the executives and the shareholders will be aligned.

There remains the possibility of stock performance being affected by factors altogether unrelated to the executive's performance. He or she might simply be lucky—or unlucky. Some executives might, over time, damage the company's longer-term prospects by pumping up the stock price for personal gain.

The necessity of consent in the increasingly transparent, accountable world of twenty-first-century leadership prompts an ongoing negotiation between executives and those they serve. Such negotiation establishes shared understandings of the value of their contribution. It also reinforces the service orientation of individuals entrusted with power.

---◆---

In today's wired world, individuals entrusted with positions of power are accountable to empowered stakeholders, both inside and outside of their organizations. The resulting process of ongoing negotiation can be challenging. At times, even in the private sector, it requires an attention to public communication resembling that of public officials. While not an unmixed blessing, it helps maintain focus on those to be served.

To paraphrase Churchill's view of democracy—it's the worst system—except for the alternatives.

---◆---

5. LEADERSHIP IS A DYNAMIC RELATIONSHIP.

In the past, leadership was often seen as a status. So, too, the relationships built around leadership tended to be static. There was a template: persons moved up a defined career "ladder" to attain high positions of authority. Corporate, military, governmental and many not-for-profit enterprises were bureaucratic, centralized, hierarchical and change-resistant.

With the rising empowerment of individuals, leadership relationships are continually subject to renegotiation. Leadership is becoming an open source project, where many people and organizations apply their expertise or assert their views and values. Those being served increasingly have the power not only to define or expand the project, but to terminate it.

Leadership is about change. Change is mastered by invincible adaptability. Adaptability renders one able to serve in new and often unfamiliar circumstances.

Leaders—both individuals and organizations—must adapt to remain effective. Again, the key reference point is the service required, not the characteristics or druthers of those who would lead.

Leadership is becoming an open source project, where many people and organizations can apply their expertise or assert their views and values. Those being served increasingly have the power not only to define or expand the project, but to terminate it.

Among Winston Churchill's unique contributions in leading the United Kingdom in the Second World War was his accomplishment in raising the British people's sights toward an older, ennobling (some would say mythic) vision of their historic role. Theretofore, his long, uneven career had been marked—and its initially boundless trajectory curtailed—by his obdurate refusal to bow to any number of twentieth-century developments. Churchill early recognized within them the death knell of the British Empire he had experienced, loved and sought to preserve, beginning in his youth in Victorian England.

Against the specter of Hitlerism, Churchill's anachronistic inflexibility was recast as indomitability. As the British Empire tottered on the precipice of the abyss, he was grudgingly granted the mantle of the highest political office. His implacable stance enabled his nation to face down "the wave of the future" represented by Nazi Germany at its fearsome height.

Churchill inspired the English to transform their darkest hour into "our finest hour." He experienced the melancholy satisfaction of seeing Hitler's vaunted "one-thousand-year Reich" utterly vanquished amid the unfathomable destruction it unleashed. The maimed remnant of the Nazi regime surrendered unconditionally on 8 May 1945.

In July 1945, with the cheers of his nation ringing in his ears, Churchill and his government were voted out of power.

As personally devastating as it was for Churchill, there was some logic in the electoral verdict. That he was extraordinarily effective in the exceptional circumstances of a war for national survival did not necessarily mean his approach to leadership was suited for the new world of the peace. The victory he made possible released long-suppressed expectations of change.

Many citizens concluded that Churchill's effectiveness as a warlord did not augur well for his transition into peacetime leadership.

No relationship remains static. This includes leadership—all the more when the stakes are high. A relationship can be strengthened or weakened or renegotiated and reset. The imperative of service decrees continual change. Those who would lead must adapt or be cast aside.

The bitter cup that Prime Minister Churchill tasted in 1945 is an ever-present possibility today. The world moves much faster. The tenure of CEOs and others holding high positions is far shorter than that of their predecessors of recent generations.

Some leaders adapt and add value as the needs for service change. Others cannot. Or, perhaps more accurately in many cases, they choose not to.

There is widespread misunderstanding on this score. Many headhunters seek to "match" companies with executive candidates possessing characteristics fitting the enterprises' current circumstances. If adaptability is not included as a critical trait, today's "ideal" candidate may be unsuited for challenges later in the corporate life cycle.

There's No Such Thing as a "Leaderless Organization."

The extraordinary dynamism of twenty-first-century leadership places all traditional organizations at risk. They must evolve to survive.

A notable development is the emergence of networked groups, established formally or informally, to undertake specific tasks or advance a shared vision. Networks may cut across silos within organizations. They may extend to other organizations or individuals. Many are altogether independent of traditional organizations.

In a sense, the power of groups is a longstanding phenomenon. Preeminent leadership authority Warren Bennis writes of the efficacy of great groups as vehicles for extraordinary leadership and accomplishment. Such groups, Bennis explains, are not likely to last long. They may well light the sky—and abruptly disappear. At the least, they may show the way for others to go further than previously imagined possible.

The internet has taken the potential for groups to a new level. They can assume infinite form. They can assemble or disassemble or reassemble with astonishing fluidity and rapidity. In this sense, they resemble natural organisms or ecosystems more than machines. Unlike the latter, they are not amenable to having a "boss" in the traditional sense.

This does not mean they are "leaderless organizations." Management guru Seth Godin proposes a useful way to understand many of the groups made possible by the internet and social networking: "tribes." In his book of the same name, Godin explains, "A tribe is a group of people connected to one another, connected to a leader, and connected to an idea." He adds, "You can't have a tribe without a leader—and you can't be a leader without a tribe."

As the *New York Times* reports, "Few concepts in business have been as popular and appealing in recent years as the emerging discipline of 'open innovation.'" There is a significant qualifier: "Open innovation models succeed only when carefully designed for a particular task and when the incentives are tailored to attract the most effective collaborators."

The management of such groups is distinct from traditional, hierarchical organizations whose structures often resemble the monolithic office buildings they commonly occupy. The need for leadership toward defined ends—casting a vision, attracting and directing resources in the most effective way—remains.

The dynamism of the Information Age engenders relationships of all types and intensity. Our language does not yet include terms precisely capturing them. That such evolving relationships are not uniform suggests leaders have the potential to serve more effectively, in more ways.

One thing is certain: the dynamism of twenty-first-century leadership should not be underestimated. Even Joe Trippi, the visionary political strategist who spearheaded the introduction of the internet into politics in Howard Dean's 2004 presidential bid, has been caught by surprise. Trippi predicted, in a book published in early 2008, that it would likely be 2016 before "bottom-up politics" would be "in full force… [sufficient to] thrust a minority into the presidency."

Ooops…

6. THERE IS NO UNIVERSAL LEADERSHIP STYLE.

A vast amount of ink has been expended on the question of leadership style. Many "experts" attempt to isolate the specifics of the approach of renowned leaders to cobble together a universally applicable template.

One might well question whether the quest for a universal leadership style was ever particularly fruitful. At the dawn of the twenty-first century, it's altogether fruitless.

One need not look far to identify fads in management thinking. The 1990s saw a cult of "charismatic" business leadership. Jack Welch of General Electric was often cited as an exemplar.

These winds soon shifted. Scandals rocked companies headed by "charismatic" individuals such as Bernie Ebbers of Worldcom and Dennis Kozlowski of Tyco. Many observers now argue against supposed "rock-star" CEOs.

Jim Collins, author of *Good to Great*, identifies what he calls "Level 5" leaders. These tend to be "anti-charismatics." They exhibit "extreme humility." They are dependable, somewhat stolid figures of manifest drive and commitment to their enterprises. Collins focuses, for example, on Darwin Smith, the longtime CEO who guided Kimberly-Clark to astounding returns, far outpacing high-profile companies such as Hewlett-Packard, General Electric, and Coca-Cola.

Smith had a "shy and self-effacing nature." His style stands in contrast to less effective, celebrity CEOs studied by Collins. These include well-known executives such as "Chainsaw Al" Dunlap of Scott Paper and Lee Iacocca of Chrysler. Collins concludes: "The key step is to stop looking for outsized personalities and egocentric celebrities, and instead to scrutinize for results."

Collins' analysis tends to conflate charismatic leadership with egocentrism. He writes: "The good-to-great leaders never wanted to be come larger-than-life heroes. They never aspired to be put on a pedestal or become unreachable icons. They were seemingly ordinary people quietly producing extraordinary results."

Such a definition might make for good friends and neighbors and agreeable colleagues. But there are times when outsized personalities—even those who brazenly seek to become larger-than-life heroes—are best-suited to achieve outsized results.

Surely it was the case with Winston Churchill.

His service contribution—the ultimate in charismatic leadership—altered the course of history. It is difficult to argue credibly that any other individual could have been as effective. Churchill's example truly stands as monumental—as he intended.

Churchill was notably self-centered. He told a colleague, "Of course I am an egotist. Where do you get if you aren't?" Even taking into account the Victorian class distinctions he presumed as his due, he could be callously indifferent to the feelings of others.

His self-belief was, literally, historic. He imagined a pageant of titanic personalities and events and saw himself in their midst. The reactions of his contemporaries ranged from amused to unsettled by this aspect of Churchill's personality. One called his World War I memoir, *The World Crisis*, "an autobiography disguised as a history of the universe." In our time, psychiatrist Anthony Storr, a sympathetic observer, concludes that Churchill's belief in his destiny of greatness was part of an "inner world of make-believe."

At least in retrospect, such aspects of Churchill's personality were part and parcel of his effectiveness. His identification with the British nation and her history and people was so intense that he unselfconsciously personified them at their mutual moment of truth.

Darwin Smith, or other "Level 5" leaders Collins cites, would have been much easier to work with than Winston Churchill. Would they have comprehended, much less provided transformational leadership against Hitler's Third Reich?

Collins attempts to force Churchill into his template. He asserts Churchill "understood the liabilities of his strong personality, and he compensated for them beautifully during the Second World War." A number of those who worked with the great man might have smiled wearily, knowingly—especially as they emerged bleary-eyed, squinting in the early morning sun, having been kept up most of the night in compliance with the prime minister's unorthodox schedule. Few individuals come to mind who were so able to bend high office into conformance with their will and whim. Later in the book we will encounter further examples of the difficult, self-centered aspects of this greatest of leaders.

It is hard to imagine any of Jim Collins' eminently respectable "Level 5" leaders taking England from "good to great" in May 1940. More likely, with every good intention, they would have overseen her descent from peril to ruin.

To be sure, Winston Churchill might not have thrived at Kimberly-Clark, either.

The leadership style is best which is most effective in serving others in any given time and place. What constitutes the most effective leadership style is negotiated with, and ultimately determined by, those to be served. Effectiveness results from their consent and subsequent alteration of their values, thoughts and actions in furtherance of the leader's vision.

Nonetheless, some persist in searching for a universally recognized, one-size-fits-all approach for the new era. Such a pursuit may be an unconscious echo of Industrial Age thinking. It reflects a perspective from the top-down, from the inside-out. In the twenty-first century, change, innovation, adaptation and ultimate progress will be achieved through a multiplicity of management arrangements. What at first glance appears disorderly can, when held to account, comprise an effusion of experiments unleashing unforeseen accomplishment.

What's needed is not so much a universal leadership template, but systems of thought which can be applied to serve effectively in any setting.

There is no universal leadership style. A leadership style serving people well in one time and place may not work in another time and place — even serving the same people. The appropriate leadership approach is the one that enables you to serve most effectively in the circumstances at hand. A bottom-up, outside-in perspective mandates flexibility, innovation and adaptability.

7. LEADERSHIP ROLES ARE CONVERGING.

In the twentieth century, leadership was customarily assumed to be based on expertise or experience specific to one industry or situation. Transferring from one industry sector to another was unusual. Lateral moves between government agencies, not-for-profits or corporations were noteworthy.

In the twenty-first century, as the focus of effective leadership shifts to a bottom-up, outside-in orientation, the tasks of leadership in various sectors are converging.

This was foreseen, like so much else, by Peter Drucker. He recognized fifty years ago that prospective leaders in business could learn from effective leaders in other fields, such as the military and politics.

Now it's moving from the visionary to the commonplace. Ambassador Barbara Barrett, a dynamic leader in the public, private and not-for-profit sectors, suggests that the convergence results from the transparency and accountability made possible by the Information Revolution. The new world of twenty-first-century leadership affords extraordinary opportunities for individuals and organizations to serve—and lead—in multiple ways.

Bill Gates found spectacular success as an entrepreneur and Fortune 100 CEO. Now, along with his wife and colleague Melinda, Gates is breaking ground as a catalyst for public-private ventures across the world.

Bono has leveraged his musical celebrity into social activism. Mitt Romney served effectively as a corporate management consultant, a not-for-profit CEO, and governor of a populous American state. Bill Clinton moved from the presidency to pioneering networks combining public and private entities with NGOs to meet public needs. T. Boone Pickens segued from legendary oil man to national spokesman for energy independence through alternative sources.

Frank Blake, the highly intelligent and respected recent CEO of Home Depot, is representative of the new era. He has a breadth of experience. He has served at the highest levels of management in government, the law and business. He was part of the Jack Welch team at General Electric. Teaching leadership at Home Depot, Blake refers to the examples of three very different leaders. In addition to Welch, he cites two others best known for their accomplishments outside the corporate sector: Ronald Reagan and George H.W. Bush.

In this new environment, it is not surprising that Jim Collins' selection of the "entrepreneur for this decade" is not in business per se. He points to the not-for-profit sector, to Wendy Kopp, founder of Teach for America. By all accounts, Kopp's brainchild—bringing recent college graduates into classrooms as teachers in under-performing public schools—is having a positive impact. Kopp's concept challenges the exhausted, at times self-serving complacency that settles like a soupy fog on so many American public schools. Her organization suffuses government with private sector energy and innovation, and a not-for-profit sensibility.

Amid such change, many individuals are finding their jobs and careers redefined. Pollster Mark Penn points to the emergence of "quasi-government workers." This refers to workers and executives in businesses which are government-owned or -directed. Penn identifies more than a million workers who have shifted from the private to the public sector.

Inevitably, many organizations, like individuals, are crossing boundaries to serve in new ways.

Google was deeply involved in the highly productive internet fundraising undertaken by the Obama campaign. The company then assisted the Obama administration in developing technology policy. This represented a departure but is consistent with the company's core mission and undoubted expertise.

Google is also moving into unanticipated spaces such as mobility and energy. Other Silicon Valley fixtures are serving diverse fields such as health care and consumer ratings.

When the Association of National Advertisers selected the marketer of the year at their annual conference in 2008, they passed over familiar favorites such as Apple and Zappos. Instead, they recognized a politician: Barack Obama. Why not? His presidential campaign made effective use of talent in disparate fields, including political campaign management, web design and social networking, community organizing and film production.

This may be disorienting to those seeking security and predictability. It can be exhilarating for those determined to serve others.

Various names are put forward to define new, emerging, unfamiliar constructs. Some speak of "philanthro-capitalism." Some see "social capitalism." Others speak of "capitalism 3.0," "conscious capitalism" and so on.

There is no end to the possible descriptors, because there is no limit to the potential variations of networked enterprises and individuals. These are mutually reinforcing trends. As the velocity of change occasions untold leadership opportunities, the convergence of leadership roles accelerates.

A majority of the world's largest economic entities are now corporations rather than nation-states. This, combined with the transparency of the Information Age, means the numbers and expectations of stakeholders served by CEOs of major companies increasingly resemble those encountered by similarly situated politicians and government executives. This is very different from the experience of their recent predecessors, the bureaucratic administrators of large American corporations in the post-World War II period.

John Mackey, co-founder of Whole Foods, personally experienced the consequences of this transition. He wrote an extensive op-ed for the *Wall Street Journal*, advocating a free-market approach to health care reform.

A significant segment of the Whole Foods customer base rebelled. Some organized boycotts. They had assumed that Mackey—a vegetarian, advocate of animal welfare and organic agriculture—adhered to the range of conventional liberal political views. Such critics believe, at least implicitly, that a corporate CEO should not express political opinions at variance with consumers.

In turn, many on the right, who had held corresponding misconceptions of Mackey's views, were delighted to discover his longstanding dedication to free-market principles. Some conservatives urged a "buy-cott," whereby like-minded consumers would demonstrate support for Mackey, purchasing more Whole Foods products.

There is historical precedent for the melding of public and private functions and accountability. More than two hundred years ago, the great parliamentarian Edmund Burke assailed the British East India Company as a "government in merchant's clothing." Now it's not only corporations. NGOs and ad-hoc networks are assuming prerogatives previously entrusted to governments. This runs the gamut from extraordinary economic power, to dissemination of information, to the deadly force wielded by terror networks.

Walmart was viewed by many as more effective than the ill-starred Federal Emergency Management Agency in its emergency response in New Orleans in the immediate aftermath of Hurricane Katrina. In many localities, Walmart has become a larger factor in many people's lives—for good or for ill, depending on your point of view—than some government agencies. This trend continues, as seen in Tesla's commitment to restore power to the Puerto Rico following two devastating hurricanes in 2017.

> *Companies today are bigger than many economies.*
> *We are little republics. We are engines of efficiency.*
> *If companies don't do [responsible] things, who is*
> *going to? Why not start making change now?*
> —INDRA NOOYI

FEMA notwithstanding, expectations of—or, at the least, demands on—government are also rising. People accustomed to using ATM machines at banks and grocery stores are stunned by the glacial speed of public agency procurement. Customer service improvements in the private sector render the uneven performance of high-profile government bureaucracies, such as the U.S. Postal Service, all the more difficult to endure with equanimity.

From the vantage point of those served, the divisions among public, private and not-for-profit mean less, just as the hierarchies within enterprises mean less.

In all sectors, subject matter specialization is much less prized when information is so widely available. Front-line employees are apt to know much more about any number of relevant matters than those higher on the organization chart.

When facts are "free," that elusive quality, *judgment*, is elevated as a defining characteristic of an effective leader. There is rising recognition of the value of the so-called "right brain" competencies of emotional intelligence and creativity, popularized by Daniel Pink, Daniel Goleman and others.

The capacity to empower others, to obtain their best performance, is prized—and increasingly recognized as universally applicable. Collaboration need not be limited by boundaries erected for other purposes, in earlier times.

Effective service in the Information Age can transcend bureaucratic trench warfare and its dysfunctional, self-serving aspects (such as silos in large organizations). Web-based networking creates the capacity for bureaucracy—corporate, not-for-profit, even government—to be bypassed altogether.

You don't need to spend years attempting to reform a civil service system that reflects the best thinking of the 1880s. You don't need to overcome entrenched labor-management practices dating from the 1930s. You don't even have to show endless fealty to graying NGO functionaries eager to exhibit their moral superiority going back to the 1960s.

Using the power of networking, you can cobble together ad hoc arrangements to respond to circumstances and opportunities.

You can achieve results by transcending outdated bureaucratic arrangements. As this becomes more common, perhaps the survival instincts of corporate and government bureaucrats will move them from a default position of resisting change to initiating it.

The skills required for effective service in a networked world—collaboration, information management, cross-disciplinary and cross-cultural understanding, the capacity to engage diverse, changing, multiple stakeholders—are similar whether you're working in a company or a not-for-profit, in the military or a government agency. In one sense this convergence makes possible a welcome flexibility in individuals' careers. It also means that those who would serve effectively must be cognizant of and ready to learn about other sectors. In today's world a corporate CEO must have more than a nodding acquaintance with how government agencies and NGOs operate. Leaders in government agencies, NGOs and the military should have corresponding understanding of other sectors.

IBM implicitly recognizes and fosters this convergence in its innovative Corporate Service Corps. The company deploys promising leaders to work with NGOs, entrepreneurs and government agencies in emerging markets. *McKinsey Quarterly* reports that the company has found value not only in opening prized markets, but also in enhanced leadership development—and increasing participants' commitment to "Big Blue."

To be sure, not everyone recognizes the applicability of these trends to their own spheres. One encounters executives who acknowledge the convergence of leadership roles in other sectors and organizations and circumstances—while regarding theirs to be the great exception. After the fact, when such changes have been forced upon them, they too acknowledge the new world.

Leadership convergence is not simply an ideal, it's a reality. Are you prepared to seize the new opportunities?

> What leadership roles have you observed converging? Are there additional roles you might play to add value in new ways and better advance your most deeply held values?

8. A LEADER'S UNIQUE TASK IS TO IMAGINE AND ADVANCE A VISION.

One familiar aspect of leadership remains unchanged: a leader uniquely has the task of crafting and advancing a vision. As ever, it requires a future orientation and a bias for action. What is new is the need for ongoing persuasion to engage stakeholders and obtain (or maintain) consent.

What is a leadership vision? It may be a new way of comprehending a situation. It may reframe longstanding, widely shared ideas of reality. It may mean discerning future possibilities and reasons for optimism amid dizzying, confusing, current conditions. It may mean deliberately offering your life as an example, inspiring others to reflection and action.

The most compelling visions draw from both art and science. They must be clear and comprehensible enough for measurement and accountability, yet flexible enough to spur and incorporate the contributions of others.

An inspiring vision is built on the hard ground of truth—and requires artistry to reach the summit. Casting and advancing a vision is necessarily about change, growth, innovation and adaptation. Effective leadership spurs new, creative, unexpected associations of ideas and individuals within a vision, melding them within a framework making the vision actionable.

◆

An inspiring vision is built on the hard ground of truth—and requires artistry to reach the summit. Effective leadership spurs new, creative, unexpected associations of ideas and individuals, melding them within a framework making the vision actionable.

◆

Amid the extended, deepened relationships made possible by the Information Revolution, a leader's vision can be filled out and expanded through ongoing communications with those she would serve. So, too, the missions emerging from a vision can be continually improved.

In the end, the role of the individual leader remains decisive. There is no more powerful way to advance a vision than to personify it. In the new world of the twenty-first century, your capacity to serve can be devastated if you lead your own life in a way perceived as contradictory to your expressed values.

9. LOVE IS THE HIGHEST LEVEL OF LEADERSHIP RELATIONSHIP.

Pursue love.
—1 CORINTHIANS 14:1

What is done in love is done well.
—VINCENT VAN GOGH

Love is the highest level of relationship. This includes the relationship between leaders and those they serve.

To be sure, using the term *love* in this context can initially seem awkward. The English language is notable for absorbing many words and nuances of meaning from other languages. Surprisingly, where many of them distinguish one type of love from another, English is at a linguistic loss.

This lapse has consequences. We lack the vocabulary to readily describe and inform various positive, productive relationships. As our language is imprecise, our thinking is inexact.

Think beyond romantic love, family love, and love of country. There's the love of comrades-in-arms. There's the love of teammates in sports and business. There's the love of customers for a company, or a company for its customers. There's the love of a profession, a tradition. There's love for future generations.

Such relationships share a fundamental aspect. At the highest level, people unreservedly serve others.

The essence of love in action is service; the summit of service is sacrifice. Placing your own desires, even your life on the line for others, draws upon and unleashes an escalating series of virtues. It might begin with simple good manners, being considerate of others' feelings. It might culminate in universally recognized physical or moral courage. It is not an accident the word "courage" is derived from the French for "heart." Lao Tzu had it right: "Being deeply loved by someone gives you strength; loving someone deeply gives you courage."

Some misconstrue what a loving relationship entails. In business they might say, "the customer is always right." In politics they might say, "the people are always right."

Such notions are altogether wrong. As English essayist G.K. Chesterton wrote, "'My country right or wrong,' is a thing that no patriot would think of saying. It's like saying, 'My mother, drunk or sober.'"

One of the greatest evidences of love is to risk a valued relationship by acting in a way you believe necessary for the welfare of those you are serving—even against their expressed wishes.

A coward is incapable of exhibiting love;
it is the prerogative of the brave.
—MAHATMA GANDHI

Service is an expression of love at the highest transformational level.
—REV. RICHARD MARAJ, UNITY CHURCH

10. CHARACTER IS A COMPETITIVE ADVANTAGE.

Many people assume there is a necessary conflict—or at least demarcation—between ethics and business success. Some see the same division in the not-for-profit and government spheres. Knowingly or unknowingly, they accept Machiavelli's dark premise: a good person seeking worthy ends must be willing and able to employ ruthless means to prevail.

Many regard "business ethics" in the same category as "military intelligence." It is a contradiction in terms, or at least a modification suggesting something distinct from the norm.

To be sure, numerous people who strive to act ethically have lost their way in business. They often do not know who they're serving, other than themselves.

They may be working in a large enterprise far removed from their customers. Perhaps they see only a tenuous connection between their work and the ultimate product. Perhaps they are so occupied serving a "boss" that they lose sight of their customers. Perhaps they serve in representative capacities in which they routinely advocate propositions at odds with their personal values. Perhaps their entire career is an exercise in self-advancement.

In the recent past such ethical disconnects could be viewed as rational, even necessary for "success." Many people assume without question that to succeed in business you must put your self-interest ahead of concern for others. We hear the call for "service" as something other than, even antithetical to business. Some say they are leaving private enterprise to "give back." The implication is they were acting selfishly rather than serving as they achieved financial success.

Many of the scandals and other leadership breakdowns of recent years reflect the notion that you can compartmentalize your life. You might choose to be amoral and self-seeking in business—and kind in your family and community circle. Or you might be ethical and effective in business dealings—and treacherous in your personal relationships.

As we have been reminded in recent years, there is more than a little truth behind the Hollywood stereotypes of wicked, rich executives, or the devious, self-serving politicians and the like.

And yet...a transition is underway. Character is, increasingly, a competitive advantage.

In the twenty-first century, for individuals and organizations, character is making a comeback. The CEO of LRN, Dov Seidman, tells Thomas Friedman:

> In a connected world, countries, governments and companies also have character, and their character—how they do what they do, how they keep promises, how they make decisions, how things really happen inside, how they connect and collaborate, how they engender trust, how they relate to their customers, to the environment and to the communities in which they operate—is now their fate.

Seidman elaborated his view in an essay in *What's Next?*, edited by Jane Birmingham. Acknowledging the fundamental change encompassed in the emerging relationship-based society, Seidman discerns "a rare opportunity, *the opportunity to out-behave the competition.*"

Others are simultaneously having the same insight. Advancing shared values creates value. When Google proclaimed its employee-generated slogan, "Don't be Evil," it was acting in the most practical, bottom-line focused way. In the same vein, one company markets itself with the declaration: "It's more profitable to be ethical."

The wired world is changing the game. What technology is making possible, events are making urgent.

Corporate CEOs and other high-position executives face new realities. They are on call 24-7. Their off-hand emails or throw-away remarks may be scrutinized by millions.

Technology has thrown open the curtains, exposing a panorama of relationships with a multiplicity of stakeholders. Individuals and organizations find their zone of privacy narrowing perceptibly. An ex-CEO of Home Box Office learned this firsthand.

Accusations of violence against a girlfriend resulted in his being cashiered. So, too, a recent CEO of the Red Cross was fired for an extra-marital affair with a subordinate. The "pervnado" that swept through Hollywood and Washington in 2017-18 suggests the winds of change are far from spent.

One person's zone of privacy is another person's area of accountability.

Just a few years ago, would prominent CEOs and politicians have lost their positions if they were viewed as otherwise effective? In the eyes of many in older generations, longtime understandings of the boundaries between public and private lives are being breached.

Google executive Eric Schmidt points out, entertainer "Johnny Carson smoked, and for thirty years he was never pictured smoking a cigarette. Today, that would be impossible."

Schmidt extrapolates: "It's fair to say there will be no heroes. Heroism requires understanding the person in the absolute best light. I'm not sure this is good. What was Barack Obama like in elementary school? 'Oh, yeah, here's a picture of him picking his nose. God, he's no longer a hero.'"

That is one possibility. It is not the only one.

Schmidt's "hero" is a brittle, one-dimensional construct.

Another possibility is that people will find much to admire and learn from role models who serve in more ways, with more aspects of their life in alignment. In the proper context, even grievous errors and shortcomings can add value. (*See*, e.g., Churchill, Winston S.)

Younger generations, far from resisting the blurring of work and personal life, are accelerating it. Millennials—born in the 1980s and 1990s, coming of age at the dawn of the twenty-first century—have experienced their entire lives in the digital culture. Information Age norms unnerving to Gen Xers and Baby Boomers are part and parcel of what rising generations regard as "normal."

Many Millennials enter the workforce with expectations that their careers will be molded around their personal lives and values. It may be a hopeful sign that their conceptions of work and life will better aligned than in recently preceding generations.

The Industrial Age, culminating in the twentieth century, was marked by a hard boundary separating work and life. Sigmund Freud implicitly accepted it in his oft-quoted summation: "Love and work…work and love, that's all there is."

In the twenty-first-century, love and work are coming together.

Deeper, more extensive leadership relationships include deeper, more extensive claims on the lives of leaders. If your ultimate concern is service, your life and work can become one. You can achieve integrity.

Service is the essence of leadership—and character is the key to service.

Perhaps Tom Peters has it right, after all. The tasks and practices of leadership are as new as the computers in our midst. And yet, the underlying principles for effective twenty-first-century leadership would be familiar to our distant ancestors. In fact, they might be more familiar to them than to our twentieth-century predecessors.

Twenty-First-Century Leadership is Different.
Act Ethically to Create Sustainable Value.
Serve to Lead.

WAIT A MINUTE!—*MY OFFICE IS LIKE THE OFFICE!*

The emerging trends of twenty-first-century leadership are clear enough. Many people express frustration that their own business environments remain stuck in the older ways.

This is undoubtedly true. These changes are ongoing. They are reaching various sectors, various enterprises, even various parts of enterprises, in various ways, on various timelines.

You may work for a "boss" who personifies practices reminiscent of Steve Carrell's memorable character in the television series, *The Office*.

The organizations and individuals who are exemplars of aspects of twenty-first-century leadership in this book themselves fall short time and again.

Apple CEO Steve Jobs is recognized as an archetypal twenty-first-century leader in many respects. And yet, he was not reliably forthcoming about his health, which was of unquestioned significance to many, many people he served. Apple failed to meet the highest standards in dealing with backdated stock option grants to key executives. So, too, the company has been criticized for not being as transparent or forward-looking on sustainability as its marketing implies.

Barack Obama pioneered an extraordinary, twenty-first-century presidential campaign. And yet, his administration all too often defaulted to a quite conventional, regrettably familiar, politics-as-usual approach to governing.

Any individual, any enterprise assuming the risks of leadership will encounter criticism. Some will be fair, some not. As Bob Dylan said in response to intemperate attacks occasioned by his decision to move from acoustic to electric guitar: "There are a lot of people who have knives and forks, and they have nothing on their plates, so they have to cut something."

What is notable today—and different—is that when leaders fall short of ethical standards, they illuminate a space susceptible to accountability and competition. Doing the right thing is, increasingly, a competitive plus. Self-serving decisions may yield short-term benefits in isolated transactions—but they also represent opportunities for others to serve more effectively in our ever more relationship-based world.

When leaders fall short of ethical standards today, they illuminate a space susceptible to accountability and competition. Doing the right thing is, increasingly, a competitive plus.

Having explored *why* twenty-first-century leadership is different, we'll now explore **how** you can achieve extraordinary performance—from yourself and others—to prevail in this new world.

The first, omnipresent question is: *Who Are You Serving?* It is the focus of the next chapter.

RECAP
DEFINITION & TEN PRINCIPLES
OF TWENTY-FIRST-CENTURY LEADERSHIP

◆

Twenty-first-century leaders inspire others to alter their thoughts and actions, in alignment with an empower vision.

◆

1. Everybody Can Lead, Because Anyone Can Serve.

2. The Most Valuable Resource of Any Enterprise is its People.

3. We Are in Transition from a Transaction-Based World to a Relationship-Based World.

4. Leadership is a Relationship Between Empowered, Consenting Adults.

5. Leadership is a Dynamic Relationship.

6. There is No Universal Leadership Style.

7. Leadership Roles Are Converging.

8. A Leader's Unique Task is to Imagine and Advance a Vision.

9. Love is the Highest Level of Leadership Relationship.

10. Character is a Competitive Advantage.

TWENTIETH CENTURY	TWENTY-FIRST CENTURY
Leadership	Service
Transactions	Relationships
Inside-Out	Outside-In
Top-Down	Bottom-Up
Hierarchies	Networks
Boss to Employee	Leader to Leader
Administer	Empower
Efficient	Effective
Centralized	De-Centralized
Information	Judgment
Value in Natural Resources, Products	Value in People
Individual Accomplishment	Collaboration
Tangible Value	Intangible Value
Credentials	Lifetime Learning
Quantitative	Soft Skills
Linear	Intuitive
Inputs	Outputs
Time Management	Value Management
Security	Adaptability
Specialist	Adaptable Generalist
Hidden Liabilities	Undiscovered Value
Autocrat/Micro Manager	Coach, Conductor
Workaholic	Integrated Life
Male/Patriarchal Model	Female/Inclusive Model
Brick-and-Mortar	Virtual
Organization Chart	Digitized Information String
Speak	Listen
National	Global/Local
Authority Conferred	Consent Earned
Small Array of Leadership Styles	Infinite Leadership Styles
Retirement	Redeployment
Failure	Stepping Stone
Authoritarian	Renegade
Answers and Assertions	Questions
Broadcast and Inform	Narrowcast and Engage
Employees	Team Members
Work-Life Separation	Work-Life Integration
Career Path	Life Path
Servant/Ethical Leadership	Leadership

PREPARE TO SERVE

— What changes in twenty-first-century leadership have you observed and experienced?

— How would you evaluate the following individuals through the prism of twenty-first-century leadership? Martin Luther King, Jr.? Mahatma Gandhi? Winston Churchill? Adolf Hitler? Karl Marx? Vladimir Lenin? Mao Zedong? Theodore Roosevelt? Franklin Roosevelt? Eleanor Roosevelt? John F. Kennedy? Ronald Reagan? Bill Clinton? Hillary Clinton? Bernie Sanders? Ralph Nader? Donald Trump? Cesar Chavez? The Beatles? Lance Armstrong? Jackie Robinson? Margaret Thatcher? Henry Ford? Jack Welch? Bill Gates? Mother Teresa? Rick Warren? The Dalai Lama? Fidel Castro? Nelson Mandela? Cindy Sheehan? Harvey Milk? Oprah Winfrey? Dr. Phil? Rush Limbaugh? Steve Jobs? Jon Stewart? Bono? Taylor Swift? Beyonce? Maya Anjelou? Madonna? Tiger Woods? Mia Hamm? Barack Obama? Sarah Palin? Bill O'Reilly? Glenn Beck? Montel Williams? Dave Ramsey? Wendy Kopp? Jacqueline Novogratz? Muhammad Yunus? Greg Mortenson? Who else would you add for discussion? How would you evaluate your own leadership?

— Considering your own experiences, who are the most effective leaders you have encountered? Why? Who are the least effective? Why?

— How are you developing your personal approach to meet the challenges of twenty-first-century leadership? What are your strengths? Your areas for focused improvement? What do you need to unlearn?

— How do you see various sectors—public, private, not-for-profit—evolving in the new environment? How is your area of work changing? How are you adapting to meet the new needs?

— Do you recognize new opportunities to serve—and lead—in the emerging world of twenty-first-century leadership? What's different? What remains the same? How would you advise young people to plan their careers and lives? Are you taking the same approach to your own career and life?

Who Are You Serving?

Every moment of every hour of every day of your life, you're serving someone.

You're serving someone when you go to work in the morning. When you decide what clothes to wear. When you choose what food to eat. When you are in conversation. When you decide whether or how to exercise your body. When you interact with colleagues. When you interact with customers. When you check your emails, or cruise the internet. When you meet people in chance encounters. When you select your friends. When you think about your investments. When you pay your bills. When you decide how to spend those precious few quiet moments you've carved out of your otherwise totally scheduled day. When you plan your future—and whether and how you begin to act on it.

In the big things you may take for granted, in the small things which rarely cross your mind, you're always serving someone. It may be your family; it may be your boss; it may be your community; it may be your God.

Or, as when you reach for a chocolate éclair, you may be simply serving yourself.

One of the most important things you can do to transform your leadership—and your life—is to pose the question through your life, minute-by-minute, hour-by-hour, day-by-day: *Who Are You Serving?*

The Four Questions apply equally whether you are analyzing your own leadership, or that of other individuals, an organization or a team. They apply with full force to a CEO or to an intern; to a corporation or a military unit or a not-for-profit or a government agency.

This chapter will help you apply The Four Questions to develop your own, unique leadership capacities.

WHO ARE YOU SERVING?

Getting this question right is the indispensable first step to extraordinary, transformational leadership.

> *When your ultimate concern is those you're serving, your vantage point necessarily is from the outside-in, not the inside-out.*

It takes forethought, discipline, experience and humility to apply the question effectively.

We all recognize that individuals can access untold capacities in themselves by focusing on serving others.

Think of the recurring situation of a mother whose young child has become trapped underneath an automobile. She suddenly, remarkably, lifts several tons of metal in the service of her child.

If anyone had asked the same woman just a day before to lift a lawnmower, she might well have scoffed at the notion. Yet when the moment of need came, her intense focus on serving her child overcame her deepest preconceived notions of her capacities.

Something similar can happen with wounded soldiers left to die on the battlefield, or sailors adrift at sea. Those who survive such ordeals may have given their all to maintain the faintest flicker of life—solely because of an invincible determination to see their spouse or children.

A common denominator among many Medal of Honor recipients and other war heroes is their relentless drive to defend fellow soldiers with whom they have bonded in service. They overcome objectively insurmountable odds—including apparently certain death—to serve their comrades-in-arms.

Time and again, when you search for the root of extraordinary performance, you come upon a commitment to serve.

The classic film *Chariots of Fire* follows the saga of two young men competing to become champion runners in the 1924 Olympic Games. Harold Abraham was inspired in part to gain acceptance as a Jew in an anti-Semitic environment in early twentieth-century England. Eric Liddell strove to overcome discouragement of his athletic ambition by authority figures who believed it to be inconsistent with the tenets of his church. Liddell had faith he could best serve God—and his country—by developing and applying his physical gifts.

People accomplish extraordinary things when they commit to service. For some it may be taking part in an idealistic political campaign to change their city, state or nation. For others it may be creating a new product enabling people to have better lives. For others it may be achieving financial security for their family. For others it may be overcoming a longtime fear in order to serve effectively—such as a disabling anxiety about public speaking. For others it may be putting their lives on the line in war or other catastrophes. For still others it may mean caring for an ailing relative.

Thinking about your own life experience, who were you serving at times of your greatest performance or accomplishment? Were you inspired to serve a person, a cause, an ideal? Are you performing at that level now? If not, why not? Do you intend to do so in the future? What concrete steps are you taking? Do you observe others performing at that level? What are you learning from them?

ACCOMPLISHMENT CAN OCCASION LEADERSHIP.

Focusing on service can translate seamlessly from individual high performance into leadership.

The example presented by an accomplishment can constitute a powerful, dynamic aspect of leadership. Its influence can extend far beyond what could have been foreseen. How many generations of young people were inspired by Harold Abraham and Eric Liddell? Their circles of influence reached well beyond the sport of running, beyond Great Britain, beyond the 1920s.

Sometimes, an accomplishment can inspire simply by the fact of its occurrence. For decades runners across the world were vexed by the apparently insuperable barrier of the four-minute mile. Once Roger Bannister achieved it in 1954, many others followed in his wake.

Dara Torres broke similar ground in the 2008 Olympics. At the age of forty-one, newly a first-time mother, she won the silver medal for the fifty-meter freestyle. She was a mere hundredth-of-a-second behind the gold medalist. Her achievement will surely inspire many to test the limits presumed for various age categories.

In 2009, golfer Tom Watson's startling late-career performance prompted Thomas Friedman to quip, "59 is the new 30."

As Theodore Roosevelt observed, there is nothing more powerful than example. Such leadership is not defined or limited by one's position in society or in a company or other organization.

Rosa Parks galvanized the civil rights movement in 1955, igniting the legendary Montgomery, Alabama, bus boycott. She refused to yield her seat to a white passenger as then required of African-Americans under Southern apartheid laws. Parks was arrested and charged with disorderly conduct. Her example of personal courage constituted a leadership act of the first magnitude. She was well aware—as were those whose authority she challenged—that she was serving Americans generally, not merely herself.

Rosa Parks emerged as a leader whose example continues to inspire decades after her heroic moment. In contrast, only professors of history recall the "important people" who occupied positions of power over segregated public transportation. Almost no one today could tell you who was then the head of the transit authority, who was the mayor of Birmingham, or who was the governor of Alabama. All but a few would be hard-pressed to identify who was then the president of the United States.

The emblems of status and power from a lost era are long since swept away. Yet we all remember Rosa Parks.

EACH INSTANCE OF EFFECTIVE LEADERSHIP IS EFFECTIVE IN ITS OWN WAY.

Any consistently high-performing organization or individual is, by definition, effectively serving others.

This is true of Microsoft and Coca-Cola, of the Girl Scouts and the Special Forces, of the New York City Public Library and the Crystal Cathedral Ministries in Garden Grove, California, of Warren Buffett and Oprah Winfrey.

In each case, there is an unswerving focus on those being served. The leadership approach is, to that extent, the same. The practices differ, serving numerous people in countless ways.

This is to be expected when leadership is understood as coming from the outside-in, rather than the inside-out.

There are as many effective leadership styles as there are situations in which you can serve. The principle is constant and universally applicable; the applications are ever-changing, evolving to meet specific needs.

LEADERSHIP FAILURES RESEMBLE ONE ANOTHER.

Effective leadership can assume an infinite variety of forms. Leadership failures tend to resemble one another.

They can all be traced to confusion or misdirection about who one is serving.

The greater the leadership failure, the more likely one will find, at root, a self-serving orientation.

Consider recent scandals in authority positions throughout our national institutions:

— High-flying CEOs such as Ken Lay of Enron and Jim Kozlowski of Tyco were brought low by a series of legal travails. In these and similar scandals in recent years, vast numbers of shareholders—including pensioners—were defrauded. In legal terms, it may be difficult or time-consuming to prove guilt in some such cases. There are often, however, warning signs in revealing, "small" things. When Mr. Lay used his company jet to fly his dog across the country, or Mr. Kozlowski threw a grotesque bacchanalia at company expense to celebrate himself and his then-wife…. *Who Were They Serving?*

— Time and again, the watchdogs at the gate—supine corporate boards, timorous regulatory and watchdog agencies, vulpine lawyers and accountants and other "professionals," and compliant, complicit middle management—declined to challenge obvious derelictions…. *Who Were They Serving?*

— Several recent presidents of the United States perjured themselves in office. They deployed executive power to protect themselves and to harm others…. *Who Were They Serving?*

— When the CEOs of major American charitable organizations were caught in the act of embezzlement or other malfeasance, or took massive salaries any high school student would recognize as excessive in light of their charitable missions…. *Who Were They Serving?*

— When the Roman Catholic Church hierarchy closed ranks to shield from the law those in their midst who had used their moral authority to coerce children into sexual encounters (and subsequently stood by in conspicuous, enforced silence as helpless victims pleaded in vain for assistance from disbelieving families and communities) .... *Who Were They Serving?*

— When politicians of all stripes engage in campaigns of methodical mendacity, bringing discredit to themselves as well as their opponents; when legislators of both major political parties gerrymander voting districts, selecting the voters they prefer, limiting citizens' capacity to benefit from competitive elections.... *Who Are They Serving?*

What's common to all these leadership failures—to all leadership failures—is a misdirected, self-serving focus. A somewhat tongue-in-cheek article in the *Harvard Business Review* critiqued the faulty decision-making of "jerks" in the recent, historic U.S. financial crisis. All such cases, large and small, can be analyzed by focusing on those you're serving.

ASCERTAIN WHO YOU ARE SERVING

When you examine leadership situations through the prism of this simple question, so much becomes clear.

If people forget or are unclear about who they are serving, it is simply not possible for them to achieve sustained effectiveness as leaders. Clarifying who you're serving can also sort out many other issues.

The principle applies from the highest levels of positional authority all the way to the humblest business or local community activity.

Consider the following positions and those who can be served:

Presidents of the United States
— the general public
— their political party
— their political campaign teams
— the armed services
— constituent and interest groups
— the financial system

— the business world
— the workplace
— public employees
— citizens and governments of other nations
— future generations
— their successors
— the legacies of their predecessors
— the institutions of public and private life
— their families
— citizens whose recourse for assistance is the presidency
— all those who may be affected by their actions
— all those who may be affected by their example

CEOs of Large, Publicly Held Companies

— their shareholders (who may range from the general public to equity funds to pension funds)
— their boards of directors
— financial institutions
— their employees (including part-time and other limited, defined arrangements)
— their vendors and contractors
— their customers
— the organizational arrangements of their companies
— the legacies of their predecessors
— the outside institutions which support their companies (from educational institutions to labor unions)
— the general public
— the communities in which they are located
— the industry of which they are a part
— regulatory agencies
— NGOs and other watchdog groups
— their families
— future generations, both inside and outside the company
— their company's brand

Can you list others who are served by holders of these, or comparably high positions?

— all those who may be affected by their actions

— all those who may be affected by their example

These examples are of exceptionally high-level positions. Those who occupy them aren't necessarily consequential as leaders. Some are; some aren't. You can be in a high position of authority yet not be an effective leader. Even if you have little or no formal authority—such as Rosa Parks or Harold Abrahams or Eric Liddell or Dara Torres—you might become an effective leader by dint of your service.

Such a review illuminates the practicalities of service in positions of power and authority. Analyzing such high positions can also be instructive for divining your aspirations for service

As the list of those you serve grows longer, more and more of your life becomes focused on service. Presidents of the United States are potentially serving anyone they meet. This applies not only to other heads of state and government, but to the persons who clean their offices, or numerous others who may be affected for life by a friendly smile, a sincere expression of interest in their lives, or by their example of how people should treat one another.

As you examine your own life in this way, you may find you have a wider ambit of service than you had previously considered. In fact, aren't *you* potentially serving everyone you meet?

Reflect on your experience: *Who Are You Serving?* Write down a list. Think about those you are serving effectively and how you might do better. In what ways are you simply serving yourself? What areas of your life, and your service, do you regard as most effective? Why?

Are you serving the same people and organizations and causes as in the past? Do you intend to serve different people and organizations and causes in the future? How will you decide? How have you decided in the past?

For most of us, the list of *who* we are serving is at once constant and changing. Even if your list remains entirely intact, *how* you can best serve may adjust according to circumstances.

HOW CAN YOU BEST SERVE?

Getting right *who* you are serving is the fundamental, first step. Then you must determine, from the vantage point of those you would serve, *how* you can best serve.

CREATE AND SUSTAIN A RELATIONSHIP.

If you would serve someone or something, your first task is to create a relationship. If you have been brought together, initially, in a fleeting way, or in a discrete transaction, you will want to move toward a relationship. Any service is made more effective by transforming it into a deepening, evolving relationship.

FOCUS ON CONTRIBUTION.

Peter Drucker declared: "The effective person focuses on contribution.... The focus on contribution is the key to effectiveness." He found, "The great majority of people focus downward." That is, they focus on their own efforts, their own goals and needs. Intently serving others necessarily fixes your attention on contribution.

EVALUATE THE RELATIONSHIP FROM THE PERSPECTIVE OF THOSE YOU SERVE.

Your contribution is evaluated by those you serve. *Their* interpretation, based on *their* goals, and *their* needs, is the critical metric.

This requires an orientation of working from the *outside-in*. Effective listening and empathy are essential. Ensuring that those you are serving recognize tangible results from your application of those skills is also important.

Many enterprises or individuals, in complete good faith, work from the inside-out. They may have developed, for example, a new product or service. They see marketing and sales as one-way communications in which they seek to convince others to purchase their wares.

Such an approach is exactly backwards. Thinking as leaders, they would find greater effectiveness by focusing on what others need, rather than what they would like to sell.

> *True marketing starts…with the customer, his*
> *demographics, his realities, his needs, his values.*
> *It does not ask, "What do we want to sell?"*
> *It asks, "What does the customer want to buy?"*
>
> —PETER DRUCKER

If you're a lawyer, what is your product? From your point of view, it may be legal advice. It's what you went to law school for; it's what your working experience has prepared you for.

Your client's point of view may be decidedly different. There may be additional, important things she is seeking. Perhaps she places high value on the authority associated with you or your firm. Perhaps your client finds value in being able to confide in you, tapping your judgment on issues far removed from purely legal questions.

Another familiar example is residential realtors. Their job description is to assist in the purchase and sale of houses. Yet, given that a home has so many roles in the lives of families, a realtor, too, may play many roles. She may be a listener able to translate visions of a new lifestyle into reality. She may reflect, in her bearing, clothing and automobile, the lifestyle to which prospective buyers aspire. She may be a skilled negotiator who exhibits creativity in reaching agreements. She may be a source of confidence and comfort as a family endures the anxiety so often suffusing one of the largest financial transactions of their lives.

The key is to listen to those you are serving to discover how you can add value from *their* point of view.

VALUE IS BASED ON RESULTS, NOT EFFORT OR MOTIVATION.

Results—what is achieved from the vantage point of those served—constitute value. The extent of effort expended, and the admirable motives which may be present even when an enterprise falters, are not ordinarily relevant.

> [T]he single most important thing to remember about any enterprise is that results exist only on the outside. The result of a business is a satisfied customer. The result of a hospital is a satisfied patient. The result of a school is a student who has learned something and puts it to work ten years later. Inside an enterprise, there are only costs.
>
> —PETER DRUCKER

YOU MAY HAVE TO RISK A RELATIONSHIP TO BEST SERVE SOMEONE.

A relationship of love is not one of unquestioning or universal acceptance of every judgment or whim of those you would serve.

A relationship of love—whether of a family member, friend, a team, a colleague or customer—sometimes requires you to go against their immediate wishes. You may conclude you must express hard truths which could jeopardize the relationship. Objective, trusted observers of your relationship may confirm or enlarge your understanding.

In some situations, we must have the courage to express our love in a way which puts the relationship at risk. The courage to risk the relationship you value may, in the end, make the relationship stronger than ever.

This applies in all relationships, including business.

You could say it's a matter of perspective. Serving someone with a short-term focus can verge on being little more than a transaction. Love that is focused on the longer term, that is intended to last, must be sustainable. To allow or enable others to act in ways inconsistent with in their long-term interest is not sustainable. This is every bit as true in business or politics as in families.

YOUR BEST SERVICE MEANS DOING YOUR ABSOLUTE BEST.

Your first reaction might well be: *Duh!!* But linger for a moment: how often have you really done your *absolute* best? Not just tried hard, kept your head down…but given *everything* you have to give?

If you're like most of us, when you reflect on it, there are relatively few times when you have given your *absolute commitment* to a task. It's unusual enough to be memorable.

If work is love made visible, we demonstrate our love through unconditional engagement. As performance psychologist Jim Loehr points out, "Full engagement requires drawing on four separate but related sources of energy: physical, emotional, mental and spiritual."

> *If it falls your lot to be a street sweeper, sweep streets as Raphael painted pictures, sweep streets as Michelangelo carved marble, sweep streets as Beethoven composed music, or Shakespeare wrote poetry.*
> —MARTIN LUTHER KING, JR.

As a leader, your goal is to create and nurture a relationship by focusing on how you can best serve.

The deeper, more extensive the relationship, the more value it can create, the more durable it can become. This is no different from other relationships in our lives. The ultimate connection is love.

In all relationships aspiring to love, it can be helpful to have the assistance of objective third parties. Do you have individuals assist you in examining your relationships? They may well enable you to recognize additional factors which have escaped your notice.

You might well object: *What if I hate my job? What if I'm not being compensated fairly? Should I still devote my completely engaged, best efforts?*

The answer is yes. This does not mean you should not seek to improve the situation. The fact is, the likelihood of improving the situation may be increased by extraordinary performance. A manager who's neglectful of his responsibilities may belatedly come to recognize the value you bring. Sometimes, simply persevering can occasion unforeseen opportunities. Even if you conclude it's best to look for a new position, giving your all in adverse circumstances might be appreciated by a prospective employer evaluating your capacity to serve.

As we all know from our own experiences, relationships have peaks and valleys. Demonstrating full engagement and commitment can provide a strong basis for positive change in difficult circumstances.

Reflect on your relationships of service. Are you giving your complete best, your *fully engaged* commitment? If not, why not? When in your life have you given your *absolute* best? What can you learn from the experience? If you have trusted colleagues, you might also seek their evaluation of your performance.

FOCUS ENTIRELY ON THE MOMENT AT HAND.

Part of doing your absolute best is focusing your entire attention to the matter at hand. This is about striving for complete presence of mind, body and spirit.

Even well-meaning people fail to give their very best when their attention is divided. They may be thinking about family problems while at work. They may be thinking about the smart girl or athletic boy while in calculus class. They may be thinking about the time in the past when something went wrong. They may be daydreaming about an idealized future. They may be distracted or paralyzed into inaction by misguided perfectionism.

A notable example of the power of focusing comes from the record-breaking New England Patriots of the National Football League. As his team maintained a remarkable winning streak, Coach Bill Belichick's approach remained constant. In the words of the *New York Times*, Belichick exhibited a "single-minded focus on the here and now: on this moment, this day, this game."

As the Patriots won game after game, Belichick reminded everyone—most especially his players—"It's been one week at a time for us all year."

Belichick recognizes that allowing distractions would be self-serving and self-defeating.

DO YOUR BEST BY DOING WHAT'S REQUIRED.

In stern days Winston Churchill declared, "Sometimes it is not enough to do our best; we must do what's required."

Churchill's point is that external requirements—what's required for those we're serving—can elicit more than we believe we possess. This is the outside-in perspective in action.

The mother who lifts the car to save her child is doing what's required. The team or individual who achieves extraordinary performance time and again is doing what's required.

Ernest Hemingway expressed it well: "For a long time I have tried simply to write the best I can. Sometimes I have good luck and write better than I can."

This is true for you as you strive for your top performance. It's also true of those you seek to serve by leading. As David Novak, longtime CEO and chairman of Yum Brands (including KFC, Pizza Hut, Taco Bell and Long John Silver's) observes: "What...a great leader does, a great coach does, is understand what kind of talent you have and then you help people leverage that talent, so they can achieve what they never thought they were capable of."

And yet, even your very best performance may not be enough. You must also be able to serve better than anyone else.

ARE YOU MAKING YOUR UNIQUE CONTRIBUTION?

This question is vital—and often unsettling. It has several aspects.

Most importantly, are you making a *unique* contribution, serving better than anyone else?

When you ask individuals if they, or their company, or their team can serve better than anyone else, more than a few become noticeably uncomfortable. Some are concerned that they cannot meet such a standard. Others regard it immodest to make such a claim.

It's only immodest if you're thinking of it from the inside-out, rather than the outside-in. The ultimate answer to the question will not come from *your* perspective. It must be validated by those you are serving. They have an absolute right—and obligations to those *they* are serving—to demand the best available service.

This is not to be confused with regarding yourself "indispensable." Charles de Gaulle sardonically observed, "The cemeteries of the world are full of indispensable men." To think of yourself in this way would be a symptom of pride, entitlement—the antithesis of service.

It *is* about making a unique contribution. If you don't believe with all your heart and mind that you can serve better than anyone else, you need to take a hard look at how you can best serve. It's time to update and revise your priorities.

> *Never do things others can do and will do*
> *if there are things others cannot do or will not do.*
> —AMELIA EARHART

If your product or service is unique so as to evade classification, you will have no competition. From the vantage point of those you're serving, your relationship can approach the exclusivity of love.

> *You do not merely want to be the best of the best.*
> *You want to be considered the only ones who do what you do.*
> —JERRY GARCIA

I don't sound like nobody.

—ELVIS PRESLEY, AGE 18, SEEKING TO CUT DEMO

As with each of The Four Questions, this applies equally to managing yourself, a team, or an enterprise of any size or complexity. A common thread is the potential realized by identifying and achieving your calling—and enabling others to do the same.

STRIVE FOR THE IDEAL RELATIONSHIP: LOVE.

As you seek to create and deepen relationships, you move across a continuum toward an ideal: love.

On the one hand, the ideal is challenging. On the other hand, it is something we can all understand and potentially achieve. The Biblical injunction, "love thy neighbor," is so often repeated that it is rarely, truly heard. Yet, it's profound in its universal reach.

Our work and working relationships, when most effective, are based on love. They are based on service we provide without an accountant's calculation of precise reciprocity.

> *The more love we give away, the more we have left. The*
> *laws of love differ from the laws of arithmetic.*
> *Love hoarded dwindles, but love given grows.*
> *If we give all our love,*
> *we will have more left than he who saves some.*
>
> —SIR JOHN TEMPLETON

Love denotes the highest level of service. Often it occasions us to accomplish things far beyond what we imagined possible—at least possible for us.

> *Work is love made visible.*
>
> —KAHLIL GIBRAN

The further we move toward love, the more we escape the limitations of a consciousness centered on the self. We master ourselves.

Moving toward love, we abandon ego. We transcend the limits we have imposed on ourselves by our interpretation and internalization of our life experiences. Because such constraints are self-imposed, so, too, they can be overcome by our own decisions.

Observers from Aristotle to Winston Churchill declare courage to be the ultimate virtue, because all the other virtues flow from it. What we honor as courage puts ourselves at risk—all the way to loss of life—in service of something outside ourselves.

If all the other virtues flow from courage, so courage flows from love. It's worth reiterating: the etymological root of "courage" is "coeur," the French word for heart.

There is no fear in love, but perfect love casts out fear.
—1 JOHN 4:18

IDENTIFY AND PURSUE YOUR CALLING.

To be the best in the world necessitates your drawing upon all your capacities. In the doing, you will draw on what is unique in yourself. No one can replicate it.

In serving others purposefully, effectively, you will find your calling. Individuals are not the only ones who can have a calling. A team, a network, a company or a not-for-profit or government agency can have a calling. In every situation, it is critical that those who aspire to leadership identify and seek to achieve their calling.

The notion of a calling comes from religious traditions. The term "vocation" initially referred to a spiritual quest. It sounds somewhat awkward to many today. It suggests a unity of work and life.

Regrettably, many of us view our work as something separate from the essence of our life. Our job may pay our bills, but it may not be fulfilling. It may not draw upon our greatest talents. It may not be aligned with our values. In various ways, our work may be inconsistent with—even at war with—what makes us unique.

Striving primarily for money or status is antithetical to the concept of a calling. It suggests you're serving yourself rather than unreservedly serving others.

Theologian Frederick Buechner defines a calling as "the place where your deep gladness and the world's deep hunger meet." In our terms, it's the place where your passion, seeking expression from the inside-out, becomes one with your service, comprehended from the outside-in.

> *No leader sets out to be a leader per se, but rather to express him- or herself freely and fully. That is, leaders have no interest in proving themselves, but an abiding interest in expressing themselves.*
>
> —WARREN BENNIS

A calling occasions deep engagement. It summons spiritual resources. It elicits a greater contribution than you may have realized you could make. It unifies all aspects of your life: work and play, spiritual and temporal.

Most important, it results in more effective service. Your ultimate concern in achieving a calling is service. The more your self-focus is overcome, the more the energy, passion and aspirations of others can be incorporated into your performance. It's a ruthless simplifier, getting yourself out of your own way.

Dr. Wayne Dyer elaborates:

> Purpose is about serving. It's about taking the focus off of you and your self-interest, and serving others in some way. You build because you love to build. But you build to make others happy. You design because your heart directs you to. But those designs are in the service of others. You write because you love to express yourself in words. But those words will help and inspire readers.

How do you discover your calling? It's the result of a process of active learning and disciplined reflection. First, identify what you love to do. What are you so good at, so committed to, that you are willing—indeed impelled—to engage it without reserve? What comes so naturally that it blurs the line between work and play?

Orison Swett Marden wrote a century ago, "It is what we do easily and what we like to do that we do well." If you love your work so it becomes an extension of yourself, you can bring to bear every fiber of your being.

Mark Twain is widely regarded to be America's greatest writer.

What work I have done I have done because it has been play. If it had been work I shouldn't have done it. Who was it who said, "Blessed is the man who has found his work"? Whoever it was he had the right idea in his mind. Mark you, he says his work—not somebody else's work. *The work that is really a man's own work is play and not work at all.* Cursed is the man who has found some other man's work and cannot lose it. When we talk about the great workers of the world we really mean the great players of the world. The fellows who groan and sweat under the weary load of their toil that they bear never can hope to do anything great. How can they when their souls are in a ferment of revolt against the employment of their hands and brains? *The product of slavery, intellectual or physical, can never be great.* [emphasis added]

> *The biggest mistake people make in life is not trying to make a living at doing what they most enjoy.*
> —MALCOLM S. FORBES

The German poet Rainer Maria Rilke famously wrote to an aspiring young poet:

No one can advise or help you—no one. There is only one thing you should do. Go into yourself. Find out the reason that commands you to write; see whether it has spread its roots into the very depths of your heart; *confess to yourself whether you would have to die if you were forbidden to write.* [emphasis added]

This does not mean every moment will be easy or pleasurable. It does mean you will be able to summon up your greatest capacities to serve in a way that reflects your unique combination of gifts, experiences, skills and values. As Sir Roger Bannister—knighted for his achievement in breaking the barrier of the four-minute mile—says, "The man who can drive himself further once the effort gets painful is the man who will win."

That kind of drive enables you to endure risks, reversals and criticism. And make no mistake, the more you chart your own course, the more you will encounter all manner of obstacles.

An executive at Decca Records, Dick Rowe, earned a historical footnote for his pointed rejection of a rising Liverpool group, the Beatles. He dismissed the soon-to-be "Fab Four," patronizingly informing their manager Brian Epstein: "Groups are out; four-piece groups with guitars particularly are finished." Rowe's rejection was not the most egregious. Other studios declined to grant auditions.

Even at the height of their popularity and creativity, the Beatles were not exempt from harsh criticism. A *New York Times* reviewer found little to admire about the album now viewed as their masterwork: "Like an over-attended child, *Sergeant Pepper* is spoiled. It reeks of horns and harps, harmonica quartets, assorted animal noises, and a 41-piece orchestra." The critic concluded it to be an "album of special effects, dazzling but ultimately fraudulent."

At the workaday level, some habitual naysayers take aim at those whose independence stands as an implicit, unmistakable rebuke to their cowardice. That often underlies the stereotypical hostility of corporate and government "lifers" to entrepreneurs and other risk-takers.

A preexisting "job" is, by definition, a role designed by someone else with *their* goals in mind. *You're living the dream; is it someone else's dream?* Can you reasonably expect to express your uniqueness in such circumstances? The apparent security of a regular paycheck, or the imprimatur of a great enterprise on your business card, can exact a high cost.

Many people are imprisoned within negative thought patterns, invariably assuming that work must be drudgery. They can only imagine work—which consumes most of the waking time of our lives—which is unpleasant, unfulfilling and inescapable. Such thinking is deleterious to yourself and others. Like all habits of thought, it represents your decision. To choose to maintain it is self-serving as well as self-destructive.

What are your driving passions? What brings you the most influence or satisfaction? What are the values you regard as primary, which determine your decisions and fulfillment? Do you have tasks that you feel you would die if you were forbidden to undertake them? Does your work meet these goals? Is it time to recalibrate your priorities? If you had just one year to live, how would you live differently?

Remember: no matter what your life expectancy, you aren't assured of any tomorrows.

In recent years the business press has written extensively about the negative consequences of misaligned values and work in the elite, highest-paying professions: law, medicine and finance. The *New York Times* reports that top law firms are losing large numbers of young associates. About 20 percent of lawyers are said to suffer from depression.

In the face of such evidence, some people nonetheless hold themselves back. They may be disabled by an overly developed self-consciousness. They may sense that in achieving self-expression through their calling, they would make others feel small. In *A Return to Love*, Marianne Williamson untangles such misguided thought patterns:

> We ask ourselves, who am I to be brilliant, gorgeous, talented, fabulous? Actually, who are you *not* to be? You are a child of God. *Your playing small doesn't serve the world.* There's nothing enlightened about shrinking so that other people won't feel insecure around you. We are all meant to shine, as children do…. And as we let our own light shine, we unconsciously give other people permission to do the same. As we're liberated from our own fear, our presence automatically liberates others. [emphasis added]

Live on your own terms and in your own eye.

—EPICTETUS

Identifying and achieving your calling can be difficult. There is hard work to be done, forging your passion into something of value for those you would serve. But the payoff is incomparable.

When a man feels within him the power to do what he undertakes
as well as it can possible be done, this is happiness, this is success.
—ORISON SWETT MARDEN

WHAT ARE YOU LEARNING?

Life is about change. Leadership involves creating change and maximizing opportunities in its wake. At all times, individuals, groups and organizations are improving or deteriorating; they cannot remain in place.

The needs of those you're serving are ever-changing. If you would serve effectively, you must adapt continually.

Are you improving your leadership as reflected in your answers to the first three of The Four Questions? There are several mental habits which stretch your capacities to lead by serving:

STRIVE FOR ADAPTABILITY AND CONTINUOUS IMPROVEMENT.

Charles Darwin distilled his theory of evolution: "It is not the strongest of the species that survives, nor the most intelligent, but the one most responsive to change."

If you're focused on service, you must always be prepared for change. Change is the sole constant; it decrees ceaseless improvement.

To be committed to service means you will never "arrive." No status is secure. You cannot view yourself as entitled to a certain position.

Change—and the uncertainty it sows—is not something you resign yourself to. You should embrace it with open arms, head and heart. Change represents the ever-evolving opportunity to serve more effectively, better meeting the needs of more people.

A life of leadership must always be, in Gandhi's and Emerson's evocative term, an experiment. The greater the scope of the experiment, the greater the prospective service.

> *Do not be too timid and squeamish about your actions.*
> *All of life is an experiment.*
> —RALPH WALDO EMERSON

Experiments sometimes proceed as planned. More often they involve trial and error. Viewing life as an experiment encompasses the understanding that you're putting yourself on the line. Gandhi's example displays the transformational potential of such an approach, when built on a foundation of forethought, reflection, discipline and courage. It also illuminates the risks of failure, including the profound disappointment of seeing some of your most cherished aspirations left in ruins.

Experiments reliably move in unforeseeable directions. Acknowledgment of this reality can sustain faith amid setbacks. Apparently unimportant or random events may serendipitously point the way to breakthroughs—as when Sir Alexander Fleming chanced upon the homely mold that, in his skilled hands, emerged as the twentieth-century miracle drug, penicillin.

As Louis Pasteur declared, chance favors the prepared mind. Habits of adaptability can be developed. You can make yourself a vehicle of improvement through a devotion to learning.

CULTIVATE A GROWTH MINDSET.

If you closely observe a leader who is effective over time, you'll find a commitment to learning. This is true in *any* field—from sports to politics, from business to religion, from music to the military.

Stanford University psychologist Carol Dweck draws an important distinction in her fine book, *Mind-Set: The New Psychology of Success*. Dweck suggests that individuals internalize two generic thought patterns about intelligence. One is a "fixed mindset"; the other is a "growth mindset."

The ultimate "truth" of the fixed mindset is that individual intelligence is static. Standardized testing, for example, is thereby understood to reveal the bounds of one's potential. This point of view is reinforced in some educational settings. Teachers may directly or indirectly implant the notion that examinations reliably establish a pupil's capacities. The score is quantifiable and set, like a person's height. Students may then internalize views of themselves as "gifted" or "smart" or "slow."

Dr. Dweck catalogs a multitude of problems with the fixed mindset. From our perspective, it fosters a self-focused, risk-avoidant approach. Individuals may internalize a mistake or failure as indicative of greater truths about their inability to excel. Those who maintain such a thought process are liable to place undue reliance on credentials. They may believe that their superiority or inferiority in terms of intelligence is immutable. Most of us would never deliberately decide to invest such significance in scholastic tests or any single incident. Yet that's exactly what people with the fixed mindset tend to do.

The alternative approach is what Dweck calls a growth mindset. People with this perspective act on the assumption that intelligence resembles a muscle. As such, it can be developed and strengthened through well-directed application. Her examples of growth mindset CEOs include Jack Welch at General Electric, Lou Gerstner at IBM, and Anne Mulcahy of Xerox.

[Some] assert that an individual's intelligence is a
fixed quantity which cannot be increased.
We must protest against this brutal pessimism.
—ALFRED BINET, IQ TEST PIONEER, 1909

The illiterate of the twenty-first century will
not be those who cannot read or write,
but those who cannot learn, unlearn and relearn.
—ALVIN TOFFLER

The vitalizing insight is that a growth mindset or a fixed mindset represents a choice. As with any thought pattern, you have the power to decide whether to maintain it, whether to alter it.

LISTEN, LEARN, GROW.

A growth mindset prepares the ground for continuous, actionable learning. Today, when value comes from the bottom-up and the outside-in, anyone who seeks to serve effectively must develop skills in listening, observation and empathy.

Formal education can be valuable if used appropriately. Nonetheless, having a diploma or other such credential has much less reliable long-term market value than in the recent past. It may indicate that a person was at one time a successful student. It may suggest that the individual at one time had opportunities to learn. It does not answer the all-important question whether that person remains committed to learning as a part of living.

Did a graduate's "education" consist primarily of memorizing the knowledge and theories which were fashionable when he was in school? If so, he may bring limited—and declining—value. With knowledge advancing so rapidly, and access to data so widespread, the best teaching of prior decades has a very short shelf life. *What* you learn in school is not as valuable as it once was.

On the other hand, learning *how* to learn is more valuable than ever. To become—and to remain—the best in today's competitive world, you must approach life from a perspective of continuous learning. No diploma or certificate or past accomplishment can substitute for the determination to grow and develop, hour by hour, day by day.

If you view graduation as a *commencement*, a beginning, it can be a foundation for future value creation and service. That is the exact opposite perspective from those who mistakenly imagine that their credentials constitute an entitlement.

It's no accident that leaders in various fields are voracious learners whose imaginations are defiantly unbounded by the often-artificial strictures and structures of formal education or academic disciplines.

Bill Gates and Steve Jobs dropped out of college. Paul McCartney and John Lennon were not formally trained in music; neither could read notes at the time their songwriting altered the course of popular culture. Leonardo da Vinci was self-taught. Winston Churchill, Richard Branson and Ernest Hemingway were not university-educated. Frank Lloyd Wright and Le Corbusier did not hold degrees in architecture.

These individuals are extraordinarily creative. Their careers are unconventional, breaking new paths from the examples their predecessors bequeathed as guides. They are unafraid of learning new things. They are uninhibited in recombining longstanding, accepted notions in unusual, even unprecedented ways. They are not hobbled by the acute self-consciousness afflicting many people possessing extensive formal education. Having bypassed much of the shared canon, they find joy and novelty happening upon ideas others overlook as commonplace.

Such learners are insatiably curious and fearlessly adaptive. Their eyes and ears are always open and alert; their imaginations are always in play, at play. In Apple's famous slogan, they "Think Different." In Steve Jobs' formulation, they refuse to be limited by other people's thinking. They're been able to find—and express—their own, unique voice.

You must strive to safeguard the learner's mindset—an unabashedly adventurous mindset, the mindset of the beginner. Hemingway—a writer of such vast and lasting impact that it's easy to underestimate the magnitude of his contribution—said," All my life I've looked at words as though I were seeing them for the first time." Violet Bonham Carter located the same quality in her lifelong friend, Winston Churchill:

First and foremost he was incalculable. He ran true to no form. There lurked in every thought and word the ambush of the unexpected. I felt also that the impact of life, ideas and even words upon his mind was not only vivid and immediate, but *direct*. Between him and them there was no shock absorber of vicarious thought or precedent gleaned either from books or other minds. His relationship with all experience was firsthand.

[T]o Winston Churchill everything under the sun was new—seen and appraised as on the first day of Creation. His approach to life was full of ardor and surprise…. His mind had found its own way everywhere. [H]e was intellectually quite uninhibited and unself-conscious. The whole world of thought was virgin soil.

Reading presents the opportunity to learn from the greatest minds in the world. The internet expands this exponentially. The laptop computer you tap at your neighborhood Starbucks can throw open the doors to a world-class library.

History exposes us to the wisdom and experience of countless others who have confronted challenges at least as daunting as our own. Applied effectively, there is no better guidebook to facing the future. We don't study history to replicate the things earlier people did. We seek something far more precious. We learn how they thought, how they happened upon what worked, what did not.

We turn to history not to predict the future, but to prepare for it. When combined with related disciplines such as literature, history enables us to attain a perspective far greater than those who rely entirely on their own experience or that of their time.

If you doubt its real-world value, reflect on the financial crisis that gripped the world beginning in 2007. Historian Niall Ferguson persuasively argues that the lethal risks on the loose in the world's securities and housing markets were more likely to be discerned by those with a sense of the past than those confined within the illusory certainties fostered by overreliance on quantitative analysis and their own experience.

A sense of history can impart both the confidence and humility necessary to master the mystery of the future. It can enable us to imagine the world in our children's eyes, looking back on our own lives fifty years hence.

History can place our circumstances in context. If our own moment in time appears lackluster or adrift, we can direct our attention to vitalizing examples bequeathed by prior generations.

Competition is another valuable source of learning and improvement. It can be a spur eliciting high performance. It is often closely related to inspiration.

The Beatles' musical development exemplifies this. They incorporated sounds from American rock-and-roll, rhythm-and-blues and Motown. They stretched themselves in response to conceptual breakthroughs of their contemporaries, such as Bob Dylan. They did not hesitate to snatch bits here and there, such as the use of feedback by the Yardbirds.

They admired, studied and sought to surpass others. Paul McCartney recalls the challenge posed by the Beach Boys' immediately acknowledged classic, *Pet Sounds*. Their *Sgt. Pepper's Lonely Hearts Club Band* was in part an attempt to achieve similar creative range.

McCartney and Lennon's talent and energy combined with such influences to create—in the words of the title of one of their American albums—*Something New*. Lennon customarily deflected questions attempting to categorize the Beatles' oeuvre. He referred to it simply as "our music."

Lennon and McCartney's creativity and productivity were sharpened amid the pressures of competing with the greatest talents of their field. It so happened they encountered the best in the world in one another. They are comprehended not so much as equals, as each associated with another whose talent was greater in some ways than his own. Their collaboration is notable for a striking combination of competition (pieces they wrote separately) and cooperation (helping or inspiring one another to improve or refine their work).

Some of the Lennon-McCartney songs predominantly reflect the work and sensibility of one of the principals. Even those often benefit tangibly from their mutual influence. Some are marked by signature effects of McCartney and Lennon combined; in others they are connected in contrasting sequence. Examples include vocal harmonies (such as "If I Fell") or bridge sections constituting a significant change of pace, style and voice (such as "A Hard Day's Night" and "A Day in the Life.").

McCartney acknowledges what producer George Martin calls their "creative rivalry": "If he did something good, I'd want to do something better. If I did something good, he'd want to do something better. It's just the way we worked."

McCartney has said that he and Lennon "were often answering each other's songs." Biographer Bob Spitz explains that Lennon's nostalgic return to Liverpool in the psychedelic "Strawberry Fields Forever" prompted McCartney's corresponding journey in the music-hall-influenced "Penny Lane." It is fitting that these memorable songs were pressed together on a 45-rpm single release.

Producer Martin encouraged and guided their rampant experimentation. His unusual background, including classical music and contemporary popular entertainment, was integral to the group's progress.

Martin famously told biographer Philip Norman that Lennon was lemon juice to McCartney's olive oil. He modestly declined to note his own vital role, getting the balance right.

The McCartney-Lennon musical partnership yielded a catalog of nearly two hundred songs. Dozens have become standards. Many are part of the internal soundtracks of millions of lives, spanning generations. Their growth as creators and performers continues to astonish nearly five decades later. They vaulted from the simplicity and directness of "Love Me Do" to the complexity and subtlety of *Sgt. Pepper's Lonely Hearts Club Band* in the same amount of time that students routinely move from middle school through high school.

LEARN FROM MISTAKES AND FAILURE.

How mistakes and failure are comprehended and utilized is based in no small part on the perspective you decide upon. In the words of the poet Rilke, "[I]f you are being asked to achieve an ending somehow, this also means that you are receiving an order to begin anew...."

Failure can be viewed as a learning tool. One of America's paramount competitive advantages is our cultural acceptance of failure. We're a people of second chances—even third chances. Students change their course of study when things don't work out. Business failures are overlooked and overcome. Immigrants come to start again.

Mistakes and failures are a constant at every level of leadership. Consider Winston Churchill. Today he is reverently recalled as one of the great leaders of history. During his lifetime, especially prior to the Second World War, he received decidedly mixed reviews. One assessment of Churchill's pre-1940 career, by Robert Rhodes James, bears the evocative, unsparing title, *Churchill: A Study in Failure*.

Churchill held senior government offices from a precociously young age. In his mind, as well as many others', he appeared destined for the highest post. That would change soon enough.

Churchill's record included disasters such as his advocacy of the doomed invasion of Turkey at the Dardanelles in World War I. This resulted in hundreds of thousands of casualties and his removal from the cabinet. Several years later his acknowledged talents propelled him back into office. He soon stood against prevailing opinion, forlornly advocating military action to overthrow the new Bolshevik regime in Russia.

In the 1920s, Churchill served as the minister in charge of the treasury. There he approved the fateful step of returning Britain to the gold standard. This is generally understood to have wrought unnecessary, calamitous economic consequences. In the 1930s, he courted controversy in speaking for the dwindling band of diehards opposing increasing autonomy for colonial India. This reactionary stance severely damaged his credibility, limiting the persuasive power of his subsequent warnings of the emerging menace of Hitlerism.

Any single instance among this truncated summary of Churchill's missteps would have derailed most careers. Instead, in the words of journalist A.G. Gardiner, "Like the chamomile, the more he is trodden on, the more he flourishes."

I should have made nothing if I had not made mistakes.
—WINSTON S. CHURCHILL

Ever tried. Ever failed. No matter.
Try again. Fail again. Fail better.
—SAMUEL BECKETT, PLAYWRIGHT

Any endeavor which routinely occasions success and failure in public arenas draws upon a capacity to constructively learn from mistakes and rejection. Resilient individuals avoid being defined by their failures or shortcomings. To allow yourself to become distracted or consumed by such negativity would be self-serving.

Framed as occasions for learning, mistakes and failures can result in more effective service. This requires receptivity to negative feedback combined with the discipline not to be unduly influenced by others' discouraging opinions. There is never a shortage of critics who would curtail your service because of a single error. Maintaining undiminished focus on how you can best serve is the right thing to do. It removes your ego as an impediment to your greatest contribution.

> *A failure ought not to be a disappointment*
> *for those who take on the most extreme challenges and*
> *do not settle comfortably in what is modestly proportioned;*
> *it is the calibrated measure of our endeavors that is*
> *not even meant to be referred to our feelings or*
> *to be used as evidence against our achievement,*
> *which after all incessantly reconstitutes itself*
> *from a thousand new beginnings.*
>
> —RAINER MARIA RILKE

FORGE NEW BEGINNINGS THROUGH "CREATIVE DESTRUCTION."

Individuals and organizations aiming to serve effectively over time have no alternative to an ever urgent, never ceasing focus on improvement. As Henry Ford declared, "Failure is the opportunity to begin again, more intelligently."

There is a corresponding danger when organizations and individuals slacken their focused dedication to ongoing reinvention. Peter Drucker warned, "Whom the gods would destroy, they first give forty years of success."

For leadership—for service—to be sustainable, it must be protean in its adaptability. Franklin Roosevelt moved seamlessly from leading America through the Great Depression to leading the Allies in World War II. As he put it, he shifted from being "Dr. New Deal" to "Dr. Win-the-War."

One sees this in durable popular entertainers who evade categorization. Some change in sync with their audiences. The interaction resembles a dance, in which the roles of lead and responder move back and forth between the participants. Thus the Beatles continuously changed and grew, taking much of their audience with them. Madonna famously adopts new personae on a regular basis, moving from youth into the further reaches of middle age.

Continual improvement—from the vantage point of those you serve—is so important that if you don't sense it's being called for, you may decide to precipitate it. Economist Joseph Schumpeter wrote famously of the "creative destruction" of capitalism. The old is continually cleared, making room for the new. That is arguably truer today than when he offered the observation in the twentieth century.

In every situation, the key is to focus relentlessly on those you're serving. If you confine yourself within the bounds of your natural temperament, your own history or experience, or succumb to the comfort of ongoing "success," you're choosing to be insufficiently adaptive to serve sustainably at a high level.

§

Now you're in position apply the *Serve to Lead* System to your life and work.

Following the questions and summary below, you can begin to draft your *Service Map*. This is a living document. You can change it, improve it, and update it at any time.

Your *Service Map* is built around your use of The Four Questions. It is a tool for reflection, planning and accountability.

The next four chapters will apply The Four Questions to specific applications: customer service, management, general communication, and persuasive communications.

The final chapter, "What Are You Becoming?" picks up where this chapter concludes. You'll be equipped to complete your *Service Map*, to turn it into reality with new skills and tools. Thereafter, you'll carry the questions—and your own answers—to empower you in the new world of twenty-first-century leadership.

RECAP
WHO ARE YOU SERVING?

— ◆ —

One of the most important things you can do to transform your leadership—and your life—is to incorporate The Four Questions into your ongoing thoughts.

Minute by minute, hour by hour, day by day, pose the challenge: Who Are You Serving?

— ◆ —

Who Are You Serving?

— Everybody can lead, because everybody can serve.
— Every moment of every day, you're serving someone.
— Serving others underlies many accomplishments, which thereby become occasions for leadership.
— There are as many effective leadership styles as there are situations in which one can serve.
— Leadership failures often stem from confusion about who one is serving.

How Can You Best Serve?

— Create and sustain relationships based on serving others.
— Focus on contribution.
— Evaluate your service from the vantage point of those you serve.
— Value is based on results as understood by those being served; effort and motivation are not ordinarily relevant.
— Be prepared to risk a relationship to best serve someone.
— Your best service means doing your *absolute* best.
— Focus entirely on the moment—and task—at hand.
— Follow Churchill's dictum: do what's required.

Are You Making Your Unique Contribution?

— Identify and pursue your calling.
— Find the courage to follow your heart toward your unique contribution.
— Your unique contribution can be found at the place where your passion to express yourself from the *inside-out* (representing your deepest values) coincides with your commitment to serve others from the *outside-in* (focusing on their needs and potential).

What Are You Learning?

— Heed the value of adaptability to serve effectively in changing circumstances; make it real through continuous improvement.
— Cultivate a "growth mindset."
— Listen, learn, grow.
— Decide to learn from mistakes and failure.
— Forge new beginnings through "creative destruction."

PREPARE TO SERVE

Create Your First Draft *Service Map*: Complete and review your first draft list in response to the question: *Who Are You Serving?* Include not only those you serve in your work, but also in your family and elsewhere. Then you can apply the subsequent questions in the case of each of those you're serving: *How Can You Best Serve? Are You Making Your Unique Contribution? Are You Getting Better Every Day?*

Don't be concerned if your list is tentative, if the answers aren't complete. You'll be utilizing this way of thinking through the remainder of the book. In the final chapter, you'll have an opportunity to elaborate and refine your Service Map for future use.

As you draft your *Service Map* consider the following:

Who Am I Serving? Are you satisfied with your current list? How has it changed over time? Do you intend to expand it in the future?

How Can I Best Serve? Have you identified how you can best serve those you are committed to serve? Are you doing your *absolute* best? If so, how do you know? If not, why not?

Am I Making My Unique Contribution? What are the priorities you have established for your service? Are you making your unique contribution? Have you in the past? Will you make changes to continue to do so—or to begin to do so—in the future?

What Am I Learning? What are you doing to render your current level of service sustainable? Are you smarter, more effective in your work and personal life than a year ago? Five years ago? Ten years ago? Why—or why not? How are you improving your capacities? How do evaluate your improvement?

PART 2

Serve to Lead

3

Serve Your Customers

There is only one boss: the customer.
And he can fire everybody in the company,
from the chairman on down,
simply by spending his money somewhere else.

—SAM WALTON, FOUNDER &
FORMER CEO, WALMART

Our primary goal is not to increase transactions;
it's to increase the experience in our stores.

—HOWARD SCHULTZ, FOUNDER &
FORMER CEO, STARBUCKS

We're not trying to maximize every transaction.
We're trying to build a lifelong relationship with
each of our customers, one call at a time.

—TONY HSIEH, CEO, ZAPPOS

I f you're working in retail—selling shoes or cars or coffee or clothes—you're all about serving customers.

If you're working at Google or Apple or any of the thousands of technologically based startups striving mightily at this moment, you're all about serving customers.

If you're working in government, whether in the local post office or in the White House, you're all about serving customers.

If you're toiling at a not-for-profit organization, aiming toward the loftiest ideals, you're also all about serving customers.

And yet...we all know the world doesn't always work this way.

We all know because *we're* all customers.

An enduring caricature of customer "service" was presented a generation ago by comedian Lily Tomlin. Her legendary character, Ernestine, was the ultimate officious and incompetent telephone operator. Invariably, with more than a touch of the passive-aggressive, she rejected even the most reasonable, mundane customer requests. Her signature line: "We don't care. We don't have to. We're the phone company."

In the intervening thirty years the world has changed beyond recognition. The Soviet Union collapsed into the ash heap of history. Even amid global economic uncertainty, there is greater wealth and opportunity in every corner of the globe than previously imaginable.

"The phone company" Ernestine represented no longer exists.

Somehow, plenty of "Ernestines" remain.

Telephone calls are a lot cheaper than thirty years ago—but just try changing your plan. For that matter, simply try to understand the mass of ill-identified charges and fees and taxes that add up to a small fortune on your phone bill.

More often than not, the term "customer service" sounds like an ironic notion from *The Onion*.

Don't think for a moment that you're alone in encountering poor service. Type "bad customer service" into Google. You'll stir up several million results in seconds.

That web search illustrates transformational change. In the Information Age, the customer is empowered as never before. Thirty years ago, a top executive might regard effective customer service as a second-tier priority. Today, it is an absolute necessity for success—even survival—of any competitive enterprise.

To be sure, organizations may get away, for a time, with disappointing customer service. In the short-run, they may wring profits from customer inertia. Some, such as regulated telecommunications companies or public utilities, may not face the full fury of competition which ruthlessly scours every nook and cranny of the world in pursuit of value. Such outliers may not see you as their direct customer. They may not feel there are immediate consequences for bad service.

And yet...*No one* can long evade accountability in today's world. Tired of disappointing service from ATT? Suddenly, there's Skype. Tired of paying for first-class mail and getting third-class treatment from Postal Service employees? Use email or United Parcel Service or FedEx.

Tired of waiting for education to improve in your community? Follow the example of New York City reformer Eva Moskowitz. Having been frustrated in the pace of change she was able to spur as a politician, she moved into direct, entrepreneurial action. Moskowitz founded the Success Academy Charter Schools. No matter what their ultimate effects, her enterprise is challenging the status quo in a notoriously difficult environment. At least as importantly, she's setting an example for other reformers everywhere.

Unable to get malarial treatments from your public health agency? Contact the Bill and Melinda Gates Foundation.

In the twenty-first century two new realities have merged. The customer has more power, more options to obtain service than ever before. Simultaneously, the capacity of individuals and organizations to serve has never been greater.

Yes, Ernestine is very much alive. But in the new relationship-based world of the twenty-first century, her days are numbered.

ONE DAY, TWO EXPERIENCES

On a recent Saturday, Jane experienced the best and worst of customer service. Jane is methodical about her scheduling. A thirty-something mother of two, she works flat-out in business and at home. Her days and nights blur into one another. Even the small change of her time budget—a few moments here, five minutes there—is precious. Jane thinks of her time as a "life account." She treats it with the same care she directs to her bank statements.

When Jane strode purposefully into a familiar discount store, she was on task like a military commander.

Jane entered as a longtime customer of this vast retail establishment. We'll call it "Dollar House." She was organized, ready for action. She reliably arrived with a list of items to purchase. This was as much to protect her time as her money.

Her primary need on this visit was a key chain. Her list included other items if time allowed.

As Jane looked around, she realized her well-laid plans were disrupted. Dollar House had rearranged its inventory.

Jane pushed her shopping cart forward tentatively. She scanned the newly unfamiliar terrain. She searched in vain for a welcoming table with updated store maps. Though mildly disappointed, she smiled knowingly. Jane had worked in retail while she was in school. She wondered if Dollar House had brought in consultants with "new" ideas about product placement. Perhaps they peddled the very old notion that customers who spend more time in the store inevitably purchase more items.

As it was, Jane had little time to linger or reflect. She spotted the women's jewelry and watch section. She rapidly made her way over. No one was behind the counter. Unable to locate an attendant, she searched in vain for key chains.

After glancing at her watch, she spotted the new location for women's clothing. Reaching the section, she was relieved to find a uniformed employee re-stocking clothes. Jane pushed the basket in her direction. She politely asked where key chains were located.

The twenty-something employee was not nearly as polite in response. She appeared vaguely annoyed at the interruption. Without even a forced smile, she responded, offhandedly, "I have no idea…. It's not here…."

Jane gently persisted. "Where would you suggest I find them?" The employee reacted as if to a clueless, bothersome child.

"Well, I really wouldn't know…. As I said, I just work in *this* section… plus we just moved everything all around."

Jane felt her blood pressure rising. She was striving to maintain an appearance of imperturbable patience. "*Well*…how would you suggest a customer find the key chains…I'm in a hurry…that's all I need."

"Hmmm, you might want to ask the manager…she might know…."
"OK," sighed Jane in manifest, restrained frustration. "And where will I find the manager?"

"Uh…I dunno…She's real busy with the move and all. She moves around a lot and all…." The clerk turned away, resuming her restocking.

Jane was beginning to feel more like a customer service trainer than a customer. "Do you think the manager might want *you* to help *me* find what I came here for?"

The young Dollar House "host" turned her head around. She regarded Jane with the vacant condescension familiar to every parent of a sullen teenager. "You'll have to ask *her*. *She* told me to do *all this*." She returned to her listless stocking.

Time was passing all too fast. Jane had nothing to show for the rapidly rolling minutes at Dollar House. Her right eyebrow arched, her mouth agape, she scanned the cavernous warehouse in search of another section she thought might have key chains: automotive.

Locating a distant placard hanging from the ceiling, she wheeled her still-empty basket nearly half-way across the cavernous store. Reaching her destination, she searched each side of two aisles. She turned up nothing.

Jane's frustration was rapidly escalating. *She had carefully planned her time…. She didn't have time for this…. Most importantly, the people in her world who depend on her didn't have time for this.* Her mind summoned up a long-lost phrase from her parents—was it French? Spanish?—*People count the faults of those who keep them waiting.*

With some difficulty she maneuvered the heavy, unwieldy, still-empty basket to an adjacent section, sporting goods. She located two young male employees, each wearing the familiar Dollar House apron. They were chatting. Neither acknowledged Jane's approach. She thought about her own children. She hoped they were learning better habits than these kids.

Jane stopped directly in front of them. The two boys willfully maintained eye contact with one another, talking among themselves.

Jane raised her left arm rather conspicuously, checking the time on her watch. She politely, firmly interrupted their desultory discussion of high school life. The boys evidently were annoyed. They turned toward her in unison, regarding her blankly. One sighed deeply in a feeble bid for dramatic effect. Addressing them both, Jane asked yet again where she could find key chains.

One of the boys, assessing Jane with an elevator stare laced with bemused contempt, replied, "I wouldn't know...can't you see we're in *sports*?"

Continuing, he snorted, as if for emphasis, "Don't think we have 'em here, but you're free to look...." He glanced toward his fellow Dollar House "host" with a self-satisfied smirk, apparently anticipating his approval.

Jane was more aware by the moment of the loss of her valuable time. The Dollar House "hosts" had no clue that they were supposed to be serving their "guests." The annoyance level from this experience was building. She was finding it difficult to maintain her composure.

"Are you suggesting I wander around the store and look on every shelf?"

One of the boys appraised her quizzically. "What*ever*...We can't know where everything is...especially now with everything moved all around..."

Incredulous, Jane defiantly, noisily wheeled her cart around 180 degrees. She headed toward the exit. Her gait started fast and picked up speed. Her head was bowed in determination.

She was really frustrated—her anger was rising, palpably, by the moment. Jane knew that the days were long past when store clerks were informed about products. This was a step too far. If they could not even assist customers in locating items, what's the point of their presence?

About halfway down a main aisle she realized she was urgently pushing an empty basket. Scarcely missing a step, Jane surveyed an aisle to her left. It was bereft of shoppers or employees. She scornfully heaved the basket inward. She didn't pause to watch it come to a stop. She heard the loud clang as it landed a glancing blow against a metallic shelf. Making her way past lines of customers at checkout, she pressed her now crumpled list of intended Dollar House purchases into her purse.

As she broke through to the open space beyond the registers, Jane noticed a woman in a Dollar House uniform. She was older—at least older than the "hosts" she had encountered thus far. Perhaps she was in her late thirties or early forties. Getting closer, Jane saw from her name tag that she was the manager.

Finally. Relieved, Jane paused. She stood by, waiting patiently while the manager concluded her assistance to another customer.

When her turn came, the manager smiled and asked pleasantly, "How can I help you today?"

"I am so *happy* to find you. I have just spent at least ten minutes wandering around this store, receiving no help from your employees.... I'm just looking for a key chain."

"As you see we've just moved things around," she smiled, "so I don't even think *I* know where a key chain would be now. Have you tried women's jewelry?"

Jane was thunderstruck. She has not anticipated that the manager would be so cavalier, so unhelpful. Didn't she even care, for her own sake, if customers weren't being well-served?

Jane's eyes widened, then narrowed. "You know, you're getting paid for this time.... God knows *why*.... you're costing me time and money...." "I can see you're upset.... You feel you've been inconvenienced...."

Jane plunged her old college debating rapier straight in. "Excuse me, are you presuming to speak for me? I believe I can speak for myself just fine, thank you! Do *not* characterize my thoughts unless I ask you to.... What makes you think *you* have the capacity to accurately assess my view of the situation, much less articulate it?...There *is* a problem here and it's *not* a mere *inconvenience*...the problem is that all of you regard your customers as an inconvenience...."

The manager looked at Jane with manifest detachment. Perhaps it was something she picked up in customer service training. "I understand your frustration. I'm sorry you if feel inconvenienced. I'm sure if you'll bear with us and keep looking you'll find what you're looking for.... I think we used to carry key chains but I'm not sure.... Anyway, I have to assist other people now, especially because everything has been moved around. I'm sure you understand."

Jane's eyes appraised this pitiable functionary. She thought to herself: *The Soviet Union was out of business. Dollar House must have been her second choice.* Jane's eyes held the manager's. Jane regarded her coldly. Jane was about to say more, but she held her tongue. She thought of what she often told her children: *One can only lose in an argument with a fool.* Jane forced her pursed lips into a perfunctory smile. She shook her head slowly, turned around and strode emphatically toward the bright daylight beyond the doors. The tap, tap, tap of her practical heels hitting the hard floor was the final outside indication of her reaction to her experience as a "guest" at Dollar House.

In about a quarter-of-an-hour, Dollar House had fractured a decades' long customer relationship. With each passing moment, Jane's memory called up other frustrating incidents from recent months and over the years. Jane resolved to transfer her loyalty to Dollar House's competitors. It would be easy to remember and follow through on this resolution. She wouldn't need to write it down on a list.

For the moment, that lay in the future. Jane's immediate problem was the unnecessary, counterproductive disruption of her carefully planned Saturday morning schedule.

She drove as fast as she could to Costco. For quite a while she had followed a ritual of listing in advance which items would be better bought at Dollar House or Costco. On arrival, she burst through the front door with adrenaline-fueled speed, flashing her membership card. She pulled her Costco list from her purse. She moved smartly, directing her large shopping basket from aisle to aisle with total focus. She checked discounts. She weighed alternatives. She made decisions rapidly, dropping items into her basket with a clanging finality.

The coffee section was familiar territory. Costco generally carried several high-quality coffees that she and her husband enjoyed. Examining the selection, Jane noticed the store's brand was marked down. It was about 20 percent below its usual price, far cheaper than comparable offerings. She lifted three bags from the dwindling supply and sped ahead toward check-out.

The lines were long, very long. That's the downside of Costco, Jane thought. She found one that looked as good as any. She settled in for the inevitable wait, moving slowly toward the front.

She was next in line to load onto the conveyer when she felt a tap on the shoulder. "Ma'am, I'm opening a new line, next one over…Looks like you're next if you want to come over."

Jane was delighted. As she pushed her cart, she recalled a similar situation at Dollar House. She was stuck in a long line for what seemed an eternity. A young man threw open a nearby register, shouting for anyone to come over. Because she was so near the front of her interminable line, she was stuck in place while those behind her fled to the new line. Jane's time was further wasted—and her frustration soared—as she stood idly by, watching any number of customers who had arrived after her being checked out. One more thing Costco got right, she thought, they have the mother wit to respect their customers' places in line.

Jane watched the computerized register as the cashier scanned her groceries. She noticed that the bags of coffee were not discounted. As the receipt cascaded out of the register printer, Jane remained in place. She wanted to review the prices charged prior to exiting.

She perused it rapidly. Sure enough, the discount was not included. "Miss, I believe the coffee is on sale, but it didn't ring up that way." "Oh… let me try scanning one of them again."

The repeated scan confirmed the non-sale price.

Jane continued, "I'm pretty sure about this…I was just in the aisle looking at it."

The cashier nodded. She was polite but non-committal. She waved a young assistant over. She asked him to go to the shelf and check the price. He took off in a semi-sprint. Jane waited at the end of the check-out area while the cashier assisted the next person in line.

Returning quickly, short of breath, the assistant explained to the cashier, "Actually, this coffee is not on sale, but the ones that are supposed to be on sale are sold out."

The cashier turned to Jane, "I understand the problem. We'll ring it up at the sale price as soon as I finish this customer, and credit the difference to you. Would that work for you?"

Jane was delighted. "Thank you *so* much!"

Jane had always liked Costco. Now, in the immediate aftermath of the Dollar House debacle, she liked Costco *a lot.*

WHO ARE YOU SERVING?

Every enterprise declares its purpose to serve customers. Many if not most appear to believe they are doing it effectively.

Nearly all of us think *we* would *never* make the kinds of customer service missteps that Jane encountered. And yet, somehow, we all suffer through such "service" all the time.

The Gallup Poll has found customers' pet peeves include two of the issues confronted by Jane in Dollar House: clerks continuing to talk among themselves rather than greeting customers with a welcoming smile; clerks saying they "don't know" in response to a product question—and making no effort to find out.

Such findings were reinforced in a poll by Covergys, reported in the *Harvard Business Review*. More than half of customers in the survey reported a "bad service experience," and 40 percent of the aggrieved group discontinued their customer relationship with the company in question.

The Convergys survey found that more than two-thirds of customers urged that companies create metrics which would result in more knowledgeable front-line workers, able to address customer needs in a single contact. These polls confirm the common experience of lackluster customer service. They also reinforce that many, many people tasked with serving customers simply do not understand—at least in a meaningful, actionable sense—who they are serving.

The Dollar House employees—including the manager—did not understand who they were serving.

Presumably the front-line employees thought they were complying with what management asked of them. Presumably the manager thought she, too, was doing the right thing for the store.

In the end, such sentiments mean little. The bottom line: from the customer's point of view, they were serving themselves.

In today's unremittingly competitive environment, the consequences of dysfunctional customer service can be swift and severe. For example, many observers reasonably conclude that it was a significant reason why Circuit City, a fixture in many malls for years, was forced to close its doors.

In contrast, the Costco employees understood exactly who they are serving. Had they thought primarily of themselves, they might have sought advantage in the transaction. Certainly, since the mistake was Jane's, they would have been justified in charging her the full price. Instead, they sought to understand Jane's perspective. As if by instinct, they seized an opportunity to strengthen a customer relationship.

Costco's customer service stands out. Generic slogans and mission statements notwithstanding, many other organizations and individuals exhibit confusion about who they are serving.

Ultimately, management is responsible for clarifying the situation. In many companies, "customer service" is understood to be a cost center rather than a profit center. In some situations, employees may be rewarded for cutting the expenses of ongoing customer service. Customer follow-up calls may be discouraged by hard-to-navigate telephone systems. Returns and repairs may be short-staffed and short-changed. As occurred at Home Depot and other top retailers in recent years, the number of employees available for in-store consultation may be slashed.

The organization structure may be conceived from the *inside out*— reflecting the druthers of company management—rather than from the *outside in*—reflecting the needs and experiences of the customers.

Government agencies are notorious for bad service. In theory, they serve all of us. In practice, it often seems they serve none of us. Public employees may understandably feel they are serving a supervisor, or a union, far more than their taxpayer customers. Without the spur of competition, their performance may vary wildly, depending on their individual standards or those of their direct managers.

On the other hand, organizations and individuals who are intent upon serving their customers can reap tremendous rewards. Their laser-like customer focus can simplify a raft of otherwise vexing decisions and issues.

The way to ensure that members of an enterprise maintain focus on those they should be serving is by creating a culture of service.

Jim Sinegal, longtime CEO of Costco, underscores that serving customers is his—and his company's—ultimate concern. When other stakeholders Costco must serve—such as Wall Street investors—clamor for higher returns, Sinegal held the line for relatively low margins. This orientation strengthens Costco's customer relationships. Most importantly, it expresses priorities in action.

> Who are you serving in your work? Do your practices reflect that your ultimate concern is serving them? How do you monitor yourself to ensure that you're serving them, from their point of view? How do you guard against rationalizing your actions as serving others when you're actually serving yourself?

HOW CAN YOU BEST SERVE?

As I write these lines, I'm sitting in a spacious Starbucks in Scottsdale, Arizona. This bustling café is a regular part of my life.

My computer is in my lap, logged into a wireless internet service. I'm checking and responding to emails. I'm here in the middle of a weekday afternoon, handling paperwork between appointments.

To avoid unwanted conversation and other interruptions, I'm plugged into an iPod. Now and again, I glance up, look around.

All manner of people come and go I smile at the endearing sight of young couples with toddlers. They're at once harried and joyful. As often as not, they appear somewhat dazed in their manifest amazement at the little creatures they brought into being who've turned their world upside down.

High school kids come and go. They're coltish, self-conscious, scarcely able to contain their astounding physical energy.

Business people confer, sometimes portentously. Sales people chat. Some attend to their emails.

Presumptively single men assemble in small groups. They often speak behind cupped hands, harmlessly conspiratorial. Some appear to have notably high self-regard. The insignificance of their conversation is revealed by their habit of turning their eyes and attention toward physically attractive women who pass by.

There is plenty of opportunity to observe people in this Starbucks. Its predominant design feature is an extended walkway, perhaps a hundred feet or longer.

Numerous young women stride down the walkway, bypassing the side door. Some have purposefully chosen the long way toward the coffee bar. A few appear self-aware as they brush past clusters of people at tables or seated separately. Some exude confidence, others vulnerability. Some combine both, not unlike new models on a runway. Some appear oblivious to the watchful gaze of people on all sides. Others cannot resist looking to see who might be observing them.

Their younger sisters, often sporting Hanna Montana gear, come and go in little platoons. For many, the easily recognized Starbucks logo on a cup is a fashion accessory. Perhaps those carefully designed cups, with their up-to-date colors, represent the kind of sexy sophistication and status that formerly lured teenagers to cigarettes.

Young professionals are sometimes alone, sometimes in groups. A few plainly, plaintively, are seeking companionship or romance. Starbucks can be a refuge from the tired and tiring bar scene.

Across the room I notice two thirty-something women who are regulars. They're studious. They're earnest. They're attractive. They're good friends. Each works intently at her computer. They're sometimes seated side-by-side at a long table with fixed lamps, recalling a college library. Other times, they face off.

They're a matched set. One is a brunette with olive skin; the other is blonde with a fair complexion. Their concentration is destined to be interrupted by importuning men—generally young men, though a few are noticeably older. Some approach intrepidly, without evident encouragement. If they've done preparatory reconnaissance, they know they face long odds. A few suggest ill-equipped bomber pilots taking off to certain death over heavily fortified targets. Depending on the whim of the objects of their attention, such intruders may be well-received or rather devastatingly rebuffed. Anyone who wants to watch can see it all happen.

Young, married moms breathlessly snatch scarce time with old friends, out of the house, away from the children. They're coming up for air. Sometimes, they visibly enjoy being women in the world again. Now and again, one or more engages, with evident delight, in harmless flirtations. Soon enough, they will walk out the door, resuming their all-consuming identities as mothers and wives.

An older couple, tanned and self-possessed, strides my way. They are elegant but not showy. They nod amiably as they situate themselves in easy chairs facing me. They're visiting from Grenoble, France. They're eager to chat about their "American-style" president, Sarkozy. After a few minutes, we exchange cards. We say we'll stay in touch by email. This presumptively empty ritual is given some weight by the fact that they're emailing friends back home from their laptop.

Several would-be Hemingways and Jonathan Safran Foers are at work. Or, at least, they appear to believe they appear to be artists at work. Now and again they're joined by an aspiring poet or songwriter. Some are on break from nearby restaurants and bars and retail stores where they earn their living and gather experiences to feed their creativity. Some want to be writers, some want to write, some are content to daydream. They survey their domain, at once present and detached.

New Starbucks product offerings abound. There are gift cards with stylish artistic designs. Music is played and made available for purchase, connecting artists and consumers in new relationships which might not otherwise have occurred. You may see the new work of rock royalty from your youth (or your parents' or grandparents') such as Paul McCartney or Carly Simon. Local musical groups occasionally play on-site. Books and book clubs are featured. Quotations are placed on paper cups to stir thought, provoke discussion.

Omnipresent and engaging, presiding over the entire scene, is the dynamic general manager, Jenn. She somehow keeps the diverse personalities and demands of her team in sync with the kaleidoscopic personalities and demands of her customers. Behind a nondescript door at the rear of the coffee bar, she must reconcile the commitment to customers' experience of a warm, welcoming "third place" with the cold, unforgiving metrics of corporate accounting. Jenn occupies the challenging point where romance and reality come together.

Amid this moveable feast, some customers have come to Starbucks primarily motivated by the coffee. What is striking is how many other ways Starbucks serves its customers. The customers seek—and find—value from many things. An individual customer may find value in different aspects of the experience at different times.

Starbucks has achieved extraordinary success by nurturing customer relationships—with confidence that the transactions will follow. Each store comprises an intricate web of service relationships. The company's goal is to constantly deepen and broaden those relationships.

The underlying question in every interaction in which Starbucks is a party: *How Can We Best Serve?*

Coffee is a necessary part of the answer. But it's nowhere near the complete answer. As the company states in a marketing campaign: "You and Starbucks. It's bigger than coffee."

> *Unlike many other places that sell coffee, Starbucks built the*
> *equity of our brand through the Starbucks Experience.*
> *It comes to life every day in the relationship*
> *our people have with our customers.*
> *By focusing…on the Starbucks Experience, we…create*
> *a renewed level of meaningful differentiation*
> *and separation in the market between us*
> *and others who are attempting to sell coffee.*
> —HOWARD SCHULTZ

CREATE VALUE FROM THE OUTSIDE-IN.

The Starbucks "experience" is unique. The thinking behind it is not.

A limitation of many traditional organizations is their tendency to work from the inside-out. There has long been an assumption, often unspoken or unexamined, that a centralized group of experts would come up with the best ideas for products or services. In turn, the enterprise would produce and sell them.

This mindset can be found not only in the private sector, but also in the not-for-profit and government arenas.

By contrast, effective twenty-first-century organizations create value from the outside-in. They engage those they would serve. They listen to and learn from them. That learning is not simply about how to better sell their wares. They attempt to divine how to create products and services and experiences that best serve their customers—even if, especially if, that points to necessary innovation.

Do unto others as you would have them do unto you.
Of course, you would have them do unto you what you would choose—not necessarily what they would choose.
So too, you must provide what they would choose.

Many costly errors would have been avoided had companies listened more carefully to those they were serving. Even Dell Computer has stumbled when not focusing on its customers' perspective.

Founder Michael Dell recalls his company's immense investment in a series of breakthrough products over the years. One, the Olympic line, was intended to propel the retail giant to a new level of technological sophistication and market preeminence.

Dell scientists and experts were fascinated by their own handiwork. Unfortunately, the dazzling new products encountered customer indifference. The Olympic project failed in the marketplace. Michael Dell faced the downside of working from the inside-out:

> [T]he most important lesson was to involve our customers early and often in the development process. We had created a product that was technology for technology's sake, rather than technology for the customer's sake.

By contrast, Amazon created its wildly successful Kindle product by working from the outside-in. According to CEO Jeff Bezos, speaking to *Fast Company*, his team was not distracted by any non-customer point of view. They were determined to work from the outside-in:

> There are two ways to extend a business. Take inventory of what you're good at and extend out from your skills. Or determine what your

customers need and work backward, even if it requires learning new skills. Kindle is an example of working backward.

If you listen with care, you may discover that the value customers find in a commercially successful product is different from what its creators initially intended or anticipated. Jim Cramer, the hyperkinetic host of CNBC's *Mad Money,* recounts a striking example. Cramer's teenage daughter wanted a new iPod. Cramer was surprised; he had recently given her an iPod for the holidays. His daughter, likely exasperated at this inexplicable lapse of parental understanding, explained that she wanted another I-pod in a different color. *Duh!!*

Until that moment, Cramer had thought of the iPod as an MP3 player. His daughter regarded the extraordinarily well-designed product as a fashion accessory.

Toyota found a niche market with its gasoline-electric "hybrid," the Prius. Some competitors have manufactured products with comparable performance, reliability and price points. Nonetheless, while sales of Toyota's hybrid soared, its competitors' versions struggled for consumer acceptance.

It soon became evident that part of the value of the Prius to its customers is its unusual, readily recognizable design. Many owners not only want to drive an environmentally friendly, advanced technology motor vehicle—they desire recognition. It's a question of status and self-expression. Competitors who designed hybrid vehicles indistinguishable from popular gasoline-powered offerings had not internalized their customers' point of view.

> *The critical issue is not what you are selling—it's what your customers are buying. Uncovering the latter may require deep engagement and applied imagination.*

BREAK THROUGH THE SILOS.

Outside-in approaches expose the heavy costs of corporate "silos." The term refers to the tendency of organizations to "stovepipe" inflexibly along functional lines. Ideally, structure and function should reflect and respond to the needs of the customers. Silos represent attempts to define the relationship from the inside-out.

Silos are about serving yourself.

High-velocity twenty-first-century information flow and competition has knocked down silos in many enterprises. To be sure, one still finds great bureaucratic resistance in less competitive sectors. The U.S. auto industry and government agencies come to mind (even before General Motors and its federal overlords combined forces in their improbable Mastermind Alliance).

Ultimately, the most challenging silos to break down are those of habit and custom: silos of the mind.

The most challenging silos to break down are those of habit and custom: silos of the mind.

When one looks back to the Fortune 500 list of 1955, one notices that companies tended to have set ideas as to what they were selling, how they could best serve. A steel company or a coffee company tended to be just that, with few fundamental questions likely posed or pondered. Today it is clear that such inside-out thinking among so many Industrial Age companies limited their capacity to adapt to customer needs. Many of the companies from fifty years ago are gone. Others are adapting well, depending on their capacity to respond to competitive pressures.

Busting silos—on organizational charts, in the mind—enables you to serve effectively by discerning customer needs and adapting appropriately.

TRANSCEND THE FALSE CHOICE OF SOCIAL RESPONSIBILITY VS. SHAREHOLDER VALUE.

In the 1960s and 1970s there was fierce debate in academic and political circles about the "social responsibility" of companies. Some urged that companies focus solely on their "core" business. A steel company, they might say, should stick to manufacturing steel. It should not attempt to ameliorate, for example, social ills in the communities where its facilities are located. That could be viewed as reducing shareholder value on the balance sheet.

Both sides of the debate shared an underlying assumption that social responsibility and business success are invariably at odds. Where they differed was in their prescriptions. One side concluded that market capitalism must be altered or abandoned to achieve social concerns; the other held that companies should ignore social concerns to create and protect shareholder value.

In the twenty-first century, that debate is as outdated as Austin Powers and flower power. Effective companies establish deeper customer relationships by engaging a broader range of stakeholder concerns. They serve more and more people in more and more ways. Far from being antithetical to shareholder value, they're discovering ways to create value in the historically neglected terrain of externalities.

Corporate environmental strategy is a striking example. In response to public consternation about pollution, since the 1970s many companies have sought to portray themselves as "green." To be sure, no small amount of this has been limited to "feel-good" advertising campaigns. Some "environmental" initiatives are ham-handed attempts to alter public perceptions of longstanding regulatory and legislative issues affecting companies' bottom line. Major oil companies, for example, have become visible donors to environmental advocacy groups. Some of this has been dismissed, rightly, as "greenwashing."

And yet...something more is going on. Coca Cola has established a program to protect supplies of clean water worldwide. Marriott is undertaking a program to sequester carbon, to cut the creation of greenhouse gases contributing to global warming. Starbucks is working with Conservation International on a series of initiatives encouraging sustainable coffee farming practices. Pursuing the vision of Richard Branson, and under the direction of its first CEO, Fred Reid, Virgin America committed to use clean fuels in its jets.

Even Walmart, the bête noir of many activist groups, initiated a series of internal and external efforts to promote sustainability. In early 2008 the company reported it had sold 145 million compact fluorescent light bulbs, saving electricity equivalent to that produced by three coal-fired power plants. Similarly, as government agencies, industry and activist groups debated the safety of a chemical used in popular baby bottles, Walmart banned future in-store sales. Suppliers immediately responded with alternatives intended to be safer.

In the ensuing decade, Walmart has taken other significant steps The Bentonville behemoth gathers and disseminates information from its suppliers about a range of sustainability issues. The full force of Walmart's $400 billion market share is being leveraged to establish standard criteria for socially responsible organizations globally.

Such corporate initiatives can be far more consequential, in terms of results, than the work of all but a few environmental advocacy groups. So, too, they can bypass or even surpass government efforts. They can also have a significant effect on the public sentiment that determines the bounds of agency and legislative action.

Walmart has built its sustainability initiatives from its public relations needs. The company is seeking to respond to various, often longstanding stakeholder concerns. It also understands that its existing customer and employee base—as well as potential new market segments—find value in these efforts.

Though sustainability initiatives remain controversial in some quarters, they are increasingly recognized and embraced as a new source of value through expanded notions of service. For example, *McKinsey Quarterly*, authors Sheila Bonini, Timothy M. Kohler and Philip H. Mirvis surveyed corporate social responsibility programs to ascertain their financial value.

The McKinsey team concluded that the most effective companies successfully crafted metrics demonstrating value of environmental, social and governance programs in traditional terms: growth (markets, products, market share, innovation, reputation); returns on capital (operational and workforce efficiency, reputation/price premium); risk management (regulatory, public/community, supply chain, risk to reputation); and management quality (leadership development, adaptability, long-term strategy).

The McKinsey report cataloged numerous examples of companies—including Coca-Cola, IBM, Telefonica, Novo Nordisk, Verizon, Cargill, and Nestle—breaking ground, serving in new ways.

Corporate initiatives to advance sustainability represent an attempt to better serve more stakeholders, at deeper levels. They are intended to align business strategy with social goals, beyond the traditional, short-term, twentieth-century bottom line. Such initiatives can spawn innovation and activity far beyond what is foreseen at the outset. The logic of ever-increasing service, once embraced, tends to spread across the entire internal and external life of an organization or individual.

Serving customers effectively—and sustainably—now includes advancing their broader aspirations and values. Because of the internet, such expanded notions of service are rising not only in the wealthy West, but across the planet.

Today, you can create market value by sharing and visibly advancing the personal values cherished by your customers. The relationship can be dramatically intensified if they see themselves as living their values by purchasing and utilizing your products.

EMPOWER YOUR CUSTOMERS AND STAKEHOLDERS TO SERVE.

In today's information-laden world, we are aware that all our actions have consequences. At a neighborhood super market we can purchase food from around the world. For many years that was viewed as a notable achievement. We now recognize the effects on people and the environment issuing from each step in the process of bringing food to market—from land and labor, to manufacturing and packaging, to distribution and delivery.

Taken together, our actions as individuals—from how much gasoline we consume, to the kinds of products we purchase from other nations—make an immense difference across the globe. Each such effect represents an opportunity to serve.

Armed with this awareness, more and more of us want to serve by knowing that part of the revenue from our purchases will be deployed to advance our values. In turn, various enterprises realize that they can create value by responding to our desire to serve. In a recent advertising campaign, Starbucks declares: "Everything we do, you do." The company recites a litany of actions it is taking to protect the environment and improve communities.

Starbucks is merely one among an increasing number of companies striving to create customer value in this way. Apple Computer and other consumer standouts have joined the Product Red campaign. Prospective purchasers are informed that a portion of the price will be donated to a fund to ameliorate the plight of AIDs victims in Africa.

Yvon Chouinard, founder of Patagonia outfitters, established "One Percent for the Planet." Patagonia and other signatory companies commit to donate one percent of their sales revenues to environmental protection causes. Patagonia's service extends even further—surely further than it could have initially foreseen—by the power of its example. A compelling case in point: it's reported that Walmart's ongoing sustainability initiatives are influenced by Patagonia's experience.

> *Customer indifference is the enemy. Mutual passion—customer and company—is the prize.*

In the end, it's about the relationship. Customer indifference is the enemy. This is true not only of Starbucks, but of every enterprise in today's new world.

For an enterprise to thrive over time, its goal must be to create service relationships at the highest level: love.

ARE YOU MAKING YOUR UNIQUE CONTRIBUTION?

Ideally, your customers will conclude that no one else can do what you can do. The relationship between you and your customer becomes exclusive.

This is where the relationship approaches love. It's partly rational. The relationship may have an objective basis in forethought and objective analysis. It's also about emotional connection.

"Chemistry" may keep the relationship strong when it might otherwise seem irrational to maintain it. It's one-of-a-kind. Those caught up in it grow together. They may become powerfully entangled, like sturdy vines. What they become, when joined, can't be entirely foreseen. Nor can it be replicated.

> *Our relationship with our customers is one of love.*
> *The customers are not always right—but they always deserve respect.*
> —MIKE FAITH, FOUNDER, HEADSETS.COM

Kevin Roberts of Saatchi & Saatchi writes of "lovemarks." They are distinct from run of the mill brands. A lovemark may enter one's life like any other. Or it may be love at first sight.

You purchase shoes or clothing or a car or a motorcycle or an iPod or download a song. It all seems unexceptional. Yet, there may be something so compelling about a particular product or service that it sparks a special relationship.

Think of self-satisfied Mac owners who would be mortified to be seen with a PC. Think of middle-aged women, wearing otherwise unremarkable tee shirts, who feel supersonic because of the impossibly loud label emblazoned in silver letters across their chests: *Bebe.* Behold young people—and their aging Baby Boomer parents and grandparents—with iPods. Summon up visions of the middle-aged and older men—from dentists to drill instructors—astride Harley-Davidson bikes with customized boots and jackets. Some, in a spectacular act of devotion, declare undying love for their "hog" with tattoos.

A relationship of customer love can be created in unexpected places. Watches are quintessential commodities. The technology is not unique. A digital timepiece costing less than $10 can keep time flawlessly. The designs are not often path-breaking.

Nonetheless, numerous high-end watchmakers have created lovemarks. Watches may be commodities, but their place in our lives can be a gateway to intimacy.

Rolex forges a link to excellence, achievement and financial success. If you wear a Rolex, you are tying yourself to celebrities of diverse accomplishments and disciplines. Mont Blanc uses celebrities in advertising to connect its watches to social responsibility. One campaign, for example, promised a portion of profits would go to the Heal the Bay environmental organization in Santa Monica, California.

French watchmaker Patek Philippe directly associates love for its product with love as we all experience it. Their "Generations" men's advertising campaign has reached iconic status. It focuses on the relationship between father and young son, declaring: "You never actually own a Patek Philippe. You merely look after it for the next generation." The success of that campaign prompted a corresponding approach to women: "You don't just wear a Patek Philippe. You begin an enduring love affair."

Lovemarks, at their peak, interact to reach an ever-deeper level of customer engagement. Consider the Prius owner who declares her computer allegiance with an Apple sticker on her car. She wants the world to know that she not only *thinks* different, she *lives* different. She's become an advertisement for the products she loves. (Have you ever seen a vehicle emblazoned with a decal proclaiming undying devotion to the Windows PC?...*Just sayin'*....).

Apple has long nurtured a manifest connection with one of the historic lovemarks: The Beatles. Apple Corps, the ubiquitous Beatles' trademark, inspired Jobs from the start. The words and graphics of Apple Computer (now Apple Inc.) bring to mind—and heart—the singular and astonishing creativity, productivity and engagement the "Fab Four" represent to millions around the world. The shared symbolism of the Apple Inc. trademark bonded Jobs' products with many consumers in the immense market of first-wave Baby Boomers who came of age with the Beatles in the 1960s. This vast demographic cohort is distinguished for finding individual fulfillment and validation through mass conformity—a desirable market by any reckoning.

To a significant extent, Apple Inc. has piggybacked on the branding established by the Beatles' Apple Corps. Both Apple brands represent hip style within bounds of decorum; they tweak the establishment yet are safely subversive; they're perpetually innovative while maintaining reliable quality. Even the decades-long lawsuit entangling Steve Jobs' Apple in a trademark dispute with the Beatles' Apple kept the connection alive in the public mind. So, too, did the cat-and-mouse game around the questions of how and when the Beatles' catalog would be made available on iTunes.

Loving customers means nurturing a relationship that remains with the customer long after the sale. This is a tenet of Joe Girard, renowned as the world's greatest salesperson. He holds the *Guinness World Record* for selling 13,001 individual cars over the course of fifteen years at a Chevrolet dealership near Detroit. He told the *Harvard Business Review*:

> People are sick to death of sitting around in service departments. When I was selling cars, my right-hand man could go to the service department while the customer's car was at the curb and get three or four mechanics to come right out with toolboxes and take care of the customer in 25 minutes. Sometimes they would install $15 or $20 worth of parts—a lot of money back then—and the customer would say, "How much do I owe you?"
>
> "Nothing," I'd say. "I love you. Just come back."
>
> You get service like that, where are you going to buy next time? That's what makes businesses big: word of mouth. If you create it, it'll make you. If you don't, it'll break you.

Starbucks is striving for iconic, lovemark status. Like Apple or Harley Davidson or Rolex or Patek Philippe, Starbucks seeks to enable millions of people achieve self-expression.

In recent years the Seattle-based giant has faced immense, even existential challenges. Howard Schultz returned from retirement to helm the ship through the storm. Starbucks confronts apparent secular declines in share prices and in-store sales, and decidedly mixed results on recent product launches.

Schultz spoke of new customer-centered changes to the Starbucks annual meeting in 2008. Like Steve Jobs at the 2007 Macworld conference, Schultz used a Beatles' hit to set the stage. He dramatically entered the room to the accompaniment of George Harrison's upbeat 1969 number, "Here Comes the Sun." He thereby associated Starbucks with a legendary lovemark. Selecting one of the Beatles' most beloved songs, long a standard, Schultz none-too-subtly inserted Starbucks into the intimate space where generations of people hold that song in their own lives. (Lest the connection be overlooked, they followed up with a worldwide "All You Need Is Love" campaign in late 2009.)

Though it declares on the web that "you love Starbucks," the company's actions reflect the recognition that they are not there yet. They are moving with renewed, very public vigor to entice a steady stream of customers into an enduring, mutually rewarding embrace.

Given the number of challenges before it, there are many diagnoses and remedies one might imagine. Schultz seeks to frame the various issues within his original vision for the chain. He focuses on "the Starbucks experience."

Schultz doesn't have in mind the experience of the shareholders, or the Wall Street analysts, or the management, or even the employees. He focuses primarily on *Starbucks as experienced by the customer.*

◆

A company that lives by the transaction, dies by the transaction. You should aim for a unique, durable relationship that customers value beyond any particular transaction.

◆

If its customers' primary concern is getting a cup of coffee at the lowest price, Starbucks will have to compete transaction-by-transaction, hour-by-hour, day-by-day. It will have stumbled into the treacherous no-man's-land of a global commodity battleground. Across the field some of the world's most successful fast-food enterprises lay in wait. McDonald's, Dunkin' Donuts—and numerous competitors now unknown—are digging into positions near or in territory where Starbucks is stretched dangerously thin.

Despite its short-term allure for those focused on the quarterly report, a transaction-by-transaction approach could leave customers indifferent to the company. Starbucks encourages customers to see their experiences as unique in ways large and small. Baristas are trained to memorize the first names of "guests." Their names are written by hand on the side of cups, to identify and personalize customers, and to facilitate connections among them.

Products are given unusual, often trademarked names—such as Frappuccino—signaling a non-replicable value proposition. Even the Starbucks names for drink sizes—*tall, grande, venti*—lend an aura of uniqueness. Such labels may also make it less likely that a customer would readily compare coffee prices with competitors. Do you think to equate a Starbucks *tall* coffee with a competitor's *small*? Challenged by a tough retail climate and facing invigorated competitors, will Starbucks achieve the commitment of an enduring, exclusive relationship with its customers? That will depend, in large part, on the company's capacity to innovate.

A practical question emerges: at what point does the deepening of the customer relationship come into conflict with extending to new groups of customers? Some Starbucks initiatives are aligned with left-leaning attitudes and interest groups. Inevitably, as some consumers were pulled in, others felt pushed away. Competing coffee purveyors have emerged with alternative social and political messages.

Patagonia may have reached a corresponding tipping point. Moving to a new level of engagement, the company has been outspoken in its advocacy of energy and environmental political positions, including filing suit against the United States government's regulation of public lands.

WHAT ARE YOU LEARNING?

Continuous improvement is a hallmark of effective customer service. The never-ending quest is to serve more people at a deeper level.

You might initially hit pay dirt providing a product or service reflecting your own desires or experiences. Richard Branson created novel aspects of his airlines—such as in-flight bars—based on his personal tastes.

Over time, the key is to listen and learn effectively. Ideally, you focus on the customer with the intensity of love.

Disney World strives to constantly improve in ways which reflect an unmistakable, unrelenting customer focus. Disney goes beyond what customers *expect*, to what they *experience*.

Mom and Dad and their two kids may be walking back to the car, exhausted but satisfied after a remarkable day at Disney World. A good time was had by all. Nearing their vehicle, Dad reaches into his pants pocket for the keys. Nothing. Then through all his pockets. Still nothing. His anxiety rises. He must have left the keys in the car.

No worries. You may have forgotten something; Disney World has left nothing to chance. Their team is trained and ready, on the spot in minutes. They are prepared to handle this situation rapidly, with a minimum of friction and fuss. They knew of the likelihood of this problem before you did. An incident that might have blighted your entire holiday becomes another occasion for memorable customer service.

Maintaining customer service relationships requires continuous improvement through innovative engagement. Striving to "win" the transaction is antithetical to earning and tending to a truly unique relationship.

*We got swept up. We stopped asking: How can we do better?
We had a sense of entitlement. And I'm here to tell you that's over.*

—HOWARD SCHULTZ

CREATE A POSITIVE FEEDBACK LOOP OF CONTINUAL INNOVATION.

Organizations and individuals master change by continuously improving their products and services from the vantage point of their customers. Focusing on those they serve, they can overcome any inclination to rest on their laurels, to forestall change.

Organizations and individuals focused effectively on improvement recognize that the sole constant is their quest to provide the best possible service. Circumstances within their control or influence—habitual ways of doing business, for example—are always subject to adjustment. A rapidly evolving enterprise, like a person in any exclusive relationship of love, may develop in ways which are hard to foresee.

Consider Starbucks. Can anyone say with assurance what the company will look like in twenty years? Who its primary competitors will be? What its customers will seek and find in the Starbucks experience?

If, as Howard Schultz urges, his company's ultimate value proposition is its relationship with customers, one can imagine it growing—transforming—in any number of directions.

Presumably Starbucks will maintain its base in selling coffee. What about beyond that? Given the swelling numbers of small business entrepreneurs and consultants no longer working from dedicated office buildings, might Starbucks team up with UPS or Kinko's or Mailboxes Etc. or other business service providers? The possibilities are endless, because the opportunities to serve are infinite.

Amazon continues its evolution from online bookstore to general retailer. The company purchased Zappos, the acclaimed seller of shoes and other fashion items. Amazon not only dramatically expanded its ever-growing product line; it is also grafting Zappos' extraordinary customer service culture to its own.

Will Amazon transform itself from a first-rate transaction-based retailer into a Zappos-type relationship-based enterprise?

So, too, Amazon's purchase of Whole Foods recast the entire food sector.

Alphabet, the most recent iteration of Google, is astir with similar notions. Google's partnership with Walmart bids fair to create spectacular creativity in competition with Amazon.

INNOVATION SHOULD RESPOND TO CUSTOMER QUESTIONS— BUT NOT NECESSARILY BE LIMITED TO CUSTOMERS' INITIAL ANSWERS.

There is truth in Henry Ford's dictum: "If I had asked my customer what they wanted, they would have said a faster horse."

Of course, Ford served customers much more effectively by applying his greater knowledge to their actual, unarticulated goal: enhanced mobility. Ford served by translating their ultimate aspiration into technological innovation.

◆

It's always right to serve the customer—but the customer isn't always right. Customers may hold you accountable for disappointing results from your following their expressed wishes. They depend on you to know what they would wish done —if they knew as much as they expect you to know.

◆

There is risk, of course, in presuming to reframe customers' wishes to better achieve their goals. It might require courage. A relationship of love may be strong enough to withstand such challenges, if it is recognized as such and valued by customers.

Consumer insights lead to innovation opportunities.
You must develop an appreciation for who your
consumers are and how they live,
to know their needs and aspirations.
Only then can you figure out how to deliver
the product that can improve their lives.

—A.G. LAFLEY AND RAM CHARAN,
CO-AUTHORS, *THE GAME-CHANGER*

WHEN YOU MUST FIRE CUSTOMERS.

Sometimes in our focus to serve we can forget that the relationship must be mutually satisfactory.

Customers are not the only ones who may decide to alter or sever a relationship.

You may have to fire customers if their demands impair your capacity to serve others effectively. Sometimes ongoing improvement and growth may mean that a previously rewarding relationship is no longer a "match."

Sprint made international news in 2007 when it publicly dismissed 1000 customers. The customers in question were imposing high costs. According to Sprint, some called customer care hundreds of times per month.

Those resources can now be reallocated to serve more effectively.

CULTIVATE A CULTURE OF SERVICE

Any enterprise that effectively, sustainably creates value for customers stands on the foundation of a culture reflecting and rewarding service. Such a culture can transmit and reinforce positive, empowering mindsets with lightning speed.

There are a select few CEOs who have made their companies monuments to a culture of service. Herb Kelleher built Southwest Airlines into a game-changing enterprise on the solid ground of a service-driven culture. It continues at Southwest long after his departure from the CEO chair. It is also reflected in the approach of others who view Kelleher as a model, such as Doug Parker, the highly regarded CEO of American Airlines.

Jim Sinegal at Costco reinforced a culture of service in ways large and small. He knows the business from top to bottom, and takes a manifest, methodical interest in the "little things" which are indicative of larger issues, such as a dedication bordering on obsession with cleanliness and tidiness. When he enters a store, he strives to put himself in the place of the customer. Sinegal personifies the approach to service he encourages. The result is an organization that, at its best, is so customer-centered that regular customers often encounter new offerings of items they have just started thinking about. From mobile computer cases to spa-quality towels to dress clothing to wedding rings to caskets, Costco never ceases to evolve and surprise.

CEOs as diverse as Fred Smith of FedEx and Mike Faith of Headsets. com have engendered such cultures. They recognize that no matter how service-focused they may be as individuals, the customers' experience is with the employees they encounter personally. Such interactions are not limited to call centers; they may be with the FedEx delivery person making the rounds in their office building or in the neighborhood where they live. Today, they may watch companies at work on YouTube.

> *Our competitive weapon is our culture because,*
> *as opposed to a command-and-control culture,*
> *it is constantly evolving from all directions.*
> *Our culture is based on principles of inclusion,*
> *self-responsibility, and co-creation of the future.*
> *Whole Foods is a networked organization, a sharing*
> *organization—not one where everyone is waiting for*
> *some memo about what the future will look like.*
> *[W]e're not retailers who have a mission—*
> *we're missionaries who retail....*
> *So we put our customers and team members*
> *before our shareholders. We deliver results*
> *by being a mission-driven business.*
> —WALTER ROBB, WHOLE FOODS

The bottom line: in today's relationship-based world, your single most important relationship is with your customers. To serve your customers effectively, you must serve your employees effectively.

If your enterprise is going to serve your customers better than anyone else, you must serve your employees better than anyone else.

As Margaret Heffernan explains in *How She Does It: How Women Entrepreneurs Are Changing the Rules of Business Success*, "The culture you build for employees is the culture experienced by customers. They become mirror images of each other."

Management, serving those you would lead, is the subject of the next chapter.

We recognized early on that the equity of the Starbucks brand was going to be the retail experience that the customers had in our stores. [T]he investment we made was in creating a unique relationship with our people and getting them to understand that if the battle cry of the company was "to exceed the expectations of our customers," then as managers we had to first exceed the expectations of our people.

—HOWARD SCHULTZ

RECAP
SERVE YOUR CUSTOMERS

---◆---

Whatever the nature of your enterprise, your ultimate concern is to serve your customers. You should mobilize every resource—financial, intellectual, emotional and spiritual—to serve them effectively. Ultimately, the culture you create for customers is the culture you create for your employees and others with whom you collaborate.

---◆---

Who Are You Serving?

— In today's relationship-based world, serving your customer is tending to your single most important relationship.
— Serving your boss, or your enterprise, should not be confused with or placed at odds with serving your customer.
— If you serve your customers effectively, you will necessarily serve other stakeholders—such as employees and investors.
— Top management should maintain direct ties with customers, personifying enterprise priorities, encouraging and rewarding employees who are on the front line.

How Can You Best Serve?

— Customers can be served in many ways, reflecting their diverse needs and desires; effective enterprises serve more needs of more people, more reliably.
— Create value from the outside-in. The "best" ideas may be technically or theoretically sound—but if they don't meet customers' expectations they will miss the mark.
— Ensure you understand how your product or service adds value from the vantage point of consumers. They may regard your

product or service to be something quite different from what you anticipated.

— Break through the silos. Organizational functions should reflect customer demands, not enterprise convenience or preference. Beware, too, of silos of the mind.

— The Social Responsibility vs. Shareholder Value debate has been transcended. Customers increasingly find value in enterprises which reflect and advance their own values.

— Empower customers to serve, to live their values through your products and services.

— Nurture deep, enduring customer relationships. The enterprise that lives by the transaction dies by the transaction. Sustainable relationships are of greater value to all sides.

Are You Making Your Unique Contribution?

— Customer relationships of love are the most durable—and can create the most value.

— The customer is not always right—but should always be accorded respect.

— "Lovemarks" can be mutually reinforcing when they reflect customers' emotions, values and experiences.

What Are You Learning?

— Serving customers should be viewed as a never-ending quest to serve more people at a deeper level.

— Strive for a positive feedback loop, in which your enterprise continually improves, adding more value in more parts of more customers' lives.

— Be prepared to fire exceptionally demanding customers who impair your overall capacity to serve. Relationships work both ways.

— In the twenty-first century, the enterprises which serve customers effectively are those which serve their employees effectively.

PREPARE TO SERVE

Who Am I Serving? Who are your customers? How has the list changed from one year ago? How would you like it to change in the coming year? In five years?

How Can I Best Serve? How do you determine how you can best serve your customers, from their point of view? How would you define your products or services? How would your customers define them? How do you know your customers' perspective?

Am I Making My Unique Contribution? Do your customers regard you as providing products or services better than anyone else? If so, why? Can you maintain that position? If not, why not? Do you have an action plan to achieve an enduring relationship of customer love?

What Am I Learning? What are you doing to improve your performance from the point of view of your customers? Are you serving more people at deeper levels over time? Do your customers believe you are more effective at creating value today than yesterday? Do they anticipate you will create greater value in the future? How do you know?

4

Management:
Serve Those You Would Lead

"Fail to honor people, they will fail to honor you."
But of a Great Leader, when his work is done, his aim
fulfilled, the people will say, "We did this ourselves."

—LAO TZU, CIRCA SIXTH CENTURY B.C.

People who profoundly achieve aren't necessarily those people who do so much; they're people around whom things get done. Mahatma Gandhi and President Kennedy were both examples of this. Their greatest achievements lay in all the energy they stirred in other people, the invisible forces they unleashed around them. By touching their own depths, they touched the depths within others.

—MARIANNE WILLIAMSON

Bill was blessed with one of the greatest gifts you can have, which is the ability to see the future potential of another human being. It just so happened that football was his expertise.

— COACH BILL WALSH, RECALLED BY
NFL HALL OF FAME QUARTERBACK STEVE YOUNG

He was fifty years old. His career was stalled. It would be understandable if he occasionally wondered whether it was all a mistake.

He had not achieved financial security. His wife might well have hoped for more.

He was trained to fight in war. More precisely, his education and career prepared him to lead others into battle. When his first war came—then called the Great War, now remembered as World War I—his superiors refused his request for a battlefield command. They judged his skills at training others to fight to be unique, the way he could most effectively serve.

At midlife, the pages of the calendar moved with remorseless rapidity. He was certainly extraordinarily well-prepared—but for what?

He might be forgiven a touch of envy toward his contemporaries who had gone further. Every indication was he was fated to remain a desk officer.

His indistinct public persona was confirmed the following year in a press report. He was referred to as "Colonel D. D. Ersenbeing."

We know what neither he, nor anyone else, could have known at the time. Just over three years later, Dwight D. Eisenhower was a five-star general. He would be entrusted with command of Operation Overlord, the greatest invasion in the history of the world. We remember it as D-Day, Tuesday, 6 June 1944.

The stakes were incomparable: the fate of Western Civilization hung in the balance. If successful, this invasion would signal the inevitable destruction of Adolf Hitler's Nazi regime. If it failed, the D-Day assault might result in America's becoming a mere bystander as the most destructive conflict in history abruptly shifted course. Hitler and Soviet dictator Joseph Stalin might have been left to decide the world's fate. Though locked in a titanic death struggle, they had entered World War II as wary, unlikely allies, dividing and conquering the doomed, abandoned Poles. Would they again find common cause? The future would have been very cloudy.

Everyone understood the stakes. How did it come to pass that this individual, Eisenhower, was selected for this role?

The historic significance of the selection was lost on no one. It was understood that the commander, if successful, would thereafter possess unrivalled potential for positions of future leadership—in the military and beyond.

Eisenhower's lack of a combat record meant that he was not a "soldier's soldier." His public persona was not emblazoned with the conspicuous audacity of his swashbuckling contemporary George S. Patton. He did not possess the prestige of his former boss, Douglas MacArthur. The theatrical

MacArthur had demonstrated brilliance in every aspect of military leadership. He was a heroic warrior and an effective executive.

Nonetheless, when the greatest command in history was on offer, it went to Dwight Eisenhower. Many historic occurrences seem inevitable only in retrospect. Eisenhower's selection appeared inevitable at the time. Even the hardest of the hard-bitten leaders of the war, British Prime Minister Winston Churchill, recognized that Eisenhower stood alone in his capacity as a manager of complex, high-stakes enterprises.

The relationships required for effective performance in the Second World War were complex beyond imagining. In the United States, government, industry, labor and the military were compelled by circumstances to work together in unexpected, unprecedented ways. In many cases this went against the experience and operating philosophies of the participants. And it took place under the searing, often distracting light and heat of congressional oversight, partisan politics and public debate.

The allied governments were each jealous of their prerogatives. There were undercurrents of resentment against the Americans. All understood that, should victory be achieved, the U.S. would emerge as the predominant world power.

The lines of power and authority were blurred, in constant flux. The contrived clarity of organization charts often meant little in practice. The fog of war obscured the interrelationships among progressively higher levels of command. To be effective, one had to sense when to clarify a situation, when to leave it artfully ill-defined.

Eisenhower exhibited consummate skill in negotiating this dense, treacherous thicket of relationships. He served his superiors—such as President Franklin D. Roosevelt and General George C. Marshall, U.S. Army Chief-of-Staff—with loyalty and devotion. Yet he was never a courtier.

"Ike," as he was universally known, also tended to relationships with his various co-equals. This included numerous other American military officials, as well as those of other nations.

At the same time, he developed unique rapport with those whose welfare was his responsibility, from the troops on the ground to heads of state.

Ike effectively managed change in relationships. Churchill might be in some sense his superior one day; on another he might be an equal. Most challenging for all concerned, Churchill could also find himself in a position of having little sway over Eisenhower and the surging American power he represented. Such an awkward situation might be mutually understood but not explicitly acknowledged.

Eisenhower's wartime management challenges were far afield from the mannered learning he encountered at West Point at the turn of the twentieth century. He had to deal with the range of issues arising from the advent of "total war." One moment would find him poring over the design and supply of the "Higgins boats" from which American boys would land on Normandy Beach. Another moment would find him disciplining an American officer for disrespecting a British counterpart. Or he might be reflecting on the options available to his wily adversary, laying in wait across the English Channel, Field Marshal Erwin Rommel, Germany's dreaded and revered "Desert Fox."

Ike's negotiation of this skein of relationships anticipates the sinuous, ever-changing networks that are part and parcel of twenty-first-century management. Like a skilled maestro, he orchestrated high performance and enforced accountability.

Eisenhower's extraordinary management skills matched an extraordinary moment. He was dealing with far more than other people's money. He was a leader in the war when Western Civilization was braced precariously, in the words of Churchill, on "the hinge of fate."

The two players with the greatest say in Ike's selection for Overlord recognized that the management skills necessary were distinct from the capacities of the many outstanding leaders who would serve under his command.

Army Chief-of-Staff General Marshall served as President Roosevelt's primary military advisor and strategist. Like Eisenhower, he had not had the opportunity to lead troops in combat. Perhaps this enabled him to discern and give proper weight to Ike's management skills. So, too, Franklin Roosevelt's expressed desire to serve in combat in the First World War had not been granted. President Woodrow Wilson directed him to remain in service as assistant secretary of the navy.

Roosevelt and Marshall knew exactly what they were doing. In 1942 they plucked Eisenhower from 366 more senior officers to serve as the commander of U.S. troops in Europe and North Africa (even in this capacity, he would not personally lead troops into battle). Eisenhower's success as a military leader was, in retrospect, presaged by other aspects of his career. He served as a staff officer under General John J. Pershing, an American hero of the First World War. He served as an aide-de-camp to General MacArthur, both in Washington and in the Philippines. He learned from lively interactions with Patton and other contemporaries. He had made a life study of leadership. When his time came, he was unusually if not uniquely prepared.

After the war, Eisenhower's skills as a manager were applied at high levels in other domains. He served as the first Supreme Allied Commander in Europe, forging the NATO alliance. He served as the president of Columbia University. Ultimately, he served as president of the United States.

In each task, Ike's added value was not technical skill. He had not been a professor any more than he had been a battlefield commander. He had not been a party politician or previously sought elective office.

Eisenhower's singular management skills enabled him to elicit extraordinary performance from complex organizations and networks, including in the face of existential challenges.

> *In my regiment nine-tenths of the men were better horsemen than*
> *I was, and probably two-thirds of them better shots than I was,*
> *while on average they were certainly hardier and more enduring.*
> *Yet after I had had them a very short while they all knew, and I*
> *knew too, that nobody else could command them as well as I could.*
> —THEODORE ROOSEVELT

MANAGEMENT IS A DISTINCT SKILL SET

Peter Drucker explains management:

Management is about human beings. Its task is to make people capable of joint performance, to make their strengths effective and their weaknesses irrelevant. This is what organization is all about, and it is the reason that management is the critical, determining factor. These days, practically all of us work for a managed institution, large or small, business or non-business. We depend on management for our livelihoods. *And our ability to contribute to society also depends as much on the management of the organization for which we work as it does on our own skills, dedication, and effort.* [emphasis added]

Management is encompassed within leadership. Ideally, leaders are found in every position in an organization. Yet we know from experience that many who are capable as managers are not effective as leaders. And any effective leader, especially in high positions, must cultivate management skills.

British war hero Field Marshal Sir William Slim elaborates:

There is a difference between leadership and management. The leader and the men who follow him represent one of the oldest, most natural and most effective of all human relationships. The manager and those he manages are a later product, with neither so romantic nor so inspiring a history. Leadership is of the spirit, compounded of personality and vision: its practice is an art. Management is of the mind, more a matter of science. Managers are necessary; leaders are essential.

Managers are necessary; leaders are essential.
—FIELD MARSHAL SIR WILLIAM SLIM

Drucker recognizes that management is a distinct, identifiable skill set. It comprises "hard" and "soft" skills, art and science. His examples for executives run the gamut from the military and government to business. He cites models from various times and places. Though the applications vary, the principles remain the same.

As Drucker emphasizes, most of us depend on management for our livelihoods. Yet we encounter widely varying levels of management effectiveness all around us.

It is not primarily about native intelligence or subject-matter expertise. President Eisenhower was routinely belittled for his apparent incapacity to assemble grammatically correct English sentences in press conferences. Many reporters dismissed him with the unflattering sobriquet, "bubble head."

George Washington was by no means the most intelligent of the legendary American founders. Yet all agree that Washington was the indispensable figure who brought it all together. As Carnegie-Mellon professor Randy Pausch reminds us in his farewell, even Captain Kirk was not the smartest person on the U.S.S. Enterprise.

Management skills can be learned. In the twenty-first century, with so many ways for people to organize their concerted interactions—from informal networks all the way to formal employment—management skills have become more important than ever.

Ultimately, management is a key to extraordinary service. Individual performance has the limitations of an individual. You may be a virtuoso. Yet, if you are determined to express your individuality in a more expansive way, you must develop management skills and engage others in a larger enterprise.

To achieve ever deeper relationships with greater numbers of customers and other stakeholders, you must master management. Day in and day out, that means you must serve those with whom you work, enabling them to serve ever more effectively.

No one can whistle a symphony. It takes an orchestra to play it.
—H. E. LUCCOCK

WHO ARE YOU SERVING?

As with other leadership competencies, confusion about who you are serving is at the root of nearly every management dysfunction.

Consider the common situation where individuals are "promoted' to formal management responsibilities based on outstanding personal performance. Quite often their success has been based on activities largely unrelated to the task of managing others. Why should we be surprised if they disappoint in their new role? They may have developed highly efficient, productive habits in an environment of competition for limited resources—such as high grades in school, points in sports, bonuses in business. Fulfilling the visions of their superiors, they may have served others as they served themselves. They may not have thought overmuch about who they are serving. As individual performers their interests and those of others were aligned in a pre-set path.

Individual achievement can provide relevant experiences for becoming an effective manager. In many cases, though, purely individual efforts are primarily about demonstrating one's own capacities.

It can be a treacherous transition to move toward developing and empowering *others* to effectively challenge circumstances as part of a united enterprise.

Nonetheless, many enterprises promote, almost as a matter of course, star performers from line to management responsibility.

Should a football team, in recognition of star performance, simply "promote" a star quarterback—or center, or tackle, or linebacker—to coach? Should a virtuoso violinist routinely be "promoted" to conductor?

The answer may seem obvious—but many, many organizations have taken that approach.

Survey findings reported in *Human Resource Executive Online* confirm general experience and observation: "First-time managers too often are promoted into positions without the know-how, tools or training to successfully lead a team." In the survey, conducted by i4cp, a workforce-productivity research firm, only 25 percent of respondents characterized their organizations as "good" at transitioning individual performers to management. The overwhelming

Your first task as a manager is to recognize and focus on who you are serving. A manager's primary task is to serve an enterprise by empowering others to achieve their potential.

majority, just over 60 percent, found their organizations to be doing a "fair" job in this respect; 16 percent said "poor." Such numbers may change; the challenge endures.

To be sure, many enterprises acknowledge the need for training in this transition. The training may emphasize *externals*. It may instruct organizational etiquette and customs, how to dress, how to address people, and so on. It may shed light on recurring work situations among employees. Such lessons can be useful, but are likely not sufficient. The harder, more important work is on the *internals*. Your underlying thought process must put others first as a matter of course, even instinct.

This, truly, is a moment to change perspective from *me* to *we*.

Before you become a leader, success is all about growing yourself.
After you become a leader, success is about growing others.

—JACK WELCH

There is one arena of individual achievement that can prepare you well for management responsibility. That is superior performance as a teacher, a coach or any capacity where you serve by assisting others to reach their potential. In such roles, personal accomplishment is absolutely linked to service. This was the foundation of Eisenhower's management genius. So, too, for many others.

The bottom line is that in today's world, where value in every enterprise is primarily based on human capital, managers' ongoing task is to serve their employees (and others with whom they collaborate in various relationships, such as free agents, consultants, franchisees, vendors and participants in formal and informal networks). In this way, those with management accountability—and their enterprise as a whole—can best achieve their ultimate concern: serving customers. To the greatest possible extent, every person, every resource should be mobilized.

Hour-by-hour, day-by-day, the primary way managers serve their customers is by serving their employees.

For many people, this necessitates a wrenching change in outlook. In the twentieth century, serving customers and serving employees were often viewed as at odds. Adversary labor-management relations were endemic, accepted as inevitable.

Twenty-first-century leadership has turned this on its head. Effective management is based on the recognition that the interests of customers and employees are aligned.

In speaking and working with hundreds of corporate and not-for-profit CEOs, elected and appointed government officials, military officers and other leaders in positions of management authority, I've found their *universal* declaration to be that their most important management role is to serve their employees.

> *If you serve your employees well, everything else—from shareholder value to customer service—will fall into place.*
> —FRANK BLAKE

> *Happy team members make happy customers. Our job as management is simply to make that a reality.*
> —WALTER ROBB

HOW CAN YOU BEST SERVE?

The twentieth-century command-and-control management model was aptly summarized by Frederick Winslow Taylor: managers should seek efficiency from "knowing exactly what you want your men to do, and then seeing that they do it in the best and cheapest way."

This assumes that preponderant value derives from the "manager." Employees are simply a factor of production.

> *In the past, the man has been first; in the future, the system must be first.*
> —FREDERICK WINSLOW TAYLOR, 1911

The twenty-first century has turned Taylor's approach upside down. Now, the *employee* is first; the *system* must serve the employee rather than the other way around.

Command-and-control is totally *over*. The kinds of "bosses" we recall from Dilbert, *The Office, 30 Rock*, and *The Simpsons* are humorous because we've all encountered them. Some of us still work for them (a few among us *are* them—might that include *you*, dear reader?). Their days are numbered. Such autocrats of the conference table will not thrive amid the frenetic change and value creation of the Information Age.

The fact is, serving such a "boss" is antithetical to serving your customers. At the least it is a distraction; at worst, it is suicidal. Once again, what is ethical is merging with what is practical.

> *I think the "servant leader" ...matters because of the nature of the current business world. Perhaps there was a time when it was possible for a leader to know enough to call all the shots and when expertise was all that was required to establish and execute on a clear vision. What is obvious is that it's now gone.... It is no longer possible for a single individual to know enough, so leadership becomes about building functional teams that can.*
>
> —MARGARET HEFFERNAN

Twenty-first-century managers empower others. The principles they follow are shared; the specific approaches will be as varied as the individuals and enterprises they serve. While there is value in some degree of specialized technical experience, twenty-first-century managers must be able to work across and within a multiplicity of disciplines. As such, their skills can be transferable across industries (e.g. Alan Mullaly from Boeing to Ford), and across professional boundaries (e.g. numerous lawyers and marketers serving as CEOs). To an unprecedented extent, managerial skills and experience are transferred across economic sectors (back and forth between government and the military, not-for-profits and businesses). Reflecting the needs of customers, many of the traditional lines are being erased. Management practices, in turn, must be adaptive to enable enterprises to serve effectively.

There is no such thing as the right way for
a manager to operate or behave.
There are only ways that are appropriate for specific tasks
in specific enterprises under specific conditions.
—THEODORE LEVITT

◆

Levitt's insight is even more apt today. There is no universal set of management rules to apply in all situations. There is a universal set of management principles, based on serving and empowering others. There are an infinite number of new and evolving organizational arrangements. This affords extraordinary opportunities for individuals to serve effectively in a range of circumstances which were unimaginable even recently.

◆

Going forward, managers have three ways in which they can best serve: *Inspire, Empower, Hold to Account.*

◆

Twentieth-Century Management:
Command-and-control.
Twenty-First-Century Management:
Inspire, Empower, Hold to Account.

◆

INSPIRE

A leader serves by inspiring those she serves with a vision of the future which is compelling, achievable and provides a context for understanding their ongoing experiences. Such a vision connects the employees and customers.

In addition to a vision—which may be enterprise-wide—there is need for clarity of mission. Mission is the down-to-earth linchpin fusing individuals' daily work into enterprise accomplishment.

If vision is the sine qua non of a leader, mission is the fundamental focus of the manager.

The most effective leaders are also effective managers. The most effective managers are also effective leaders.

The mission to implement the vision can itself be inspiring. These would include the "big hairy audacious goals" identified by Jim Collins in organizations going "from good to great." Audacity itself can unleash formidable force. Collins says, "A true BHAG is clear and compelling, serves as a unifying focal point of effort, and acts as a clear catalyst for team spirit. It has a clear finish line, so the organization can know when it has achieved the goal."

> *We cannot exaggerate the significance of a strong determination to achieve a goal or realize a vision—a conviction, even a passion. If there is a spark of genius in the leadership function at all, it must lie in this transcending ability...to assemble...a clearly articulated vision of the future that is at once simple, easily understood, clearly desirable, and energizing.*
>
> —WARREN BENNIS AND BURT NANUS

EMPOWER

In the twenty-first century, the managers who create the most value are those who best empower others.

◆

As a manager, your ultimate task is to hire, motivate and develop leaders for your enterprise. You serve your enterprise—and your customers—most effectively by empowering your team to unlock their potential, individually and in combination with others.

◆

Empowerment occurs in big and small ways. The big ways include a culture of relentlessly pushing authority and capacity for action to the level closest to the customer. Effective delegation is not a static concept. It is dynamic, constantly evolving.

The new world of 24-7 customer service and just-in-time supply chains necessitates employee empowerment. It is simply not possible to create maximal value through a traditional, centralized management system. Empowering individuals to make decisions, on the front line, in real time, is the order of the day.

Like flowers blooming from seedlings scattered by the winds, examples of management based on empowering employees are found everywhere.

—Home Depot. Recent CEO Frank Blake was accountable for the performance of a public company comprising more than 2,200 stores. No two stores are alike. Many reflect unique features of their customer base. What is constant is that the manager is "critically important." A manager can literally take a store up…or down. Blake views the CEO role as empowering in-store managers. This includes assisting them in developing the "associates" with whom customers primarily interact.

◆

Empowering management may begin as a top-down initiative to create value. The logic of empowerment dictates that, as it gathers force, it will inspire yet additional value creation. Even the most brilliant, well-intentioned top managers may not foresee the directions it takes.

◆

—Whole Foods. The healthy lifestyle leviathan has long been distinguished as much for its team-based management system as for its innovative food selections. Authority has migrated from company headquarters, to stores, to teams of employees in stores. Any number of traditionally top-down decisions—from hiring, to food purchasing and product placement—are based significantly or entirely on in-store team input.

—**The U.S. Military.** The workaday world of the military is, justifiably, viewed as one of the most command-and-control, hierarchical. Yet, even in the Second World War the organization chart would not necessarily reveal the entire story. Stephen Ambrose, the distinguished historian of D-Day and its aftermath, demonstrates that many of the critical decisions and actions resulting in American success were made in the lower ranks, far from command direction.

In the twenty-first century, those earlier, informal, ad hoc arrangements are being enshrined in military doctrine. Journalist Robert Kaplan chronicles how the Information Revolution has expanded the scope of decentralized authority and independent action. The traditional command-and-control approach has given way to explicit recognition of the need to empower leaders of small units to assess and act rapidly in response to local conditions. The brigade combat team has replaced the division as the central maneuver unit, the organizing structural component of the U.S. Army.

This trend has been accelerated by the deployment of the military for various civilian-related and peace-keeping missions. It is bolstered by the rising numbers of highly educated service members. Such individuals are desirous and capable of greater operational flexibility and responsibility. Chronic shortages of resources for many functions in the post-Cold War era also have encouraged military personnel to learn from relevant private sector innovation, such as supply chain management.

The result: "military management" no longer elicits a reflexive, dismissive reaction. Numerous companies recognize that the management skills from the military can be directly transferable.

—**Enterprises of all types** are finding they can create value by empowering their employees to accomplish tasks in ways consistent with their individuality. Cox Communications enables installers to telecommute and communicate through computers. Jet Blue's legendary telephone customer service is built around hiring high-skill women in flexible arrangements, including working from home. Law firms are offering flexible work and career arrangements, from telecommuting to sabbaticals. More unusually, some CEOs, are experimenting with such arrangements for themselves, including working from home. The negotiation between employees and contractors and the enterprises they serve can yield a great variety of approaches, best creating value in specific, ever-changing circumstances.

> *Robert Altman won the lifetime achievement*
> *Oscar about three or four years ago....*
> *Mr. Altman said, "the role of the director is to*
> *provide a space where actors and actresses can become*
> *more than they ever dreamed of being" ....*
> *Now you say Hollywood, I say everybody....*
> *The same thing exactly is true with a housekeeper in a hotel,*
> *with a junior accountant in the finance department.*
> —TOM PETERS

EMPOWERMENT, DAY BY DAY.

Many enterprises claim they empower their employees. Some have great policies—but woe to the career of anyone who would utilize them. Even some organizations which get "big" things right, may drop the ball on what they view as "little things." Those "little things" often determine, day in and day out, whether employees thrive and grow and achieve their own life callings.

> *The leader finds greatness in the group.*
> *And he or she helps the members find it in themselves.*
> —WARREN BENNIS AND PATRICIA WARD BIEDERMAN

THE ERA OF DAILY "DECENCIES," "SOCIAL INTELLIGENCE," AND THE "NO ASSHOLE RULE."

A spate of business books reflects rising recognition that how people are treated on a regular basis—the "little things" of daily life—has significant consequences for the value created by an enterprise. What was once dismissed as "touchy-feely" is now understood as going to the core of a sustainably high-performing team or organization.

Consider some recent titles: *The Power of Nice: How to Conquer the Business World with Kindness*, by Linda Thaler and Robin Koval; *The Human Equation: Building Profits by Putting People First*, by Jeffrey Pfeffer; *The Manager's Book of Decencies: How Small Gestures Build Great Companies*, by Steve Harrison; *The Cost of Bad Behavior: How Incivility is Damaging Your Business and What to Do About It*, by Christine Pearson and Christine Porath.

Managers serve themselves rather than their employees when they treat them with disrespect, incivility or indifference. Such behaviors can be costly. Many empirical studies confirm the obvious: poor treatment of employees increases turnover, decreases productivity and detracts from team and enterprise achievement.

These behaviors are often easy to identify—and can be challenging to eradicate.

Celebrated executive coach Marshall Goldsmith identifies a recurring, self-focused perspective that tugs managers into dis-empowering actions: the desire to "win."

Many managers—especially new managers promoted based on individual accomplishment—may be habituated to looking for "wins" in their interactions with others. They want the last word. They want to demonstrate their intelligence or experience. They may sincerely believe they are adding value—even when their interjections and interventions demoralize those they should be serving.

In our terms, the whole notion of "winning" is wrong. It reflects a self-serving, transactional perspective.

Today, if an organization is to prevail against the competition in globalized, instantaneously moving markets, it must be managed to create "winners" throughout its ranks.

I suppose leadership at one time meant muscles;
but today it means getting along with people.

—MAHATMA GANDHI

Goldsmith's compelling book, *What Got You Here, Won't Get You There*, lists twenty counterproductive habits often found among managers (and all of us). The common thread: each is the result of serving oneself. From "winning too much," to "making destructive comments," to "making excuses," they are all errors arising from indulging oneself rather than empowering and encouraging those one is entrusted to serve.

> *Rudeness is the weak man's imitation of strength.*
> —ERIC HOFFER

There is a golden thread linking the positive habits which can replace them: cultivating a habitual, instinctual perspective of constantly, persistently, effectively serving others.

Some people are so accustomed to dysfunctional workplace environments that they are unable to see the very real costs imposed. Yet, nearly everyone recognizes the positive impact of encouraging, empowering relationships. We recall our best teachers, coaches and mentors for their *confidence* in us (that is, they treated us *with faith*), and their *enthusiasm* for our efforts (thereby tapping the universal spirit of God, *en theos*).

Reflect on your life. Which teachers, coaches, mentors and friends had the most impact on your development? Why are they effective? When have you been most effective in mentoring and encouraging others? Are you applying those lessons in your workplace?

As a manager, you should be no less empowering. A useful way to incorporate this approach is to ask yourself before speaking with a direct report or colleague or superior: *How Can You Best Serve This Person?* Try it for an hour; try it for a day; try it for a week.

This can be a significant change for those who view management positions as granting license to give voice to every passing thought. It shifts the burden to consider your words prior to uttering them. When in doubt, you should simply not add anything—other than, perhaps, a sincere compliment.

> Prior to speaking to anyone in your enterprise—superior, colleague, direct report—pause to ask yourself:
>
> *How Can You Best Serve This Person?* Are you treating them as leaders worthy of respect? If not, why not?
>
> Strive to empower them, to impart *confidence* in and *enthusiasm* for them and their capacity to achieve and grow. Accord them the reverence due the leaders you can help them become.

Many of your most important communications are nonverbal. Yielding to a sigh or a yawn—or checking your Blackberry while someone is speaking—can have far-reaching consequences.

As in all relationships, it can be useful to get unvarnished feedback. You might turn to a full 360-degree review, based on analysis of confidential reports from the range of people with whom you interact. As a start, simply turn to trusted colleagues in a position to observe you in various settings. They can reinforce your empowering behaviors—and let you know when your well-intended communications may be misdirected or misinterpreted.

A good place to start is that vitally important, ubiquitous management exercise: meetings. Are you assisting others in developing their ideas—or are you seeking to exhibit your knowledge or experience? Are you serving others, coaxing them to take risks for the enterprise—or are you making them anxious? Are you *en*couraging others—or are you *dis*couraging them? In short, are you serving those with whom you work? Or are you pursuing an outdated management approach? Are you too often serving yourself?

Robert Rubin, secretary of the treasury under President Clinton, might easily have become an intimidating presence in meetings, demoralizing and deflating those with whom he worked. Instead, a *New York Times* profile noted, "Mr. Rubin often prefaces his opinions by saying, 'I don't know much about this,' and then proceeds to lay out his argument by asking questions of those around him."

When they are offered in a supportive rather than prosecutorial way, questions—rather than declaratory statements—can empower others and tap a wealth of relevant information and insight.

HOLD TO ACCOUNT

The greater the autonomy, the greater the accountability. This combination holds the prospect of ever-rising value creation in twenty-first-century management.

> *Never tell people how to do things. Tell them what to do,*
> *and they will surprise you with their ingenuity.*
> —GENERAL GEORGE S. PATTON

In earlier times management added value by directing *inputs*. This ushered in the tyranny of the timesheet. This was acceptable in Frederick Winslow Taylor's era, when managers were intended to be bosses.

Now, effective managers support employees and hold them accountable for *outputs*, for completion of *tasks*. They empower others to identify and apply their own approaches to problems. The manager may have relinquished the power to direct or control, but she gains the prospect of unleashing new energy and creativity from individuals and teams.

There are innumerable metrics to establish accountability.

Jack Welch famously applied a forced ranking approach at General Electric. Every employee was rated against others and placed in numerical order. One of Welch's protégés, former Intuit CEO Steve Bennett, elected a variation. Eschewing numerical rankings for individuals, he chose to group people in "buckets"—from top performers, to strong performers, to the lowest.

Metrics based on outputs necessarily push managers toward empowering those who report to them. As the output measures become more demanding, the futility of a command-and-control approach becomes more apparent. Capacity-stretching, ambitious goals depend on previously untapped creativity and ingenuity.

Enforceable accountability for outputs underscores the need for *enterprise* loyalty, fidelity to the shared mission. This contrasts with misplaced *personal* loyalty that prompts some misguided managers to overlook poor performance. That is "office politics" at its worst.

Transparency in accountability ensures that good performance is recognized—and failure called out. It promotes a sense of fairness and ensures that managers focus on effective service.

Thomas Friedman coined the term "super-empowered individual." As several financial institutions have learned to their detriment, accountability is even more urgent when individuals have the capacity to produce extraordinary value—or destroy it.

> *As he was leaving, [Averell Harriman] noticed the blow-up Life cover (1938) of [Franklin D. Roosevelt]. He...said, "You know why he was a great President?...Because he did not yield to feelings of personal loyalty. He picked men, gave them jobs to do, gave them plenty of discretion. If they did the job well, fine; if not, he cut them off without a second thought. He did not allow personal loyalty to get in the way of public business." ...I reminded him of Emerson's statement on Napoleon: whatever else could be said for or against him, everyone had to admit that Napoleon "understood his business." Averell said, "President Roosevelt sure understood his."*
>
> —ARTHUR M. SCHLESINGER, JR.

ARE YOU MAKING YOUR UNIQUE CONTRIBUTION?

As we have seen, this question has several management implications. It can be critical for setting priorities.

If you can't credibly evaluate yourself, your organization, your product, as the best to serve your intended customers, you're in serious trouble in the marketplace.

Jack Welch made it company policy: if GE could not achieve and maintain a position of number one or number two in an industry segment, the company would move its resources elsewhere.

Welch was aligning resources with strategy. His approach ensured that GE focused its necessarily limited resources in the areas where it could serve better than anyone else. It motivated GE team members to give their utmost efforts to lift their divisions to the top tiers to earn or maintain their place within the company.

In the early twenty-first century, Welch's insight is, if anything, even more apt. Seth Godin explains, "Beating 98 percent of the competition used to be fine. In the world of Google, though, it's useless. It's useless because all of your competition is just a click away, whatever it is you do. The only position you can count on now is best in the world."

> *The only position you can count on now is best in the world.*
> —SETH GODIN

If your offering is not best in class, you're not making your unique contribution. (In fact, if you're aware of the deficiency and not rectifying it, you're in the worst possible place: serving yourself.) If your product or service is a commodity which can be provided equally well by others, competition will drive the price down, down, down as customers seek the best service and greatest value.

THE WAR FOR TALENT CHANGES THE GAME.

Today, with human capital more valuable than ever, the war for talent is intense. You must be prepared to compete with the best anywhere in the world. The empowerment of individuals—especially those possessing a portfolio of marketable, transferable skills—is unprecedented. Employees who serve effectively as leaders in their own right—and that is an important goal of enlightened employers—have options.

The fleeting, post-World War II American moment of large enterprises, lifetime employment and assured "retirement" has passed. The "creative destruction" that is part of today's economy often leaves precarious work arrangements in its wake.

More and more people find themselves to be "at will" employees. They can be hired and fired at the whim of their employers. Others work in innumerable, ad hoc arrangements aimed at isolating their wealth creation and minimizing their fixed costs. This is the basis of what Daniel Pink calls "the free agent nation."

We're all entrepreneurs now.

Many companies attempt to condition employees to a kind of unexamined one-way loyalty. Employees, especially in the younger generations, recognize that such loyalty must go both ways. They're not fooled. They're not sentimental. They never had the post-World War II paternalist template in their minds.

> *We live in a world where we ask employees to give more of*
> *themselves than ever before. In return, they need to know*
> *that this is a mutual relationship, that the employer is also*
> *going to give more than ever—and that they care.*
> *This is especially true of our next generation, the Millennials.*
> *They want to understand what a company stands for, what*
> *its values are, how it is making a difference in the world.*
> *If you want to retain these types of employees, you must*
> *understand that these questions are important to them.*
> *Only then will you have the opportunity to make them happy.*
> —JULIA STEWART

More and more employees recognize that they're empowered vis-à-vis their employers. With scales off their eyes, they see employers' challenges in assembling and retaining outstanding talent. Employers are often every bit as much "at will" as their employees—if not more so.

Employees increasingly find themselves to be "at will" employees—they can be fired at the whim of their employer. Yet, in today's networked world, employers can find themselves equally to be "at will" vis-à-vis their employees. High-performing employees increasingly have the resources and opportunities to move if they are dissatisfied.

In these circumstances, there is no higher priority for enterprises than to serve their employees. The way to prevail in the war for talent is to aim for the most reliable relationship, one of love.

Evidence of the high stakes in the war for talent is found in the extraordinary steps taken by organizations in highly competitive sectors. They ask a lot of their employees—and offer a lot in return.

Google famously provides many of the accoutrements of home and community on-site—from workout rooms to pool tables, gourmet meals and clothes cleaning services.

Other companies, such as Microsoft, Cisco, and DreamWorks, have created one-of-a-kind campuses with work conditions intended to elicit one-of-a-kind value creation. They seek to unite the work and personal lives of their teams. Even those least cuddly enterprises, large corporate law firms, are moving in this direction. Improbably, one has announced a "happiness committee." This is a world away from Charles Dickens' *Bleak House*.

> *There used to be this idea of having a separate work self and home self. Now they just want to be themselves. It's almost as if they're interviewing places to see if they fit them.*
> —RICHARD FLORIDA

In a time of recession, some wonder if the balance may shift decisively in favor of employers. Wise enterprises will win loyalty and respect in good times by showing loyalty and respect in hard times.

CREATE A RELATIONSHIP OF LOVE FROM THE START.

As exemplified by Whole Foods' hiring practices, a deep relationship with employees must begin from the start. When human capital is of such great value, you must make it an executive priority every bit as much as traditional financial issues—even in a down economy.

If you regard it as a relationship of love—meant to be enduring—you realize that the initial matchmaking can be decisive. You wouldn't ordinarily choose a spouse on a whim, or in the midst of a Las Vegas weekend. The same goes for your personnel choices.

Though people are increasingly recognized as the greatest assets of enterprises—at least rhetorically—personnel functions all too often remain marooned in their traditional, secondary roles. That is a relic of the Industrial Age. Many enterprises devote more resources to decisions about equipment than they do about hiring.

This is one area where nearly every enterprise can focus usefully, bringing its practices more into line with its principles.

LOVE YOUR CUSTOMERS, LOVE YOUR EMPLOYEES.

As we have seen, if you would serve your customers better than anyone else—achieve a relationship of love—you must do the same with your employees. As Gandhi said in another context, there can be no compartmentalization.

This is not wishful thinking. It's the essence of practicality and enterprise achievement. Wharton School finance professor Alex Edmans examined the *Fortune* annual list of the "100 Best Companies to Work for in America." Based on analysis of the years 1998 to 2005, he found that the better employers returned 14 percent per year, against an overall market average of 6 percent per year. This is far from an outlier. Subsequent studies yield similar findings.

> *You have to treat your employees like customers. When you treat*
> *them right, then they will treat your outside customers right.*
> That has been a powerful competitive weapon for us....
> *We've never had layoffs. We could have made more*
> *money if we furloughed people. But we don't do that.*
> *And we honor them constantly. Our people know that*
> *if they are sick, we will take care of them. If there are*
> *occasions for grief or joy, we will be there with them.*
> *They know that we value them as people, not just*
> *cogs in a machine.* [emphasis added]
>
> —HERB KELLEHER

One might say that today's managers are in ménage a trois with customers and employees. In today's wired world, ineffectual management can find itself the odd one out. On the other hand, thoughtful management can be more effective than ever before.

Companies and other large institutions are becoming attuned to this. Even Walmart has reacted in recent years to public concern about its treatment of employees. In a memorable case, the Bentonville behemoth withdrew from a lawsuit and declined to assert its rights against an employee facing extraordinary health insurance expenses. The company recognized that its customers and employees had been brought together through news stories and internet buzz. Unaddressed, the controversy could have resulted in lost value in the marketplace—even damage to its brand—or exposure to cascading political, regulatory and legal liabilities.

> *[I]n the final analysis, our attitude is how can't you provide*
> *[excellent health insurance coverage] for your employees?*
> *If you can't, what you are going to wind up doing is losing them or*
> *they are going to put themselves into a very difficult position, and*
> *we think that in the final analysis, when you do the right thing for*

your employees, it pays dividends, they are more productive, and
they are happier, and they don't leave you. Those are all nice things.

—JIM SINEGAL

ALIGN THE CALLINGS OF YOUR ENTERPRISE, YOUR EMPLOYEES, AND YOUR CUSTOMERS.

A relationship of love between management and employees is one in which three callings intersect: enterprise, employees and customers.

At its core, the calling of the manager must be to nurture, develop and elicit the calling of those who report to her. This results not only in an enduring relationship that approaches love; it also holds the prospect of extraordinary value creation.

A person's purpose is to become the-best-version-of-himself
or -herself. Finding a way to create an environment that
helps employees become the-best-version-of-themselves,
while at the same time moving the company toward
the-best-version-of-itself, may seem impossible to many;
to others, these purposes may seem diametrically opposed;
but in reality, they are astoundingly complementary.

—MATTHEW KELLY, THE DREAM MANAGER

Enabling your employees to achieve their own callings requires that your managers regard them as individuals. To be sure, you must also have the analytical grounding to make judgments on the enterprise or its parts. But such metrics should inform your capacity to treat your employees as individuals.

Many companies are taking actions to merge their employees' personal callings with their corporate callings. The most effective do so in the same space that engages their customers. Green Mountain Energy is representative of many renewable energy companies in providing "green" employee benefits. The goal: to deepen the company-employee relationship by linking the values of the employees with their work at the company.

Zappos pioneered the internet shoe sales space and expanded to a range of retail offerings. CEO Tony Hsieh found the sweet spot by focusing on the happiness of his employees and customers. His attention to customer relationships inevitably points Zappos to comprehensive training. It is intended to inculcate the perspective and cultivate the skills necessary for their development as leaders. The company reinforces the managers' relationships by encouraging non-structured time with other employees, as well as out-of-office socializing.

Unlikely as it may seem, Walmart is joining in. The world's largest retail company, with more than 2 million U.S. employees, is attempting to create a relationship of love. Recent CEO Lee Scott referred to the calling that binds employee and company:

> No company can make the difference that Walmart can make. You have the opportunity to go to work every day...to help people live better... and to help make the world a better place. And you can do that without having to be somebody you're not—or being a company we are not. You can be yourself and live the culture, the mission and the values of your Walmart.... In the end, there is no higher calling for ourselves or our company.

Walmart's recent actions in the sustainability space exemplify the power of simultaneously engaging management, employees and customers. The company's "Personal Sustainability Project" comprises more than half-a-million employees. They undertake a range of commitments, such as using less fuel and exercising more, which improve individuals' health and productivity, increase their value to the enterprise, and enable them to advance community goals as part of their work. They join "green teams," bringing innovation to corporate environmental issues, such as waste management and energy use. This is part of company strategy to gain competitive advantage through improved environmental performance. It extends to supply chain and customer relationships, further connecting key stakeholders.

No one will mistake Walmart for an eleemosynary institution. These steps, taken together, hold the promise of extending the company's reach, significantly increasing value.

The Information Age makes it possible for an enterprise to better serve the deeper needs, the callings of its customers. Where there is alignment of the three callings—enterprise, employees, customers—the prospects are breathtaking.

MANAGE WITH LOVE WHEN THEY'RE SHOOTING WITH REAL BULLETS.

The ultimate test of loving one's employees or team is putting oneself on the line to serve them.

There is no better example than the military. When one examines the careers of successful military leaders—from Lord Nelson to George Washington to Napoleon to Dwight Eisenhower, and many, many others—one finds the golden thread of a commander's love for those for whom he (or today, she) is responsibility.

A vivid example is offered by Theodore Roosevelt. TR's meteoric political ascent—from a subcabinet post to the presidency in four years—was supercharged by his renowned battlefield leadership in the Spanish-American War, Cuban campaign of July 1898.

TR exhibited courage. He visibly put himself in harm's way for his troops. He led from the front. He made himself a tempting target in battle, conspicuously mounted on horseback while most of his troops were on the ground. Roosevelt took pardonable pride in the fact that the percentage of officers killed and wounded in his regiment was far greater than among the troops.

Roosevelt reliably maintained the perspective of the soldiers he served. He tangled with the bureaucracy to procure suitable food and equipment. Here again, TR put himself on the line. He broke protocol, signing a public letter to shame the recalcitrant military brass into relocating his troops outside a malaria-plagued area. This was understood to have been a factor in TR's failure to receive the Medal of Honor he coveted. That malicious bureaucratic oversight would not be rectified until a century later.

The intensity of Colonel Roosevelt's relationship with the "Rough Riders" is noteworthy. He handpicked them, trained them, led them into battle, and maintained close personal contact with them for the rest of his life. As president of the United States, TR would interrupt the business of state to attend to a request or an impromptu visit from an old comrade. The mutual devotion between commander and troops proved an enduring bond.

> *Sound leadership—like true love, to which I suspect it is closely related—is all powerful. It can overcome the seemingly impossible and its effect on both leader and led is profound and lasting.*
> —SYDNEY JARY, RENOWNED BRITISH
> COMMANDER, WORLD WAR II

For companies, the stakes tend to be much lower, but the principle is the same. Managers who demonstrate love for their employees can elicit extraordinary performance and value creation. A manager who puts herself on the line may well inspire others to do the same, throughout the organization. The excitement and energy around the return of Steve Jobs to Apple and Howard Schultz to Starbucks in part reflected this. Jobs and Schultz were risking their records of success in attempting to lead their companies back to profitability.

> *You have to love the people you serve so much that you're willing to give up your own fun and joy, because that's what it takes. [W]hat I'm saying is that leaders have to have a special role, and it takes love to do it. That is, we have to give up some of our fun in order so that persons we're serving cansoar, can experience their humanity.*
> —DENNIS BAKKE, FOUNDER, AES CORPORATION

DOES LOVE MEAN NEVER HAVING TO SAY YOU'RE SORRY? APPARENT EXCEPTIONS TO THE "NO ASSHOLE RULE."

Robert Sutton, author of *The No Asshole Rule*, reports: "As soon as people heard I was writing a book on assholes, they would come up to me and start telling a Steve Jobs story. The degree to which people in Silicon Valley are afraid of Jobs is unbelievable. He made people feel terrible; he made people cry. But he was almost always right, and even when he was wrong he was so creative he was amazing."

Given Job's track record at Apple, it is hard to argue that he did not effectively serve his team and other stakeholders. He plainly had a genius for obtaining superior performance on an ongoing basis, resulting in technology and design breakthroughs. He led the company to spectacular profitability. Apple has achieved a unique relationship with a devoted customer base.

By many accounts, Jobs could be a trial to work with. An employee might find himself treated as brilliant at one moment, worthless the next, and back again—all without warning or apparent reason. Jobs' vaunted volatility and expressed ambivalence toward specific individuals has been compared to an unstable love affair.

There is no question that Jobs loved Apple Inc. He helped found it, nurtured it to success—and then lost control of it. With the company's survival at stake, Jobs returned. He not only brought Apple back; he guided it to new heights. As long as the company achieved outsized results, Jobs appears to have achieved a relationship of love with his employees—one of sufficient durability to survive his otherwise self-serving, disempowering actions. Even when he was, in Professor Sutton's parlance, a "total asshole."

There are other apparent exceptions to the "No Asshole Rule"—where the stakes were immeasurably higher.

We have noted Winston Churchill's historic leadership in the Second World War. It also must be acknowledged that, at times, his management team suffered from the same unreasonableness and resolve that he deployed against Hitler.

In June 1940, Churchill's personal conduct prompted what historian Geoffrey Best rightly says "must be the most remarkable admonition ever addressed to a Prime Minister." It was written by his incomparable wife, Clementine.

> My Darling, I hope you will forgive me if I tell you something that I feel you ought to know. One of the men in your entourage (a devoted friend) has been to me and told me that there is a danger of your being generally disliked by your colleagues and subordinates because of your rough sarcastic and overbearing manner—It seems your Private Secretaries have agreed to behave like schoolboys and "take what's coming to them" and then escape out of your presence shrugging their shoulders—Higher up, if an idea is suggested (say at a conference) you are supposed to be so contemptuous that presently no ideas, good or bad, will be forthcoming....

> My darling Winston—I must confess that I have noticed a deterioration in your manner; and you are not as kind as you used to be.... I cannot bear that those who serve the Country and yourself should not love you as well as admire and respect you.... Please forgive your loving, devoted and watchful Clemmie....

Churchill's conduct reportedly improved somewhat for a time thereafter. It would, however, surface as a concern time and again. Best draws a useful distinction in understanding Churchill's managerial approach. In some cases, there was "unintended offensiveness." He acted in an unattractively self-centered manner, including thoughtless, dismissive, peremptory argumentation. On occasion, the prime minister stooped to hurling papers at colleagues.

The episodic outbreaks of a disempowering management style predictably occasioned dismay, distraction, anger, frustration and hurt. Nonetheless Churchill prevailed in leading his government with astonishing effectiveness. He maintained the respect and affection of nearly all those around him. Surely this reflects in part their recognition of Churchill's devotion to Great Britain. Just as surely, allowances were made for the parlous circumstances in which they all found themselves. Best suggests that Churchill at other times deployed "intended offensiveness." He could be unrelenting in seeking information, assigning accountability, or ensuring performance.

This, too, could bruise feelings. In some circumstances it could nonetheless be effective. In dealing with complex, hidebound bureaucracies at a moment of existential peril, such behavior could be condoned even when not objectively justified.

> *I just didn't like him as a person very much. I don't think he*
> *was a very nice man. I think he was a very great man....*
> *I shall always be grateful to him...for giving me the*
> *chance to serve a raging genius which he was.*
> —LORD BOOTHBY, BRITISH POLITICIAN WHO REPORTED
> DIRECTLY TO CHURCHILL IN VARIOUS CAPACITIES

> *Anyone can become angry, that is easy—*
> *but to be angry with the right person at the right time,*
> *and for the right purpose and in the right way—*
> *that is not within everyone's power and that is not easy.*
> —ARISTOTLE

You may find yourself navigating between intended and unintended —appropriate and inappropriate— offensiveness in service of your team. Seek out third parties who can assess the relationships and provide an accurate, unbiased and actionable assessment of your interactions with others.

There are times when an organization requires a martinet who remorselessly wrings out value through a tyrannical approach. One thinks of Gunnery Sergeant Emil Foley, the character made unforgettable by Louis Gossett Jr.'s performance in *An Officer and a Gentleman*. Certainly, street punk Zach Mayo (Richard Gere) found him to be insufferable. Foley belittled, undercut and humiliated Mayo—with a relish not evident in his treatment of other recruits. By the end, even Mayo understood that Foley's harsh medicine had been the best way he could serve Mayo. The Sergeant's tough love made possible his unlikely transformation into an officer and a gentleman.

DO THE THINGS ONLY YOU CAN DO.

As with an enterprise, an individual manager performs most effectively when she is doing the things which only she can do.

First, that points to how a manager directs her efforts. Can she serve more effectively than anyone else in her tasks? If the answer is no—if some else can serve as effectively at any given task—then the manager is not serving at full capacity.

This applies at every level of an organization. As Samuel Taylor Coleridge wrote of George Washington: "He had no vain conceit of being himself all; and did those things which only he could do." To undertake tasks which others can perform equally well or better is self-serving.

> *He had no vain conceit of being himself all;*
> *and did those things which only he could do.*
> —SAMUEL TAYLOR COLERIDGE, ON GEORGE WASHINGTON

One of the important aspects of higher levels of formal management responsibility is the capacity to attain perspective. Individuals in such positions are entrusted to comprehend the context within which their organizations operate. Whether based on additional information or exceptional judgment, they can thereby add value.

Internal and external relationships converge on managers. That includes relationships with those to whom you report, your direct reports, and colleagues of equal or indeterminate power relations elsewhere in the enterprise. That also encompasses outside relationships which affect your capacity to serve.

As straightforward as it sounds, effectively navigating such relationships may be easier said than done. Shirley Williams (Baroness Williams of Crosby), a longtime center-left political leader in Great Britain, has discussed the failure of a gifted colleague to reach the top rung of politics. She observes that he was effective in dealing with those "above" him, effective in dealing with those "below," but not with "equals."

Many of us have temperamental or other tendencies which incline us to attend to some types of relationships more productively than others. To allow such preferences to affect your actions routinely is self-serving. The better approach is to prioritize your relationships based on your judgment of what best advances the interests of those you serve.

Top managers are positioned—and accountable—for monitoring of the relationship between an enterprise and its customers. Many CEOs, like Theodore Roosevelt, use "managing by walking around" to observe, comprehend, stimulate and encourage their teams in action. This can be used to evaluate and strengthen the relationship with employees. In some cases, it also enables C-level managers to observe the enterprise-customer relationship firsthand.

Other companies urge top managers to spend significant time in direct communication with customers. This can ensure that accurate information is received. It can also be a counterweight to the tendencies of large organizations to harbor bureaucratic interests and imperatives distinct from those they serve (even as they claim to be acting for their customers).

Doing the things which only you can do as a manager means you must be highly adaptive, open to change in your own life. You must be prepared to undertake assignments and adopt roles far afield from your experience or comfort zone. You must be recognized as giving more of yourself than you ask of others.

Doug Parker, CEO of American Airlines, is a case in point. His early career achievements were built on his widely recognized analytical and quantitative abilities. He was named CFO of America West at the age of thirty-three. As he rose rapidly through the ranks, Parker realized that to continue to serve effectively he had to transcend his reserved, introverted temperament. To engage his airline's employees and other stakeholders—from flight mechanics to pilots to flight attendants to managers to board members to the range of outside stakeholders—Parker mastered communication skills.

In other cases, a leader in a high position must focus on one task of the enterprise to serve the whole most effectively. Bob Parsons, the flamboyant founder of Go Daddy, the web domain-name registrar, was frustrated that his company's market share did not reflect the value offered. His segment was becoming commoditized; he sought a way to break out.

Parsons turned his attention to marketing, marketing and marketing. He was confident that as people became aware of his company and its offerings, the sales would follow. He set his sights on the Super Bowl. Go Daddy burst into public consciousness with a memorable, calculatedly controversial television advertisement. A pneumatic model, wrapped in a shirt with the *Go Daddy* logo stretched across her improbably proportioned chest, parodied the recent Janet Jackson "wardrobe malfunction" before a suitably old and priggish congressional committee. Viewers were invited to the Go Daddy site for products—and to see additional, racier ads that were said to have been banned by censors. The "Go Daddy Girl" became a phenomenon.

Parsons tells *Inc.* that advertising is "where I see the biggest impact on our bottom line." He subsequently formed Go Daddy Productions, creating advertising for much lower prices than outside agencies.

At the same time as Go Daddy relies heavily on advertising, Parsons explains, "We don't have an advertising budget." They simply search for opportunities and pounce. Thus it was that Parsons subsequently selected Indy 500 racer Danica Patrick as a "Go Daddy Girl."

Leaders in positions of authority are also entrusted to possess the judgment to recognize when procedures and metrics are serving the enterprise—or when the enterprise begins to serve procedures and metrics. They have to "know" when to break rules or alter systems that are otherwise productive.

So, too, they are responsible for the stewardship of the structure of their organizations. Among the puzzling aspects of the historic Wall Street meltdown of 2008 is that *not one* high-profile financial sector CEO had taken a public stand against the decades-long orgy of manic greed and gambling with other people's money. The historical credibility of investment houses such as Lehman Brothers and Bear Stearns lured credulous investors to assume unprecedented, often highly leveraged risk in opaque instruments. Financial writer Michael Lewis convincingly marks the shift of the investment banks from partnerships into public corporations as a fateful inflection point. The culture of the new companies was unmoored from the longstanding sense of public obligation of the venerated Wall Street partnerships they succeeded.

If you're entrusted with a high position to guide an enterprise, you're uniquely responsible for determining how changes in structure could unleash transformational consequences. In contrast to their flashy corporate successors, previous partners in the legendary, if sometimes stodgy, Wall Street firms had a clear, at times conspicuous sense of who they were serving.

WHAT ARE YOU LEARNING?

James McNerney became the CEO of Boeing after an acclaimed career at General Electric and 3M. He is manifestly dedicated to continuous enterprise improvement through developing people:

> I start with people's growth, my own growth included. I don't start with the company's strategy or products. I start with people's growth because I believe that if the people who are running and participating in a company grow, then the company's growth will in many respects take care of itself. I have this idea in my mind—all of us get 15 percent better every year. Usually that means your ability to lead, and that's all about your ability to chart the course [for your employees], to inspire them to reach for performance.... I tend to think about this in terms of helping others get better.

I am convinced that if the rate of change inside an organization is less than the rate of change outside, the end is in sight.

—JACK WELCH

Management must also enable the enterprise and each of its members to grow and develop as needs and opportunities change. Every enterprise is a learning and teaching institution. Training and development must be built into it on all levels—training and development that never stop.

—PETER DRUCKER

To create value, the improvement must be customer-centered. Again, the ideal is the ménage a trois of customer, employee and manager.

Today's digital world affords extraordinary opportunities to learn by listening; indeed, your opportunities to learn are as limitless as others' capacities for self-expression. Organizations and individuals have access to vast amounts of information to comprehend the views and needs and experiences of those they would serve.

Innovation breakthroughs tend to arise not only from methodical attention to customers, but also to the base of the organization. Intuit's Scott Cook tells *Inc.* that he was influenced by the history of Hewlett-Packard in this regard. Younger employees—and others who maintain the openness, energy and exuberance of youth—can be an asset. Cook set up "Idea Jams," intended to elicit, recognize and back innovative ideas which can create value.

Just as valuable innovations can come from the bottom-up, so, too, they increasingly come from the outside-in. In the new world of twenty-first-century management, one result is what C.K. Prahalad terms "co-creation." This is the essence of "crowd-sourcing." Rather than attempting to conceive new products and services on their own, companies add value through customer participation in the development process. In the most compelling cases, this means designing products or platforms enabling customers to continue their participation as they use the product, sharing personalized, unique experiences of wide applicability. Prahalad's useful book, *The New Age of Innovation*, points to examples such as the iPod. So, too, the iPhone, following initial attempts to limit third-party programs, soon welcomed the "apps" that have become a cultural phenomenon.

There are always more smart people outside your company than in it.
—BILL JOY, CO-FOUNDER, SUN MICROSYSTEMS

Innovative enterprises strive to conjoin bottom-up and outside-in streams into a powerful force.

These examples reflect the ongoing transition from command-and-control to the twenty-first century management approach: inspire, empower, hold to account.

In the Industrial Age, organizational structures tended to resemble architecture. The notion of "structures," and the schematic renderings of traditional organization charts, reinforced such a perception. Such constructs often seemed inanimate if not immutable, conditioning people to adjust accordingly.

In the Information Age, with value rising from the bottom-up and the outside-in, enterprises in globally competitive spaces increasingly resemble organisms and ecosystems. They have functional elements, but are distinguished by short-term adaptability fostering long-term evolution.

> *Innovation—creating what is both new and valuable—is not a narrowly defined, technical area of competence. It cannot be reduced to a single frame of reference, way of thinking, or set of methods. Innovation emerges when different bodies of knowledge, perspectives, and disciplines are brought together.*
>
> —JOHN KAO, INNOVATION NATION

> *When asked in 2007 how Toyota was handling proclamations that the company had reached number one status globally as both an automaker and corporation, Tomoni Imai, a twenty-five-year Toyota employee and group manager… was quick to laugh. "Mr. Watanabe [then-President and CEO]," he says, "will never say Toyota is number one." The reason, Imai explains, is that rankings of size, profit and customer satisfaction reflect what the company did yesterday. Being number one isn't possible because Toyota is focused primarily on the customer, and the customer is always changing. "The customer," he says, "is a moving target. The customer always wants more."*
>
> —DAVID MAGEE, HOW TOYOTA BECAME #1

Many people associate structural transformation with faltering enterprises. The *McKinsey Quarterly* has published research on corporate transformations. McKinsey found that "defensive transformations," reactive to external stimuli of the market, regulatory crises and the like, had a mere 34 percent rate of success. In contrast, "progressive transformations," initiated to empower strong performers to reach the next level (e.g., "from good to great"), had a 47 percent rate of success.

Seizing the initiative to serve more effectively is more likely to create value than defensive actions conceived and implemented within the confines of a reactive, self-concerned perspective.

Change is the law of life. Those who would serve most effectively must anticipate and respond to it. This requires adaptability and an outside-in mentality. It can elicit courage. The benefits of enterprise transformation may appear theoretical, while the costs may be immediate. Cisco, for example, reportedly has lost as many as a fifth of its top executives amid transition to a more collaborative culture.

> *The most effective way to manage change is to create it.*
> —PETER DRUCKER

MAKE USE OF MISTAKES.

Any attempt to systematically improve and learn opens one to mistakes, missteps. How should managers use them to empower and develop individuals and organizations?

> *We are not gods, we are not infallible.*
> *Sometimes even Tiger Woods misses a shot.*
> —SHOICHIRO TOYODA

Nokia Bell Labs is noted for its internal mantra: *Fail Fast, Learn Fast, Scale Fast.* Daniel Pink urges that one make "excellent mistakes." On a day-to-day basis, managers often hold the key to whether mistakes have empowering or disempowering consequences.

Southwest Airlines is committed to overlooking—even encouraging—mistakes which are reasonably intended to serve their customers.

Founder Herb Kelleher recounts an incident illustrating what this means in real time:

> I got a note once from a customer service agent at Baltimore/Washington International Airport who was still in her probationary period. She said, "Herb, I hope you mean what you say, because last night weather prevented our flight from BWI to Islip. So I hired three buses to take our passengers to Islip." I wrote back and said, "I not only mean what I say, but I want you to know that we're going to give you an award." Now, there's no union protection, no job security whatsoever when you're on probation, but, boy, she launched ahead, she got those buses, she took 'em to Islip. Isn't that wonderful?

Obviously, this was, in part, a mistake—a costly one. Yet Kelleher was able to turn it into a teachable moment, obtaining value from it in various ways.

History is replete with mistakes, missteps and serendipity setting the stage for breakthroughs. Many discoveries and inventions are testament to that. Scientists are understood to be experimenting; explorers traverse uncharted territory. Leaders such as Jim Sinegal regard their work in the same light. When Costco announced that it would shutter its ill-starred home stores, Sinegal characterized it as "a valuable experiment for us."

Nonetheless, some managers take perverse pleasure in highlighting others' mistakes. They serve themselves, asserting spurious superiority. A few go further, attempting to define others' prospective contribution based on their missteps, rather than their high points.

Legendary San Francisco 49ers coach Bill Walsh chose an empowering approach. He expressed the view that if he saw a player deliver superior performance *one time*, he knew, with proper coaching, the player could perform at that level routinely. This insight underlay his determination to develop two quarterbacks initially regarded as unexceptional. Joe Montana and Steve Young ultimately became Hall of Fame standouts. So, too, Walsh stood behind Jerry Rice, who, after erratic professional performances emerged as one of the greatest (if not *the* greatest) wide receiver in National Football League history.

Every man has a right to be valued by his best moments.

—RALPH WALDO EMERSON

I saw the angel in the marble and I carved until I set him free.

—MICHELANGELO

John Wooden's peerless record garnered him recognition as "The Greatest Coach of the Twentieth Century." He achieved this in part by his attention to factors beyond winning games. He expanded the metrics for success—and mistakes. Wooden held the Bruins accountable for their performance as team members rather than as individuals. He demanded maximal effort always. This included practice, as well as games where his fearsome U.C.L.A. Bruins held an apparently insurmountable lead. He also monitored the players' work in the classroom. Wooden regarded it as indicative of the character traits that would ultimately distinguish extraordinary team performers on the basketball court.

What about a "mistake" verging on insubordination? How much "play" should be left in an organization to encourage experimentation and innovation?

Taylor Clark reports that Starbucks top management long resisted moving beyond the traditional, hot offerings that formed the foundation of the company's early success. CEO Howard Schultz was initially dismissive of the idea of a cold, blended drink suggested by stores in Southern California, where smoothies were popular. Behind Schultz' back, several managers persisted, working with store partners to formulate, test and market a new concoction.

That awkward birth yielded the "Frappuccino"—with annual revenues exceeding one billion dollars. The Starbucks organization had sufficient adaptability so that the company culture could incubate and execute an innovation its upper management initially resisted.

MANAGERS MUST MAINTAIN THEIR SELF-IMPROVEMENT, TOO.

We all have experienced newly minted managers who believe they have "arrived." They feel they have been certified as knowledgeable, able to direct others' affairs more effectively than the people themselves. Far from regarding their new role as requiring ongoing personal improvement, they regard it as confirmation that their learning is complete.

Such a view is entirely inconsistent with a service orientation. The more opportunity you have to serve, the more you must continually learn and grow and improve. The needs of those you serve are always changing—and the wired world affords them a new range of options—so you must evolve as never before.

As you improve yourself, and spur the improvement of your team, you sustain a virtuous cycle. As with other twenty-first-century leadership issues, doing the right thing creates a competitive advantage. John Hagel, John Seely Brown and Lang Davison make a vital point: "Talented workers join companies and stay there because they believe they'll learn faster and better than they would at other employers." Is this dangerous and destabilizing—or is it an unprecedented opportunity for ever-better service, enhancing the lives of managers, employees and customers? That's your decision.

> *Growth takes place whenever a challenge evokes a successful*
> *response that, in turn, evokes a further and different*
> *challenge. We have not found any intrinsic reason why*
> *this process should not repeat itself indefinitely....*
> —ARNOLD TOYNBEE

§

Communication has always been an essential element of leadership and management. In the twenty-first century, when consent must be earned and information is available everywhere at the click of a mouse, it's more important than ever.

The new opportunities to communicate are accompanied by unaccustomed accountability. Andy Grove, the legendary leader of Intel, provides a telling anecdote in his essay, "A Random Walk: One Man's Evolution into Leadership."

As CEO, Grove made it a point to address groups of new employees in their orientation. He would take questions from the participants. Unsurprisingly, the questions were wide-ranging. Grove explains that if his answers about a company policy gave him "discomfort," he knew "something was wrong with what we were planning to do." He added: "Nowadays, I would supplement this test by asking myself how comfortable I would be explaining the contemplated action on *The Daily Show with Jon Stewart*." Or, perhaps, even more, how comfortable he would be discussing his practices on the stormy seas of social media.

For twenty-first-century leaders, in the words of David D'Alessandro, former CEO of John Hancock Financial Services, "It's *always* showtime."

The next two chapters explore communication aspects of twenty-first-century leadership.

RECAP
MANAGEMENT: SERVE THOSE YOU WOULD LEAD

◆

Management comprises a distinct skill set.
As a manager, your primary task is to
hire, motivate and develop your employees (and others
for whom you have responsibility) as leaders.
You serve by eliciting the best possible
performance of others.

◆

Who Are You Serving?

— The sole way to achieve a lasting relationship of service with your customers is to have a corresponding relationship with your employees.
— Hour-by-hour, day-by-day, your primary focus should be on serving your employees. Serving your employees effectively is your best means to achieve your ultimate concern: serving your customers.
— "If you serve your employees well, everything else—from shareholder value to customer service—will fall into place."

How Can You Best Serve?

— There is no universal management style, effective in all circumstances: "There are only ways that are appropriate for specific tasks in specific circumstances under specific conditions."
— The twentieth-century approach of command-and-control has given way to a new model. In the twenty-first century, an effective manager's service has three elements: *Inspire, Empower, Hold to Account.*

» **Inspire:** A manager inspires by fusing the vision of the organization with the mission of her team.

» **Empower:** A manager's most important task is to hire, motivate and develop leaders. Your primary mode of operation should be empowering them, not directing them.

» **Hold to Account:** Managers add value by holding employees accountable for *tasks* and *outputs*. "Never tell people how to do things. Tell them what to do, and they will surprise you with their ingenuity."

Are You Making Your Unique Contribution?

— "The only position you can count on now is best in the world."

— Employees are increasingly "at will." So, too, employers are increasingly "at will" from the point of view of the employees. Employees with demonstrated talents have more opportunities to serve—more ways to create value—than ever before.

— To prevail in the "war for talent," enterprises must strive to create relationships of love with employees as with customers.

— An ideal is a *ménage a trois* of management, employees and customers.

— Treating employees with respect in a loving, durable relationship is essential (as in life, tending to a vital relationship may necessitate overlooking or forgiving disappointing behavior).

— Just as managers must ensure that their enterprise is serving customers better than anyone else, they must also ensure that their own service is focused on what they can do more effectively than anyone else.

— Managers are the stewards of internal and external relationships vital to organizational success.

What Are You Learning?

— Managers must ensure that their enterprise "is a learning and teaching institution."
— Improvement must be customer-centered, linking the ménage a trois of enterprise, employees and customers.
— To enable their enterprises to prevail amid accelerating "creative destruction" in the globalized economy, managers must initiate ongoing change.
— Mistakes and missteps are inevitable. You should render them experiments, learning opportunities. How mistakes are defined and measured, penalized or rewarded, are ultimately important management decisions. Just as "objective" metrics are derived from a series of judgments, so, too, how you will use metrics to manage mistakes is based on judgment.

PREPARE TO SERVE

Who Am I Serving? Who are you serving as a manager? How do you evaluate other managers? To what extent have you served your teams effectively? Have you had a third party review your answers?

How Can I Best Serve? How do you determine how you can best serve your employees? Are you serving by *Inspiring, Empowering, Holding to Account*? How do you receive feedback on the relationships involved? Over the course of an hour, a day, even a week, ask yourself, before speaking to anyone with whom you are working: *How Can You Best Serve This Person?*

Am I Making My Unique Contribution? Do your employees regard their work experience as uniquely beneficial to them? On what do you base your opinion? Considering how you spend your time as a manager, do you focus on those areas where you can serve better than anyone else? Review your calendar for the past month. Do you find areas where others—such as your direct reports—can serve equally well or better than you? If so, can you transfer those tasks? If not, why not? Conversely, are others of a higher organizational rank doing tasks you could handle as well or better?

What Am I Learning? How are you making your organization a learning enterprise? How has your enterprise improved and grown in the past year? Past two years? Past five years? What are your metrics for continuous organizational improvement? How are you growing and improving as a manager? Do you encourage and reward experimentation and risk-taking? Or do you and your organization tend to respond to circumstances imposed by others?

5

Serve through
Effective Communication

All the world's a stage, and all the men and women merely players. They have their exits and their entrances, and one man in his time plays many parts.

—WILLIAM SHAKESPEARE

Once a human being has arrived on this earth, communication is the largest single factor determining what kind of relationships he makes with others and what happens to him.

—VIRGINIA SAFIR

[T]o transfer the point of concentration outside of yourself, is a big battle won.

—SANFORD MEISNER

A young state senator from the Midwest, in Los Angeles for the 2000 Democratic National Convention, was departing earlier than he had planned.

He had been unable to obtain a pass to the convention floor. He was thereby barred from moving freely among the movers and shakers who might advance his prospects. Adding insult to injury, his credit card was rejected when he sought to rent a car. This followed his overwhelming defeat, several months earlier, for his party's nomination for a U.S. House seat.

Four years later, that little-known state legislator delivered the keynote address to the Democratic National Convention in Boston. Because of his dazzling oratory, Barack Obama was immediately, universally recognized as a new star in the political firmament.

Three months later, in November 2004, Obama was elected to the U.S. Senate. Before the end of his second year in Washington, he had begun his presidential campaign. Without a deep record of accomplishment, Obama's ascent was based almost entirely on his communication skills.

In September 2008 another star was born. Alaska Governor Sarah Palin was a relative unknown when John McCain tapped her to be the first female vice-presidential nominee on the Republican ticket. Palin was forty-four years old. Like Obama, her public record was thin compared to most first-tier national aspirants. She had served as mayor of Wasilla, Alaska. She had upended her state's political establishment, defeating an incumbent Republican governor (and longtime U.S. senator)—a mere two years earlier. For five days after the surprise announcement of her selection, political opponents and many in the press flayed Palin with scurrilous rumors and full-fledged attacks on her credibility and competence. Some floated the possibility that she would be forced to withdraw from the ticket in disgrace.

As a result, the world tuned in expectantly to hear Palin speak to her party's national convention. Appearing undaunted by the controversy, Palin strode across the dais. Her speech was compelling, memorable in design and presentation. Notably self-assured, she did far more than merely hold her own in the most challenging circumstances.

Though their political views are quite different, Barack Obama and Sarah Palin vaulted to the highest level of national politics based on their exceptional abilities to communicate. Obama's skills would take him into the White House. They also were the basis for the Nobel Peace Prize he was awarded in the early months of his presidency, in encouraging anticipation of future achievement. In contrast, Palin's performance proved erratic as the campaign unfolded. Popular opinion of her rose and fell in large part based on her effectiveness as communicator.

Death and life are in the power of the tongue.
—PROVERBS 18-21

*Talkers have always ruled. They will continue
to rule. The smart thing is to join them.*

—BRUCE BARTON

COMMUNICATION IS CENTRAL TO LEADERSHIP

Obama and Palin follow a long tradition of American political leaders propelled to prominence on the power of a single speech.

Abraham Lincoln—a former one-term congressman and unsuccessful U.S. Senate aspirant from Illinois—cemented his national reputation with a stirring speech at the Cooper Union in New York City in 1860. In 1896 a former two-term congressman from Nebraska, thirty-six-year-old William Jennings Bryan, electrified the Democratic National Convention with his "cross of gold" speech. He walked away with the first of three Democratic presidential nominations. In 1956, first-term Massachusetts Senator John F. Kennedy won praise from another Democratic National Convention—and from millions watching on television—for his gracious concession after being passed over for the vice-presidential nomination. In 1964, Hollywood actor Ronald Reagan inspired millions with a nationally televised plea for Senator Barry Goldwater's doomed presidential candidacy. "The Speech," as it was known to Reagan's admirers, was the first step on his unprecedented path from Hollywood to the White House.

Communication is central to leadership. Every aspect of leadership—from casting a vision to managing relationships with employees, colleagues, customers, competitors and other stakeholders—is built upon a foundation of effective communication.

Twenty-three-year-old Winston Churchill marveled at the power of speech:

> Of all the talents bestowed upon men, none is so precious as the gift of oratory. He who enjoys it wields a power more durable than that of a great king. He is an independent force in the world. Abandoned by his party, betrayed by his friends, stripped of his offices, whoever can command this power is still formidable.

It is not self-regarding "presentism" to observe that there are now more avenues and opportunities for serving through communication than even Churchill could have imagined. When he wrote in 1897, a small number of individuals holding positions of authority wielded much greater power in free societies than today. In the twenty-first century, to an unprecedented extent, far more people can become "independent forces," with "formidable" power.

In the past, people in positions of authority controlled much of the "reality" presented to and experienced by others. In post-World War II America, a clique interpreted and disseminated information through a handful of broadcast media corporations. They generally looked alike and thought alike and lived alike in the environs of New York City and Los Angeles.

That coterie of institutions and individuals assumed the role of documentary producers of the nation's narrative. They transmitted their vision and version of reality through centralized technologies. There was limited reciprocal communication.

The Information Revolution is turning that world upside down. Today, individuals and groups are empowered to communicate, to an astonishing extent, on their own terms.

In the new world of communication, everyone has access to a camera and film-editing software. Anyone can create and publish a video documentary. The information monopoly held tightly by individuals and organizations in positions of authority is nearing its end.

In the twenty-first century the absence of—or even a brief lapse in—disciplined communication can have dire consequences. This is true for anyone, anywhere. It's true for CEOs of great corporations. It's true for people in marketing, sales, management or any other part of an enterprise.

Shakespeare's adage — "all the world's a stage" — has a whole new meaning in today's digital, 24/7 world.
No matter what we might wish, we're all actors on that stage.

IN THE TWENTY-FIRST CENTURY, COMMUNICATION CAN NO LONGER BE A SUPPORT FUNCTION

Given the ever-increasing importance of communication, one would expect its significance to be universally recognized. Yet time and again organizations and individuals undervalue it.

One might assume that any large twenty-first-century enterprise would make communication a central part of its decision-making process. When considering a course of action—establishing relationships through social networking online, introducing a new product, disclosing financial results, or responding to a crisis—a company would be well-advised to incorporate communication into business strategy from the start.

Many, if not most, enterprises do not follow this approach. They routinely turn to communication issues *after* strategy is set or decisions are made. They see communication primarily—or solely—as a support function. They act on the assumption they already know what's best for those they seek to serve. It's the equivalent of not listening in a conversation, simply interjecting one's views.

Some enterprises take an additional, intermediate step. They include communication specialists at the table from the start—as observers. The intention is that their spokespersons will be better able to present the ultimate decision. Unless communication is factored into the decisions themselves, this too is insufficient.

Many executives glibly assert that communication is everyone's task. All too often it means that no one's accountable for results.

The optimal approach for individuals or organizations in leadership roles is to make communication a *primary basis* for decisions and actions. Systematically listening to and seeking to serve numerous, empowered stakeholders—customers, shareholders, prospective investors, communities, NGOs, regulatory agencies, the financial press, bloggers—should be built in from the start.

Jack Martin, of Hill+Knowlton Strategies, urges that communication be accorded "the fifth seat" at the boardroom table, along with the familiar, longstanding representation of financial, legal, accounting and management functions.

Every corporation has some sort of communications program designed to reach "the public." But the messages transmitted are often disconnected by corporate divisions, and diluted by a lack of focus. Information disseminated by a company must support a cohesive brand in the marketplace, in the courtroom, on Wall Street, and on Capitol Hill. [Communication functions should be represented in] the CEO's inner council, ensuring that public opinion is used as a strategic asset for short- and long-range planning.

—JACK MARTIN

The urgency of this task becomes apparent when you look at what today's CEOs do, hour-by-hour, day-by-day. Their work is converging with that of high-level government executives and politicians. Often without realizing it, many companies are adopting communication approaches akin to political campaigns and governance. This is the inevitable consequence of serving ever larger audiences, and being held accountable by more stakeholders, themselves possessing independent means of communication. Twenty-first century "authority" is accompanied by 24-7 accountability.

CEOs are not the only ones who must comprehend all their actions as communications—and all communications as having consequences. Even the largest enterprises can be affected by communications arising from, or relating to employees far down the formal chain of command.

Consider the American military. Young soldiers in combat zones in Iraq and Afghanistan—many of whom are mere months out of high school—know they are subject to being filmed at any moment. The press is everywhere. Television networks and websites seek film clips from anyone willing to share them. Individual citizens and fellow soldiers have the capacity to record events. Just as the brass are ceding operational authority to those closer to the front lines, many are realizing that their traditional near-monopoly on public communication is over (though, to be sure, resistance remains, as reflected in the Marines' ill-conceived attempts to ban use of Twitter, Facebook, and other social media).

In a sign of the convergence marking twenty-first-century leadership, Admiral Michael G. Mullen, former chairman of the Joint Chiefs of Staff, enunciates a position comparable to that of Jack Martin in the private sector: "Strategic communication should be an enabling function that guides and informs our decisions…. To put it simply, we need to worry a lot less about *how* to communicate our actions and much more about *what* our actions communicate."

In twenty-first-century communication, truly everybody can be a leader, because everybody can serve. You really have no choice. Peter Drucker long ago explained that everyone, at every moment, is marketing. His prescient insight is turbocharged today. Through the internet and digitization, every action you take can have consequences.

This presents breathtaking opportunities for those who embrace it. Yet even the most intelligent and articulate individuals and enterprises are at risk if they ignore the changes, vainly clinging to familiar ways and vanishing prerogatives.

◆

Everyone faces unprecedented opportunities—and challenges—in the new world of twenty-first-century communication. Any interaction with customers or other stakeholders can be turned into a relationship at their discretion—and they possess unprecedented capacities for communication and consent. Individuals and enterprises accustomed to one-way communications within their prerogative can be especially vulnerable to disruption.

◆

LARRY SUMMERS' LESSONS IN LEADERSHIP COMMUNICATION

In January 2005, Lawrence Summers, then president of Harvard, inadvertently ignited a media firestorm. It initially distracted and ultimately destroyed his administration over the course of the following year.

The conflagration was sparked by Summers' own words. Summers was not speaking at a major public event. He was not speaking to a notably influential audience. He was not speaking about his ambitious, controversial agenda of educational reform for the nation's most widely recognized university.

The Harvard president had chosen to speak "off the record" (that is, without public attribution) to an audience of academics of the National Bureau of Economic Research. His topic was the underrepresentation of women in scientific positions in academia, compared with their percentage of the population.

Summers rambled through a self-indulgent exploration of gender issues and science in society. He related his observations of his young daughters' invincible preference for role-play as mothers rather than truck operators. He noted the underrepresentation of Catholics in investment banking. He made light of the dearth of white players in the National Basketball Association.

Summers—renowned for exacerbating resistance to his Harvard administration because of his overreliance on a conspicuously limited array of interpersonal skills—thereby set off an uproar among many professors, students and alumni. This preternaturally proud man subsequently was forced to flagellate himself pathetically at a faculty meeting that, according to reports, resembled a Stalinist show trial of the 1930s. Harvard's discomfiture became an occasion for commentary from Rush Limbaugh and Bill O'Reilly, to Time and the Wall Street Journal.

How did Summers, indisputably intelligent and well-spoken, unleash a communications disaster that many less gifted individuals never would have approached?

The answer is clear: he was serving himself. Summers' preface to his fateful remarks tells the tale:

> I asked Richard, when he invited me to come here and speak, whether he wanted an institutional talk about Harvard's policies toward diversity or whether he wanted some questions asked and some attempts at provocation, because I was willing to do the second and *didn't feel like* doing the first. And so we have agreed that *I am speaking unofficially* and not using

this as an occasion to lay out the many things we're doing at Harvard to promote the crucial objective of diversity. [emphasis added]

Summers, whose words received public attention solely because he represented a great institution as its titular head, declared that on this occasion he would *not* serve those he represented. Rather than deploy his presence and words in service of his agenda for Harvard, he elected to amuse himself and his immediate audience.

Summers simply disregarded who he was serving. It was all about Larry.

The subsequent fusillade of criticism was catastrophic for the far-reaching goals Summers held dear for his tenure as president. In the minds of many the imbroglio raised questions about the innate capacity of male economics professors to serve in positions of institutional authority.

When he resigned a year later, commentators cited the controversy over his comments on women's roles as the "tipping point" in the steep downward trajectory of his administration.

By his self-imposed travails in leadership communication, Summers may have provided more valuable instruction to more people than he ever could have done in a Harvard classroom.

WHO ARE YOU SERVING?

Had Larry Summers asked himself this question in advance of his fateful speech he likely would have remained president of Harvard indefinitely. He also might have been selected, rather than passed over, for the position of secretary of the treasury a few years later. Instead, he was tapped for an advisory role, without primary management or public communication responsibility.

Had Summers been just another Harvard professor, shielded by lifetime tenure from any controversies his words might occasion, his comments would have entirely defensible. It would have been a question of freedom of expression vs. "political correctness."

Summers was not serving as a professor. The issue was not freedom of expression—it was leadership. He spoke as the president of one of the preeminent educational institutions in the world. Summers had the opportunity to serve with every breath he drew. He also had obligations. His public actions and utterances inevitably would be scrutinized by innumerable audiences and constituencies.

Summers' priority was serving the university itself. This included the Harvard Corporation that governs the institution, as well as students, faculty, alumni and other stakeholders.

As he spoke to the National Bureau of Economic Research he sought to limit himself to serving the audience of academics in the room. He foreswore, for the moment, his status as Harvard president. He would share some "personal" reflections.

Regrettably for Summers, the Harvard brand affords too potent a platform to be so casually cast aside. Summers doubtless thought his comments would amuse those in the room at the moment. At most, though, that would have been to serve only his immediate audience and himself.

Summers should have known better. His self-absorbed commentary and awkward wisecracks had thrown up unnecessary obstacles during prior stints of high-level government service. He should have foreseen that his words, as president of Harvard, would be transmitted by his attendees into their institutions and professional networks. Reports of his remarks—even clandestine taping or filming or texting—might well make their way to television and radio outlets, as well as newspapers and internet publishers.

Summers ultimately used this incident to improve his capacity to serve in the future. He publicly acknowledged his error: "I think it was, in retrospect, an act of spectacular imprudence. There are enormous benefits to being the leader of a major institution, but there are also costs and limitations. I thought I could have it both ways, and I was wrong."

I thought I could have it both ways [serving himself
while president of Harvard], and I was wrong.
—LAWRENCE SUMMERS

Of course, it was not only a problem "in retrospect." It all could have been avoided had he paused to reflect on who he was serving.

Anyone speaking must first consider what audiences they're serving. A larger leadership role means a greater number of audiences.

The prospective significance and consequences of the communication rises accordingly. It may require sophistication to take into account the divergent needs of various groups, crafting a message to reach multiple stakeholders in a single speech or piece of writing.

This can be seen in any communication situation. If you seek to communicate effectively with CEOs, you must focus on what concerns them, understanding their backgrounds and the demands they face. The same is true whether you are communicating to middle managers, sales teams, sports teams, the military, or a community or spiritual group.

The first and fundamental question to ask yourself at every moment of any communication is:
Who Are You Serving?

To the extent that would-be leaders do not focus on serving their audiences unreservedly, they are acting in a self-interested way.

GET OUTSIDE YOURSELF—WORK FROM THE OUTSIDE-IN.

To succeed in communication, you must strive to move beyond *inside-out* thinking, replacing it with an *outside-in* approach. You must transcend *self*-consciousness, achieving *audience*-consciousness. That is the "secret" to which the legendary twentieth-century acting teacher Sanford Meisner refers in an epigram to this chapter.

This perspective is paramount in public speaking.

Numerous opinion polls confirm that public speaking is among the greatest fears of millions across the world. Manifestly strong and accomplished men and women find their hands trembling, their mouths gone dry and their brains frozen….and that's when they're facing a crowd of well-wishing colleagues and supportive friends earnestly awaiting their words. Most people can only imagine what it means to face an overtly hostile crowd.

Polls have found that
nearly half of Americans
list public speaking as one
of their greatest fears.

As Jerry Seinfeld puts it, "At funerals, most people would rather be the one in the casket than the one giving the eulogy."

The most timid individual finds vocal power if she sees a fire in a theatre, or if he needs to warn his straying child away from an oncoming automobile. Others find that they can mimic or impersonate others to much greater effect than they can speak on their own—and many professional actors are surprisingly shy or reserved in their "roles" as themselves.

Questioner:
Did you ever overcome your serious stutter?

Actor Rowan Atkinson ("Mr. Bean"):
It comes and goes. It depends on my nerves, but it can be a problem. I find that when I play a character other than myself, the stammering disappears. That may have been some of my inspiration for pursuing the career that I did.

Just as serving yourself is the antithesis of leadership, self-consciousness is the enemy of effective performance as a communicator. If you're one who flinches at the thought of speaking in a public setting, think for a moment of your own reaction to speakers.

If you're like most people, you'll notice a common element. Whether you were moved or unimpressed, you likely did not give their performance that much thought either way.

We may be quite certain that Jones cares more for where he is going to dine, or what he has got for dinner, than he does for what Smith has done, so we need not fret ourselves for what the world says.

—WINSTON S. CHURCHILL,
QUOTING BRITISH HERO, GENERAL GORDON

To the extent you internalize that you're serving others—and take the focus away from yourself—all the performance aspects of communication fall into place.

Focusing on those you are serving, rather than yourself, is the greatest single factor in effective communication. Everything else is built on this foundation.

HOW CAN YOU BEST SERVE?

Once you've ascertained who you're serving, you're positioned to decide how you can best serve. Your goal is to engage your audience, to establish and strengthen a relationship.

THERE ARE NO UNIVERSAL "RULES" FOR EFFECTIVE COMMUNICATION.

Just as there is no single leadership "style" applicable in all circumstances, there is no generic set of communication "rules." It's all about what's effective from the standpoint of those you're serving.

To be sure, there are many "rules" you can find in books and seminars about communication. In the case of public speaking, for example, there are long lists of "rules" from professed "experts." Such experts offer the prospect of removing all anxiety and uncertainty from the speaker. They present rules to deal with everything you might think of. How long should you speak? How many points should you make to convey information? What kinds of words should you use? How should the audience participate? Should you rely on PowerPoint or other visual aids? If so, how? Should you stand behind a podium? Should there be handouts? If so, when should they be supplied? How should you dress? How much should you speak about yourself or your own experiences? Should you arrive early? Should you linger afterward? Should there be a question and answer period?

These and many other questions can seem daunting—and never-ending!—*if you focus on yourself as the speaker*. On the other hand, when you forget yourself, strive to serve your audience, any situation becomes crystal clear. The more you aim to serve, the more you will transcend the limits of your own knowledge and experience. As you connect with your listeners, you will draw unforeseen strength, tapping into their thoughts, motivations, emotions and experiences.

For example, how long should you speak? There is no unalterable "rule," the "experts" notwithstanding. It depends entirely on your audience. Some specialists may expect a forty-minute talk; children's attention might be hard to hold for more than a few moments. John F. Kennedy, Ronald Reagan and Mark Twain, extraordinarily effective public speakers all, each concluded that twenty minutes was about all a general audience should be expected to sit in what Reagan called "respectful silence."

To determine how to communicate, you need to know what your audience expects. Knowledge? Inspiration? Motivation? Confidence? A vision for the future? Reassurance of your character or judgment? In some cases, an audience might have little concern for what a speaker says, but intense curiosity about her character, as discerned from her presence and presentation.

Experts relying on "rules" rather than principles can offer as many rules as there are situations. The problem is that the situations are always changing. Technologies and audience expectations evolve. Such manuals can never be complete. Instead, if you focus on serving, you can bring your individuality to bear, using your empathetic understanding of your audiences to craft compelling communications.

HONOR YOUR AUDIENCE.

Your intended audiences decide how you can best serve. They constitute the sole determinant of your success or failure in a communication.

*Eloquence is the power to translate a truth into language
perfectly intelligible to the person to whom you speak.*

—RALPH WALDO EMERSON

To know how best to serve your audience, you must strive, as far as possible, to put yourself in their place. You must comprehend how your communication will add value from their point of view.

You might deliver what you regard as a well-crafted speech or blog entry—but it cannot be considered a "success" if the intended audience rejects it.

The *Los Angeles Times* reported a humorous example along these lines:

> Kindergarten kids in ritzy L.A. suburb Calabasas have been coming home and talking about the "weird man" who keeps coming to their class to sing "scary" songs on his guitar. The "weird" one turns out to be Bob Dylan, whose grandson…attends the school. He's been singing to the kindergarten class just for fun, but the kiddies have no idea they're being serenaded by a musical legend—to them, he's just Weird Guitar Guy.

In the same vein, the *Washington Post* conducted an experiment demonstrating that even the best performance in the world will fall flat if it's not in sync with the audience.

During a wintry, early morning rush hour, the dynamic violin virtuoso Joshua Bell delivered an impromptu recital in a Metro station in the nation's capital. There was nothing to distinguish him from any other busker at work. More than a thousand people passed by during his spirited rendition of classics on a Stradivarius.

Seven people paused briefly to experience the performance. Twenty-seven dropped money into his plate—leaving a grand total of $32. The *Post* asked: "IF A GREAT MUSICIAN PLAYS GREAT MUSIC BUT NO ONE HEARS… WAS HE REALLY ANY GOOD?"

Joshua Bell was, surely, really good in a technical sense—but his performance was not about serving the audience in the Metro station. Bell was serving the Post reporter, the Post's audience and himself. In that sense he succeeded spectacularly.

Award-winning actor William H. Macy sums up:

I really believe in the audience. I started in the theater, and at the end of the day, we always said, "There's one god, and that's the audience." They're never wrong. You either believe in the audience or you don't. I've done a lot of movies, but *Wild Hogs* is the one that everyone's seen me in.... I can't look at the audience and say, "Well, you're wrong because I've done better work or more sophisticated work." If that's what they like, then that's what they like. They're never wrong.... Everything is based on them.

The value you place on your performance may differ significantly from the value your audience places on it. The audience's evaluation is determinative.

LISTEN, LISTEN, LISTEN.

The only way you can learn how best to serve an audience is to listen to them, to learn from them.

It is striking that there are innumerable training opportunities in speaking and writing—but next to none in listening.

It is simply not possible to serve effectively as a communicator without highly developed listening skills. That means transferring your focus from yourself to truly taking in the entirety of others' verbal and nonverbal signals.

> *When people talk, listen completely. Most people never listen.*
> —ERNEST HEMINGWAY

William K. Reilly, the widely respected former administrator of the U.S. Environmental Protection Agency, observes that the people who need to listen the most—individuals holding high positions in organizations—often listen the least. Perhaps this is a holdover from the past, when "leading" from high positions was more akin to dominating than serving.

> *Many leaders don't listen, and it is one of the greatest methods*
> *we have of learning. You need to listen to those under your*
> *supervision and to those who are above you. We'd all be a lot*
> *wiser if we listened more—not just hearing the words, but*
> *listening and not thinking about what we're going to say.*
>
> —JOHN WOODEN

For any audience—most especially larger audiences—listening should open the path to informed imagination and empathy.

Ronald Reagan's emergence as "the Great Communicator" was based, in no small part, on his highly cultivated capacities to listen and observe. These are workaday tools for professional actors. They enable them to keep their audience in the front of their minds at all times.

Looking back late in life, Reagan explained that a "secret" of his success was his custom of imagining he was speaking to the people he recalled from a neighborhood barber shop when he was a young man. He could see them in his mind's eye. He could relate to their outlook. He did not seek to impress them with big words or unnecessarily complicated concepts—that would have been serving himself. He sought to serve them, to take part in a conversation that flowed back and forth without distraction.

> *When I was a sports announcer, I learned something*
> *about communicating with people I never forgot.*
> *I had a group of friends in Des Moines and we all happened*
> *to go to the same barber. My friends would sometimes sneak*
> *away from their offices or other jobs when I was broadcasting a*
> *game and they'd get together at the barbershop to listen to it...*
> *I'd try to imagine how my words sounded to them and*
> *how they were reacting, and I'd adjust accordingly and*
> *spoke as if I was speaking personally to them.*

There was a specific audience out there I could see
in my mind, and I sort of aimed my words at them.
[W]hen I'm speaking to a crowd—or on television—
I try to remember that audiences are made up of individuals
and I try to speak as if I am talking to a group of friends...
not to millions, but to a handful of people in
a living room...or a barbershop.

—RONALD REAGAN

Reagan constantly sought to listen and learn to enhance his communications. His longtime aide Michael Deaver recalled how Reagan differed from other professional speakers. Many routinely cut short their social time with hosts or audiences. They skip introductory cocktail events and even the dinners preceding their speeches. Reagan made it a point to arrive early. He sought opportunities to mingle with attendees. This yielded the raw material he could use to engage his audiences on matters closest to their heart.

There is one approach that invariably yields valuable information on how best to serve: ask questions. Before producing any spoken or written communication, don't hesitate to ask question after question, to learn, as far as possible, what your audience would regard as a successful performance—and why.

◆

In preparing any written or spoken communication,
don't hesitate to ask numerous questions in advance
to determine how you can best serve. Your audience,
and those representing it, may have ideas altogether
different from what you would have anticipated.

Collaborative preparation may result in a product more
compelling than you or they independently envisioned.

◆

ENGAGE YOUR AUDIENCE.

There are as many ways to engage your audiences as there are audiences. Reagan's connection was enhanced by including extended question and answer sessions following his speeches. Some questions would reveal that his presentation had not conveyed the points he intended. Others pointed toward unforeseen concerns of his listeners. Still others suggested an intensity of viewpoint that might not have been clear in polls or other, more formal, soundings of public opinion.

In his 1966 run for governor of California, such question and answer sessions informed Reagan of the depth of voter sentiment about student demonstrations and the general breakdown of order throughout the University of California system. This issue, theretofore underestimated by conventional politicians and pollsters, became central to his successful campaign.

Many effective presenters engage their audiences in customized, unconventional ways. Charlotte Beers, a high-profile Madison Avenue executive, was renowned for her capacity to woo and win clients. For example, she impressed Sears Roebuck executives by taking apart and reassembling a power drill at the same time as she delivered a pitch for their business.

In the Information Age there are innumerable ways to engage your audiences. At the same time, maintaining engagement has become more challenging. People will, literally, not sit still for an extended period. Many are unaccustomed to focusing their attention more than momentarily, at least absent ongoing audio-visual stimulation. Some, especially young people, multitask with laptop computers or personal digital assistants during speeches and other presentations. If you're losing your hold over them, you may soon confront an audience using Twitter and other instant messaging to incite and exchange unfavorable, even derisive reactions in real time.

You're likely to serve your audiences better if you adapt to and incorporate such developments rather than resist them. For example, you might encourage people to text or "tweet" you during a presentation, or in a question and answer period.

The single best way to engage an audience is to supply — or suggest — an answer to a question they consider important. It may be a question they have articulated — or your presentation may point them toward an issue they are facing but previously had not framed clearly.

ONCE YOU'VE DONE YOUR HOMEWORK, FEARLESSLY EXPERIMENT WITH FORM.

As the examples of real-time communication suggest, flexibility and adaptability are as important in this area as in others. Attempting to adhere to what's in your own comfort zone would be to serve yourself. Memorably effective communications tend to have been innovative, even unconventional in their original context. This is true of one of the most influential: Abraham Lincoln's Gettysburg Address.

Lincoln's masterwork has long since been rendered conventional. It's a part of the American canon. It's a trove of ready quotations for leaders in various sectors and situations, worldwide. It has been memorized by generations of American schoolchildren.

At the time it was delivered, Lincoln's speech was highly unconventional.

The president was not the primary speaker at the consecration of the Gettysburg battlefield site on Thursday, 19 November 1863. That distinction was accorded the venerable Massachusetts politician Edward Everett. Everett was widely regarded as the nation's greatest orator.

As might be expected of a former governor, U.S. secretary of state, candidate for vice president, ambassador to Great Britain and president of Harvard University, Everett's oration was erudite, ornate. Consistent with the significance and solemnity of the occasion, his address found context and inspiration in centuries of history and literature. It was replete with familiar reference points and subtle allusions, ranging from ancient Greek and Roman history to the Bible and Shakespeare.

Everett used his two months of preparation well. The press reported his oration was powerfully delivered. He maintained the audience's rapt attention for fully two hours.

Lincoln was a study in contrast to the keynote speaker. He was not college-educated. He was self-taught in the Western canon. Having been invited a mere two weeks prior to the event, Lincoln's direct preparation would be much less than Everett's. Unlike Everett, despite the protocol due a president, Lincoln was asked only to offer a "few appropriate remarks."

Lincoln did not attempt to match Everett's virtuoso performance, at least on its own terms. The president, like Everett, wrote his own speech. Beyond that, there was little similarity. Lincoln's presentation was direct in message, taut in construction. It was a mere ten sentences, 271 words. It was delivered in Lincoln's characteristic, unprepossessing monotone, tinged with a Midwestern twang.

It was reported that the Lincoln address engendered a tepid response from the audience on hand, but the performance element was not paramount. He was reaching out to a multiplicity of audiences. Among them were many people who would read the entire speech in newspaper reprints (made accessible because of its brief, austere format, easy to fit on a single page).

The Gettysburg audience may not have comprehended the situation, but Edward Everett did. Everett may have scored the most points that day—but Lincoln changed the game.

I should be glad, if I could flatter myself that I came as near the central idea of the occasion in two hours, as you did in two minutes.
—EDWARD EVERETT, IN LETTER TO LINCOLN

How far should you experiment with form? The answer can only be derived from a thorough understanding of your audience. The deeper your comprehension, the more you can improvise with confidence. A knowledgeable third party's opinion can be invaluable in attaining perspective.

Today, vast numbers of relevant technologies are opening vistas of creativity in design and presentation. Audience expectations are correspondingly high.

Garr Reynolds, in his invaluable guide, *Presentation Zen*, limns the creativity that can result from cross-fertilizing various forms of storytelling.

For presentations, he suggests people move away from traditional modes such as PowerPoint. Documentary films include elements which can be used in live presentations, such as narration, interviews, still images and on-screen text. Reynolds notes that comics can be "amazingly effective at partnering text and images that together form a powerful narrative which is engaging and memorable."

Your readiness to experiment with form reflects your commitment to meet the needs of those you're serving.

Graphic design can be compelling. A symbol—representing an idea, an ideal, even good and evil—can convey a fact or evoke an emotion. An outstanding resource, including many historical examples, is Edward R. Tufte, *The Visual Display of Quantitative Information*.

MAKE IT BIGGER BY MAKING IT SIMPLER.

To engage large audiences, and to move people's emotions as well as intellect, communications must be crafted for simplicity.

When you strive for simplicity, you can reach others' hearts and minds in the places we all share. The most important messages in life—in all our lives—are simple, because they are universal.

The challenge is to pare and hone critical messages, to convey complex information reliably and accurately. As Einstein said, "Make everything as simple as possible, but not simpler."

Threading that needle requires forethought and informed, unswerving audience focus. Lincoln's Gettysburg Address transmits complex, significant, controversial messages through a methodically crafted, disciplined, polished presentation.

Four score and seven years ago our fathers brought forth on this continent, a new nation, conceived in Liberty, and dedicated to the proposition that all men are created equal.

Now we are engaged in a great civil war, testing whether that nation, or any nation so conceived and so dedicated, can long endure....

The world will little note, nor long remember what we say here but it can never forget what they did here. [T]his nation, under God, shall have a new birth of freedom. [G]overnment of the people, by the people, for the people, shall not perish from the earth.

Lincoln's words are moving to adults and memorable by children. They point to lofty aims, credibly justifying the inconceivable brutality, loss and intractability of the Civil War at a palpably dark, uncertain moment. He stood on the cold, damp ground, an ungainly, unlikely warlord whose decisions dispatched hundreds of thousands of his countrymen to mayhem and death. Lincoln's hard-earned, painstakingly crafted simplicity engaged audiences then and now.

———————————— ◆ ————————————

*Effective communications engage audiences.
A communicator may offer a recital reflecting talent and
preparation, but not necessarily engage an audience.
Edward Everett's speech at Gettysburg was appreciated much
as one might appreciate a virtuoso musical performance.
Lincoln, in contrast, may not have made a comparable
impression on the scene, but his message endured, engaging
more and more audiences at many more times and places.*

———————————— ◆ ————————————

Lincoln understood that the larger the audience—and the more that is asked of them—the greater the need for simplicity in communication.

Theodore Roosevelt was a compelling, self-taught communicator. TR explained that communications to mass audiences rely on the directness of posters, not the subtlety of etchings. This was not to rationalize limitations on Roosevelt's part. TR was able to rouse—or tame—a crowd of roughnecks in the mining country of the West, or, as the occasion demanded, challenge scholars as president of the American Historical Society.

The quest for simplicity disciplines the crafting of the messages. Home Depot CEO Frank Blake believes "clearer and simpler is better." He quotes his mentor Jack Welch's leadership dictum: "Complexity is not your friend."

Blake recalls receiving management signals during his service in the Reagan administration. Reagan's messages were unmistakable. No matter what their location in the vast organization chart of the federal bureaucracy, Blake found that everyone had a pretty good idea of what Reagan wanted done: *strengthen defense, cut taxes and regulations*. Blake follows the same approach today as he steers Home Depot through the stormy seas of economic, financial and management challenges.

> *Complexity is not your friend.... Clearer and simpler is better.*
> —JACK WELCH AND FRANK BLAKE

Achieving simplicity on the other side of complexity can be demanding. It tends to require extensive preparation, collaboration and pre-testing with your audiences.

Among the key elements:

—**Simple Words are Best**. Winston Churchill summed it up: "Broadly speaking, the short words are the best, and the old words best of all."

> *He has never been known to use a word that might send a reader to the dictionary.*
> —WILLIAM FAULKNER ON ERNEST HEMINGWAY

> *Poor Faulkner. Does he really think big emotions come from big words? He thinks I don't know the ten-dollar words. I know them, all right. But there are older and simpler and better words, and these are the ones I use.*
> —ERNEST HEMINGWAY ON WILLIAM FAULKNER

Author Adam Gopnik reports that Lincoln told an acquaintance in 1860: "Among my earliest recollections I remember how, when a mere child, I used to get irritated when anybody talked to me in a way I could not understand." As a result, Lincoln sought to express himself "in language plain enough, as I thought, for any boy I knew to comprehend."

—Simple Words Can Convey Great Meaning. Churchill declared: "All great things are simple, and many can be expressed in single words: freedom, justice, honor, duty, mercy, hope."

Choice of words is significant. Today, when so many people use words carelessly, it can be all the more important.

According to British writer Virginia Woolf:

[The] power of suggestion is one of the most mysterious properties of words. Everyone who has ever written a sentence must be conscious or half-conscious of it. Words, English words, are full of echoes, of memories, of associations—naturally. They have been out and about, on people's lips, in their houses, in the streets, in the fields, for so many centuries. And that is one of the chief difficulties in writing them today—that they are so stored with meanings, with memories, that they have contracted so many famous marriages.

A word may be heard to have entirely different meanings depending on context. As a communicator, you should comprehend it from the vantage point of your audience.

One approach is to aim for legalistic precision of expression. The downside is you may thereby limit the space for play of a listener's imagination.

Alternatively, you might aim for the greater room to roam afforded by the calculated ambiguity of poetry. The risk is that your message may be diluted or misunderstood.

The genius of the Gettysburg Address arises from Lincoln's applying his lawyerly skills of drawing fine distinctions in concert with his capacity for poetic expression.

—**Pare Words to the Greatest Extent.** Hemingway once challenged an editor to open to any page of one of his books and find *any* word that could be removed without damage to the text. *That* is concision.

In his classic *On Writing*, William Zinsser exhorts: "Be grateful for every word you can cut."

Lincoln's economy of words was methodical. He famously mocked another speaker: "He can compress the most words into the smallest ideas of any man I ever met."

The assistance of a skilled editor can be invaluable in excising words which are extraneous, inexact, confusing, or to which a writer is unduly attached.

—**Repeat, Repeat, Repeat.** If you seek to convey information to a large audience or large number of audiences, you must be prepared to repeat, repeat, repeat. Thoughtful simplicity and ruthless concision help make this effective. In the Information Age, when people are bombarded with communications, repetition retains potency.

> *If you have an important point to make, don't try to be subtle or clever. Use a pile driver. Hit the point once. Then come back and hit it again. Then hit it a third time—a tremendous whack.*
> —WINSTON S. CHURCHILL

The necessity to repeat messages within a communication—and to repeat an entire communication—can be daunting. It's a challenge familiar to professional actors. You can use the repetition to improve, refining the performance that your audiences experience. You can wring out any lingering self-consciousness to reach the next level of engagement.

For example, you can experiment with voice modulation and enunciation. You can modify timing. You can practice pauses. You can customize otherwise identical presentations for various occasions.

The key, as ever, is to strive to serve your audience. In most circumstances, the messages you're delivering aren't repetitive to them. Even if they are, your presentation need not be.

USE STORIES TO MAKE INFORMATION "STICKY" AND ENGAGE YOUR AUDIENCE.

Every communication tells a story. People tend to organize their thoughts, to comprehend their experiences, through stories.

Many of the most effective communicators are renowned storytellers. Ronald Reagan, like his salesman father Jack, was gifted in this regard. He took it seriously, collecting jokes and humorous anecdotes for every occasion. This was not only to amuse his audiences. It was a keystone of the substantive effectiveness of his presentations.

Lincoln's Gettysburg Address was audacious exercise in purposeful storytelling. Entire books have been devoted to interpreting those ten sentences.

Against the backdrop of the ongoing Civil War, Lincoln was communicating that the nation's foundational document was not the revered Constitution of 1789. Instead, the Declaration of Independence should be viewed as the ultimate source of the American notion of government. Familiar debates about the Constitution—and its contradictory, conditional acceptance of slavery—would be superseded. The Civil War would resolve the constitutional infirmity. The way forward would be found in the earlier ideals, the first principles, of the Declaration.

Lincoln was simultaneously unveiling the scaffolding that he would elaborate in his Second Inaugural address on 4 March 1865. This was another masterpiece of brevity. With unforgettable, balanced phrasing and imagery—"with malice toward none, with charity for all"—the president offered a hand of reconciliation to the Southern states. The two narratives—the rationale for war, reconciliation in peace—were interlaced. Each was part of the broader, united vision flowing from his pen, from his imagination. Lincoln's craft resulted in many listeners accepting his narrative initially as inevitable, later as commonplace.

Stories can be especially suitable for conveying complex information. Ideally, they can be passed along from audience to audience, extending the reach of an important message, enhancing it through the give-and-take of subsequent conversations and iterations.

Anne Mulcahy, former CEO of Xerox, emphasizes the importance of storytelling to her leadership. Noting that employees were concerned about the future of the company at a turbulent time, Mulcahy enlisted their participation in creating the story of their future.

> We wrote a *Wall Street Journal* article, because they had been particularly nasty to us, dated five years out. It was about where we could be if we really stood up to the plate. And people loved it. No matter where I go, people pull that article out. They personalized it.

Mulcahy adds that stories are found throughout organizations. They can create momentum, enabling individuals at every level, across every function, to participate, to find ways they can add value. She concludes: "It's much more powerful than the precision or elegance of the [business] strategy."

Stories can be powerful vessels to convey information. They can be the means by which information is translated into action, bringing to bear the energies and thoughts of others as they gather force and break out into multitudes of subsequent conversations.

RESIST CROSS-PRESSURES AGAINST SIMPLE OR DIRECT COMMUNICATION.

Not everyone will react favorably to the simplicity that marks effective communication with general or diverse audiences.

Some sophisticates and intellectuals presume that knowledge not expressed is knowledge not possessed. Even if they concur with your argument, they may dismiss the capacities of a communicator whose presentation is engineered toward general audiences.

Some communicators are thereby enticed to alter their approach. This poses the danger of serving yourself rather than your audience.

Robert Kyosaki, author of the fabulously popular *Rich Dad, Poor Dad* series, offers a memorable reminder for communicators: *Do you want to be the best writer—or do you want to write a bestseller?*

◆

Individuals unaccustomed to being interviewed often become separated from their audience. Reporters may browbeat or belittle interviewees. They may be tempted to respond with demonstrations of their intelligence or erudition. In so doing, they may serve themselves, serve the reporter—and quite possibly not serve their intended audiences.

◆

[Here's] the most important lesson you will ever learn about being interviewed. Ignore the question you're asked and make your best argument. Your aim isn't to please the interviewer but to influence the audience.

—WILLIAM F. BUCKLEY, JR.

The need for simplicity—from the vantage point of the audience—encompasses your medium as well as your message. Your message must be readily accessible. Engaging people of diverse socio-economic backgrounds and generations may suggest a variety of approaches. Some may be reached best by telephone, others by internet; some by snail mail, some by email; some by words, some by music; some by Power Point, some by words spoken face-to-face. Some may be reached best through a customized combination.

Zappos, for example, creates extraordinary value by integrating a self-contained internet experience with extensive telephone-based customer service. The result, as intended, is notably deep relationships, built around customer preferences (the flexibility, speed and information density of the internet for orders; the personal touch of live, unhurried telephone service to deal with an individual customer's problems, concerns or special circumstances).

> *The more elaborate our means of communication,*
> *the less we communicate.*
> —JOSEPH PRIESTLEY

PREPARE, PREPARE, PREPARE...THEN PREPARE SOME MORE.

You would not presume to speak to an audience in a foreign nation without extensive, carefully tailored preparation. You would consider what language would be used. You would study cultural norms and nuances. You would understand that you must consult with others to get it right. Having focused on serving your audience in an intelligent, methodical manner, you would succeed brilliantly.

Closer to home, many people assume they can rustle up a presentation based solely on their preexisting knowledge and experience. Some give no more forethought to a speech than they would to a casual conversation at their neighborhood Starbucks. They are giving little or no serious consideration to those they are serving.

Preparation is an essential element enabling you to serve to the greatest possible extent.

When you examine the practices of great communicators, you invariably find extensive planning and rehearsal. The best strive for presentations which appear seamless, natural. Ronald Reagan often said he aimed "to make it look easy."

That does not mean you should aspire to having no anxiety about a speech. Jitters, dry mouth, brain freeze, even all-out stage fright have stalked stage actors as renowned as the twentieth-century titan, Sir Laurence Olivier. You can make it easier through preparation. Repeated, excellent practice can help you overcome any lingering preoccupation with yourself. You can emerge less distracted, better able to serve your audience.

Mal Evans [The Beatles' road manager] had always said that
the Beatles as a group were nervous before shows. "It shows that
they are real stars. But that's what it's all about, ya' know.
It's a good thing, being nervous; it's a sign of a star to me."
—LARRY KANE, *LENNON REVEALED*

If anxiety detracts from your effectiveness, you may find it useful to serve—in your mind—a third party. You might dedicate your performance to someone you care about deeply—perhaps a family member or other loved one, or the memory of someone who inspires you. In every case, your goal is to get outside yourself to get closer to those you are serving.

Theodore Roosevelt added another element in preparing for major public addresses or articles: enforced self-scheduling. He would prepare an initial draft as far in advance as possible. He would place a copy in a desk drawer. He would circulate it among others who might have useful comments. Roosevelt would return to it whenever ideas rose from his subconscious, or when subsequent, relevant learning or experiences came his way. Incorporating such inputs, TR's preparatory reviews brought to bear new, fresh sets of eyes—others' and then, after an extended interval, his own. This custom enabled Roosevelt to mix more of himself, of his life, into his communications.

Paul McCartney speaks of the Beatles' taking a similar approach in their cultivation of creativity. He explains, "There's a lot of random in our songs. By the time we've taken it through the writing stage, thinking of it, playing it to the others and letting them think of bits, recording it once and deciding it's not quite right and do it again and find, 'Oh, that's it, the solo comes here and that goes there,' and bang, you have the jigsaw puzzle."

This approach requires that you overcome the procrastination inhibiting the productive creativity of many people. You must schedule your time—and hold to it—to attract and utilize such wide-ranging input. If you leave it to the last moment, you're likely to leave a lot of value unexplored and untapped.

Preparing in this way can bring forth your greatest capacities. It can give you the benefit of the second bite at the apple that otherwise could be lost by hasty drafting. You can avoid the disappointment of coming up with a brilliant idea only after the fact, what the French call *l'esprit d'escalier*, the Germans *treppenwitz*.

PREPARE TO BE FLEXIBLE ON THE SPOT.

Preparation should not metamorphose into paralysis. Paradoxically, effective preparation can displace your self-consciousness to an extent that you can react spontaneously in performance. Think of it like jazz: innovation in performance is made possible by rigorous forethought and disciplined practice.

Many things can go wrong in a presentation. The most methodical planning can be confounded. In the same vein, unanticipated opportunities may arise.

Either way, with the self-possession derived from effective preparation, you can remain open to on-the-spot adjustments. Many of the greatest speakers—Winston Churchill comes to mind—customarily planned for foreseeable contingencies such as interruptions for applause or heckling.

> *Preparation, as important as it is, is only preparation. The performance is the thing.*

In the end, preparation, as important as it is, is *only* preparation. It enables you to perform effectively. It sets the stage for audience engagement. If it results in rigidity that distracts from audience focus, it can be self-serving.

From the point of view of those you're serving, the performance is all that matters.

ARE YOU MAKING YOUR UNIQUE CONTRIBUTION?

Had Larry Summers decided—against all reason—that he would be the best person to serve as the speaker for his fateful engagement, this question would have stopped him in his tracks.

Summers' top priority in office was clear: to reform the university's curriculum and governance. A speech to the National Bureau of Economic Research was far from mission-critical.

Summers' reform agenda was sufficiently ambitious to stir numerous individuals and groups into defiant resistance. His goals were sufficiently controversial that they could be set back by any mistake, any misstep—even an otherwise reasonable action open to malicious misrepresentation. His "personal" actions and words should have been brought into alignment with his mission of service. Anything else would be irrelevant, self-indulgent and potentially destructive.

Surely others could have served better in the circumstances of the academic conference. An expert in gender studies, of which Harvard has no shortage, might have been brought in. Another economist, Summers' own discipline, would have been better suited.

This analysis does not require the benefit of hindsight. It is hard to imagine anyone credibly concluding President Summers would be the best person to speak to that group, on that subject, at that time.

Asking whether you can serve better than anyone else relates not only to management and delegation. It's also a question intended to elicit your greatest capacities as a communicator.

It's a truism that no one is indispensable. Yet, there are circumstances where one individual can add unique value.

A stirring example from our time was Senator Robert Kennedy's impromptu speech upon learning of the assassination of Martin Luther King, Jr. on the evening of Thursday, 4 April 1968.

Amid the ongoing tumult of that historic, heady year of change, Kennedy was campaigning for president in a predominantly African-American section of Indianapolis. Given the recent history of rioting in urban areas, it was foreseeable that the announcement of King's death would be, literally, incendiary. In fact, many cities across America were engulfed in flames as night fell.

Brushing aside security concerns, Kennedy was determined to share the tragic news with a largely African-American audience (this was in an era before cellular phones made general communications instantaneous).

Setting aside a draft prepared by an aide, Kennedy spoke from his own, rapidly scribbled notes:

> Ladies and gentlemen, I'm only going to talk to you just for a minute or so this evening because I have some very sad news...and that is that Martin Luther King was shot and killed tonight in Memphis, Tennessee.

Dreadful, heart-rending screams and wailing ensued. As they subsided, Kennedy continued:

> Martin Luther King...dedicated his life...to love...and to justice between fellow human beings, and he died in the cause of that effort.... My favorite poem, my favorite poet was Aeschylus. He once wrote, "Even in our sleep, pain which cannot forget falls drop by drop upon the heart...until...in our own despair, against our will, comes wisdom through the awful grace of God."

As political writer Joe Klein points out, it's hard to imagine that Kennedy's advisers would have recommended referring to Aeschylus (whoever exactly that was).

Nonetheless, Robert Kennedy, born into the highest socio-economic stratum, movingly conveyed his love to an audience largely bereft of middle-class stability, much less upper-crust privilege. His empathy was manifest.

It's difficult to conceive that at that moment, anyone other than Kennedy could have prepared and presented that speech. He reached and revealed his own essence as he dug deep to serve others.

While much of urban America burned that evening, Indianapolis remained outwardly calm.

In effective high stakes communications, the persona, the history and message of the speaker or writer meld into the unity of performance. At their best, such communications can engage the speaker at an intimate level with individuals, even if they are part of a mass audience.

WHAT ARE YOU LEARNING?

Effective service means constant improvement in this realm of leadership, as in others.

The twentieth century was marked by dramatic, rapid change in communication technology. Over the course of a lifetime one could experience the transition from mass circulation tabloids to silent films, from radio to "talking" pictures, then to television. Many individuals who mastered one medium were unable to master others.

Today's Information Age has increased the velocity of innovation even further. The only way you can reliably reach various audiences over time is through resourceful adaptability.

Any attempt to stand still risks irrelevance—with ruthless speed. Are you following notions of presentation you were taught in school? Are you maintaining approaches based on successes early in your career?

You would never wear bell bottoms and tie-dyed shirts to a presentation in the twenty-first century. Yet, many people rely on communication techniques every bit as outdated.

A notable example of changing communication techniques is seen in museums. For decades they resisted change. As a result, many lost their audiences, especially young people. Now, under the leadership of a new generation of innovators, they are incorporating multimedia capacities and establishing internet relationships with visitors, including students and others.

Countless companies are extending their internet presence. Many deploy new technologies for interactive communications with internal as well as external audiences. They are constantly refining their communication capacities, updating and deepening relationships with those they serve.

The same principles apply to any communication. Ongoing improvement is necessary; staying in place is not an option.

> Are you improving in your effectiveness as a communicator? Are you more effective than a year ago? Two years ago? Five years ago? How do you know?
>
> Are you being rewarded by the market? Are you reaching new audiences? Are you reaching rising generations? Are your messages engaging your audiences as they change over time?
>
> If someone asked you to present on a key topic of your expertise, how would your presentation differ from earlier years? Are you offering new value?

§

Communication is vital to *inform* those you would serve. Providing information to prospective customers or others may be all that is necessary. Management pioneer Peter Drucker suggests, "The aim of marketing is to know and understand the customer so well the product or service fits him and sells itself."

Nonetheless, there are many situations where you must do more than inform; you must *persuade*. There is no clear delineation on the continuum from communication which informs to that which persuades. Nonetheless, persuasive communication is sufficiently distinct to merit additional attention. That is the focus of the next chapter.

RECAP
SERVE THROUGH EFFECTIVE COMMUNICATION

◆

*Effective communication is central to leadership.
Communication was all too often viewed as a support
function in the twentieth century. In the twenty-first
century, with individuals empowered as never before,
even the most powerful organizations no longer control
communications which affect their very existence.
To be effective, organizations and individuals must
make communication a core function that
informs and drives strategy.*

◆

Who Are You Serving?

— In the twenty-first century, with 24/7 internet communications, any action can become a public communication with innumerable audiences.

— At every step in planning a communication, focus on the threshold question: *Who Are You Serving?*

— Strive to develop a *audience-consciousness* to overcome *self-consciousness*. Get outside yourself—work from the *outside-in*, rather than the *inside-out*.

How Can You Best Serve?

— There are no universal "rules" for effective communications. The preferred approach is that which best serves your intended audience, from *their* point of view.

— Honor your audience. The sole metric for determining the effectiveness of a communication is how it's received by the intended audience.

— Listen, Listen, Listen. The only way to learn how best to serve an audience is to listen to them. Ask questions to determine how you can best serve. The discussion is likely to yield results superior to what you or they could have crafted independently.

— Once you've done your homework, fearlessly experiment with form. Many of the most effective communications—including Lincoln's Gettysburg Address—were highly unconventional when initially presented. In today's Information Age there are many formats to convey information, from words to graphics to innumerable, evolving variations.

— Make it bigger by making it simpler. To be most effective, achieving the deepest relationship with the largest number of audiences, strive for simplicity. The goal is to convey the essential, shorn of unnecessary complexity.

— Follow Churchill's example:
  » Simple words are best.
  » Pare words to the greatest possible extent.
  » Repeat, Repeat, Repeat.

— Use stories to engage your audience.

— Resist cross-pressures against simple or direct communications.

— Prepare, Prepare, Prepare... Then prepare some more.

— Rehearse extensively so you can be spontaneous in performance.

Are You Making Your Unique Contribution?

— If you are in a management position, consider whether your communication goal can be as well or better achieved by someone else. Otherwise, you may disorder your priorities or simply serve yourself.

— If you can bring your life experience and persona to bear in a communication, you can make your unique contribution.

What Are You Learning?

— To cling without question to a longstanding message or mode of communication is to serve yourself. Effective communication—particularly in a time of rapid technological and cultural change—requires a commitment to ongoing improvement.

PREPARE TO SERVE

Who Am I Serving? Listen to a major address by a public figure—the president of the United States, a CEO of a major company, or another person in a high position. Focus on the question of who they are serving. List the various audiences that they are—or should be—addressing, and why. Evaluate their effectiveness. Good sources, including a variety of speakers and formats, include vsotd.com (*Vital Speeches of the Day*, and ted.com (Technology-Entertainment-Design).

— Over the course of a day, in all your conversations, ask yourself, before you speak, *Who Are You Serving?* Do you find you're learning more (improving your capacity to serve effectively) and earning goodwill, strengthening relationships?

How Can I Best Serve? As you prepare for a communication, written or spoken, how might you reposition your point of view toward others? For example, rather than anxiously replaying your concerns about how you appear, etc., seek to focus unreservedly on your task, adopting the perspective of those you're serving.

— Watch a major speech on television or computer with the sound turned off. Similarly, examine coverage of a public figure, such as the president, a CEO, or another celebrity, walking or otherwise in motion, with the sound off. How are they serving by their nonverbal communications? What messages are being sent?

Am I Making My Unique Contribution? Consider your own communications. When do you add unique value? Are there examples from your work? Are there instances from your personal life, such as a eulogy you prepared and delivered for a loved one?

What Am I Learning? Analyze your effectiveness as a communicator, posing the Four Questions. This can include not only public presentations, but also informal communications such as interoffice memoranda. In what situations are you most effective? Least effective? Why? Who are you serving in your various communications? How might you improve your performance, focusing more purposefully on the needs of those you're serving?

— Ask a trusted colleague or friend to provide feedback on your effectiveness in several communications situations. These might include giving a speech or other presentation, writing a letter, or doing business over the telephone. Follow up by reviewing what was effective and what can be improved to best serve your intended audiences.

6

Serve through Persuasion

Everyone lives by selling something.
—ROBERT LOUIS STEVENSON

The only reason to give a speech is to change the world.
—ATTRIBUTED TO JOHN F. KENNEDY

[I]n classical times when Cicero had finished speaking,
the people said, "How well he spoke," but when Demosthenes
had finished speaking, the people said, "Let us march."
**—ADLAI STEVENSON, FAVORABLY COMPARING THE POWER
OF JOHN F. KENNEDY'S ORATORY TO HIS OWN**

The highest communication function of leadership is to persuade. Persuasion is the primary means by which leaders achieve change.

In the mid-twentieth century, political scientist Richard E. Neustadt argued that persuasion, rather than the direct exercise of power, was the essence of the American presidency. Even in that more hierarchical time, individuals holding positions of authority found their capacity for independent action more circumscribed than it might appear from afar. Neustadt recounted:

> President Truman used to contemplate the problems of the general-become-President should Eisenhower win the forthcoming election. "He'll sit here... and he'll say, 'Do this! Do that!' And nothing will happen. Poor Ike—it won't be a bit like the Army. He'll find it very frustrating." ...Eisenhower evidently found it so.

This surprised many people fifty years ago. The most important "power" American presidents possess, Neustadt concluded, is the power to persuade.

It is even truer today. Twenty-first-century leadership is marked by the empowerment of a vast array of stakeholders. Consent must be earned by individuals and enterprises, including those vested with formal authority.

Persuasion is the stock-in-trade of leadership. When effective, it results in others taking actions which would not otherwise have occurred. Such actions are consistent with the vision presented by those who lead by serving. This is a golden thread through leadership in every realm, from the marketplace, to the political arena, to interpersonal relations.

Persuasive communications enable us to see familiar facts and ideas in unaccustomed ways. They enable us to discern new patterns, make new associations. In a few cases, extraordinarily effective persuasion results in people recognizing an imperative, or a truth, that impels them to disregard or overlook salient aspects of reality altogether.

A contemporary, reluctantly admiring critic of Winston Churchill suggested that his greatest contribution was "to persuade people not to look at the facts." This refers to his historic achievement in rallying the British people to fight Hitler's theretofore invincible, implacably ruthless war machine at the height of its reach in 1940. As the legendary journalist and war correspondent Edward R. Murrow observed, Churchill mobilized words into battle, in rhetoric, the art of persuasion honored since the time of Aristotle.

Leadership in all arenas relies on powers of persuasion. Arnold Schwarzenegger moved from world-class body-building, to motion pictures, into the California governorship. Schwarzenegger explains, "You have to sell, no matter what, all your life. I'm still selling now, policies, right?"

The principles underlying effective persuasive communication are the same as for general communication. Nonetheless, the applications are distinct. Every aspect of communication, connecting the performer and the audience, must have greater intensity. The relationship must be sufficiently strong to impel the receivers to make changes in their own lives.

Persuasion, as the stakes grow higher, is based on an ever-deeper relationship with those to be served. That relationship is, more than ever before, two-way. Shelly Lazarus, former CEO of the Ogilvy and Mather advertising firm, explains: "We have gone from intrusion in consumers' lives to extending an invitation to them."

Some people labor under the misapprehension that once you've "arrived," reached a high position, you no longer need to rely on persuasion. In the twenty-first century, you *never* reach a position where persuasion becomes unnecessary. In fact, such skills are ever more necessary for everyone.

The Dutch historian Pieter Geyl wrote in 1949, "History is, indeed, an argument without end." In the twenty-first century all communications become arguments without end. In our "Wiki-world," no voice is beyond questioning, no authority able to shut down discussion.

The era is long past when Walter Cronkite could, literally and figuratively, bring the curtain down with his daily valedictory: "And that's the way it is."

In the twenty-first century, you never reach a position where
persuasion becomes unnecessary. There are fewer and fewer
circumstances where formal authority can impose its will.
No one has the last word.

THE 'HARD SELL'

It's useful to start with what's not effective.

All of us have struggled to escape the clutches of a "hard sell." It may have been in a car dealership. It may have been inside your home, dealing with an overly aggressive attempt to sell a vacuum cleaner or life insurance—even a religion.

Why do we resent the hard sell? Why are we so often impelled to push back against it?

The fundamental reason: we sense *it's not really about us*. It's about the person who's attempting to persuade us. *He's serving himself.* Another's heedless assertion of self-interest, though offered in our name and wrapped in sticky-sweet flattery, stiffens our resistance.

I recently encountered a memorable example of the hard sell. It was a clear case. It was artlessly presented. It was over almost as soon as it started.

A young, strikingly beautiful woman was a fellow guest at a dinner party. Her vitality and enthusiasm invariably caught the admiring attention of the men present, and occasioned a range of reactions from other women.

Mona is a walking advertisement for fitness. She is, in fact, a personal trainer. Her physical presence is a compelling marketing tool. Any place can be a sales venue for her; everyone is a prospect.

At the dinner table, Mona's sales process started naturally enough. Appropriately for a social occasion where business is not on the agenda, it began without her prompting.

Mona was introduced as a personal fitness trainer. With the other seven attendees looking on, Michael, the CEO of a Fortune 500 company, sought her advice.

"I'd really like your thoughts. You're obviously in wonderful shape. I'd like to be, but it's so hard to find time to exercise regularly.... With family and work and being in the sandwich generation and whatever, working out just always gets pushed to the side. Plus...and I hope you don't take this personally...it's just...you know, it's just *so-o-o-o boring*! I really admire how you do it. I've recently started using an elliptical machine in my bedroom.... Betsy and I work out while we listen to the news."

There could have been no better entrée for Mona. Her authority was presumed. She was invited to exhibit her expertise. It could result in sales not only to the CEO, but to others present. What's more, the CEO is what marketing specialists call an "influencer." He could provide entrée to any number of high-end prospects.

Mona responded to this upbeat opening with an unmistakable note of discouragement. "You can *never* do that much on your own—you *must* have a trainer!... Exercise machines *never* do *any* good—no matter what you are doing on your own, a trainer can push you so much further!"

Michael smiled gently, nodding attentively while she spoke. Mona's unexpected, vehement response was somewhat jarring. Glances were exchanged across the table. Michael was worldly enough to recognize that Mona's torrent was not aimed at him personally. He chose to maintain his low-key manner.

"Are there any exercise machines you *would* recommend? Frankly, I get bored going to a gym…and it takes more time than I have most of the time, so I easily end up doing nothing…. I'd really like to find something that can occupy my mind, ideally so I can work while I exercise…. That's what appealed to me about the elliptical."

"Well," Mona continued, sighing with evident, patronizing exasperation, "You really can't *push* your body unless you're doing exercises and *nothing else*. If you're not being pushed by a trainer, it's *not* very useful anyway."

That the CEO's patience was being tried was becoming evident—evident to everyone other than Mona. His smile was shifting ever so slightly, from vaguely interested to tolerantly indulgent.

"Understanding that there might be better ways to train, if I *were* to get a machine, are there *any* you find useful? What do you use?

Mona blurted out, "I don't know.…*I* don't *sell* that kind of thing!"

There was a momentary, uncomfortable pause. The conversation between Mona and Michael trailed off like a creek into the desert. One sensed that across the table various minds were processing Mona's ultimate declaration: *So* that's *what this is about*.…

Michael's right eyebrow arched slightly but discernibly. His facial expression toward Mona was not unpleasant but implied no particular connection. Mona's would be the last words in the exchange. Michael looked down, turning his attention to his plate.

The conversation moved on. There was no further discussion of fitness or training during the long, multi-course dinner.

No sale was made. One can be sure the CEO was not inspired to tell his friends and colleagues he had encountered an outstanding new trainer.

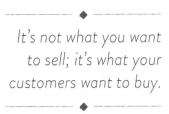

It's not what you want to sell; it's what your customers want to buy.

Mona focused intently on making a sale—and failed to serve her prospective customer.

WHO ARE YOU SERVING?

Mona's example is unusually clear. Few among us would recognize ourselves in Mona's situation; she certainly would not. Yet we all experience interactions of this sort on a regular basis.

All present could see that her focus was on making a sale. The intensity of her reactions to Michael's generic questions prompted some of the guests to wonder whether her financial circumstances were desperate.

From the point of view of her prospective customers—*and that is the only point of view that matters*—Mona's focus was on herself, not on their needs.

At first glance, that may seem unfair. Mona's a giving person. She's a single mother. She moves heaven and earth to raise a young son without financial assistance. Her motivating purpose in business is to do everything she can to make a good life for her child. That ever-present goal fuels her ambition to become a successful personal trainer.

There's no doubt that Mona means well. There's also no question that her commendable service to her family is irrelevant to nearly all her prospective customers.

Mona fell short as a sales person because she was serving herself.

Persuasive communications are most effective when there is a laser-like focus on serving the intended recipient.

It cannot be repeated too often: the prospect is not concerned with the sale, per se. In all but a few cases, the customer is not concerned with the personal life of the person offering the sale.

Customers are focused solely on having their needs met. That does not mean they are acting selfishly. After all, they, too, are seeking to serve their families and others as best they can.

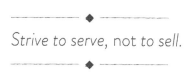

Strive to serve, not to sell.

Had Mona focused on Michael's needs, their interaction might have taken an entirely different course. She might have offered encouragement of his attempts to improve his fitness regimen. That would have conveyed her desire to serve Michael, while underscoring her capacities as a trainer.

Rather than denigrate Michael's use of the elliptical machine, Mona might have spoken of its virtues. She could have posed questions about his fitness goals. That would have drawn upon her expertise, positioning her to offer more suggestions. It might have prompted Michael to seek to follow up with her.

A benefit of striving to serve rather than sell is that it opens all participants to the potential of much greater information and creativity. It takes everyone beyond their limitations.

This applied to the dialogue between Mona and Michael. Had she offered to assist him with advice or otherwise to meet fitness goals not limited to her current role, she would be acting without regard to her perceived self-interest. Recognizing this, Michael might have begun to develop a relationship of trust with her.

Such an interaction can set the stage for innovative collaboration. Those you are serving may recognize you offer potential value you may not have considered. Had Mona served Michael effectively when they met, he might have been inspired to retain her to set up and direct a corporate wellness program. This might have expanded her business and her own capacities far beyond her plans or dreams. It surely would have enhanced her ability to serve her son.

The seller should strive to take himself out of the picture entirely. He should serve the customer unreservedly. One reason success begets success in sales and marketing—in business, politics or any other arena—is that a seller recognized as financially independent does not appear to have a "need" other than serving the customer.

> *In commerce, the suggestion that there is a bargain to be*
> *secured is far more potent than any direct appeal to buy.*
> —B.H. LIDDELL-HART, STRATEGY

Third-party endorsements and other apparently disinterested, unbiased support can be persuasive for just this reason: they shift the focus from the seller and the sale, to the customer and his needs. They can have significant impact in situations where there is a lack of familiarity or credibility. For example, many companies with mixed (or worse) histories of environmental performance seek certifications and testimonials from government agencies, not-for-profit groups, environmental advocacy groups and others trusted by the public.

The political realm presents particular challenges. Candidates for public office in contemporary America are generally self-selected. They are in the awkward position of asserting their value to voters—at the risk of making it seem more about themselves than those they would serve. For example, when Barack Obama introduced himself to Iowa caucus voters, he used the word "I" nearly one hundred times in his stump speech.

That may have been unavoidable in clearing the initial hurdles of earning credibility as a presidential contender. Nonetheless it could be viewed as self-serving. Obama sensed the danger. He directed that his victory speech in Des Moines shift to be about "us." On that occasion, Obama used the personal pronoun sixteen times.

◆

To persuade, you should, to the maximal extent, take
yourself out of the picture. Your focus should be—in ways
large and small, evident to all—on those you are serving.

◆

Communicators are often caught in a related snare: they fall in love with their own words, their own approach. What was rooted in serving their audience may slip into something subtly self-involved.

Effective communicators utilize various techniques to maintain their focus on those they're serving. As we have seen, Ronald Reagan maintained, in his mind's eye, an image of his old friends sitting around the barber shop.

Theodore Roosevelt conjured up a "typical American." TR's picture was precise—and highly attuned to the electorate of his time. He saw an older individual, likely operating a farm or a small business such as we would now call middle class. TR envisioned a man (this was prior to universal woman's suffrage) who served his nation in war, served his family always, and wanted nothing more than a "square deal" from the national government. In a similar vein, radio legend Paul Harvey aimed to make his broadcasts comprehensible and interesting to his proverbial "Aunt Betty."

Bruce Barton was a legendary twentieth-century advertising executive. He was a father of the industry that came to be known simply as "Madison Avenue." On the wall of his office at Batten, Barton, Durstine & Osborn, behind his massive desk, was a vast photograph of a crowd on the move at the Coney Island boardwalk. Barton looked to the photograph for inspiration—and to ground his creativity in the realities of those he would serve. Simultaneously, the mural, facing all who entered, sent a strong signal to his own team as well as to clients and other visitors.

To be effective in persuasion, always keep those you are serving front and center in your thoughts and imagination.

HOW CAN YOU BEST SERVE?

Having determined who you would serve, you can explore how you can best serve. This takes into account your view of your own capacities and goals. Ultimately, it should be guided by the perspective of those you would serve.

The only way to get business is to think of the
prospect's needs, of the company's needs, and
to reflect positive, admirable qualities in your own conduct.
—VASH YOUNG, TWENTIETH-CENTURY SALES LEADER

START SERVING NOW; TAP THE POWER OF RECIPROCITY.

There is no better way to initiate or strengthen a relationship of service than to give someone something they value. Ideally, this would be done with no intent other than to serve; it is about establishing a relationship entirely apart from a transaction. Depending on circumstances, this could range from a sincere compliment, to sharing an idea or information or an appropriate gift.

Such kindness, without any ulterior motive or expectation, can incline people toward trust and engender a desire to reciprocate.

The power of reciprocity can be observed in our daily lives. It's backed by scientific experimentation and evaluation. It has been validated in study after study. Robert Cialdini's classic, *Influence*, states:

> The rule for reciprocation…says that we should try to repay, in kind, what another person has provided us…The rule possesses awesome strength, often producing a "yes" response to a request that, except for an existing feeling of indebtedness, would surely have been refused.

This approach has universal power. Think of the disabled veterans' groups who send snail mail stickers pre-printed with your name and address. Or the plethora of enterprises—from realtors to environmental groups to local businesses of all kinds—who provide calendars to customers and prospects. Though sent without charge or obligation, such gifts are intended to spark reciprocation.

Simply serving others in the small ways once known as "common courtesy" can set the stage for effective persuasion. In the words of Antoine de Saint-Exupery, "True love begins when nothing is looked for in return."

ENGAGE YOUR AUDIENCE TO COMMIT TO A RELATIONSHIP BY TAKING A CONCRETE ACTION.

As those you are serving gain confidence in you, they may become amenable to taking steps indicating increasing levels of commitment. Enduring relationships can begin with small steps.

Cialdini refers to

> our nearly obsessive desire to be (and to appear) consistent with what we have already done. Once we have made a choice or taken a stand, we will encounter personal and interpersonal pressures to behave consistently with that commitment. Those pressures will cause us to respond in ways that justify our earlier decision…Indeed, we all fool ourselves from time to time in order to keep our thoughts and beliefs consistent with what we have already done or decided.

The political realm is a fountainhead of such commitments. Successful electoral campaigns create and sustain relationships with large numbers of engaged citizens. In 1981 President Reagan used television, radio, mass mailing and telephone contacts to motivate tens of thousands of citizens to contact their congressional representatives in support of his controversial tax reform agenda. Such involvement enabled Reagan to establish lasting bonds with many voters. Some took the significant step of disengaging from longstanding allegiances to the opposing political party.

The internet has taken this kind of engagement to a new level. The Obama presidential campaign used social networking to communicate on an intimate basis with millions of voters. John Heilemann reports that Obama's database at the end of his first presidential campaign included at least three million donors, two million active users and 35,000 active affinity groups on MyBarackObama.com; a million cell phone numbers from individuals asking for text messaging; and thousands of volunteers. According to Heilemann, "fully 25 percent of the people who pulled the lever for him were already connected to the campaign electronically."

As one would anticipate, subsequent campaigns absorbed these practices and gone further. The Trump and Sanders insurgencies were pioneers in deepening engagement. The right-leaning "Tea Party" and left-leaning "Resistance" movements, among many others, have continued the development of social media connections for political mobilization. Once you get started, it is hard to stop. Cialdini approvingly quotes Leonardo da Vinci, "It is easier to resist at the beginning than at the end."

A generation of young people who participated in the "Reagan Revolution" remained loyal to the Republican brand over the course of three decades. Will the social networking tools of the early twenty-first century spark corresponding loyalty in a new generation to the Democrats? Or will the speed of replication in the Information Age enable competitors to respond, make up lost ground—and pull ahead?

LISTEN TO THOSE YOU SEEK TO PERSUADE.

As essential as this is to any effective communication, it's even more important in persuasion.

How often we encounter people trying to persuade us to purchase goods or services, who transparently have been trained to present what *they* think we would want to hear. They appear to have little interest in our views, other than to alter them. Such standardized sales pitches perpetuate a disabling self-focus in those who attempt them.

> *Listen first. Then talk.*
> —CHARLES SCHWAB & CO.

One encounters the same mindset in many who seek to influence our political or religious views. You might think, since they are presenting issues relating to *your* life and death, that they would focus intently on *your* point of view. *As if...* More often than not, they resist a real give-and–take of information and ideas. Instead, they attempt to "spin" data toward their preconceived ends.

Have you experienced the stricken reaction of door-to-door religious presenters when you ask them for equal time to persuade them of *your* spiritual views? Or if you tell a cold caller selling financial services that you will listen to him—on the condition he agrees to listen to your alternative notions?

Recently defeated political campaigns often expend their final gasps placing blame for their demise. They wonder how they might have better communicated their message. They question the quality of their candidate. All the while they resist listening to and learning from members of the public they claim to seek to serve. They bring to mind Churchill's quip: "All I wanted was compliance with my wishes after reasonable discussion."

Unwillingness or incapacity to listen is a sure sign that someone is serving himself.

◆

Attempts to stifle disagreement, dissent or negative feedback are sure signs that individuals and organizations are serving themselves.

◆

Those who attempt to "persuade" from the inside-out may well believe what they are saying. But if they are seeking to impose their views, which were developed without our ongoing input, they are not serving us effectively. Even if we are persuaded in one interaction, it may be a fleeting victory. We may be unwilling or unable to accord trust.

To persuade, you must listen skillfully—not only to words written or spoken, but to nonverbal cues and context. Taking an empathetic approach, you should place yourself in the shoes of those you would persuade. You should focus on comprehending their views, reflecting concern for their needs.

How often is this done? It's so unusual, it's memorable. What we regard as "charm" is generally little more than genuinely interested, focused, purposeful listening. If your persuasion can be advanced simply by having people want to be with you—and it often can—this can make a tangible difference.

Listening denotes respect. It's a precondition for any useful service. It's also a primary learning vehicle, to identify how best to serve.

He that answers a matter before he hears
it, it is folly and shame unto him.

—PROVERBS 18:13

The more you seek to serve, the deeper the relationship sought. You must listen comprehensively, systematically, to achieve the level of trust required to persuade others to make major changes.

Barack Obama's rapid ascent exemplified the power of listening, particularly in contentious settings. Where people are polarized, they often have ceased to listen. They seek avenues to impose their will or express a grievance. When Obama was elected by his peers to become the first African-American president of the prestigious *Harvard Law Review*, his winning margin was from conservatives. They understood that Obama, a liberal, did not share their political views. They believed he would listen to them. They sensed he understood their substantive and organizational positions. Acutely aware of their minority status and marginalization at Harvard, they were promised respect, perhaps the prospect of some influence.

Obama deploys the same skilled listening in the political realm. Jodi Kantor explains in the *New York Times*, "Obama prides himself on trying to see the world through others' eyes. In his books, he slips into the heads of his Kenyan relatives, teenage mothers in Chicago, Reagan Democrats, bean farmers in Southern Illinois, and evangelical Christian voters."

In a polarized environment, listening—even without committing to compromise—has persuasive power. It's particularly effective in a time when American public discourse is marred by yelling, interruption and general disrespect for others and their perspectives.

Attentive listening, acknowledgment of the legitimacy of other points of view, can disarm those who disagree more from custom than conviction. The great philosopher Goethe explained, "Every word that is uttered evokes the idea of its opposite." Anticipating and acknowledging alternative and opposing arguments, foreseeing others' concerns, conveys a mindset of taking others into account in real time. It suggests a speaker's ultimate conclusions are intended to serve others, whether or not one agrees.

From a persuasive standpoint, incorporating other viewpoints into a presentation enables Obama to advance his policies, expressing them in the words of, or around the concerns of, many who are skeptical or opposed. In some situations, this may prompt others to accept views they would otherwise resist. Third parties who are observing may be influenced by what they interpret to be a manifest desire to serve others.

> *I will listen to you*, especially *when we disagree.*
> —PRESIDENT-ELECT BARACK OBAMA

As compelling as this kind of persuasion can be, there is another, higher level. The ultimate indication of dedication to serving others, not yourself, is to be recognized as open to persuasion by others.

If you're manifestly persuadable, you can be powerfully persuasive. Such openness makes plain that your self-interest or ego needs are not decisive. This may call upon considerable courage.

> *I have found it of enormous value when I can*
> *permit myself to understand another person....*
> *Is it necessary to permit oneself to understand another?*
> *I think that it is. Our first reaction to most of the statements*
> *which we hear from other people is an immediate evaluation,*
> *or judgment, rather than an understanding of it....*
> *Very rarely do we permit ourselves to understand*
> *precisely what the meaning of his statement is to him.*
> *I believe this is because understanding is risky.*
> *If I let myself really understand another person,*
> *I might be changed by that understanding.*
> —CARL ROGERS, TWENTIETH-CENTURY AMERICAN PSYCHOLOGIST

◆

If you are determined to persuade, be persuadable.

◆

BEGIN WITH QUESTIONS, NOT ANSWERS.

Questions are powerful tools in the hands of skilled listeners. Is there any better way to learn how you can best serve?

Nearly a century ago, John Patterson, the legendary founder and CEO of National Cash Register, established enduring sales practices. One of his insights was to shift the perspective of the sales force from themselves and their company to the customer. This was accomplished the old-fashioned way: by asking questions.

NCR salespeople learned to avoid making a direct, "hard" sell of their product in initial sales calls. Instead, they explored customers' business challenges through the trained use of targeted questions. This became the foundation of the subsequent IBM sales juggernaut.

Armed with vital customer information, NCR could determine, with highly relevant particularity, how best to serve.

Longtime Cisco CEO John Chambers is recalled for asking a simple, direct question: *What do* you *think?* Identifying this as a key to Chambers' effectiveness in sales, *Fortune* referred to it as "turning the tables on his questioners."

If you are striving to serve others, customarily asking questions should not be surprising, much less "turning the tables." Nonetheless, it is unusual enough that simply asking relevant questions can be a competitive and interpersonal advantage.

> *If you're unsure what to say, just ask questions, and I promise you that when they leave, they will think you were the smartest one in the room, just for listening to them. Word will get around.*
> —LADY BIRD JOHNSON, TO YOUNG BILL MOYERS

Relying on questions enables the sales person to move toward the customer. They can put their heads together, crafting a solution to meet the customer's goals. Ideally, the sales person will be regarded as an indispensable ally going forward.

There is a risk. If you are truly listening with a mind to serve your customer, you may conclude that another organization or individual is better suited in a given situation. Nonetheless, there may still be an opportunity for you to serve. A time-tested approach of successful sales people is to follow up when a sale has *not* been made. You can forward information about other products or ideas which may fit their needs in the future. You can establish a relationship built on proven attentiveness to their interests rather than your own.

The key, in every case, is to focus on how best to serve. Don't start by attempting to position your sale or move others to your point of view. Ask questions and listen to learn what others seek, how they think, what they view as best meeting their needs.

◆

Walk with the customer on the path toward solutions to their unique needs. Position your value proposition as the inevitable destination you can reach together.

◆

Some people resist using questions to such an extent. They believe they appear more forceful, more competent, by making declarations. There may be some settings where this concern is valid, depending on your audience. Overall, however, it's fair to say this would indicate a self-focused approach.

Many people go to great lengths to avoid "leaving money on the table" in a transaction. Yet they leave untold value untapped simply because they didn't take the trouble to ask questions and listen methodically.

ACQUIRE A "THIRD EAR."

Sociologist Lillian Rubin writes of the necessity of developing a "third ear." This refers to the capacity to listen skillfully to hear not only what is being said, but what lies beneath what is being said.

Peter Drucker explains, "The most important thing in communication is to hear what isn't being said."

As in other leadership relationships, this points to the utility of third-party input. Thus, in sales situations, many companies, such as Oracle, encourage having a "second chair." That person can observe the interaction with the prospective customer. The second chair can provide the third ear, potentially picking up signals even the most skilled listener may miss while simultaneously guiding a presentation. CEOs, trial lawyers and others engaged in high-stakes, persuasive communications often adopt the same approach.

FOCUS ON WHAT THEY'RE BUYING, NOT WHAT YOU'RE SELLING.

It is of course essential that you be thoroughly knowledgeable of your product or service or idea or vision. You must know the details of performance and relevant specifications. At least as important, you must understand the underlying principles, so you are able to customize applications to respond to evolving demands.

You must put yourself in your customers' place to understand what *they* believe they're buying. It may be quite different from what you believe you presume you're selling.

Seek first to understand, then to be understood.
— STEPHEN COVEY

In India clothes washing machines are used to produce lassi, a popular yogurt drink. If you are a manufacturer or seller of washing machines, this is critical information to serve your market in Punjab. HSBC markets itself as "the world's bank," pointing to its knowledge of local market niches such as this.

The legendary American company, Harley-Davidson, offers a compelling example. This American icon *manufactures* motorcycles and accessories; "What we *sell* is the ability for a forty-three-year-old accountant to dress in black leather, ride through small towns and have people be afraid of him." [emphasis added]

Harley-Davidson is repositioning outside its niche as a predominantly male preserve. In the tradition established by the legendary Edward

Bernays in mass-marketing cigarettes in the aftermath of World War I, Harley now presents itself as a source and symbol of freedom and empowerment for women. The company is coaxing them from the back of the motorcycle seat to the front. Female riders constitute the company's fastest growing market segment. Women who once sought a room of their own now want a Harley of their own.

A memorable example, in an entirely different context, of focusing on what the other side is seeking, comes from the career of James Woolsey. Prior to his service as Director of Central Intelligence, he was the U.S. ambassador to the Negotiation on Conventional Armed Forces in Europe (CFE) in 1989-91.

Woolsey was navigating an exceptionally complex environment at a historic moment: the ongoing demise of the Soviet empire. The treaty was negotiated and drafted in six languages; ultimately it would be 110-pages-long. After months of preliminaries, a nine-month deadline loomed.

As the experts and politicians toiled, an overarching problem emerged. The French government, representing America's longest-standing ally, was becoming a thorn in the side of the United States.

That France could be difficult in international affairs was hardly news. The government of Charles de Gaulle had withdrawn from full participation in NATO in the 1960s. This proud nation was acutely sensitive to its uncertain, declining status in the post-colonial world. By the 1980s they also faced well-known economic challenges.

Nonetheless many hoped for restored Franco-American amity in the heady moments following the collapse of the Soviet empire.

It was not to be.

Woolsey worked tirelessly with staff to overcome foreseeable points of concern advanced by the French and others. The principals convened public sessions. When Woolsey and his colleagues presented draft provisions of the carefully crafted treaty, the French ambassador objected vehemently, repeatedly. Woolsey recognized that the nature and tone of the reactions were not conducive to direct, public resolution.

The fate of the negotiation was uncertain.

Woolsey might have responded in any number of ways. He might with justification have railed against French perfidy or passive-aggressive behavior. He might have sought to isolate the French through informal alliances with other nations. Given the United States' predominant position at that moment, he might have opted to overpower them.

He chose the path of persuasion.

To nudge the French toward the U.S. goals, Woolsey sought to comprehend what was truly important to them. This meant methodically considering what they said—and striving to understand their thought process, including what was left unsaid.

Woolsey concluded that the multiplicity of French objections—as well as their robust public presentation—was largely the result of domestic political needs unrelated to the substance of the negotiation.

The treaty provided an occasion for the French government to placate elements of its electorate by venting against Uncle Sam.

Woolsey adjusted his approach. He sensed that the French diplomats saw only red whenever they encountered the American red, white and blue.

Woolsey pulled the U.S. back from center stage. He persuaded other European ambassadors to introduce sections of the draft treaty deemed essential by the American government. Woolsey went so far as to argue publicly *against* some provisions vital to American interests. This was, clearly, how he could best serve the French, better to advance his fundamental obligation to serve the U.S.

The French ambassador, witnessing the apparent discomfiture and disappointment of the American ambassador, was visibly delighted. Even after the French caught on to Woolsey's gambit, their good feeling remained. French support was forthcoming. The treaty was consummated. France and the United States each—both—achieved "success."

FRAME YOUR COMMUNICATIONS IN TERMS FAMILIAR AND OF VALUE TO YOUR AUDIENCE.

One of the most powerful tools of persuasion is the effective use of language. Attempts to persuade can be greatly strengthened by framing a discussion in terms favored by those you seek to serve.

In our approach, choosing *not* to frame your presentation in their terms would be self-indulgent.

> *It's not what you say—it's what people hear.*
> —DR. FRANK LUNTZ

The first reason to frame your communications in your audience's terms is clarity. If you speak in ways familiar to your audience, you're more likely to enter their thought processes, to be accepted rather than resisted. Sometimes, simply hearing key words may prompt some hearers to cease listening. They assume they know where you're coming from and where you're going.

> *On matters of great importance, remember that*
> *style, not sincerity, is the vital thing.*
> —OSCAR WILDE

---◆---

The greater the extent to which you communicate in a way which resonates with your audience, meets their needs, the more likely you are to reach the deeper level of connection necessary for persuasion.

---◆---

Framing your communications in the terms of those you would persuade enables you to better learn what they are seeking. A purchasing manager for a large company may have her fate intertwined with the success of your product or service. Though you're selling software, for example, that may not be the entirety of what she's hoping to learn about. She may care little for the ins and outs of the products which earn you and your employer respect within your industry. She may be focused on the credibility your company could convey should she need to call upon it in a future crisis. Would your team be convincing in backing her up before a group of skeptical C-level executives, should your product fail? Perhaps she is culling your presentation for arguments she can carry upstairs relating to entirely separate priorities, unstated or unrelated to what you're selling.

If you frame issues in familiar terms, aligned with your customer, you will be moving, figuratively, from your side of the table to hers.

A compelling use of reframing a longstanding narrative was employed by Gandhi in his campaign for an independent India, freed of British colonial rule.

Gandhi faced an adversary that included many officials who viewed the prospect of "losing" India to be against Great Britain's vital interests. The English controlled India's legal, political, financial and business structures through an intricate web of relationships that enabled them to rule with a relatively small military force. Various rebellions had been quelled over the course of several centuries. There was little reason to believe that armed resistance could be the basis of a successful strategy for Indian independence. Many, on both sides, were so accustomed to British rule that its prospective end was, at the least, disconcerting.

Gandhi's great insight was that the British could be persuaded most effectively by framing the discussion in terms of their own most deeply held and proclaimed values.

The greatest challenge to any thinker is stating the problem in a way that will allow a solution.
—BERTRAND RUSSELL

Gandhi declared: "Whenever you are confronted with an opponent, conquer him with love." Toward the British, Gandhi's love was tough. He asked sardonically, "What do I think of Western civilization? I think it would be a very good idea."

With the world watching through his masterful use of mass media, Gandhi provided numerous opportunities for the British Empire to reveal its ultimate values.

Gandhi's non-violent protests literally disarmed the colonial government. The British monopoly on legitimate force was neutralized. Gandhi, formally educated in England, had a sure sense of the English national character. His movement touched their conscience and quickened inchoate but increasingly uneasy public sentiment against the politicians and interests who sought to maintain the status quo.

Eventually, the British lost the will to contest the rising tide of independence. In the frame of reference created by Gandhi, they could have maintained their imperial power *only* through actions indisputably inconsistent with their self-image and expressed values.

Gandhi's example resonated in America as elsewhere. Martin Luther King, Jr. brought the non-violent approach to bear against a century of Southern "Jim Crow" laws and customs oppressing American citizens classified as non-white. This would shock the American conscience were it seen in any other nation. King challenged the majority to make change based on their own traditions and values.

His framing of the dialogue was masterful. Perhaps the apogee was his legendary "I Have a Dream Speech," delivered on Wednesday, 28 August 1963, as part of the "March on Washington."

Every aspect of this historic event was planned with care.

King spoke from the base of the Lincoln Memorial. The venue was redolent of recent, relevant history. The beloved singer Marian Anderson had performed there on Easter Sunday 1939—after the Daughters of the American Revolution declined to allow her, an African-American, to perform in Constitution Hall. In June 1947, President Truman had selected the Lincoln Memorial as the site for his landmark statement committing his administration to expanding civil rights.

The vital link was Lincoln's legacy. King worked from this familiar tableau to summon the nation to fulfill the Great Emancipator's vision. Like the president at Gettysburg, King reached back to the ideals of the Declaration of Independence, as well as our shared spiritual roots, to comprehend contemporary challenges. Millions who as schoolchildren had recited Lincoln's words would feel the full force of King's vision.

Cognizant of a worldwide television audience, King and other organizers ensured that the demonstration would be peaceful. Hundreds of thousands of participants maintained a respectful tone as they assembled, many in Sunday dress, amid monuments to heroes and institutions they were simultaneously honoring and challenging.

King's address sought to reframe the national discussion. The African-American minority was not seeking to be conferred unique rights and privileges. They were calling due the "promissory note" held by every American, written into the foundation of the nation.

Invoking the nation's most deeply held and oft-expressed values, King ensured that the majority would not evade a necessary dialogue about the meaning of being "American."

> Five score years ago, a great American, in whose symbolic shadow we stand today signed the Emancipation Proclamation. This momentous decree came as a great beacon light of hope to millions of Negro slaves who had been seared in the flames of withering injustice….But one hundred years later, we must face the tragic fact that the Negro is still not free…When the architects of our republic wrote the magnificent words of the Declaration of Independence, they were signing a promissory note to which every American was to fall heir….

Understood in this way, it was inconceivable that a result other than legal equality could be consistent with the American story.

In the early 1960's, President Kennedy also strove to reframe public discussion about Southern apartheid laws. Many defenders of the status quo argued that the self-criticism explicit in the civil rights debate undercut the nation's global reputation. Kennedy turned this on its head. He reminded Americans that racial prejudice and discrimination were sources of international embarrassment. Ambassadors from African nations were unable to drive across Southern states in which they would be denied travelers' accommodations. At a moment when the U.S. sought to make our system attractive to others in the ideological struggle against communism, we were exhibiting a very unattractive side, inconsistent with our professed ideals.

The same practice can be seen in other examples of successful large-scale persuasion. In the 1950s, President Eisenhower advocated a system of interstate highways to be financed primarily by the federal government.

The idea was not new. Ike broke a historic impasse by reframing the issue as one of national defense. The new highways would be dual-use (civilian and military), strengthening the nation's military capabilities during the Cold War.

A contemporary example involves the political conflict that has immobilized U.S. energy policy for nearly half a century. James Woolsey describes how reframing a discussion can bring antagonists together:

> I was testifying before a congressional committee about how climate change really was an issue and one of the members of the committee didn't believe it.
>
> I said, "Congressman, you realize that seven of the nine things I've suggested would improve our resilience substantially against terrorist attacks," and he said, "Oh, well if you do them for that reason, it's fine." People are willing to cooperate on substance as long as they don't have to lose the argument.

These aren't examples of "spin," twisting the truth perilously near the breaking point. They illustrate the power of framing the discussion—and, ultimately, thought—in terms familiar and consistent with shared values and concerns.

The greater the change you seek, the more you should frame your arguments in terms of the values, history, customs, traditions and aspirations of those you seek to persuade. The uncertainty you would introduce to longstanding understandings and arrangements should be informed by and accompanied with expressed respect for the hard-earned certainties of old verities.

COMMUNICATE IN A FORMAT TO WHICH YOUR AUDIENCE IS RECEPTIVE.

If you wish to serve others effectively, you must go where they are.

In the late 1970s, Kay Warren realized that many people—especially young people—had lost interest in attending church services which seemed distant and irrelevant to their lives. Working with her husband, Pastor Rick Warren, she introduced rock and roll music into the repertoire of what would emerge as their incomparably successful Saddleback Church.

Tyler Perry incorporates moral, often explicitly religious messages into his brilliant plays and television programs. Many touch upon areas of controversy. His manifest love for his audience enables him to confront issues which others sidestep. From *The House of Payne* to his trademark character Madea, Perry communicates in ways which speak powerfully to his core African-American audience. The universality of his messages reaches more broadly as well.

John Lennon methodically used his songwriting and performance skills to persuade his listeners to seek peace through direct action. *Lennon Revealed*, by Larry Kane, includes Lennon's explanation of the strategy behind his enduring anthem, *Imagine*:

> The song says, "Imagine that there was no more religion, no more country, no more politics," which is basically *The Communist Manifesto*. I am not particularly communist, nor do I belong to any movement…Now, I understand what you have to do. Put your political [ideas] across with a little honey. This is what we do above all, Jerry (Rubin), Yoko and the others—it is to try and change the apathy of young people.

It is widely recognized that the Beatles had profound political influence during the 1960s, including behind the Iron Curtain. In 2003, Russian President Vladimir Putin escorted Paul McCartney on a tour of the Kremlin. Putin, formerly a KGB operative, intimated he had been a Beatles' fan—even though their music had been classified "propaganda of an alien ideology." With pardonable hyperbole, a 2009 documentary examined "How the Beatles Rocked the Kremlin."

Endless treatises about America's impending entitlement crisis have been written by earnest, would-be reformers. They stand, undisturbed, moldering on neglected, dusty library bookshelves everywhere.

Writer Christopher Buckley chooses another approach: humor. His satirical novel *Boomsday* pits the rising generations against aging Baby Boomers. An advocacy group uncannily resembling the American Association for Retired People seeks more and more subsidized benefits, including Botox injections and motorized scooters for oldsters who seem to live forever in gated retirement communities. A young firebrand, Cassandra, incites riots, proposing incentives for the elderly to gracefully depart the scene sooner than medical science would otherwise allow.

The persuasive potency of satire and humor should not be underestimated. It can be a solvent, dissolving the foundation of even the most formidable fortress. Author Ben Lewis chronicles the jokes that helped undercut the legitimacy of the Soviet Empire. His book *Hammer & Tickle* carries the subtitle: "The Story of Communism—A Political System Almost Laughed Out of Existence." Example: *Why, despite all the shortages, was the toilet paper in East Germany always two-ply? A: Because they had to send a copy of everything they did to Moscow.*

General George S. Patton was renowned for his capacity to inspire troops under his command. Though he was highly educated and from an aristocratic background, he was legendary for communicating in the tough, coarse terms that could motivate young GIs facing the most grievous risks.

On Monday, 5 June 1944, Patton addressed the massed, anxious men who would constitute the vanguard tasked with piercing the steel and savagery of Hitler's *Wehrmacht*. On D-Day, Tuesday, June 6th, the Allies might have the moral high ground. But Nazi gunners lay in wait, nested in the fortified high ground, atop jagged cliffs toward which scores of young Americans would run straightaway to their fate.

Historian Charles Province has reproduced the text of Patton's remarks. They are far earthier than suggested in public reports or the movie *Patton*.

All through your Army careers, you men have bitched about what you call "chicken shit drilling." That, like everything else in the Army, has a definite purpose. That purpose is alertness…I don't give a fuck for a man who's not always on his toes…. If you're not alert, sometime, a German son-of-an-asshole-bitch is going to sneak up behind you and beat you to death with a sockful of shit!

There are four hundred neatly marked graves in Sicily. All because one man went to sleep on the job…But they are German graves, because we caught the bastard asleep before they did.…

Don't forget, you men don't know that I'm here. No mention of that fact is to be made in any letters. The world is not supposed to know what the hell happened to me. I'm not supposed to be commanding this Army. I'm not even supposed to be here in England. Let the first to find out be the Goddamned Germans. Someday I want to see them rise up on their piss-soaked hind legs and howl, "Jesus Christ, it's the God-damned Third Army and that son-of-a-fucking-bitch Patton.…"

There is one great thing that you men will all be able to say after this war is over and you are home once again. You may be thankful that twenty years from now when you are sitting by the fireside with your grandson on your knee and he asks you what you did in the great World War II, you WON'T have to cough, shift him to the other knee and say, "Well, your Granddaddy shoveled shit in Louisiana." No, Sir, you can look him straight in the eye and say, "Son, your Granddaddy rode with the Great Third Army and a Son-of-a-Goddamned-Bitch named Georgie Patton!"

Patton's performance remains the gold standard of extraordinary leadership communication in high-stakes circumstances. Reflecting its time and place, his speech is a classic in the tradition of the eve of Saint Crispin's Day speech in Shakespeare's *Henry V*.

◆

For effective persuasion, your format should engage your intended audience. The higher the stakes, the more fundamental the emotions and commitments sought, the more directly and deeply your format should engage those you serve.

◆

APPEAL TO INTEREST, NOT INTELLECT.

Benjamin Franklin urged, "If you would persuade, you must appeal to interest rather than intellect." Warren Buffett's partner Charlie Munger elaborates: "This maxim is a wise guide to a great and simple precaution in life: Never, ever, think about something else when you should be thinking about the power of incentives."

Persuasion can be exceptionally effective when the audience understands that what is offered furthers their interests. An appeal to change backed by relevant incentives is far more likely to succeed than an appeal based on reason, intellect or sentiment.

That said, it is important to understand how those you would persuade comprehend their interests. A perennial curiosity of American politics is that many proclaim their virtue in voting for candidates because of factors beyond their own short-term material interest—yet are perplexed that voters on the other side choose opposing candidates because of factors beyond *their* short-term material interest.

To presume that others' perceptions are the same as yours would be to serve yourself.

◆

To best serve others, discern and appeal to their perceived self-interest to the greatest possible extent. To persuade others to alter their ways of acting or thinking, you must understand the mix of interests and incentives to which they will most readily respond. You can transform your interaction into a joint endeavor applying your contribution to their areas of greatest concern.

◆

KNOW WHEN TO STOP.

When you've made the sale, stop talking. *Immediately.* Anything more is self-serving, placing your transaction or relationship at entirely avoidable, unjustifiable risk.

First, always ask for the order,
and second, when the customer says yes, stop talking.
—MICHAEL BLOOMBERG

ARE YOU MAKING YOUR UNIQUE CONTRIBUTION?

BE THE FIRST, BE THE ONLY.

The guaranteed way to serve better than anyone else is to be the first and only.

If you're recognized as the first mover, offering something that your audiences recognize to be unique, you get powerful advantages. You're indelibly linked in people's minds—and hopefully, hearts—with your value proposition.

The first mover can frame the terms of discussion. In a negotiation, a credible initial offer can anchor the subsequent give-and-take. If you open with a strong argument fixing the value at $1000, all parties are likely to accept that as a baseline. If the discussion is anchored at $100, the give-and-take will tend to occur nearer that point.

Seeing yourself as the first-and-only empowers you with the belief your product or service or idea will add more value to the purchaser than anyone else's.

You can't fake that kind of commitment. Others sense it. To be sure, you might, for a time, skate by with slippery claims. That may suffice for a single transaction. It could be fatal, though, to any chance of an ongoing relationship. In the Information Age, anyone trying this is about as likely to succeed as the feeble-minded losers who persist in robbing banks at gunpoint in front of ubiquitous security cameras.

Entrepreneur Felix Dennis, in his entertaining book, *How to Get Rich*, points to the persuasive power emanating from Winston Churchill's "astonishing...self-belief." Dennis argues that the course of history was altered "by one old man's belief in his own destiny, by his insane, unprincipled self-belief, and the belief in the destiny of his country and of freedom in Western Europe."

Churchill was an egotist by any reckoning. That egotism was no small part of his absolute conviction that he was uniquely suited to serve his nation—indeed, the world—at a moment of existential peril. As Dennis suggests, such unwavering self-belief can be irresistible. In the case of Churchill, it was combined with acknowledged if erratic genius and service without reserve.

In the dire circumstances faced by Britain at the outset of the Second World War, Churchill displayed a degree of love for his nation that overcame longstanding, well-founded, widely shared qualms about his judgment. Unprecedented—in the minds of many, unimaginable—events appeared uncannily suited for his curious combination of virtues and idiosyncrasies.

In more commonplace situations, you can readily exhibit such dedication, earning an exclusive place in others' hearts and minds. A reliable path is illuminated by William James' dictum: "The deepest craving of human nature is the need to be appreciated."

Striving to be attuned and responsive to others can render your proposition appealing and even unique. Being that way in small things can increase their comfort with you on larger matters, where the stakes are high and the facts available for decision may be sparse.

When the conduct of people is designed to be influenced,
persuasion, kind unassuming persuasion, should ever be adopted.
It is an old and true maxim that "a drop of honey catches more
flies than a gallon of vinegar." So with people. If you would win a
person to your cause, first convince them that you are their sincere
friend. Therein is a drop of honey that catches their heart, which,
what they will, is the great high road to his reason, and which,
once gained, you will find but little trouble in convincing him of
the justice of your cause, if indeed that cause really is a good one.
—ABRAHAM LINCOLN

CREATE COMPETITION TO ESTABLISH UNIQUE VALUE.

What about situations where value is not readily measured? Sometimes, it can be difficult to establish value, especially for something asserted to be unique.

Donald Trump recommends that a negotiator "create competition." Such competition suggests scarcity to the purchaser. It can clarify value in terms of status or other benefits derived from being the first to own an exciting new product. Recent, prominent examples include the highly anticipated releases of the iPad, iPhone, J.K. Rowling's Harry Potter novels, remastered Beatles collections, Google's "Wave," and Facebook's rollout of dedicated URLs for its pages.

> *GENEVA—In the rarified world of watch collecting,*
> *where Wall Street investment bankers and Asian*
> *millionaires buy and sell at auctions, a timepiece can*
> *command a higher price than a luxury car.*
> *At an April event here, a 1950s Omega platinum watch*
> *sold for $351,000, a price that conferred a new peak of*
> *prestige on a brand known for mass-produced timepieces.*
> *Watch magazines and retailers hailed the sale, at an auction*
> *in the lush Mandarin Oriental Hotel on the River Rhone.*
> *Omega trumpeted it, announcing that a "Swiss bidder" had offered*
> *"the highest price ever paid for an Omega watch at auction."*
> *What Omega did not say: The buyer was Omega itself.*
> —WALL STREET JOURNAL

The *Wall Street Journal* provides another memorable example of creating competition to raise value. It involves the late Jack Valenti. Valenti was a renowned negotiator. Early in his career he was a trusted aide to President Lyndon Johnson.

Valenti served for many years as the CEO of the Motion Picture Association of America. In this capacity he dealt with the top talent and management in Hollywood, as well as national politicians.

Fay Vincent, who served variously as CEO of Columbia Pictures and later as baseball commissioner, observed Valenti's skill in persuasion in action.

Barry Diller, then CEO of Paramount Pictures, called Vincent about the renegotiation of Valenti's MPAA contract. Diller explained that Valenti was being courted by team owners as a prospective commissioner of baseball. Diller was anxious to do everything possible to ensure that the MPAA maintain Valenti's services. The prospect of losing Valenti focused the attention of the most important MPAA decision makers. Valenti and the MPAA soon concluded a new, suitably generous contract.

Years later, when Vincent became baseball commissioner, he learned the back story. An influential team owner, Bud Selig, had been approached by a fellow owner, legendary Washington lawyer Edward Bennett Williams. Williams asked Selig to invite Valenti to lunch at the tony Metropolitan Club, near the White House. Williams explained he merely wanted Valenti to be seen with Selig at that exclusive venue of power brokers; what they discussed would be irrelevant.

As Williams intended, news of the lunch flashed across the country—straight to Hollywood (this was long before Twitter). The implication was plain: soon-to-be free agent Valenti was being wooed to become the next baseball commissioner.

In fact, Fay Vincent learned later, the baseball owners never had interest in Valenti.

Williams, serving as Valenti's advocate, established Valenti's value by creating the credible appearance of competition.

In some cases, it may be more difficult. Many products become commodities—the opposite of being unique. Many services—for example much legal and accounting work—also become commoditized. The seller can face a permanent disadvantage if the customers' primary point of comparison is price.

If you find yourself in this situation, it is a clear warning that your value proposition must be updated and improved. It is a customer feedback signal that goes straight to your capacity to serve.

To avoid commoditization, you may be able to customize your offering. Some law firms, for example, add value by assembling and managing teams in an array of related services, brought together to solve clients' problems. This can include, in litigation situations, scientific, communications, project management and other relevant expertise.

What if you face a situation where you conclude you are *not* able to serve better than anyone else? When it's clear to you that someone else could better serve the customer?

The ideal response is to share your judgment with the prospect and point him toward that alternative. You may lose a sale—while attaining a high level of trust, undergirding a lasting business relationship. What if your personal situation makes that approach seem impossibly idealistic? You may believe that serving your employer precludes your serving your customers to that extent. Perhaps your need to provide for your family or other personal goals distracts you from a total focus on your customer's needs.

Should you find yourself in such a situation, don't go into denial. You must recognize that you are not best serving your customers. You may "get away" with this temporarily, for example if you have a strong preexisting relationship. But you've received a warning you must not ignore. If you're part of a large organization, send the information up the management chain; they need to know there's a problem. If you're unable to see your way clear to correcting the situation, you'd be well-advised to seek employment alternatives.

The bottom line: if you don't believe you're offering unique value, you're limiting your persuasive capability. Your difficulty is based on a substantive reason: someone, somewhere can serve more effectively than you. You need to get ahead of change—lest change get ahead of you.

ENCOURAGE THIRD PARTIES TO MAKE YOUR CASE.

Creating competition is not the only way to establish value by reference. In many situations, third parties can credibly convey that your product, service or idea will best serve others. They can overcome the inevitable tension created by the appearance of self-serving when you're presenting your offering as unique.

In the past, third-party advocacy was generally from authority figures, including subject-matter experts and celebrities.

Today, those who speak with greatest credibility are often people we recognize as sharing our values and experiences. Amazon reviewers and other online sources can be compelling. The telephone call or email from a neighbor or fellow member of an interest group on behalf of a political candidate may have more impact than the endorsement of a governor or senator. The internet newsletter writer or blogger who proclaims the merits of a new computer software program (or a book, for that matter) may add more value than a celebrity pitchman on television. Social networks such as Facebook and Twitter enable an extraordinary range of third-party communications.

The bottom line: similarly situated third parties are often credible and effective in conveying unique value propositions.

CAST A VISION INTO WHICH OTHERS INCORPORATE THEIR CALLINGS, THEIR MISSIONS.

As discussed in Chapter 1, casting and communicating a vision is a foundational service that all leaders perform. It's a core, non-delegable task.

A leader continually seeks to persuade others to take actions in furtherance of her vision. When the actions taken are significant, and would not have otherwise occurred, her value is greatest.

> *The central issue is never strategy, structure, culture, or systems. The core of the matter is always about changing the behavior of people...In highly successful change efforts, people find ways to help others see the problems or solutions in ways that influence emotions, not just thought.*
> —JOHN KOTTER, HARVARD BUSINESS SCHOOL

> *One thing hasn't changed at all and never will, and that's the importance of a big idea. That's the real value we bring to clients...*

[Y]ou have to have an idea to begin with.
It's the one thing that will survive.
—SHELLY LAZARUS

A vision must be simple. It must be flexible and easily communicated by others, so it can be adapted by many people, in many circumstances. The most compelling visions encompass narratives for broadly comprehending reality. They are in sync with, and advance, others' visions for their own lives. They engender missions. They set the stage on which individuals can create and perform in narratives to which they can contribute. Ideally, the visions of the individual and the enterprise become one.

In the Information Age, interactivity makes possible an unprecedented mutual engagement. Whether you seek to change behavior relating to a product or an idea, you have many new avenues to connect with your audience.

Numerous companies have turned to "crowd-sourcing," seeking online engagement to co-create their brands or design their offerings. Diet Coke, Mentos, Converse, Firefox, Doritos, Dell, and Apple each have looked to the public for advertising ideas and submissions.

Although the mind may be part of your
target, the heart is the bull's-eye....
For the leader, storytelling is action oriented—
a force for turning dreams into goals and then into results.
—PETER GUBER, MOTION PICTURE PRODUCER

People choose whether to become characters in a narrative you've conceived. It should include space for others to fill and elaborate in ways unique to themselves. This enables them to find value in extending their own stories. They simultaneously contribute to the vitality of the vision, expand it, refine it, take it in new directions.

As they seek to make a sale, realtors often, purposefully, leave parts of a house incompletely furnished or decorated. They preserve space for a prospective purchaser to imagine his family home. This is akin to how a leader leaves a place in her narrative for her audience to recognize their own contributions as important, to see that the greater vision is consistent with their personal histories and callings.

A vision can provide a narrative in which individuals find answers to great questions. It can also seed their imaginations as they comprehend their lives in new ways. The result is a creative process in which the vision evolves.

As the great mathematician Blaise Pascal said, "We are generally the better persuaded by the reasons we discover ourselves than those given to us by others." A skillfully crafted narrative enables audiences to recognize their own rationale within a frame of reference offered by the leader who serves them.

A great storyteller is devoted to a cause beyond self.
That mission is embodied in his stories, which capture and express
values that he believes in and wants others to adopt as their own.
Thus, the story itself must offer a value proposition
that is worthy of its audience.
—PETER GUBER

LIVE YOUR VALUES—*YOU* ARE THE MESSAGE!

The most compelling persuasive communications come from individuals whose personae, life experiences and verbal messages coalesce.

The leader who personifies her vision can transform her life into an ongoing narrative. That can be a tangible service, inspiring countless others.

You Are the Message. To most effectively serve your audience, you must fuse ever greater parts of yourself into your message. Your values, your hopes for the future, your life history, your habits of living and working, the very clothes you wear... these can all become elements of your communication arsenal.

What kind of advertisement am I for myself?

—BRUCE BARTON

Consider the example of Gandhi. Gandhi foreswore his youthful adoption of the finery associated with British-educated lawyers such as himself. He chose instead the clothing, bearing and lifestyle of the non-privileged people he sought to serve in India. Winston Churchill, who vehemently opposed Gandhi's political project in the 1930's, recognized the power of his adversary's self-presentation. Churchill sought to marginalize him as a "half-naked fakir."

Like Gandhi, Churchill was, to a notable extent, self-created as a communicator. He overcame a distracting speech impediment. He educated himself to compensate for his failure to attain the university degree then customary among top-rung English politicians.

Churchill's dedication to oratory culminated in his stirring Second World War speeches. The inspiration imparted by his words was reinforced by his signature "V for Victory" sign, as well as his customary hats, cigars, bow ties, waistcoats, walking sticks and "siren suits." He harnessed his facial and verbal expressions into unceasing service, conveying indomitable English resolve against "Corporal Hitler." Historian Andrew Roberts quotes Churchill's advice to a fellow member of Parliament: "Never forget your trademark."

More recent examples of embodying one's message include President Kennedy's decision to wear neither hat nor overcoat at his bitterly cold inauguration in 1961. This accentuated his evocation of generational change. Kennedy, the youngest elected president in American history, sought to convey a vivid contrast to the older, departing Eisenhower team.

President Reagan adopted a similar approach at the high-stakes Geneva nuclear arms summit in November 1985. Reagan was the oldest president in American history. Having outlived a series of doddering Soviet premiers, he found himself in an unfamiliar, potentially uncomfortable position. His latest adversary would be new, fresh, legally trained, highly articulate and media-savvy.

Reagan was thoroughly prepared for their first face-to-face meeting. Their initial encounter would be recorded by the cameras of the world. Mikhail Gorbachev arrived in an unpretentious Volga limousine. He wore the familiar, sensible hat favored by Soviet functionaries, matched with a funereally somber overcoat against the winter cold.

Assuming command, Reagan stood at the entrance to their meeting place, awaiting his Soviet counterpart with the confidence of a genial host. In contrast to the bundled Gorbachev, Reagan pointedly wore nothing more than a suit. The preliminary public dynamics of the closely watched negotiations redounded to Reagan's advantage.

In business, one thinks of Steve Jobs. Many made light of the Apple CEO's rather scruffy, vaguely art-school attire. Yet, who can doubt the forethought embedded in Jobs' personal presentation? He embodied Apple; indeed, his indelible image continues to do so. His apparel and bearing seemed entirely appropriate for the varied audiences—from teens to aging baby boomers—who identify with the brand that prompts millions to believe that each of them "thinks different."

Several the companies considered in this book—including Apple, Berkshire Hathaway, Microsoft, Google, Patagonia, Amazon, Zappos, Virgin, and Dell—maintain public roles for their founders. Such leaders are uniquely able to personify vital aspects of the enterprise's value proposition (in some cases their presence is such a recognized asset that succession planning takes on added urgency). Equally important, their presence helps sustain the continuity of a vibrant organizational culture.

Act well your part, there all the honor lies.
—ALEXANDER POPE

You do not create a style. You work and develop yourself; your style is an emanation of your own being.
—KATHERINE ANNE PORTER

Despite the manifest value of this aspect of communication, some people nonetheless resist cultivating the requisite skills. They dismiss them as "acting." Ailes draws a critical distinction: acting is impersonating someone else; performing is presenting yourself in the most effective manner.

Political strategist Dan Schnur says experience bears out what one would expect: "the greatest mistake a leader can make is to try to be something they're not." As Reagan often said, the camera doesn't lie.

British Prime Minister Margaret Thatcher is recalled as an extraordinarily effective leader, the epitome of the "conviction politician." An admiring journalist, John O'Sullivan, recalls, "Margaret Thatcher was not yet Margaret Thatcher" in her early years as a national political figure. O'Sullivan reports that she was regarded as "shrill" and ineffective in parliamentary debate. She turned to experts to assist in developing her ideas. She sought out advice in presentation, including from the legendary actor Sir Laurence Olivier. She altered her clothing and hair style. The results were tangible. In July 1977, after she unexpectedly dominated a critical parliamentary debate, a hard-bitten journalist declared: "If Mrs. Thatcher were a racehorse, she would have been tested for drugs yesterday."

O'Sullivan believes this to have been a defining moment in her emergence as a consequential leader.

As she sharpened her presentation, Margaret Thatcher in no way trimmed her sails ideologically. She did not camouflage her beliefs. She was doing the hard work of bringing the entirety of her talents, gifts and experience to bear to advance her message.

One of the greatest strengths of a leader is the capacity to summon up everything she is, and can be, into her service. We live in a time when many people in high positions in corporate and political life routinely deliver speeches drafted by others. Invariably this occasions a vague, sometimes distracting disconnect, akin to the sensation of watching films in which the audio and video tracks are slightly out of alignment. Breaking from the pack, crafting and communicating your own words and thoughts, can be singularly compelling.

When your authenticity is deployed with passion to serve others, your communications, at every level, can be transformed. Your relationship with your audience may intensify toward love, moving further and further from the confinement of self-concern.

My life is my message.

—MAHATMA GANDHI

◆

The most effective communicators strive to make their lives a cavalcade of teachable moments.

◆

SAFEGUARD YOUR CREDIBILITY.

You might well be thinking: *I admire Gandhi and Churchill, but I'm not striving to be a Gandhi or a Churchill. I just want to serve my company and community.*

Fair enough. But the fact is, in today's wired world, your life is melding into your message irrespective of your wishes. The internet has rendered our lives more or less open books. It's as if everyone, everywhere, lives together in a small town.

In the twentieth century, formal authority conferred credibility. The prestige of an institution—such as a church, a corporation, a labor union or a political party—was itself an element of persuasion. Authority could be asserted by individuals based on the positions they held, or the contribution they made over time.

In the twenty-first century, the scope of formal authority is greatly diminished. Widespread malfeasance and incompetence, combined with the decentralization and availability of information, undercut its claims. The Information Age also has removed the distance that bolsters prestige.

Not long ago, the benefit of the doubt went to those asserting or representing authority. Today, at least as often as not, formal authority labors under the burden of doubt.

◆

In the twentieth century, authority conferred credibility.
Today, formal authority no longer gets the benefit of the doubt.
More often than not, it labors under the burden of doubt.
In the twenty-first century, credibility confers authority.

◆

Credibility is the watchword today; trust. The internet has actualized Ronald Reagan's credo: *Trust but verify.* Assertions of authority may get you in the door, but no longer suffice to win the business.

Nothing is more destructive of credibility than the widespread practice of "spin." In a world of irreverent late-night television and the 24-7 scrutiny of the internet, finely parsing words can shatter credibility with swift, severe, rough justice.

Consider familiar, failed instances of spin. Families blown into bloody bits by aerial bombardment are not usefully referred to as "collateral damage." Common understanding of what constitutes government-sanctioned torture is not evaded by calling it an "enhanced interrogation technique." Howard Schultz's wishes notwithstanding, a 97-percent decline in revenues for Starbucks during a recent recession was not evidence of "steady progress of our Starbucks Rewards program and the enthusiastic reception to the Starbucks Gold Card, [indicating] we are well positioned to weather this challenging economic environment."

An argument and its presentation ultimately cannot be stronger than the underlying facts.

There is no more persuasive evidence of your commitment to serve than holding fast to the truth, pursuing it faithfully—even into unfamiliar, uncertain terrain.

WHAT ARE YOU LEARNING?

As you tailor your persuasive communications, it's essential that you constantly seek to improve. This is important for deepening existing relationships, as well as establishing new ones.

The challenges of persuasive communications are great. There is so much outside your control. It's not surprising that many people seek to reduce their sense of vulnerability, falling into superstitious attitudes and inflexible routines.

A common trap is found among sales personnel trained to rely on the telephone as their primary communication tool. Some middle-aged and older people resist moving toward email. They may persist, for example, in cold calling—even against the expressed wishes of prospective or current customers. With the explosion of communication options and the multiplicity of individuals' work and personal arrangements, it is more necessary than ever to update such practices routinely.

I recently encountered this problem in dealing with a financial institution. A certificate of deposit was due to mature. The account had been established and maintained via email. I had asked for any account-related communications to be sent via email.

Nonetheless, a bank representative contacted me by telephone. He wished to persuade me to maintain the account, perhaps expand it.

As he started his spiel, I gently interrupted. I asked if he was aware of my request to be contacted by email rather than telephone. He claimed he wasn't—but said he would make a note for the future. He then asked if he could continue to share the information on investment alternatives. I agreed—provided he do so via email.

The salesman demurred. He said it was important for him to explain by phone or, even better, in person; would I come to his office for a meeting? It apparently had not crossed his mind that someone who elected to use email rather than telephone communication was focused on time management. Had he been thinking of those he supposedly was serving, would he have concluded that such a customer would likely dedicate yet additional time to travel to the company office for a face-to-face sales presentation?

I declined. I reiterated that I'd be pleased to receive the information via email. He said that was not possible. He repeated his plea for an in-person meeting.

The salesman had delighted me long enough. The conversation concluded. My previously positive view of the bank was damaged. He not only failed to win new business; his bank lost an existing customer. They were unwilling to serve me in simple, reasonable ways—even after being asked repeatedly—so my willingness to entrust them with my financial well-being came to an end.

The bank's heedless approach may have sufficed in the 1980s or 1990s. It might work with some customers today. However, maintaining such "success" may prove elusive in the remorselessly competitive market environment of the twenty-first century. Customers have options.

If you seek to persuade, every aspect of the communication should be reevaluated regularly. For example, various studies suggest gender differences in receptivity to email communications. With the usual caveats about stereotyping, some women may be less receptive to email, in part because they prefer additional levels of contact to develop relationships. Some men may lean toward email, in part because it can tamp down explicit status awareness and competition.

Many others have work demands for which interruptions, such as by telephone, can be exceptionally costly. So, too, there are often generational preferences in communication approaches.

What is clear is that persuasive communications must improve and adapt every bit as much as the products and ideas they present.

In recent years, for example, there has been increasing reliance on "sound bites" and other short forms of communicating complex issues. Skilled speakers often spoke in ten- to fifteen-second bursts. The set speech was thought to be of declining importance.

Interestingly, at the same time as the compressed-character texting of Twitter takes hold, the set speech is roaring back as a powerful tool of persuasion. This is exemplified by presidential candidate Obama's address, in March 2008, responding to controversies occasioned by the incendiary remarks of Reverend Jeremiah Wright.

Obama spoke for thirty-seven minutes, touching a range of issues relating to race and American life. Traditional news outlets handled it in various ways. Strikingly, it became the most-watched video on YouTube—with more than 1.6 million viewers tuning in within forty-eight hours.

Two things are certain in this changing environment. Technological innovation will continue, resulting in additional avenues for individuals and organizations to transmit and receive information. The communicators who will be most effective are those who adapt accordingly, in terms of both media and message. As Gandhi pointed out, "Constant development is the law of life, and a man who always tries to maintain his dogmas in order to appear consistent drives himself into a false position."

◆

Individuals and organizations which resist changing the format and substance of persuasive communications are, to that extent, serving themselves. If they fall into the trap of distorting reality to hold fast to outdated notions, they risk becoming impervious to truth itself. The resulting ineffectiveness of their persuasive communications can foreshadow a death spiral, a broader incapacity to serve.

◆

EVERYDAY SCENARIOS

The same principles of persuasive communications apply in recurring situations in business and personal relationships.

Employment Applications and Raises

The approach of The Four Questions can be effective in your efforts to obtain a new job, or to get a raise where you are.

Some people make the error of focusing on themselves in job interviews. They may place lay undue weight on their formal education, for example. The fact is, unless you're a recent graduate, your alma mater is more likely a matter of curiosity than relevance. In a similar vein, other applicants rely too heavily on prior work experience.

As critical as these factors may seem, they're generally secondary. Your degrees or past positions are relevant to your prospective employers solely as indicators of your future value to them. They are much less interested in who you are, or what you have done, than in what you can do to serve their enterprise going forward.

The Four Questions point the way. Emphasize that you understand who you would be serving in your prospective role; how you would best serve (such as examples of how you take on tasks, reflecting actionable knowledge of the prospective employer's enterprise); why you are the best possible choice for the position (may be a good place to present your relevant experience in a context important to the employer; may also be appropriate to introduce scarcity into the equation); and how you will ensure ongoing improvement, adding increasing value over time.

The most effective way to present yourself to prospective employers is to focus on how you can add value in the future, measured from their perspective.

The same principles apply in seeking a raise. No one enjoys asking for a raise—though nearly all of us feel we merit higher compensation.

Many people begin from the perspective of what they believe they "deserve." This calculation is often based on how they believe their employer should best serve them. They may compare themselves with fellow employees or competitors. Their baseline may be what they regard as necessary to maintain their lifestyle.

Unless your relationship goes further than the workplace, seeking a raise solely or primarily because of your own needs is dubious. From the start, it is an example of serving yourself rather than your employer. What's more, your employer and fellow employees likely face financial pressures every bit as daunting.

The more promising route to a higher pay grade is to persuade your employer that your service is creating additional value from her point of view. If you can demonstrate that you're serving your employer unreservedly, effectively—adding unique, measurable value—your relationship can be one of ongoing, mutual benefit.

Love and Romance

Many people who fail to pique the interest of a prospective romantic partner could have been successful had they applied the approach of The Four Questions.

Some approach possible relationships with a laundry list of what *they* want. On websites such as Match.com, one finds that many of the self-composed entries catalog item after item of what the person is looking for—and little or nothing about what they would bring to a relationship. They presume their suitability and desirability to be self-evident, based on their accompanying photographs and self-appraisals.

So, too, one hears of first dates where one or both participants put the other through a gauntlet of questions, much like supercilious job interviewers.

Should they be surprised if such self-referential approaches prompt others to view them more in terms of a transaction than a relationship?

As ever, you're most persuasive when you seek to serve others. That suggests a service orientation, not a slavish orientation.

There is a need for mutually recognized reciprocity. We expect others may serve us in a way bearing some relation to our conception of how we serve them. Indeed, if we view others as serving too much or too little, we may well become uneasy.

Kym Galloway, a top matchmaker based in California, advises her clients: "Whatever it is you are looking for in a relationship, you should also bring to that relationship." Of course, that means what you bring from the vantage point of the other person.

The persuasive communication approaches applicable elsewhere also hold for seeking romantic partners. Third parties may help you recognize patterns in your thoughts and actions. Simply taking inventory of your habitual responses and approaches can be revealing. You may find that you were serving yourself, or serving outdated notions or past relationships. In sum, you were doing things other than serving your prospective romantic partner.

Nothing is more persuasive in personal relationships than effectively communicating your desire to serve the other person. If you're seeking to persuade another to love you, persuade them by serving them as far as possible; seek to establish a loving relationship by demonstrating that you can serve them in a way that is manifestly unique.

ADAPTABILITY, AUTHENTICITY, INTEGRITY

The most effective persuasive communications comprise adaptability and authenticity.

There can be tension between the two. *Adaptability* can be constrained by too rigid a sense of what constitutes authenticity. The credibility, the force issuing from *authenticity* can be undermined if one appears to be unduly responsive to ever-changing circumstances.

Integrity unifies authenticity and adaptability. The result can be an engine of service that runs powerfully, runs true.

Effectiveness in persuasion, as in other aspects of twentieth-first-century leadership, calls upon all aspects of your life. In one sense, this is not new. The classical historian Plutarch, in *Lives of the Noble Romans*, argued that the character of leaders is revealed in small, everyday actions as well as momentous decisions.

Today, the entire world can witness and judge those small, everyday actions. Anyone seeking to persuade others of his vision must recognize that his access to larger numbers of deeper relationships is accompanied by his own life becoming an open book. An otherwise compelling vision may be undermined by digital photos of boorish behavior at a football game or other social event, or a moment of unjustifiable harshness to a spouse, a child or an elderly person. Even "liking" or sharing a social media post can be hazardous.

In the end, to be effective as a leader, you must strive—and be recognized as striving—to live the values you advocate. Persuasive communication is not the mere presentation of a vision; it's how you give it life. The greater the vision, the deeper the relationship sought with those you would serve, the more your life and work become one.

The concluding section of the book is about how you achieve such integrity: living to serve. Where the preceding chapters generally apply to both individuals and enterprises, the final chapter focuses on making service the fundamental, ultimate concern of your life.

Police your brand daily.

—ARNOLD PALMER

Writer Elizabeth Gilbert, in her book *Eat, Pray, Love,* suggests that every great city has a single word that defines it. Rome, for example, could be "Sex," Stockholm might be "conform," and so on.

What one word would you suggest represents you? Do you think others would see it the same way? Do they see you differently in your work and personal lives? How are you communicating your values? Has your one word changed over time?

What would you like your one word to be? What are you doing to merit the one word you seek?

RECAP
SALES AND OTHER PERSUASIVE COMMUNICATIONS

───────◆───────

In a time when consent must be continuously earned, persuasion is the essence of leadership. At their best, persuasive communications impel individuals and organizations to decide to act in furtherance of a leader's vision.

Casting a vision—pointing toward a shared future so vivid it can break through established world views shaped by history, custom and ongoing experience—is a fundamental leadership task. A consequential leader personifies her vision, melding ever more aspects of her life into her service. Her entire life becomes a series of teachable moments.

In the twenty-first century, even leaders serving relatively limited groups and goals must strive to conduct their lives consistently with their values if they wish to be effective.

───────◆───────

Who Are You Serving?

— Strive to serve, *not* to sell. If you focus on serving, the sale will take care of itself.

— Always keep those you're serving front and center in your thoughts and imagination.

— Ensure that your perspective is from the *outside-in*, not the inside-out.

How Can You Best Serve?

— Start serving *now*; tap the power of reciprocity. Serving others in appropriate ways, even common courtesies, can set the stage for effective persuasion.

— Listen to those you seek to persuade. *Really* listen. Unwillingness or incapacity to listen is a sure sign that you're serving yourself.

— If you would persuade, be persuadable. Being recognized as persuadable can have tremendous force, because it underscores your commitment to serve others.

— Begin with questions, not answers.

— Acquire a "Third Ear." Listen for what is being communicated— including what is *not* being said.

— Focus on what they're buying, not on what you're selling. Those you're serving may see your offering as something quite different from what you anticipated or intended. Respect their evaluation as decisive.

— Frame your communications in terms familiar and of value to your audience. "It's not what you say; it's what people hear." The greater the change you seek, the more you should frame your arguments in ways respecting, reflecting and advancing the values, history and aspirations of those you would serve.

— Communicate in a format to which your audience is receptive. Don't simply inform your audience, *engage* them.

— Appeal to interest, not intellect.

— Take yes for an answer. Then stop talking.

Are You Making Your Unique Contribution?

— Be the first, be the only.

— Create competition to establish unique value.

— Encourage third parties to make your case.

— Cast a vision into which others choose to incorporate their callings, their missions. This is one leadership task you cannot delegate.

— Live your values—*You Are the Message*. Make your life a series of teachable moments.
— Safeguard your credibility. There is no greater evidence of a commitment to serve than to faithfully pursue the truth, wherever it may go.

What Are You Learning?

— Deep, ongoing engagement means continuous improvement. To resist changing the format and substance of persuasive communications would be to serve yourself. The ineffectiveness in persuasion that inevitably results from resisting change is a harbinger of a broader incapacity to serve.
— Effective persuasive communication requires adaptability and authenticity. The two can be reconciled in the person of a leader with overarching integrity. In today's digital world, failing to strive to live your values, even in your "private" life, can decisively diminish your persuasive power.

PREPARE TO SERVE

Who Am I Serving? Consider examples of individuals you find especially persuasive. They might be business colleagues, memorably strong salespeople and marketers, or members of your family. How do they make clear who they are serving? Are there lessons you can apply? Recalling your best performances as a persuader, how did you attain the perspective of those you were serving?

How Can I Best Serve? How do you determine how you can best serve in a persuasive communication situation? What have you observed in other effective communicators as they decide how best to serve, from their audiences' point of view? How can you apply such a focus to an upcoming persuasive communication event in your work or personal life?

Am I Making My Unique Contribution? Think of significant relationships in your life and work which require you to be persuasive. Are you convinced—*truly convinced*—that you can serve better than anyone else? If so, are you effectively communicating your value? If you are not convinced that you can serve better than anyone else—or if you're failing to communicate it—how will you rectify the situation?

What Am I Learning? Are you improving your persuasive communications? How do you know? How different are your persuasive communications today than in the past? What metrics are you using to gauge progress? Are you considering how you are viewed by new audiences, including older and younger generations you may not have dealt with previously?

— Are your persuasive communications incorporating aspects of your personality, experience and values, integrating your work and personal lives? Are there areas of inconsistency which could be usefully addressed?

PART 3

Every Day's a Decision

7

What Are You Becoming?

"How many people are trapped in their everyday habits:
part numb, part frightened, part indifferent? To have a
better life we must keep choosing how we're living."

— **ALBERT EINSTEIN**

"Each day is a little life; every waking and rising a little birth; every fresh
morning a little youth, every going to rest and sleep a little death."

— **ARTHUR SCHOPENHAUER**

"In the long run, we shape our lives and we shape
ourselves. The process never ends until we die. And, the
choices we make are ultimately our responsibility."

— **ELEANOR ROOSEVELT**

S teve Jobs was dead.
Bloomberg News released its obituary for the tech titan on 27 August 2008.

The Bloomberg piece recited Jobs' multifarious accomplishments and experiences. Controversies were touched on lightly. There were notes of grace. Bill Gates, a longtime rival, lauded Jobs as "the best inspirational leader I've ever met."

In fact, Jobs was very much alive.

He might look to the example of Mark Twain, who also had the experience of reading his own, premature obituary. Twain famously responded, "The reports of my death are greatly exaggerated."

What a focusing experience, reading one's own obituary! There is a ruthless clarity imposed by the exercise of fitting a life, in all its parts, into a few formulaic paragraphs composed against the ultimate, non-negotiable deadline.

Ernest Hemingway read his own inadvertently accelerated obituaries. He is said to have carried them around, reviewing them constantly. Perhaps he found them useful in clarifying his priorities. Perhaps he thought he was denying death its dominion. Like many writers, he confronted his life much as he did a major project. His approach reflected an extraordinary self-assertion, an unbounded confidence in his capacity to forge his own destiny. Drawing upon various experiences, including proximity to combat in World War I, Hemingway said, "I got [dying] pretty good, complete with handles, because I had been breathed upon by the Grim Reaper more than once...."

> *If I were to die today and people were to write my epitaph, it would actually be a pretty damn good one. It would say she lived wisely, agreeably and well. And to me that is really how you've got to live life. You've got to say, at every point in your life, if you were to drop dead, would your epitaph be something that you could be proud of? Is your legacy something that would linger long after you?*
>
> —INDRA NOOYI

Alfred Nobel is renowned for endowing the prestigious prizes bearing his name. Foremost is the Nobel Peace Prize. Incongruously, his immense fortune was based on the invention of dynamite. It is said the magnate was moved to alter and expand his legacy after confronting an unanticipated obituary: "The merchant of death is dead."

In the normal course of things, most of us cannot expect to read our own obituaries. Nonetheless you may have moments when you sense the warm breath of death brushing the nape of your neck. Perhaps your imagination is stirred by the loss of others, a troubling medical diagnosis, or a rising awareness of the transience, the inescapable, apparent randomness and contingency of so much of life.

If you are going to decide, every day, how you will live, you must give serious thought to the life you are creating. Have you written your own obituary?

Prepare to live more purposefully by drafting your own obituary. What would you like it to say? What would you like others to remember about you and your life? What is your legacy? Draft a realistic piece—but aim for your highest goals, your ultimate concerns. You may find inspiration in reading well-crafted obituaries of memorable lives. One good collection is *Great Lives: A Century in Obituaries*, from the London *Times*, edited by Ian Brunskill. Or read obituaries from the best contemporary sources, such as the *New York Times*, the London *Times*, the London *Daily Telegraph*, and the *Economist*. As you draft yours, strive for a longer view, an outsider's perspective.

Your obituary is, most importantly, a history of the relationships of your life. You may want to share your draft with trusted friends and others who can add their points of view. In the end, others will have the last word.

In the preceding chapter you considered the *one word* you would choose to convey your essence. If you consulted others, you learned how you are perceived from the outside. Sometimes, as with public speaking, what you intend and what others experience bear less relation to one another than you might have supposed.

Now, from the perspective of a complete life, you can expand that concise summary—but just a little.

Clare Boothe Luce was a celebrated twentieth-century writer and politician. With her second husband, *Time* founder Henry Luce, she had a rare vantage point to observe world affairs, becoming personally acquainted with many of the top leaders in myriad fields, from numerous nations.

Luce reminded highly accomplished people that everyone gets only one sentence in memory. Even presidents of the United States, she said, get only one sentence—no matter how much more they might believe they merit.

Isn't Luce's insight apt for all of us? Think back on people you have known and admired or loved who have passed on. How would you summarize their lives in a single sentence?

How would you craft *your* one sentence? You can take your summary sentence, and apply it going forward as your personal *vision statement*.

Draft the single sentence that you would like to express the essence of your life. It may seem difficult initially, but limit yourself to a single sentence. Perhaps it would be the opening or closing of your obituary. Think of it as the ultimate take-away, the one, memorable, apt line that you would have others summon up in looking back on your life. Make this your *vision statement for leading your life* from this day forward.

Are you living up to your vision statement? Would others agree with your assessment? What steps can you take to align your life with your intended legacy?

> *When I was 13, I had an inspiring teacher of religion*
> *who one day went right through the class of boys asking*
> *each one, "What do you want to be remembered for?"*
> *None of us, of course, could give an answer.*
> *So, he chuckled and said, "I didn't expect you to be*
> *able to answer it. But if you still can't answer it by the*
> *time you're 50, you will have wasted your life."*
> *I'm always asking that question: "What do you want*
> *to be remembered for?" It is a question that induces you*
> *to renew yourself, because it pushes you to see yourself*
> *as a different person—the person you can become.*
> —PETER DRUCKER

In Chapter 2, you began to draft your *Service Map*. In the remainder of this chapter, you will take the steps to complete that project. The *Serve to Lead* System is presented in a format in which you can focus each week on a specific aspect of your development.

At the end of eight weeks, you will have undertaken tangible actions to *make your life a masterpiece of service.*

WHO ARE YOU SERVING?

Having made it to this point in the book, you will have incorporated this question into your daily life. Have you noticed that it cannot be compartmentalized?

You may have first used it to improve your communications with your supervisor—and realized it can also be effective in dealing with your children. Or, having found it useful in improving your time management with your family, you're now applying it at work.

Wherever you begin, you soon find that silos of service are hard to sustain. A spirit of service introduced into one part of your life is unlikely to be contained.

APPLY THE QUESTION TO YOUR TIME, MONEY, RELATIONSHIPS & THOUGHTS.

This section includes a four-week program to align your values—your aspirations to serve—with your life.

In Weeks One and Two, you will audit how you spend your time and money. This will illuminate who you're *actually* serving in your life, day-in and day-out. In Week Three you will undertake a thoroughgoing review of the relationships in your life. In Week Four, you will move to the next level, reviewing your ongoing thought patterns—the habitual ways in which you process and respond to your life as you experience it, minute by minute, hour by hour, day by day. At the end of Week Four, you will begin updating your *Service Map*, incorporating what you've learned—and decided—during your first month.

Action expresses priorities.

—MAHATMA GANDHI

 Week One: Account for Your Time

How much time are you devoting to work? Within that time, how much are you working (rather than getting to work, preparing to work, talking about work, thinking about work, etc.)?

In Week One, keep a Time Journal. Simply write down how you spend your time. Account for the entire 168 hours. Make note of things you do for even five or ten minutes.

After completing this task for a week, examine your calendar entries with care. Reflect on each increment of time, asking: Who Am I Serving?

Within your work, who are you serving? Your customers? Your supervisor? Your direct reports?

Do you find yourself watching television excessively?

Who are you serving when you read gossip magazines, or surf the web to amuse yourself?

Who are you serving in your choices in diet and exercise? Are you making decisions which enhance your ability to serve those you care about? Or are you simply serving yourself, eating junk food, methodically transforming yourself into an appendage to a recliner?

Are you attending to vital relationships, in your personal and business lives?

Does your use of time reflect your commitment to those you're serving?

How does it align with your *Service Map* you created in Chapter 2? Do you see areas where too much time is allocated to self-serving choices—including inactivity?

Notice how much time you have that is not effectively serving others—or even yourself. It's easy to fritter away an hour or more a day on activities which, essentially, serve no one.

Some people celebrate the "extra" hour they get from turning the clock back from daylight savings time in the autumn. Yet they may well assemble an additional workday each week in their midst, simply by making use of the "loose change" of moments they heretofore wasted without a thought. Over the course of a year, that can approach *two months* of additional productive time.

> *Guard well your spare moments. They are like uncut diamonds.*
> *Discard them and their value will never be known. Improve*
> *them and they will become the brightest gems in a useful life.*
> —RALPH WALDO EMERSON

> *Time is the scarcest resource, and unless it is*
> *managed, nothing else can be managed.*
> —PETER DRUCKER

 ## 2 Week Two: Account for Your Money

In your second week, audit your use of money with a *Finance Journal*. As with your time, your money is an indisputable indicator of who you're serving.

If you have access to a personal computer, you might turn to a comprehensive software program such as Quicken. Of course, a pen and paper will suffice.

As with your time audit, keep a Finance Journal over the course of an entire week. Be sure to note even the smallest expenditures. To create a useful context, also lay out, as best you can, all your spending over the course of the preceding three months, six months, one year. Don't be concerned if you don't have a complete picture of the earlier periods; reviewing the larger trends, combined with the details of one week, will yield significant data.

Do you like the portrait that emerges? Are your spending and saving habits consistent with your ultimate values?

Review your regular expenditures with a skeptical eye. Just because something is familiar doesn't mean it makes sense. How many of your customary purchases are truly necessary? Are your spending habits and career goals in sync? Are you saving today for your future years? It is easy to drop cash (or, even more insidiously, to flash a credit card) for high-end coffee, short vacations and other trifles which, with minimal lifestyle adjustment, could be redirected to finance an annual contribution to an individual retirement account. For young people, given the time value of money, the opportunity costs of misallocated spending can be staggering.

Pay close attention to your levels of debt. The Bible says it plainly in Proverbs 22:7: "[T]he borrower is servant to the lender." Regrettably, many people almost absentmindedly make decisions resulting in their dedicating much of their lives to serving lenders. "Debt service" is a term worth pondering.

Are you serving lenders for essential items, such as a home and car within your means? Are you serving lenders for investment in your future through relevant education?

Or are you serving lenders for what earlier generations called "super-fluities," which will not serve those you most care about?

 Week Three: Account for Your Relationships

In the third week, turn to your relationships. Keep a *Relationship Journal* each day over the course of a week.

First, list the most important relationships across the entirety of your life. What do your Time Journal and Finance Journal reveal about how you are serving your relationships?

Over the course of Week Three, itemize and reflect on your interactions with the people you're seeking to serve. Are you tending to vital relationships with family and friends and others?

Make note of how you interact with each person or group. To what extent are you serving yourself versus serving them?

Are you deepening existing relationships? Are you initiating new relationships? Are you making friends? Are you transforming interactions and transactions into relationships? For example, are you taking—and expressing—sincere interest in the person who makes deliveries to your office? Are you giving additional attention to older and younger people and others who face daunting challenges?

This book is about managing your mind. It presents an approach to reorient your thought patterns, moving them into alignment with your values. Above all, your default response in comprehending any situation will be to ask yourself, *Who Are You Serving?*

Your thoughts are your reality—which may be, to a great extent, independent of objective circumstances.

Over the course of one week, keep a *Thought Journal*. Jot down your thoughts as you go through your daily living.

Do you notice that certain thoughts are recurring? Are they triggered by specific circumstances?

Do you routinely have positive thoughts? Habitually negative thoughts? Do you assume the best from other people—or the worst? Are there voices—your own or others'—from your past, finding their way into your mind now? Do you recognize patterns? Do they enable you to serve effectively? Do they reinforce your ability to live more intently in the moment, to listen and observe more purposefully? Or do they distract you from being fully present?

Our minds are comparable to gardens. We should expect to spend some time attending to them. There are weeds to pull, seeds to plant, growth to guide and prune, vulnerable places to nurture with warm sun, needed nutrients and clean water.

Many people don't take the time to tend that garden. They allow destructive growth to multiply, imperiling the well-being of vital plants. They may be resigned to the presence of alien species brought in by others—or by themselves in earlier times.

> *Choice of attention—to pay attention to this and ignore that—is to the inner life what choice of action is to the outer.*
> —W.H. AUDEN

A wise saying is: *Don't believe everything you think.* Author and educator Tama Kieves asks: "Would you take advice from an insane advisor? Sure you would, and do." Disordered thinking, out-of-date thought patterns, undue worry about things which brooding cannot cure—these can constitute a disabling inner world. The result: you're listening to, giving credence to—and acting on the basis of—grotesquely distorted thoughts.

◆
What's the language of your world?
◆

The great philosopher Ludwig von Wittgenstein said, "The limits of my language are the limits of my world." What's the language of *your* world?

Your beliefs become your thoughts.
Your thoughts become your words.
Your words become your actions.
Your actions become your habits.
Your habits become your values.
Your values become your destiny.

—MAHATMA GANDHI

As with your time, money and relationships, accounting for your thoughts enables you to manage them. For a moment, imagine your life as a motion picture: your thoughts are one-part screenplay, one-part soundtrack, one-part camera work, one-part editing and production. The best result emerges if each aspect is in sync with the others, and all are consistent with your values, your ultimate intention.

A few people may be blessed with empowering habits of thought through happenstance of temperament, education and experience.

Most of us have some work to do. Having determined who we're serving, we need to bring our customary thought patterns into alignment.

Directing your attention, truly focusing on those you're serving—and repeating positive, energizing affirmations—can transform your inner dialogue into an encouraging, empowering force.

We cannot always control our thoughts, but we can control
our words, and repetition impresses the subconscious,
and we are then master of the situation.

—FLORENCE SCOVEL SHINN

As we have seen throughout this book, effectively using The Four Questions moves your perspective beyond the limitations of *self*-consciousness to the expanded world of *other*-consciousness.

Depending on your level of need and desire, you may want to experiment, making additional changes to your thought patterns:

— Louise Hay has a series of positive affirmations in her beloved book, *You Can Heal Your Life.*

— Dr. David Burns' *Feeling Good* is an accessible introduction to cognitive therapy. This is simply taking command of your inner dialogue to expose and alter your thought patterns. Burns includes exercises to identify and replace negative self-talk.

— *Managing Your Mind: The Mental Fitness Guide*, by Gillian Butler, Ph.D., and Tony Hope, M.D., is a useful compendium for developing healthy mental habits. Its premise of self-determination is consistent with a determination to serve.

After Week Four, Update Your *Service Map*: Who Are You Serving?

At the end of Week Four, you're prepared to reexamine and update your *Service Map*. Based on your accounting of your time, money, relationships and thoughts, is your *Service Map* consistent with the life you're leading? Do you wish to refine your initial thoughts about who you're serving? Are you leading your life toward the vision you've established?

The more tightly you align your resources—time, money, relationships, thoughts—toward those you would serve, the more effective you will be.

> *Our duties naturally emerge from such fundamental relations*
> *as our families, neighborhoods, workplaces, our state or nation.*
> *Make it your regular habit to consider your roles—*
> *parent, child, neighbor, citizen, leader—and the*
> *natural duties that arise from them.*
> *Once you know who you are and to whom you*
> *are linked, you will know what to do.*
>
> —EPICTETUS

HOW CAN YOU BEST SERVE?

Having clarified who you are serving, *How Can You Best Serve?* In many situations, simply to ask the question is to answer it.

Yet, there are often choices you must face.

TO SERVE IS TO CHOOSE.

Charles Dickens offered a cautionary example of misplaced service priorities in his nineteenth-century novel *Bleak House.*

Dickens' Mrs. Jellyby is resolutely committed to the "Borrioboola-Gha venture." It is a prototype not-for-profit organization dedicated to settling impoverished Britons among African natives. Its laudable mission is mutual improvement and benefit through establishment of an indigenous coffee industry.

Like a woman possessed, Mrs. Jellyby throws herself into this indisputably well-intentioned, idealistic enterprise. Regrettably, her monomaniacal approach does not suffice to create success. The forsaken English volunteers are sold into slavery by an African despot seeking funds for rum. All the while, Mrs. Jellyby overlooks the needs of her long-suffering husband and children, sowing resentment, discouragement and despair in her own household.

Dickens' tableau may strike us as melodramatic, but the underlying issue is real. Who is Mrs. Jellyby serving? To an extent, she's serving her charitable cause. Nonetheless, it fails. Her daughter Caddy, a conscript into her crusade, understandably becomes hostile to all things African. Mrs. Jellyby, "telescopic philanthropist," sees only into the distance, oblivious to what's in her midst. She neglects those who need her most, whose lives she can most readily affect.

Lest the tale of Mrs. Jellyby seem overdrawn, consider a choice faced a few years back on the *Dr. Phil* television show.

Dr. Phil (Dr. Philip C. McGraw) was working with a teenage girl facing a dilemma.

The girl had spent time serving as a student volunteer in Africa. She found fulfillment in making a manifest, positive difference in the lives of people enduring the most grievous circumstances. Returning to conventional American high school life, she felt alienated amid the self-absorbed, self-defeating behaviors she now recognized among her fellow students.

The girl was inclined toward cutting short her formal education to return to Africa. Her family was supportive of her service, respectful of her rising maturity. Nonetheless, her parents were worried about the long-term consequences of her dropping out.

Dr. Phil, with his customary combination of gentleness and forthrightness, helped her clarify her thoughts through a series of questions. She soon recognized she could provide greater service in the future if she obtained additional skills in school.

The takeaway: any decision to serve in one way necessarily affects your capacity to serve in others. Even a choice which seems inevitable constitutes a decision. Sometimes, a course which appears on its face to be serving others, is, from a broader perspective, more ambiguous.

———————◆———————

Third parties—including objective friends—can be valuable in helping sort out your service priorities and choices. Relationships that at first glance appear to be based on service can be deceiving. People in Mrs. Jellyby's situation may be acting out expressed or suppressed anger against those they believe they love. In other situations, some may not recognize subtle, destructive changes occurring in relationships initially rooted in service.

Just as foreign visitors sometimes understand other nations more clearly than the native-born, outside observers can help you see aspects of your choices which you may overlook or undervalue.

———————◆———————

AFFIX YOUR OXYGEN MASK SO YOU CAN SERVE OTHERS.

Passengers on commercial airlines are familiar with the admonition repeated by flight attendants: *In case of an emergency, be sure to strap on your oxygen mask before acting to assist others.*

This is said, of course, because most of us would instinctively move to assist others first, especially young children. Yet, to anyone assessing the situation clearly, it's obvious that you can serve more people, more effectively, if you take care of yourself first.

In a similar way, some people misguidedly say it's selfish for you to take care of your physical health. In fact, it's self-regarding not to do so. Otherwise, you simply cannot serve effectively.

> *To preserve health is a moral and religious duty,*
> *for health is the basis of all social virtues.*
> *We can no longer be useful when we are not well.*
> —SAMUEL JOHNSON

> *Take care of your body with steadfast fidelity.*
> *The soul must see through these eyes alone,*
> *and if they are dim, the whole world is clouded.*
> —JOHANN WOLFGANG GOETHE

> *Pay mind to your own life, your own health, and wholeness.*
> *A bleeding heart is of no help to anyone if it bleeds to death.*
> —FREDERICK BUECHNER

> *As I see it, every day you do one of two things:*
> *build health or produce disease in yourself.*
> —ADELLE DAVIS, DIET AND LIFESTYLE PIONEER

Every decision you make in the course of a day affects your capacity to serve. The food and drink you ingest is nothing other than a high-volume medication. Is there a more vexing sight than people consuming vast amounts of unhealthy food, washing it down with canisters of processed sugar water—and then downing a few vitamin pills in pointless penance?

Daily decisions about physical exercise can have long-range consequences. Should you walk—or drive? Should you stand—or sit? Should you work out—or "veg out" in front of a computer or television screen? These are not small things; they are consequential decisions. Many complaints about stress, anxiety and fatigue are simply the body's pleas for activity. New York Times personal health columnist Jane Brody sums it up: "You Name It, and Exercise Helps It."

Protecting your physical health becomes a rising priority over the course of advancing years. Young people tend to have surplus physical energy. They generally require discipline and guidance to develop the capacity to sit and think for the extended periods of time required for learning and work. For older people, that reverses; their default position may be sedentary. The discipline required in youth for an "iron butt" must shift, with an iron will, to stirring themselves to activity.

◆

Are you maintaining your capacity to serve effectively by giving your health the priority it requires? Are you able to set personal goals and schedules which you enforce? Are you adjusting your approach to health and fitness to reflect your current stage of life?

◆

LISTEN AND LEARN WITH A SERVANT'S MIND AND HEART.

There is no substitute, in any situation, for learning from those you would serve. They will be the source for your determination how best to serve; so, too, they will be the ultimate decision makers. Even if you conclude that they're best served by actions going against their immediate wishes, you will be ascertaining how you can best serve them, *from their point of view.* The more you can identify with them, empathize with them—and take yourself out of the picture—the more effective you will be.

HOW YOU CAN BEST SERVE CHANGES OVER TIME.

Your contribution, and the service others need, change over time. Approaches which would be self-regarding at one time in life may be necessary for service in another; what's useful service in some situations might be self-regarding in others.

Young people may be especially effective in providing service reliant on their abundant physical energy. Older people may add more value from their judgment or experience.

The needs of those you serve are constantly changing. You may be serving a growing group, seeking to deepen relationships. You may be serving them over time, their needs evolving with events. Wars end; children grow up; the sick recover; others pass on. Customers' desires and expectations change. Imagine how a person transported from the 1950s or 1960s would react to the mass affluence, freedom and heightened product quality expectations enjoyed by Americans today!

Many people assume that as they serve in various ways—family, community, work—their lives will become "balanced." In some cases that may be true; at least as often, it's not.

At one stage of life you may emphasize one area of service to the detriment or exclusion of others. Raising a child, caring for an ailing relative, dealing with an extraordinary work demand, or going to graduate school may crowd out other areas of contribution. The key is to have your life *as a whole* reflect a range of service aligned with your values. At any particular time, though, your life may be far from "balanced."

A life, viewed as a whole, may be balanced in terms of service—yet entirely out-of-balance at specific times.

One thing is certain: change will occur. You should evaluate how you can best serve at regular intervals, based on feedback from and observation of those you're serving, as well as third parties.

How is your service changing over time? How would you like it to evolve?

Beware those who would limit your service to one stage of life or another. Everybody can lead, because everybody can serve *at every time of life*. As Carl Jung observed, "A human being would certainly not grow to be seventy- or eighty-years-old if this longevity had no meaning to the species to which he belonged. The afternoon of human life must also have a significance of its own and cannot merely be a pitiful appendage to life's morning."

SERVICE IS NOT SUBSERVIENCE.

What about situations where others would manipulate you, arguing that you're best suited to serve in a way which is unfair or inappropriate?

Theodore Roosevelt's injunction remains apt: "No one has a right to ask or accept any service unless under changed conditions he would feel that he could keep his entire self-respect while rendering it."

Anyone demanding a relationship of subservience is not serving you, and not enabling you to best serve others. It is especially important to evaluate the course of relationships in which temporary imbalances may become entrenched.

DO THE BEST YOU CAN, WITH WHAT YOU HAVE, WHERE YOU ARE.

The circumstances of your best service are not yours alone to decide. You must, in words prized by Roosevelt, "Do the best you can, with what you have, where you are."

As written in Ecclesiastes 9:10: "Whatsoever thy hand findeth to do, do it with all thy might."

Doing your best—*your absolute best*—is a profound commitment.

In many situations it can be a challenge to determine what your best is. What's the standard?

In some cases there may be an objective standard. In others, there may be an accepted standard—but it may limit rather than stretch your performance goals.

You may have it in your head that someone of your age or gender or height or weight or education (or whatever—you fill in the blank) cannot do certain things. Such thinking is obviously detrimental to your capacity to serve.

Do you allow your mind to obsess on your failures rather than your best moments? In the law all but the most serious crimes have statutes of limitations, dates after which all liability is extinguished. Remarkably, many people internally (and often, externally) replay their failures, rather than their high points. They're creating a world based on visualization of mediocrity and failure. Such dysfunctional thought processes can be reinforced, in our Digital Age, by having many of our worst and most embarrassing moments memorialized in perpetuity, often online.

Have you gone sky-diving? Before you were allowed into a plane, you learned to fall. You repeatedly hit the ground from various angles. There's a lesson in it. If you resisted the fall, feared it, tried to protect your "dignity," you increased your risk of injury. If you accepted it for what it is, regarding it as part of the experience, you rapidly learned to roll into the fall and emerged unscathed.

Shouldn't we think of our missteps and failures in the same way? They're a foreseeable part of our lives. Just take them for what they are, prepare for them, learn from them, dust yourself off, and move on. Examine any memorable life of service and accomplishment; when you go beyond the surface you'll find plenty of errors and failures. In fact, you'll usually find far more errors and failures than in less notable lives.

Why should you expect your life to be any different?

Be not the slave of your own past—
plunge into the sublime seas, dive deep, and swim far,
so you shall come back with self-respect, with new power,
with an advanced experience, that shall
explain and overlook the old.

—RALPH WALDO EMERSON

You should isolate and work to overcome anything which distracts your focus from serving to the utmost of your capacities. To the extent your attention is divided, your contribution is limited.

It is immoral for a being not to make the most
intense effort every instant of his life.

—JOSE ORTEGA Y GASSET

FOCUS ON NOW.

Doing your absolute best means being present in the moment—unreservedly, unconditionally *present.*

As Albert Camus wrote, "Real generosity toward the future consists in giving all to what is present." So, too, the most fitting acknowledgment of debts to those who have served you is to master your present moment of service.

If you want to know your future,
look at what you're doing in this moment.

—TIBETAN PROVERB

Over the course of one week, ask yourself during every interaction with another, *How Can I Best Serve This Person?*

Ask this question in dealing with colleagues and customers, friends and family, strangers and acquaintances.

Your goal is to move ever further from thinking from the inside-out, toward experiencing relationships from the outside-in. It may be useful to identify alternative stances you can decide to assume in your interactions with others:

PLACE OTHERS FIRST	PLACE SELF FIRST
Listening	Speaking
Courageous	Self-Protective
Positive	Negative
Open	Suspicious
Optimistic	Despairing
Encouraging	Discouraging
Build Up	Tear Down
Empowering	Disempowering
Praising	Criticizing
Patient	Impatient
Courteous	Rude
Grateful	Entitled
Giving	Taking
Creating	Consuming
Generous	Miserly
Modest	Prideful
Initiating	Passive
Graceful	Grudging
Vital, Engaged	Indifferent, Withdrawn

Determining how you can best serve need not be limited to major moments of decision in your work or personal life. You can serve anyone who comes into contact with you with nothing more than an appropriate,

Examine your own service.

Are you effectively deploying your resources relating to time, money, relationships and thoughts toward your highest priorities? Are your deepest values and lifestyle in—or out—of alignment?

Even the best decisions of yesterday may not remain effective if unexamined today. Think of your service priorities like a diversified investment portfolio.

Now and again, reflecting subtle and major adjustments over time, you may need to reallocate resources to advance your strategy. On other occasions, you may decide to revisit the strategy itself.

heartfelt, kind gesture. Mother Teresa's ideal is serviceable: "Let no one ever come to you without leaving better and happier. Be the living expression of God's kindness: kindness in the face, kindness in your eyes, kindness in your smile."

At first glance it may seem trivial to cultivate habits of serving others in daily, customary interactions. Some dismiss it as "merely" being considerate.

There is something larger going on. George Washington, as a student exercise, transcribed "Rules of Civility and Decent Behavior in Company and Conversation." The first precept—which could be said to be basis for the rest—is: "Every action done in company, ought to be done with some sign of respect, to those that are present."

Washington recognized that serving others in small ways could build and strengthen habits of thinking, putting others' needs before your own. The result can be an instinctive inclination to serve that can be drawn upon at unforeseen moments, for the highest stakes.

Even a commonplace courtesy, remark or question, can have immense influence. Richard Adkerson, the highly intelligent, longtime CEO of

Freeport-McMoRan, traces a strand of his career achievement to a challenge from a dedicated professor.

The teacher asked Adkerson, if he, a star accounting student at Mississippi State, could achieve the top score in the state's certified public accounting exam—thereby defeating archrival Ole Miss. Adkerson took the bit and charged ahead. He not only came in at the top in Mississippi, he scored second in the entire nation. His mentor's well-aimed question continues to reverberate, decades later. Adkerson regards it as a hinge moment, helping lay the foundation for a career of ongoing growth and achievement.

Calvin Trillin's remarkable book, *About Alice*, is a memoir of his love for his late wife. A poignant incident illustrates the power of a "small" act to serve many people with "the transformative power of pure, undiluted love."

Alice, who volunteered at a summer camp, recalled "the camper I got closest to, L…, a magical child who was severely disabled." Genetic diseases precluded her from digesting food or growing. She was fed with a tube. Alice transported L. from place to place in a golf cart.

Alice recounted that on one occasion, L. asked her to hold her mail while she was occupied in a game. Alice could not help but notice a note on top. It was from L.'s mother. Her reluctance to violate the girl's privacy was overwhelmed by the force of her curiosity:

> I simply had to know what this child's parents could have done to make her so spectacular, to make her the most optimistic, most enthusiastic, most hopeful human being I had ever encountered. I snuck a quick look at the note, and my eyes fell on this sentence: "If God had given us all of the children in the world to choose from, L., we would only have chosen you."

Alice shared the note with her husband. "'Quick. Read this…It's the secret of life.'"

Such "small acts" can hold the power to serve many people, across time and space.

Three things in human life are important:
the first is to be kind, the second is to be kind,
and the third is to be kind.

—HENRY JAMES

Let no one ever come to you without
leaving better and happier.

—MOTHER TERESA

Kindness is the ultimate wisdom.

—VARIOUS SPIRITUAL TRADITIONS

After Week Five, Update Your *Service Map*: How Can You Best Serve?
After completing Week Five, review your *Service Map*. Focus on each person or enterprise you are serving, making note of how you can best serve. Are there areas of overlap? Are you setting clear priorities? Have you reexamined longstanding commitments to ensure they're up to date with your current thinking? Are your actual practices relating to time, money, relationships and thoughts consistent with your best service? Can you envision future adjustments in how you can best serve? Having posed the question—*How Can I Best Serve?*—over the course of a week, what have you learned? What can you apply to your future outlook and actions?

ARE YOU MAKING YOUR UNIQUE CONTRIBUTION?

In our terms, your unique contribution can be found at the place where your passion to express yourself from the *inside-out* (representing your deepest values) coincides with your commitment to serve others from the *outside-in* (focusing on their needs and possibilities).

Have you located the magical place that is your calling? If so, are you fulfilling it? Are you doing what only you can do? Is your contribution truly unique, bringing to bear all aspects of your life and capacities? Is your contribution valued appropriately by those you're serving?

DO WHAT YOU LOVE, FOR THOSE YOU LOVE.

To identify your calling, consider questions such as:

— what do you see as your three greatest talents or gifts?
— what do other people recognize as your greatest talents or gifts?
— when in your work do you feel the most confidence, even mastery?
— when have you been in "the zone," where your concentration is so great that time stands still?
— what work leaves you exhilarated?
— what would you like to do for a living if money were no object?
— what you do if you weren't afraid of failure?
— what has brought you greatest fulfillment?
— is there anyone whose career you would like to emulate?
— what do you have to do, irrespective of circumstances?
— what are you most passionate about?

Before a human being thinks of others he must have been unapologetically himself; he must have taken the measure of his nature in order to master it and employ it for the benefit of others....
—RAINER MARIA RILKE

Talent does what it can; genius does what it must.
—EDWARD BULWER-LYTTON

ARE YOU WILLING TO GIVE UP WHAT YOU DON'T LOVE?

Dan Sullivan, founder of the Strategic Coach program, declares, "You can have everything you love in life if you give up everything you hate." The notion is simple and powerful. That doesn't mean it's easy.

It may mean outsourcing or delegating tasks which are unpleasant, nonessential—but are nonetheless familiar and somehow comforting to undertake.

Marti Barletta, author and renowned expert on marketing to women, explains that one of the most difficult—and necessary—decisions is to turn away business opportunities. Offers may come in the door which are within your recognized areas of competence—but not in your area of unique contribution. When you're serving a group of employees, a family, and others dependent on you, now and in the future, this can be a vexing question.

Nonetheless, at some point you've got to decide: are you going "all-in"?

GO ALL-IN.

Everyone who finds their calling goes "all-in." As the old saying goes, "It's not to try, it's do or die."

Jerry Seinfeld recalls his decision to go "all-in":

> Even if I could just make enough to buy a loaf of bread and not starve to death, [being a comedian] was the greatest adventure that I could ever go on. I said, "I don't give a damn what happens to me; I'm doing this." That's the only way to really do it. I didn't know it at the time, but I was just like, as the poker players like to say, "all-in." My parents thought, "Well he'll get a job; it's just like something he's investigating."

Paul McCartney and John Lennon could only imagine playing rock and roll. According to their perceptive biographer Bob Spitz:

> Who else would have presumed to write their own songs? Or team up so audaciously with a manager?...It was never more apparent than in their long-range outlook: none of them had anything to fall back on. Their peers all had day jobs; the Beatles had never even thought seriously about punching a clock. It was only ever music, only the band, *only The Beatles*. There were no other options. This was their life's work.

Figuratively and literally, the Beatles put everything they had into their work. They went all-in. Their lives were not "balanced." Their prospects were uncertain. They did not have the backstop of a reliable precedent in terms of a career path. Every disappointment, every discouragement, every false start, every failure had to be mined for whatever it might yield for learning and advancement.

Looking back, it is easy to sentimentalize such a commitment. Looking forward from where they started, one is reminded just how daunting it was. The Beatles' first manager, Brian Epstein recalled, "John [Lennon] said rich bastards like me didn't realize what it was to want to succeed. I had the family business 'to fall back on.'"

There are always powerful arguments not to go all-in. Many—perhaps most—are entirely reasonable. You may be financially successful in a traditionally prestigious profession, such as a doctor or lawyer. Yet your passion—which only you can gauge—may lie elsewhere. For example, you might long to serve in Doctors Without Borders, or as an educator or author. While the costs to those who prefer you not to change may be clear, the benefits you can bring to others through pursuing your calling are, necessarily, hypothetical and uncertain.

For many people, the path of least resistance is maintaining the status quo, albeit with reservations and, in some cases, overhanging, omnipresent anxiety. It's as if they're driving their car toward their planned destination—with the parking brake engaged. It's enough to slow up the journey, it may inhibit performance, yet you heedlessly stay on track.

Tama Kieves recounts her response to this dilemma in her inspiring book, *This Time I Dance!* A strategic question pointed the way as she grappled with the pros and cons of leaving her apparently stable, yet stultifying (for her) encampment as a big-firm attorney, for the more precarious path of an author's life. A good friend put it plainly: "If you're this successful doing work you *don't* love, what could you do with work you *do* love?"

Following your heart to go all-in has never been easy. Nevertheless, it's never been easier than now. In the twenty-first century you have an unprecedented opportunity to alter the contours of your career. For example, you can craft what author (and recovering lawyer) Marci Alboher calls a "slash career"—e.g., Medical Doctor/Educator.

Writer Penelope Trunk proposes a variant, the "braided career." This "intertwine[s] the needs of the people you love, with the work you are doing, and the work you are planning to do, when it's time for a switch."

Trunk explains that you can be a stay-at-home mom and open a side business from the café on the corner. Or you might choose to take a corporate job. Even if it starts far from your calling, you might rack up money and frequent-flyer miles to fuel your dreams of travel or financing your own business.

If such arrangements enable you to pursue the *Service Map* you envision, they can be long-lasting. For many people, though, such hybrids are *instrumental*. They are intended as way-stations en route to the life they want, toward the place where their *fundamental* goals and values fuse into their calling.

However you conceive it, if you're determined to make your unique contribution, you'll have to go all-in. At one time in your life it may mean all-in for your family. At another time it may mean all-in for the business you love. You should not allow your instrumental choices, made for entirely justifiable reasons at one time and place, to become, by default, your *fundamental* decisions. To paraphrase Tim Ferriss, author of *The 4-Hour Workweek*, the risk of a "deferred life plan" is that you'll end up using the power of planning to systematically exclude those elements of living which are most important to you.

The vitalizing point is to recognize and treat these choices as the significant decisions they are. With each passing day, you are designing your life. The very word, "decision," is derived from the Latin, *decidere*, "to cut." In taking one path, you are forsaking others.

At the least, take the first step on the road to where you want to go. You can't be at the right place at the right time, unless you're at the right place to begin with. Put another way, in the words of the invaluable Ben Stein, "You can't win if you're not at the table."

It's a stern decree: *all-in*.

That may sound harsh until you remember that it's all about love— love for your work, love for those your serving.

[B]y any conventional measure, a mere seven years after
my graduation day, I had failed on an epic scale.
An exceptionally short-lived marriage had imploded, and
I was jobless, a lone parent, and as poor as it is possible
to be in modern Britain, without being homeless.
[Failure] meant a stripping away of the inessential.
I stopped pretending to myself that I was anything other
than what I was, and began to direct all my energy
into finishing the only work that mattered to me.
Had I really succeeded at anything else, I might
never have found the determination to succeed in the
one arena where I believed I truly belonged.

—J.K. ROWLING

In some situations, the decision to go all-in may be made more difficult by ongoing success in terms of financial rewards, status, and the approval or dependence of others. Have you gone all-in for a life consistent with your values and vision?

Week Six: Ask 'Am I Making My Unique Contribution?' During Every Task You Undertake

Throughout Week Six, as you go about your life and work, constantly ask yourself the question: *Am I Making My Unique Contribution?* Keep a *Contribution Journal* of your activities for each day.

Be especially aware of two aspects. One is managerial. Are you giving your attention to matters which could be handled as well or better by others? If you're like most of us, you've allowed a number of things in this category to slip into your routine. Another aspect goes deeper. Are you directing the scarce resources of your life toward activities which advance your calling? If not, are you nonetheless doing things which will move you closer to your calling?

After Week Six, Update Your *Service Map*: Are You Making Your Unique Contribution?

At the end of Week Six, review and update your *Service Map. Are You Making Your Unique Contribution?* Are you finding that your attempts to make a unique contribution in one area of your life are limiting your service in other areas? Are you doing work which is not meeting your goals of serving others, because you are handcuffed to a lifestyle that is entirely or primarily self-serving? Are you compromising your service in one area on a temporary basis in order to provide your ultimate service in another? If so, are you prepared to be accountable to make a change at a defined point in the future? Is your choice of work—or the allocation of your time between work and personal life—up-to-date? Or are you serving the goals and expectations you developed or absorbed from others (including, perhaps, your younger self)? Are you comfortable with your current priorities? Are you being sufficiently determined in turning away opportunities inconsistent with your highest and best service? Are you *all-in* to make your unique contribution? Are you committed to shove your stack onto the table at a specific time in the future? If not, *Who Are You Serving?* How would your *Service Map* look different if you *were* making your unique contribution? Can you alter your map to get to that point? If not all at once, can you envision stages of development, creating your future, step-by-step?

WHAT ARE YOU LEARNING?

Leadership—and service—are about change. To serve effectively, you must make ongoing improvement a surpassing priority. The greater the service, the more of yourself must be dedicated and rededicated, cultivated and elaborated.

In the twenty-first century much of your value arises from your capacity to encourage and empower others to learn and grow. You can't long inspire others unless you're inspired.

ARE YOU LEARNED—OR A LEARNER?

Eric Hoffer, a twentieth-century American social philosopher, observed, "In a time of dramatic change, it is the learners who inherit the future. The learned usually find themselves equipped to live in a world that no longer exists."

Learning, learning, learning is essential to effective service over time. A characteristic exemplar is Warren Buffett. He is widely heralded as the world's greatest investor. Buffett is quick to reveal the source of his ideas: "I just read. I read all day." His partner Charlie Munger advises, "If you want to succeed, if you really want to be an outlier in terms of achievement, just sit down on your [rear end] and read—and do it all the time."

> *If a man empties his purse into his head,*
> *no man can take it from him. An investment in*
> *knowledge always pays the best interest.*
> —BENJAMIN FRANKLIN

> *Live as if you were to die tomorrow.*
> *Learn as if you were to live forever.*
> —MAHATMA GANDHI

How do *you* read? Do you read solely for amusement? Or to confirm your pre-existing views? Einstein's admonition is apt: "Anyone who reads too much and uses his own brain too little falls into lazy habits of thinking."

We all know people who have had extensive formal education—and who believe that they know everything they need to know as a result. Others with little or no formal education make a project of lifelong learning and growth. The latter group is far more likely to serve effectively.

> *Every person has two educations,*
> *one which he receives from others, and one,*
> *more important, which he gives to himself.*
> —EDWARD GIBBON

Diplomas and degrees are not emblems of entitlement; they are licenses to learn.

NEVER STOP LEARNING.

Effective service must always be about innovation.

The "creative destruction" observed by twentieth-century economist Joseph Schumpeter relates not only to companies, industries and the broader economy. It's also an apt expression of individuals' capacity to imagine and innovate.

Failure can provide invaluable lessons in how not to do things. An even more treacherous challenge, requiring self-management of the highest order, is to continue learning and improving when you're at the top of your game, getting superior results.

A notable recent example is that of legendary athlete Tiger Woods. Woods has dominated professional golf to an extent unparalleled in any sport, indeed almost any endeavor. In 2002, at the height of his powers, Woods decided to rebuild his swing. For nearly two years thereafter, he failed to win any major championships. Ultimately, he came roaring back, breaking through to new levels perhaps only he could have envisioned. He had effectively navigated the distractions and snares of spectacular success.

Woods recalls, "People thought it was asinine for me to change my swing after I won the Masters by twelve shots…Why would you want to change that? Well, I thought I could always become better."

Something comparable occurred with the Beatles in 1966. The Fab Four were at the apex of their peerless global popularity and cultural influence. They could reasonably have left well enough alone, in terms of what they were doing and how they were doing it. Instead, they initiated a major change.

Without prior public notice, this quintessential live-performance band announced it would discontinue touring at the end of the summer.

The Beatles' final formal concert was at Candlestick Park in San Francisco, on Monday, 29 August 1966.

The group was thereafter able to direct its undivided attention to innovation in the studio. No longer would their creative powers be dissipated in the mind-numbing repetition and kaleidoscopic distractions of touring.

In November, the Beatles entered the Abbey Road studios in London for an unprecedented 129-day recording session. The result: their masterpiece, *Sgt. Pepper's Lonely Hearts Club Band*, released on Thursday, 1 June 1967.

In the ensuing decades, Paul McCartney has not rested on the laurels of his extraordinary achievements in the Beatles. He continues to set sail to explore new and uncharted territory. The legendary rock-and-roller—who was passed over by his local boys' choir—has composed well-regarded classical symphonies. A *Wall Street Journal* review called him "the great musical experimenter among the Beatles... [with a] desire to expand the boundaries of his art."

Innovation poses risks. So too it presents opportunities to increase service, to deepen relationships. Attempts to maintain the status quo can be fatal to prospects for ongoing service. Even amid circumstances which are apparently placid and stable, there is an unmistakable if easily overlooked tendency toward restlessness and reinvention. Ever-changing needs must be anticipated and met for relationships to endure. Novelist Charlotte Bronte explained, "It is vain to say that human beings ought to be satisfied with tranquility: they must have action; and they will make it if they cannot find it."

A leader must constantly act, seize the initiative, redefine frames of reference, expand others' imagination of the possible. The prize is a lasting leadership relationship encompassing the desire and demand for action and novelty and growth among those you serve. As Charles de Gaulle wrote, "A true leader always keeps an element of surprise up his sleeve, which others cannot grasp but which keeps the public excited and breathless."

De Gaulle's insight holds true in any setting—including leading your own life. Arnold Schwarzenegger asserts that "surprising" muscles by altering workouts is critical to ongoing physical development. So, too, you can enlarge your leadership by continually incorporating vitalizing elements of learning and experience.

Never relinquish the initiative.
—CHARLES DE GAULLE

*I've always believed that it's important to
show a new look periodically.
Predictability can lead to failure.*
—T. BOONE PICKENS

SELECT YOUR INNER CIRCLE WITH CARE.

Leadership expert John Maxwell writes of the importance of a leader's "inner circle." Those are the individuals to whom you look for guidance and perspective. They may be assembled into a formal or informal board of advisors. Perhaps they're longtime friends, with whom you have relationships preceding your current service. Perhaps they're mentors, or others possessing valuable, challenging perspectives. Some bring you down to earth; others help you soar.

You already have an inner circle. It includes your family and friends and colleagues. It includes the music you listen to routinely, the radio and television and internet offerings you allow into your life. It includes your inner soundtrack of people long gone from your life—including voices or echoes of your younger self.

In short, your inner circle comprises those people—and their ways of thinking and living—who you have elected to make part of your *outer* life. It also includes those people you have allowed into your *inner* life. Taken together, they have a consequential effect on your ongoing experience, the world you inhabit.

Your choice of your inner circle is a critical decision.

Scientific studies confirm what your grandmother may have told you: you come to resemble those you're around on a regular basis. If they're thoughtful, you're likely to become more thoughtful. If they've got healthy habits, you're likely to develop or maintain healthy habits.

On the other hand, if they're slovenly, or habitually negative, or mentally or physically or emotionally or spiritually slothful....

Is your inner circle providing you with opportunities to learn, challenges to grow? Do they bring out the best in you—or something else? Do they reflect your current values and aspirations for service? If not, are you prepared to decide to change?

Like any adjustment, altering your inner circle can occasion anxious moments. You have a good sense of what you'll be losing. You have no way to know in advance what you might gain by releasing more of your bandwidth to new people and experiences.

A practical question is often raised: where do you find those people from whom you can learn, whose presence inspires you toward your highest service?

Take a second look at people you know or interact with now. Are you missing extraordinary people in your midst? Are you overlooking exceptional aspects among those you encounter?

You can cultivate the habit and skill of searching for talent among individuals who improve your contribution simply by their presence in your life.

Malcolm Gladwell analyzes the roots of the Beatles' achievement in his fine book, *Outliers*. Gladwell emphasizes the value of the seven-day-a-week, eight-hour gigs the foursome eagerly accepted in Hamburg. Their stage and musical skills, as well as their teamwork, were cultivated as they struggled to satisfy the demands of rowdy, primarily German-speaking audiences in the *Reeperbahn* red-light district.

Gladwell convincingly presents the Beatles' development as evidence of his "10,000-Hour Rule." As important as those ten thousand—or more—hours of preparation were, so too it's important *who* those ten thousand hours were spent with. McCartney and Lennon, the core of the team, toiled side-by-side, knee-to-knee, each encouraged and challenged by one of the great musical talents of their generation.

It didn't just happen.

Lennon and McCartney met at a local church event in Liverpool on Saturday, 6 July 1957. Each immediately recognized the talent of the other. Nearly seventeen, Lennon was two years older. He was, primarily on that account, initially acknowledged as dominant. Lennon made the decision to bring McCartney into his band, establishing the working relationship. Imagine…had Lennon had not welcomed McCartney into his world, is it conceivable that either, alone, would have reached the heights they scaled together?

Lennon took pride in his decision: "I only ever asked two people to work with me as a partner. One was Paul McCartney and the other Yoko Ono. That's not too bad, is it?"

It's unlikely you'll happen across someone with the raw talent of Paul McCartney or John Lennon. But you may well encounter many more people of much more talent and possibility than you've assumed. When you cross their paths, are you looking and listening for their strengths? Are you prepared to embrace the challenge and change they may bring into your world?

Some people raise an additional, practical question: what if you're geographically isolated?

At one time you might have looked primarily to books and your own imagination. Now you have the internet.

Social networking platforms enable you to connect with others in unprecedented ways. If you're interested in business, there are various avenues whereby you can track the thinking and doing of many of the most interesting and innovative people on the planet. Simply picking up tidbits about their habits of living and working can raise your game, prompting you to demand more of yourself, day by day.

Those you're serving also become part of your inner circle. They, too, enter your conscious and subconscious experience.

However you go about it, assemble your inner circle with the care of a maestro assembling a world-class orchestra. Their music will echo through your life. They can help you discern and seize new opportunities, illuminating the farther reaches of your imagination and contribution.

What do you consider your greatest accomplishment?
"I am becoming the people I love."

—CARLOS SANTANA

ADOPT 'SPIRITUAL ANCESTORS.'

The twentieth-century English philosopher and polymath Bertrand Russell kept, in his office, a portrait of the seventeenth-century Dutch philosopher Baruch Spinoza. Russell referred to Spinoza as his "spiritual ancestor."

You, too, can have spiritual ancestors, figures from history who inspire you to your best service. Just as your inner circle need not be limited by place, it need not be limited by time.

Many people would never think of ascending an unfamiliar mountain trail without a map or a guide. Yet, they venture forth into the uncertain terrain of their lives without the guidance of those who preceded us.

Some people assume historical exemplars to be of scant value. They look down on those who've come before. They wonder how people with such outdated notions and odd clothing could in any sense enlighten us in our "more complex" time.

Those who came before have something important in common with us: they did not know, as we cannot know, the future. That is precisely why their examples can be invaluable: they can show us how to comprehend and master unprecedented circumstances.

Every generation discovers insights overlooked by other generations; every generation overlooks insights discovered by other generations.

Many effective leaders have relied on historical exemplars for inspiration amid the tumult and contingency of the present. The American founders looked to classical history and literature. The Civil War generation—on both sides—looked to the founders. Theodore Roosevelt, like Winston Churchill, constantly referred to historical figures, musing aloud about how they would have handled contemporary situations. Dr. King looked to Gandhi. The Beatles looked to Elvis Presley, Chuck Berry,

Buddy Holly, Carl Perkins, Little Richard and others. The same is true of leaders in every endeavor.

We have an additional advantage today. Social history has increased our awareness of the leadership and accomplishments of the many, many men and women who did not hold high positions, whose contributions were often undervalued or unrecognized. Their examples are all the more useful in the twenty-first century, when everybody can lead because everybody can serve.

Spiritual ancestors can raise your standards and expand your perspective. If the realities of your time or place are disappointing—such as W. H. Auden's evocation of the 1930s as "a low dishonest decade"—you can look to history for guidance. You can be *inspired* in the true sense—breathing in the vitalizing power of others' examples—then returning them into the world, enhanced by your own service.

RE-CREATE YOURSELF.

It's said that the body recreates itself, with entirely new cells every seven years. Whether or not that captures the biology precisely, it's reflective of a great truth.

You continually re-create yourself by your daily decisions, your choices in matters both great and small. Why not do it with forethought, advancing your values?

We're born with certain traits and gifts—but, over time, our day-to-day decisions increasingly determine our physical, mental, emotional and spiritual capacities.

◆

Over time, our day-to-day decisions determine our physical, mental, emotional and spiritual capacities as much or more than our inborn traits and gifts.

◆

Re-creation also means recreation. As the anthropologist Margaret Mead explained, "Leisure and the cultivation of human capacities are inextricably linked."

Leaders who maintain their effectiveness over time tend to have many interests and hobbies. Winston Churchill was far more than a world-class political leader. He was active as a painter, speaker, historian, and commentator on current events. He was a voracious reader and tireless traveler. Churchill spurred himself and others with the mantra, "a change is as good as a rest."

Recreation is a natural accompaniment to highly developed powers of concentration. Churchill relieved his cares through diversions, even in the most trying circumstances. Some may turn to social interaction, others physical exercise, others meditation and prayer.

Several spiritual traditions include notions of a Sabbath, a day of rest and reflection. This is the basis for the sabbatical, taking time "off" from one's customary roles to recharge and rededicate one's efforts.

Bill Gates is well-known for his semi-annual, week-long sabbaticals for study and reflection in isolated surroundings.

An increasing number of high-performing people make time in their day for meditation or related mental exercises of disciplined relaxation and refocusing. Some companies, such as Google, GE, and Salesforce.com, encourage top executives to do so. The Chicago Bulls, Los Angeles Lakers and many other top performers in the sports world do the same.

Regular rest and reflection should not be viewed as luxuries. They are necessities. Among other things, they can restore the spirit of humility necessary for sustainable service.

The whirl of daily activity often knots two contradictory strands of habitual thought. One is that you have little control over your destiny. This is reinforced by the non-stop demands of crowded hours, combined with their unavoidable unpredictability.

Alternatively, ceaseless focus on work or other routines can instill an unrealistic, inflated sense of your power over the circumstances of your life.

Recreation can enable you to listen to—to truly hear—the voices of others. You may also discern your internal voices, sometimes intuitions, that otherwise may be drowned out amid the cacophony of the workaday world. As the dancer Agnes de Mille said, "No trumpets sound when the important decisions of our life are made. Destiny is made known silently."

Through recreation—re-creation—you can rouse yourself from what Robert Louis Stevenson called the "respectable somnambulism" of the many, many people who move ever onward—without questioning, without doubt, without fulfillment—in the well-worn ruts of conventional lives.

Bill Novelli, former CEO of AARP, has re-created his life and career on several occasions. He has served effectively in the worlds of advertising, government, not-for-profits, and most recently, academia. Novelli heeds his internal clock, initiating change, bypassing the alluring inertia of recognized success.

Author and commentator Dave Ramsey has a wonderful saying for helping people refocus their financial affairs: "Live like no one else, so later, you can live like no one else."

The same notion applies to all aspects of our lives. If you aim to serve others at your highest capacity, you must take responsibility to create what the twentieth-century English explorer Wilfred Thesiger calls "the life of your choice."

Why should you not create your masterpiece of service?

To be nobody but yourself in a world which is doing its best night and day to make you everybody else means to fight the hardest battle which any human being can fight; and never stop fighting.

—E.E. CUMMINGS, POET

 Week Seven: Ask 'What Am I Learning?'
During Every Task You Undertake

Throughout Week Seven, as you go about your life and work, constantly ask yourself the question: *What Am I Learning?* Keep a *Learning Journal* of all your activities during the course of your day. Take care to reexamine habitual tasks. Include all aspects of your life—such as diet and exercise, and your use of time. Don't leave out longstanding relationships or schedules which may appear to be set in stone, both personal and business-related.

Make note of your thought patterns, your responses to circumstances you encounter, both foreseeable and unexpected.

After Week Seven, Update Your *Service Map*: What Are You Learning?

Review your *Service Map. What Are You Leaning?* Are you serving more people, more effectively, than a year ago? Two years ago? Five years ago? Ten years ago? How do you know? What metrics do you apply? How do you envision your service changing in the next year? Two years? Five years? Ten years? What specific plans for improvement have you crafted for the next three months? Six months? One year? Do you have an inner circle? Do you routinely obtain actionable input from third parties to improve your service?

MAKE YOUR LIFE A MASTERPIECE OF SERVICE

Leadership is performance art.

In various ways, with varying degrees of success, leaders present notions of how to live. They do so as they communicate their vision. Their most important offering, made even more compelling in the Information Age, is their example.

In "The Choice," the Irish poet W.B. Yeats declared: "The intellect of man is forced to choose perfection of the life, or of the work...." For those serving effectively as twenty-first-century leaders, the life and the work are merging. Everybody can lead because everybody can serve; every part of your life can be placed into service.

◆

For those serving effectively as twenty-first-century leaders, the life and the work are merging. Everybody can lead because everybody can serve; every part of your life can be placed into service.

◆

Throughout history, leaders have looked to artists for inspiration. That may be in part because of the audacity of artists, daring to create lives in accordance with their gifts and values and vision. Artists tend to resist convention. Many view life from a perspective sufficiently apart so as to yield unexpected, theretofore unexamined associations, comprehending, ordering and expressing reality in novel ways.

Yeats expressed the choice of which artists are acutely aware. It resonates widely, because it draws upon understandings of work and life familiar to so many of us.

How would you think about your life as a leader—your life of service—in artistic terms?

Some turn to musical composition and performance. This was the perspective of poet and physician Oliver Wendell Holmes, father of Justice Oliver Wendell Holmes, Jr. He warned, as did Emerson, that "Most of us go to our graves with our music still inside us, unplayed."

Others liken the art of living to making motion pictures. Winston Churchill saw his remarkable life "like an endless moving picture in which one was an actor. On the whole Great Fun!" Military historian Carlos D'Este adds, "What Churchill neglected to mention was that in the motion picture of his life he was not merely an actor but the star." One might go further. Churchill was also producer, director, screenwriter—and his own ardent, amazed, amused and most appreciative audience.

Some of the most conspicuous performance artists of life have been writers. Many recognize that their works and lives must attain unity to reach their potential. The English laureate John Milton proclaimed: "He who would write heroic poems must make his whole life a heroic poem." African-American writer Zora Neale Hurston echoed the elder Holmes: "There is no agony like bearing an untold story inside you."

Many effective leaders have been energetic if not gifted writers. Some, such as Theodore Roosevelt, Churchill, Lincoln, and King, used words first to alter their own realities, then those of others. Fred Kaplan, in *Lincoln: The Biography of a Writer*, concludes that in Lincoln, "the tool, the toolmaker, and the tool user became inseparably one. He became what his language made him."

As useful as each of those comparisons can be, perhaps the metaphor with the most power is painting. In this we can be guided by Oliver Wendell Holmes, Jr.: "Life is painting a picture, not doing a sum."

Life is painting a picture, not doing a sum."
—OLIVER WENDELL HOLMES, JR.

As you serve to lead, you stroke paint onto your canvas. Some of the cloth is virgin, entirely untouched. It awaits your work. At certain moments, its barrenness is an opportunity; at other times, it seems a rebuke. What's certain is that it's *yours*.

Much of the canvas is filled in. Some of it represents the legacy of others.

Your own earlier contributions are there, too. Parts of your prior efforts may please you. Some might even appear perfect in your eyes.

Some might be on the right track, but, as of yet, it's not quite right. It might benefit from elaboration or collaboration.

Some of it may be altogether wrong. At least that's how you see it now. It may have been right at one time. Or you may never have been satisfied with it. Did you relent too much to others' notions, struggling to please them at the cost of your calling? Perhaps you're proud of the work that's there, but regret others did not see it as you intended. They may not have recognized the value you anticipated.

Nonetheless, no space on the canvas is altogether without value. Even your worst mistakes can be put to use. Earlier experiments and errors, as they're incorporated, painted over or recovered, yield richness and depth. Their influence also may be seen indirectly, in the paths you realize you don't wish to follow.

All of this converges within the order suggested by your vision. You visualize your service, your life. You comprehend your present and your past within your conception of the future.

Your vision starts as a sketch, an outline of your notion of your finished painting. It's also a phantom. You work amid ambiguity, not knowing where the task will end. You learn as you go, buoyed by faith that your vision will, ultimately, enable you to bring it all together.

A vision requires a plan. The more imaginative, the more authentic the vision, the more important is the plan.

For the first twenty-five years of my life, I wanted freedom.
For the next twenty-five years, I wanted order.
For the next twenty-five years, I realized that order is freedom.
—ATTRIBUTED TO WINSTON S. CHURCHILL

Be regular and orderly in your life, like a good bourgeois,
so that you may be violent and original in your work.
—GUSTAVE FLAUBERT, NOVELIST

Some people regard discipline as a chore.
For me, it is a kind of order that sets me free to fly.
—JULIE ANDREWS, ACTOR, SINGER, DANCER

An artist also knows, as legendary Nissan executive Carlos Ghon of Nissan said, "You can't plan your life, because if you do it will be too narrow." Attempting to circumscribe the world's uncertainties within a self-imposed structure is prideful. It can be delusional, even dangerous. There's wisdom in the Yiddish saying: "We plan, God laughs."

You can, however, take steps toward the life you envision. The most effective planning builds on the understanding that it's necessary but never sufficient; it's instrumental, not fundamental.

Plans lend themselves to systems. Systems can elicit heightened performance, more rapid learning and application. They are simply ways to make your contributions, and those of others, more readily accessible, more readily combined for specific, real-time tasks.

Properly understood, the more effective the planning, the better able you are to respond productively to the random, the unexpected. Discipline enables you to be purposefully adaptive. You adjust, incorporating new ideas and possibilities. The tensile strength of your vision ensures that its integrity is reinforced, not diminished, as a result. You're open to others' contributions. Now, more than ever, you can learn continuously from those who contribute ideas or resources or spiritual support in a networked world, a world of relationships.

To achieve your masterpiece, you must ransack your conscious and unconscious mind, breaking through to the essence of your being. Henry James captured this, describing an artist as someone "on whom nothing is lost." Nothing less will suffice. Finding value in every trace of your knowledge, experience, intuition and faith is necessary to create the one thing that no one else can do.

In the words of dancer and choreographer Twyla Tharp, "Everything is raw material. Everything is relevant. Everything is usable. Everything feeds my creativity. But without proper preparation, I cannot see it, retain it, and use it."

No aspect of your life is out of bounds. You may find yourself rummaging urgently through the shelves of your experience. You may happen upon fragments from your past. You can take them out, view them in a new light. Your apparently random memories, your past work, ideas, accomplishments, attempts or mistakes—all these can be brought to bear. Some may have never quite made sense, may have seemed of little value. Suddenly, they fit your urgent need exactly.

In early 1967 the Beatles worked with inspired energy on the songs that would constitute *Sgt. Pepper's Lonely Hearts Club Band*. As the elements of rock and roll's first theme album fell into place, Paul McCartney's imagination and memory happened upon incomplete work from an earlier time. The main elements of the second number on the second side, "When I'm Sixty-Four," had been conceived by McCartney as a precocious sixteen-year-old.

The same phenomenon is seen in the career of Steve Jobs. He was an indifferent student in college. He abandoned traditional, "practical" classes in favor of calligraphy. He learned about serif and sans-serif typefaces and their manipulation. It might well have appeared a pointless diversion at the time. Many years later, when he was designing the Macintosh computer, Jobs reached back to that experience to incorporate the stunning typography that became a standard part of personal productivity software.

Overlooked, forgotten, neglected elements of your experience become visible amid the illumination of critical moments. They rise up, coming together, bringing the totality of your work and life into alignment. Everything is where it's supposed to be.

Winston Churchill had such a sense on Friday, 10 May 1940.

It took, he told an intimate, the imminent "Armageddon" wrought by Hitler's Germany to present him the chance to serve in the highest office of state. What's more, "there were not too many applicants for the job."

Nonetheless, as Churchill recounted in *The Gathering Storm*:

> I was conscious of a profound sense of relief. At last I had the authority to give directions over the whole scene. I felt as if I were walking with destiny, and that *all my past life had been but a preparation for this hour and for this trial…*. I thought I knew a good bit about it all, and I was sure I should not fail. Therefore, although impatient for the morning, I slept soundly and had no need for cheering dreams. [emphasis added]

As you create your masterpiece of service, immersion in work means immersion in life. Arnold Toynbee observed, "The supreme accomplishment is to blur the distinction between work and play." This is not to be confused with the workaholic, who attempts to elude life's vicissitudes amid a continuous, compulsive bustle of frenetic activity.

In the doing, otherwise disparate parts of your life coalesce into the love that is the core of your endeavor. You're inspired, motivated to persevere by your love for those you're serving.

Love brings its own challenges.

As work and life become one, consequential decisions may lay in wait, relating to people or things you love. To that extent, Yeats' melancholy choice remains. And yet, even that difficulty may be mined for greater intensity, additional power to your masterpiece of service.

A painter, like any artist or leader, cannot know exactly where her quest will end. She cannot control the outcome. To dwell on it would be distracting, self-serving.

Eighteenth-century English playwright Joseph Addison addressed this challenge in *Cato, a Tragedy*. George Washington and other American founders were keenly aware of this acclaimed work and its lessons for service and leadership. Among its enduring passages, in Act I, Scene 2:

Tis not in mortals to command success; but we'll do more, Sempronius, we'll deserve it.

You cannot know whether your service will be judged a "success." You cannot know whether you will achieve a desired result, much less a position of authority or power or honor.

> *You can't connect the dots looking forward;*
> *you can only connect them looking backwards.*
> *So you have to trust that the dots will*
> *somehow connect in your future.*
>
> —STEVE JOBS

What you can do: begin the journey by undertaking, without reserve, to serve those you love. You can know that you serve effectively, with all of your heart. That is every bit as assured as your "success" cannot be.

You can transform your life into a masterpiece of service, based on the decisions you make minute by minute, hour by hour, day by day. The power of your example is at once incalculable and assured. The twentieth-century humanitarian Albert Schweitzer expressed it well: "Not one of us knows what effect his life produces, and what he gives to others; that is hidden from us and must remain so, though we are often allowed to see some little fraction of it, so that we may not lose courage."

Courage is the indispensable, binding element, enabling you to call upon your greatest powers with artistic mastery—in the face of ultimate, unyielding uncertainty.

The worst day of a life led with courage is better than the best day of a life cosseted for safety. As your life becomes more and more enmeshed with those you serve, you break the bounds of your own experience. You are freed of the subtle shackles you have internalized from longstanding, outdated, limiting views of your capacities.

The worst day of a life led with courage is better than the best day of a life cosseted for safety.

The more you expand, extend, even transcend yourself, the more effectively you serve. You summon up strength you would not have been so bold to presume you harbor.

The poet Rilke mused: "How wonderful to grow old when one has worked on life like a true craftsman…then there is nothing that has passed away; everything is there, real, ravishingly real, it is there and has been acknowledged by and entered into something greater, and it is linked to the most remote past and impregnated with the future."

Oliver Wendell Holmes, Jr.'s metaphor of life as a painting sparked this meditation on crafting a masterpiece of service. His sentiment, expressed at the age of eighty-three, brings us toward our close: "If I were dying my last words would be: Have faith and pursue the unknown end."

> *The more you are motivated by love,*
> *the more fearless and free you action will be.*
> —DALAI LAMA

> *Where love and skill work together,*
> *expect a masterpiece.*
> —JOHN RUSKIN

HAPPINESS AND SERVICE

We all seek happiness. America's Declaration of Independence enshrines the right to pursue it. Yet we so often get it wrong. In his excellent book, *Stumbling on Happiness*, Dan Gilbert reports that people tend to misjudge what will make them happy.

Similarly, some people seek to act in what they believe to be their own interest. They, too, often get it wrong. In the end, no one among us knows enough to divine his own interest—though each of us knows enough to do our duty.

That duty is generally bound up in service. In pursuing it without reservation or distraction, we may encounter the fulfillment that is the key to happiness.

It is one of the most beautiful compensations of life
that no man can sincerely try to help another
without helping himself....
Serve and thou shall be served.

—RALPH WALDO EMERSON

Life is an exciting business and
most exciting when lived for others.

—HELEN KELLER

Albert Schweitzer summed up: "Success is not the key to happiness. Happiness is the key to success. If you love what you are doing, you will be successful." The virtuous circle: to love what you're doing for those you love.

In Gandhi's words, "Service which is rendered without joy helps neither the servant nor the served. But all other pleasures and possessions pale into nothingness before service which is rendered in a spirit of joy."

With every passing year science further establishes that health—mental, physical, emotional, spiritual—is enhanced by serving others. If you serve with love, the life force of the universe gathers around you.

Dr. George Vaillant, a professor at Harvard Medical School, directed the famous "Harvard Study" of adult development. The study tracks the adult lives of more than 800 men and women, beginning in early adulthood. The cohort was carefully selected. It comprised young people of conspicuous talent, intelligence, resilience and promise.

Vaillant offered a summary conclusion in 2008: "[T]he only thing that really matters in life are your relationships with other people."

In a subsequent video interview, Vaillant was even more succinct—and emphatic: "Happiness is love. Full stop."

◆

The essence of courage is serving others
with unconditional love.

◆

In the long run, no man or woman can really be happy unless he or she is doing service. Happiness springing exclusively from some other cause crumbles in your hands, amounts to nothing.

—THEODORE ROOSEVELT

Joy can only be real if people look upon their life as a service and have a definite object in life outside themselves and their personal happiness.

—LEO TOLSTOY

The secret of happiness is freedom. The secret of freedom is courage.

—THUCYDIDES

RECAP
MAKE YOUR LIFE A MASTERPIECE OF SERVICE

◆

Every day's a decision—a new opportunity to recast who and how you will serve.

◆

Going forward, you can clarify your values and aspirations by drafting your own obituary. From there, you can come up with the one sentence that you wish others to associate with your life. It will become the basis for your vision statement going forward. Armed with your *Service Map* (initially created in Chapter 2), you can audit your service. Take a close look at how you actually live—focusing on how you approach your money, time, relationships and customary thought patterns. You will increasingly align your values with the seemingly "small" decisions constituting your life, minute by minute, hour by hour, day by day.

You will be empowered to create your masterpiece of service.

The pursuit of your masterpiece holds the prospect of the happiness that can emerge from joyfully, effectively serving others.

PREPARE TO SERVE

Who Am I Serving?

— Your *Service Map* reflects your reality and your aspirations. Does the life you lead reflect and advance your service? How are you evaluated by those you strive to serve? Do you know how your service is viewed by third parties whose judgment you respect?

— Over the course of four weeks, follow the program to align your values with your life.

» **Week One:** Account for your time, keeping a *Time Journal*.
» **Week Two:** Account for your money, keeping a *Finance Journal*.
» **Week Three:** Account for your relationships, keeping a *Relationship Journal*.
» **Week Four:** Account for your thoughts, keeping a *Thought Journal*.
» **After Week Four:** With the information obtained, update your *Service Map*. Your journals can also be the basis for subsequent action plans to implement future *Service Map* changes.

How Can I Best Serve?

— To serve is to choose. The priority you accord to serving particular people or enterprises may change over time.
— Make sure your oxygen mask is on before you serve others. You must protect all aspects of your health to serve at your best.
— Listen and learn with a servant's heart.
— Service is not subservience.
— "Do the best you can, with what you have, where you are."
— Focus on now. Be unreservedly present in the moment.
— How you can best serve changes over time. You have a valuable contribution to make at every stage of life.

» **Week Five:** Ask yourself before every interaction with another: *How Can I Best Serve This Person?* Create a *Best Service Journal.*

» **After Week Five:** With the information gathered, update your *Service Map.*

Am I Making My Unique Contribution?

— Do what you love, for those you love.

— Give up what you don't love.

— When you identify your calling, go all-in. "It's not to try—it's do or die."

» **Week Six:** Ask yourself regularly as you undertake your tasks: *Am I Making My Unique Contribution?* Create a *Contribution Journal.* Ask the question not only in your work, but also in your personal life. Identify areas where you're making your unique contribution—and where you're not. Reflect on changes you could undertake to identify and achieve your calling.

» **After Week Six:** With the information gathered, update your *Service Map.*

What Am I Learning?

— Are you learned—or a learner? Effective service requires a commitment to a way of life; ongoing, never-ending learning is its fuel.

— Select your inner circle with care. Your choice of those who populate your inner and outer lives is of defining significance.

— Adopt "spiritual ancestors."

— Re-create yourself.

» **Week Seven:** Ask yourself regularly as you undertake your tasks: *What Am I Learning?* Create an *Improvement Journal.* Ask the question not only in your work, but also in your personal life. Identify areas where you're improving on a consistent basis—and where you're not. Reflect on changes you could undertake to make continuous improvement part of your life going forward.

» **After Week Seven:** With the information gathered, update your *Service Map*.

Create Your Masterpiece of Service: Week Eight and Beyond

— Gather together the items prepared in the program outlined in this chapter, including:
   » your draft *obituary*
   » your "*one word*" summary (originally from Chapter 6)
   » your "*one sentence*" summary
   » your *vision statement*
   » your *Weekly Journals* (*Time Journal, Finance Journal, Relationship Journal, Thought Journal, Best Service Journal, Contribution Journal, Improvement Journal*)
   » your *Service Map* (originally from Chapter 2)
— Update your *Service Map* to reflect the information. Create additional *Service Maps* for thee-month, six-month, nine-month, and one-year periods, as appropriate. Sketch visioning *Service Maps* for five- and ten-year periods.
— Create *Action Lists* with metrics and deadlines for each three-month period.
— At the beginning of each year thereafter, prepare an *Annual Report* on your service. Your goal is to focus accountability, measure progress, and stretch your goals.
— Continue to engage the *Serve to Lead* System, as necessary to reinforce ongoing learning and growth.
— Enlarge your circle of service by teaching the system to others.
— To analyze any situation going forward, pose and apply The Four Questions.

Make your life a
Masterpiece of Service.

Begin today:
Every Day's a Decision.

From this moment forward:
Who Are You Serving?

About the Author

JAMES STROCK is a bestselling author and speaker on leadership. His firm, the Serve to Lead Group, serves clients worldwide, including companies, professional services firms, not-for-profit organizations, government agencies and the military.

He has appeared in many media outlets, including the *New York Times*, *Wall Street Journal*, *USA Today*, *Fox News* and *CNN*.

In addition to extensive business experience, Strock has served at high levels in government, including as the founding Secretary for Environmental Protection for the state of California, the chief law enforcement officer of the U.S. EPA, and general counsel of the U.S. Office of Personnel Management.

His prior books include *Disrupt Politics: Reset Washington*, *Theodore Roosevelt on Leadership: Executive Lessons from the Bully Pulpit*, and *Reagan on Leadership: Executive Lessons from the Great Communicator*.

Strock served to captain in the U.S. Army Reserve and is a member of the Council on Foreign Relations.

Website: **servetolead.org**
Twitter: **@jamesstrock**
Facebook: **/servetoleadgroup**

Image Credits

Frontispiece

Malala Yousafzai, by Simon Davis, 2015. DFID-UK Department for International Development. Creative Commons 2.0 via Wikipedia.

Chapter One

President Lyndon Johnson meets with Dr. Martin Luther King, Jr., in the White House Cabinet Room, 1966, by Yoichi Okamato. Licensed under public domain via Wikipedia.

Chapter Two

Isaiah, by Michelangelo, 1509. Licensed under public domain via Wikipedia.

Chapter Three

Tony Hsieh, Delivering Happiness Book, 2009. Creative Commons 2.0 via Wikipedia.

Chapter Four

General of the Army, Dwight D. Eisenhower, 1945. Signal Corps. Licensed under public domain via Wikipedia.

Chapter Five

Theodore Roosevelt, speaking from the balcony of the Hotel Allen, Allentown, Pennsylvania, 1914. Unknown photographer. Licensed under public domain via Wikipedia.

Chapter Six

Abraham Lincoln, by Alexander Gardner, 1865. Licensed under public domain via Wikipedia.

Chapter Seven

Helen Keller, sitting holding a magnolia flower, circa 1920, by *Los Angeles Times*. Licensed under public domain via Wikipedia.